THE BETZ CELL

By the same author

EMBRYO

THE BETZ CELL

KEITH BARNARD

SOUVENIR PRESS

First published 1991 by Souvenir Press Ltd,
43 Great Russell Street, London WC1B 3PA
and simultaneously in Canada

ISBN 0 285 63048 2
Phototypeset by Intype, London
Printed in Great Britain by
Mackays of Chatham plc, Chatham, Kent

To
Betty Barnard, my mother,
affectionately known as Min

ACKNOWLEDGEMENTS

Grateful thanks are due to:

Tom Docherty, Senior Chief Technician, Department of Clinical Neurophysiology, Wessex Neurological Centre; Elaine Glasspool, Chief Technician, Department of Clinical Neurophysiology, Wessex Neurological Centre; Colin Bowles, author of *G'DAY! – Teach Yourself Australian*; my wife, Ann; Dennis and Sylvia Stuart; David Baker, Ll.B.; Roger Hancock T.D. M.A.; Police Constable Len Hall.

Betz Cell: A large cellular structure found in the cerebrum, in the inner pyramidal layer of the grey matter. It is thought to be associated with the powers of abstract thought and intellectual processes that are unique to the human brain.

PROLOGUE

The sun upset his vision temporarily, despite the dark glasses. Maybe he hadn't recognised the face; after all, he was fifty feet up in the air. Paul Sansome tapped his skis together to shake some of the snow from them, and watched the particles drift down to the piste below. The single chair-lift was slow, and he was impatient to be off; but it was relaxing to be here, breathing the Austrian mountain air, approaching the top of the Astberg for his first run of the holiday. He had chosen this one because it was fairly easy, but steep enough in parts to get him tuned up for more exciting runs to come. Then he could go farther afield, get away, away from the pressures of his work, the threats, the secrets. Try and forget the real reason why he was here, even though he was already sure that he would reject the offer he anticipated was going to be made at the meeting his wife had arranged.

And something else – he had to concede the fact: away from Christine. It was not really so shocking to admit it. He wanted to get away from his wife. Being a much better skiier than she, going off for a day on the Grossraum circuit was giving him just that freedom. He thought of their parting, ten minutes earlier.

'I suppose I shan't see you until this evening.' Christine was almost as tall as he, with striking jet-black hair. She had a classically beautiful face, and managed to look elegant even in her bulky ski-suit and woolly hat.

Paul gave her his best please-be-nice-to-me hang-dog expression. He was pretty good at it – he had to use it often enough. 'It *is* my first day. It'll take me a while to get my ski-legs back. I need a good run.'

'I can see I'm wasting my breath. I suppose I'll find something to do.'

'You can use the local lifts and have a gentle run yourself. The conditions are excellent.'

'Maybe for you.'

Paul didn't want to prolong the discussion. He could feel the tension returning already. And there was a queue beginning to form for the chair-lift. He'd give her the martyr's cue, that should do it.

'Look, I'll stay with you if you really want me to.' He tried hard to look earnest, praying she would not take up the offer. He need not have worried.

'No, it's all right. You go.' Just the right dose of resignation spiced with a dash of self-sacrifice. She applied the mixture as before. 'I suppose it is meant to be business *and* pleasure. Go and enjoy yourself.'

'Are you sure?' He tried not to sound tentative.

'I'll see you back at the hotel.' Christine turned and clumped away in her ski-boots, heading for the restaurant next to the lift station and a large *gluhwein*, even though it was only nine-thirty.

The vision of another woman floated into his mind. She would not rush off in search of alcohol at every opportunity; if she were here, she would want to be with him, sharing the experience of a day on the mountain, enjoying just being together, enjoying —

Paul's thoughts were interrupted by the arrival of the lift. He stood up at the right moment, and skiied away to his left and the start of the run down to the village. The piste was quite narrow here, cut into the side of the mountain, and stayed that way for about a kilometre before widening into a glorious open expanse where there was plenty of room for speed. It was a bit icy, because the weather was superb and the sun had been melting a little of the surface by the end of the day. He set off, did a couple of turns, stopped, checked everything. He felt great. He waited while a weaving crocodile of novices skiied past, their instructor shouting encouragement. Suddenly the way was clear. This was going to be good.

He rounded the second bend well in control, but was taken completely by surprise by a piste-basher coming the other way. The rush of wind in his uncovered ears had prevented him from hearing its approach. There was barely room to pass. The driver moved the broad machine over to the wall cut into the mountain, and beckoned Paul to go by. There was only a yard or so between the machine and the edge of the path. It was quite a steep drop, with a lot of trees — not too threatening, but care was needed. He pushed off, slid by the machine, and made to do a sharp parallel turn inwards as he passed the snow-tractor. It was a mistake.

There was a patch of ice that had not been scarified by the machine, right where he chose to perform the manoeuvre. His reflexes were just not good enough yet, and before he could think what was happening he was over the edge. Sky and snow whirled past; one bump, two, a tree branch lashed his face, then an abrupt halt. He felt very strange, then orientation returned as he realised he was upside-down, on his back, head down the steep slope. His left knee hurt like hell. He tried to roll over. It took him several attempts before he could right himself, and the pain made him feel weak and nauseated. He still wore the ski on the injured side, and it was tangled in a small conifer. That must be the cause of his injury. He was furious with himself, cursing fiercely under his breath, his only thought that this could ruin his holiday before it had really started. Panting heavily, he leaned forward and squeezed the binding hard. It snapped open, and he managed to remove the ski, then looked upwards, catching some movement out of the corner of his eye.

Someone was coming down to help. He had fallen about 60 feet, but in the still air he could clearly hear a man's voice. It was oddly familiar, speaking accented English.

'Hold on. I'll be there in a tick.' The figure then turned to shout to someone Paul couldn't see. 'It's OK, I'll take care of it. You go on.'

Paul squinted up towards the advancing man, but the bright sun was dazzling him and he had lost his sunglasses in the fall. He tried to stand, so that he could greet his helper, but as he got almost upright a searing pain knifed down his leg from his knee to his foot. The knee gave way, and he fell onto his back down the incline, panic rising as he gathered momentum. His knee gave another agonising twinge as it snagged on an obstruction, he slowed, then stopped, hanging head down the slope. He was just beginning to think that he was safe, when he felt further movement. The snow-covered mountain side absorbed almost all the sound of his cry, as wood pulped scalp and splintered cranial bones. Paul Sansome's long black sleep had begun.

CHAPTER 1

'It's good news, Mrs Sansome.'

The doctor smiled as he came into the room, and looked encouragingly at the attractive woman who stood on the opposite side of the bed. Between them lay the still form of her husband. Monitors winked, green traces followed each other in repetitive sequence across oscilloscope tubes, the ripple mattress pump buzzed. A drip feed went into one arm, a naso-gastric tube was taped to his cheek. The patient lay on his back, his pale, gaunt face staring up at the ceiling through unseeing eyes.

Christine Sansome seemed surprisingly unmoved by the glad tidings.

'I thought you were going to turn that ventilator off three weeks ago.'

'But Mrs Sansome, if we had done that then, he would probably have died. Now he's actually breathing on his own. I'd have thought you would be delighted.'

'He's still in the same state now as he was then. There's nothing there, no reaction. His brain is dead.' Her face tightened with tension.

The doctor looked at her sympathetically. 'There's still hope, Mrs Sansome.'

'Really? Look at him!' Her tone had a despairing quality.

'The electro-encephalogram does not show your husband to be brain dead, Mrs Sansome.' The doctor's reply was firm.

'He might as well be. How do you think *I* feel?' She sounded resentful. 'He's just in limbo. I can't talk to him, decide anything, sort out his affairs, nothing.' She looked at the figure on the bed, bitterness etching her face. 'My life has come to a complete stop. It can't start again until he recovers. Or dies.'

'He is *not* going to die.' The doctor could not control the exasperation in his voice. He turned and left without speaking again.

'Just look at you, Paul Sansome.' The woman spoke to her husband, her fine features shadowed with anguish. She turned away and followed the doctor.

Sister Yeates, the nurse who was attending the comatose man, stood at the head of the bed, white-faced and trembling, and watched her go. When the door had closed, she moved round to the side of the bed, took his left hand in hers, and with her right, gently stroked her patient's brow.

★ ★ ★

Claire felt the hand start to move up her thigh. It was no more than she expected, and maybe, at another time, she might not have objected. But she did not want to deal with the complications of sexual involvement just now. She pushed the hand away, gently but firmly, and held onto it.

'I'm sorry, Ted, but I'm not in the mood.' She cast her eyes down over the Australian's large bulky frame, then up to his face, and gave him a sympathetic smile.

Why do I always seem to attract such hulking great men? she asked herself, not for the first time. She had her theory that it was because she was so small. Big men felt protective towards her. Or was it that they felt she might be an easy conquest? She was certainly tiny, barely five feet tall, and was slim, but not skinny. She took pride in her well-proportioned body, and tried to make the best of her straw-coloured hair and pale grey eyes.

Ted withdrew his hand from hers and leaned back on the sofa, hands behind his head.

'Blown it again, have I?'

'No, it's not your fault.' She tried to reassure him. 'I just seem so preoccupied lately.'

'Since Paul Sansome became a vegetable, you mean?'

Claire was angry at that. 'That's a very unkind way of putting it.'

'Sorry. I know you admire the guy. But you've got to face the fact that's what he's become, poor bastard. You've been to the hospital, spoken to the doctors. Rumour has it even his missus has stopped visiting him.'

'Why is everyone in so much of a hurry to give up on Paul? People can come out of a coma after *months* of unconsciousness. He's only been like it for six weeks. There's still plenty of time.' She tried to keep a note of desperation out of her voice.

'Did you fancy havin' a naughty with him, or something?' The big Australian gave her a leer.

She responded with a look of derision. 'Don't be so ridiculous. I liked him, sure, but what upsets me most of all is that he was a great scientist, and was on the verge of a fantastic discovery. You're involved in it too — doesn't the research mean anything to you?'

'Of course it bloody does.' Ted sat forward on the sofa, his arms resting on his knees. 'I've put countless hours into the computer programming, and you know it. I'm pissed off that it's all ground to a halt, too. But I can't see the point in wishing the poor bugger back from the living death he's in now. If he recovers he'll probably have no memory, and if he has it probably won't go further than him playing in his pram.'

'Oh, Ted. Don't be so cruel.'

'I'm not being cruel. I'm just being realistic. I know you harbour fond images of popping in there with a tape-recorder and playing a few bars of his favourite tune, and he'll open his eyes and say, "Good morning, Miss Donaldson. Give me the computer analysis on the last batch of Vocab. EEGs, will you?" And you'll look at him with your eyes all big and shiny, and say, "Welcome, back, Dr Sansome," and then the background music will swell to a crescendo while — *ouch*!'

Claire dug her knuckles fiercely in his ribs. 'Get out of here!'

'Already?' He rubbed his injured side. 'You invited me in for a coffee, and I haven't had one yet.'

She stood up. 'You don't deserve one. You needn't think you can buy my favours with a nice meal and your crass antipodean humour. Especially if you keep insulting my life's work.'

The Australian got to his feet, towering over her, and looked at her with wide, innocent eyes. 'I didn't mean to hurt your feelings, Claire. Honest.'

She looked at his puppy-like expression for a long moment. Maybe I shouldn't be so sensitive, she thought. Maybe I should take what comfort I can get. 'All right. I'll make some coffee, and you can think of something more encouraging to say about Paul.'

She moved towards the kitchen, but he pulled her to him as she went past. He gave her a gentle bear hug, and she responded. He looked down at her. 'OK now?'

She had to smile at him. 'OK.' She went to move away, but he held her tight. His left hand went up under her T-shirt and moved round to her bare breast, his pelvis pressed against hers. Claire's mood changed instantly. She thumped him on the chest with her fist and twisted away.

'For Christ's sake, Ted! Why do you have to behave like a whale-shark on heat? Haven't you got any finesse?'

His expression darkened with frustration. 'I kinda sensed you needed some comforting.'

'I kinda think I do. But that doesn't mean you can just jump on me like some passing kangaroo!'

This was all too subtle for Ted. In his book a girl either wanted it or she didn't. She had his erections going up and down like a bicycle tyre with a slow puncture, and he couldn't stand it any longer. 'I think I'd better choof off.'

Claire couldn't help herself from responding, 'So do I.' She watched him turn and march across the room. She took a few paces after him, called out, 'Thanks for the meal.' The words were lost in the slamming of the door.

'*Damn*!' She swore to herself and flopped back onto the sofa. Nothing was going right since Paul Sansome's accident. Her whole future seemed in the balance. One minute she was wrapped up in an exciting project, research assistant to a man whose work was so revolutionary that associates were talking in terms of the Nobel Prize — and she was a key part of it all, she, Ted, and Paul. But the next minute — nothing. For the last six weeks, although she had turned up for work every day at the Clifton Neurological Research Institute, little had been achieved. Some people from the Regional Health Authority had visited, and there were rumours that the whole project might be closed down. As always, money was tight. It was only because of the extraordinary advances they had made in the past eighteen months that they had not been threatened before.

Claire felt frustrated and angry. She was ambitious, intelligent, knew she was good. She had always been determined to fulfil her potential, and this project was her golden opportunity. And now, because Paul was so damn keen on his bloody skiing, it was all finished.

She lay back, depression overwhelming her. Come on, woman, you might as well admit it. At the age of 28 your big chance has come and gone. He's never going to regain consciousness, and you know it. All that knowledge you need is locked up in that brain, and there's no way you can get it out.

She sat up suddenly, a curious feeling sweeping over her, a strange mixture of fear and excitement. *Maybe there is a way*! An avalanche of ideas engulfed her. She unsuccessfully tried to dismiss them as being impractical, impossible, impermissible. But she could not.

She lay awake most of the night, willing the time to go by until she could get to the hospital in the morning.

CHAPTER 2

Claire knew the neurosurgeon's name was Gerard Porthenoy. She smiled to herself. Christ, what a name! She had only met the consultant once before, just after Paul Sansome had been flown home from Austria by air ambulance, when Porthenoy had performed a craniotomy to remove a blood clot that was pressing on the brain. He had seemed all right then, if a touch pompous. But then with a name like that she had expected someone pretty impressive.

At the time he had appeared quite optimistic that the operation would increase Paul's chances of recovery considerably. Wonder what he thinks now. Soon find out, she told herself as she entered his office.

'It's very good of you to see me,' she began when the formalities were over, 'I appreciate how busy you must be.'

He sat back, displaying a richly patterned waistcoat beneath his expensively tailored jacket. 'Your comments on the phone sounded so intriguing, young woman, that I could not resist.'

She ignored the patronising sexism in his remark. Don't get up his nose just now, she warned herself. She was trying to formulate a diplomatic response, when he continued.

'I knew Paul Sansome quite well, you know. It's very distressing to see him like this. Very distressing.' He paused to ensure his concern carried sufficient weight to his audience. 'He spoke very highly of you. Very highly indeed.'

Claire made a mental note: *Repeats key phrases for emphasis.*

'So of course I was prepared to listen to what you have to say, if it can possibly help my colleague's recovery.'

Porthenoy's knowledge of Paul could make this a lot easier than she had thought, Claire realised. 'You know quite a bit about Dr Sansome's work, then?'

'Haven't spoken to him about it in a long time. But I know he was researching into electro-encephalogram interpretation. Certainly an area that needs it. Not a very exact science at all, is it? I've always found that rather surprising. Rather surprising.'

Claire was well aware of the truth of that. Measuring the minute electrical activity of the surface of the brain was frequently carried out, mainly to help with the diagnosis of gross lesions like epilepsy and brain tumours. But a lot of the guesswork had been taken out of the detection of physical abnormalities by such techniques as CT scanning and Magnetic Resonance Imaging, and measuring brain waves had become of limited value.

'We've been approaching electro-encephalography from a completely different angle,' she explained. 'Up till now the electrical potentials have only been measured from the surface of the brain, except very occasionally during open surgery. What we've done is to use computerised analysis to try and look at the electrical potential differences from tiny areas deeper in the brain, and to try and make some sense out of what we've found.'

'Quite so. Lot of problems, though, I gather?'

'Well, there were initially. But we've got most of them ironed out. One of the most difficult to overcome was the background noise effect. There are millions of tiny electrical discharges being emitted all the time, as all the brain cells communicate with each other constantly, even when nothing is going on. That background electrical activity obscures what is happening in a particular area. Like thought processes — and speech. They were our main target areas.'

'Hmm, yes. I remember Sansome getting quite excited about this background noise problem. Said you used a technique rather like the "anti-noise" chaps use with sound waves.'

'That's right.' Claire's enthusiasm was growing as she talked. 'We recorded the background electrical activity, the computer averaged it out, then played it back, but inverting the potentials. It virtually cancelled out the background interference, and left us with pure active signals from the area we were looking at.'

'Well, of course, I'm only a humble surgeon,' Porthenoy said with unconvincing modesty, 'so all that's a bit beyond me. Bit beyond me. Just what is it you want to do now?'

Claire took a deep breath. 'I want you to let me run some tests on Dr Sansome.'

He looked at her with a studied frown. 'Do some research on him, you mean?'

She could read the warning signs in his tone. 'No, no, not research as such. I'd be using research techniques, but not for the sake of pure science.'

'For what, then?'

'I want to try and communicate with him.'

'You what!' Porthenoy almost spluttered over the words in his haste to get them out. 'Don't be ridiculous, woman.'

Claire tried to keep her temper. 'But you don't understand. I think we've got far enough in our research to try it.'

'I think I do understand all too well, all too well.' Porthenoy sat upright in his chair, interlocked his fingers under his chin. 'You've done a few tests, and now you think you've got a prize guinea-pig to try out your results on, and next you'll be telling me that if you could only ask the poor bugger he'd say he didn't mind because he'd be supporting his own work.'

Claire was not sure how to counter this hostility. 'We haven't just done a few tests,' she protested, 'we've done a tremendous amount of animal work, and —'

'On monkeys, wasn't it?'

'Well, yes, but —'

'And just what were you doing with these sub-human species?' There was barely disguised derision in the question.

Claire wasn't sure whether Porthenoy really wanted an answer. She waited, but he continued to look at her expectantly. She decided she had nothing to lose. 'We used chimps. They had been taught sign language. It can be done, you know; in several centres they have —'

'Yes, yes, I know all about that.' He looked pointedly at his watch.

Claire tried to condense six months' complex research into a couple of minutes. 'We used three probes to triangulate a focus on tiny areas of the brain — mostly in the subcortical association fibres of the parietal lobe mid-zone. It was almost a fluke that we found it after only three months.'

She barely paused for breath, but he pushed her along. 'Found what?'

'An area of the brain that responded to the sign language a few milliseconds *before the monkey actually did it*!' She still felt the thrill of the discovery.

'You're trying to tell me you recorded a *thought*?'

She looked at him, her eyes bright. 'Yes. Exactly that.'

'Nonsense. Must have been an artefact. Or you were just recording the motor nerve activity.'

'They weren't artefacts. They were predictably and accurately reproducible signals. We could distinguish them from the motor nerve signals that followed.'

'Hmm. Sounds pretty fantastic to me.'

'But that's not all.' Claire rushed on, undeterred. 'We could differentiate different signals for different activities — and they were the same every time!'

'Come along, girl! I've seen EEGs. They're a load of infinitely variable wiggly lines. How the devil can you identify an individual pattern and give it a particular significance?'

'By using a computer. Ted Parkes – he's a superb programmer – could teach the computer to sift through and analyse hundreds of thousands of signals, eliminate the dross, and pick out recurring patterns. The same pattern emerged each time the monkey thought about a particular response.'

'And just how do you get your probes into the part of the brain you want to study? I presume surface electrodes are no good?'

'No, they're not. We drill a minute hole in the skull with a laser, and then thread a fine cobalt steel wire into the brain. It's only a few microns thick, so does no detectable damage.'

'Now let me get this quite clear. You want to drill some holes in

Dr Sansome's head, stick some wires in it, and then measure what happens?'

'That's a very simplistic way of putting it, but —'

'And you think that's going to contribute to his recovery? Because that's all I'm interested in. All I'm interested in.'

'I can't promise that it will help him out of his coma. It may do, I just don't know. But he will be helping us all.'

'Helping you, you mean. So you can ride on the back of his research and publish a paper or two for your own glorification.'

'No! That is *not* what I want to do.'

'Then spell it out to me. What, exactly, my dear girl, *do* you want to do?'

Claire looked him directly in the eye. 'I've told you. I want to find out what's happening in his betz cells.'

'In his —! Words of one syllable, please, woman.'

Claire kept her voice even. 'I want to try and read Paul Sansome's mind.'

CHAPTER 3

Joanne Yeates waited at the traffic lights in her ageing Ford Escort and thought about her day. So much of her mind these days was taken up with the patient in Side Room 3, Dr Sansome. She had volunteered to have this man in her special charge. The staff nurses and students did a lot of the nursing, of course, but she had a particular concern for his welfare. The senior nursing officer and the neurosurgeon, Mr Porthenoy, had welcomed her interest, and given her a specific brief to pay close attention to his care, although in this case she needed no directives.

She always did a professional job with her patients at the Bristol General Neurological Unit, and did not differentiate between the good, the bad, and the ugly. They all got her best efforts. But this was an unusual situation. An eminent medical researcher, laid waste by a coma, a man who had devoted his life to studying brain activity, was now a victim of a malfunction of that very organ. She could understand the strong desire of everyone involved to try particularly hard to work for his recovery. As for herself, she often had difficulty concealing her own special devotion to the task.

The traffic was moving again now, out of the centre of Bristol. She'd soon be home. She wondered whether Lucinda would be there yet. Her four-year-old daughter went to a playgroup every weekday afternoon, and Joanne's mother brought her home if Joanne was on a later shift.

Sister Yeates turned off the A38 south of Bristol into Bishopsworth, and drove along a street of modest modern semidetached houses. She had been used to something a little more spacious, but when her husband had left her this was all she could afford with her share of the sale of their former home.

Her mother's car wasn't outside, she noted — obviously not home yet. She glanced at her watch: yes, she was back a bit earlier than she had expected.

Leaving the car outside the garage in the short drive, she let herself in, and closed the door behind her. It took a moment for her to comprehend what she was seeing. Part of the hall carpet was torn up; water was coming from under the kitchen door; the hall table lay broken, the carriage clock damaged; a family portrait was torn from the wall, the glass in the frame smashed.

She opened the door to the kitchen, and cried out in shock. The room was devastated. Everything had been thrown out of the cupboards onto the floor and broken glass and crockery were everywhere. Several doors had been torn from the units, drawers hung limply from bent runners. Both taps were running full pelt and something was blocking the sink, so that the overflow could not cope. Water cascaded onto the floor, which was awash.

Joanne felt faint, shut her eyes. Then opened them wide as she thought she heard a noise. From upstairs. *God! Are they still here, the maniacs that did this*? She listened again. The same sound, like a — like a weak, pathetic wail. Her fear became almost overwhelming, she had to fight to stop her bladder emptying. Please no! Don't let that be Lucinda! Don't let her have been here when they came!

Her fear of the intruders was forgotten as she raced up the stairs, the mother's instinct to preserve her young overcoming the weakness of her legs. She stepped over a broken chair on the stairs, hardly noticing the damage and destruction on the landing. Almost on the run, she threw open the door to her daughter's bedroom.

The sight that confronted her made her stop dead. Her stomach heaved, and she vomited a stream of acidic bile onto the carpet. She clung to the door frame, eyes tightly shut, hanging on until the retching subsided. She wiped her face, felt it wet and clammy with cold sweat, then forced herself to look again.

Lucinda's pet, an affectionate grey and white cat, lay mutilated but still alive in the middle of the devastated room. Joanne tried not to look too closely, did not want to contemplate the poor creature's injuries. She could see its body fluids, and could also see the use to which the animal's blood had been put.

Written on the wall opposite were twenty words. Neatly spaced, properly punctuated, no hasty graffiti, this. The neatness was spoiled where some of the blood had run in small rivulets down the Wedgwood-blue paint. Joanne read the message again, suppressing her sobs, trying to keep control.

> *Welcome home, Sister. Pussy first, Lucinda next. Unless you help me. We'll be in touch. Soon. No fuss. No fuzz.*

She'd had to cope with all sorts of horrors before — children ravaged by cancer, terrible injuries, suicides, tragedy. But nothing like this. She needed all her professional training to force herself to think rationally. The phone was dead. Ignoring the bloody warning, she went to a neighbour's house and called the police.

CHAPTER 4

As soon as she left the hospital, Claire called Ted. There seemed to be no hard feelings after their previously less than amicable parting. She arranged to meet him for lunch. They sat on opposite sides of a small table.

'So, how did you get on with the pompous old shirt-lifter?'

Claire laughed. 'Pompous, yes, but why do you think he's gay?'

'Just a feeling. Or maybe it's the name. How can you be normal with a handle like that? Anyway — how'd it go?'

'Not very well. I thought it would be easy — Porthenoy knew Paul some time back, and was aware of his work. But he pooh-pooh'd our results with the chimps. He said he'd let me work with Paul — but only passive stuff, and only if it was directed to aid his recovery. No holes in the skull. No research.'

'For *no research* read *no experiments.*'

Claire nodded. 'That's about it.'

'For a bloke who's in that much trouble, I would have thought it wouldn't make much difference to the poor bastard.'

'That's what I said, only more politely. I've read up a fair bit about long periods of coma, and it's clear that Paul has already reached the chronic stage. Eye-opening is occurring, and sleep-wakefulness cycles are appearing. He's breathing on his own, and his cardiac state is good.'

'So what does that mean? Is it promising?'

'No. The opposite. It's likely he's entered a period of what the books call chronic vegetative existence.'

'Poor sod. A cabbage.'

Claire swallowed and hung her head. 'Yes.'

Ted reached out and covered her hand with his. 'Sorry, old girl. Too blunt, as usual.'

'It's all right. I've got to face the truth, it doesn't matter much how you phrase it.'

Ted blew out his cheeks. 'So. What the bloody hell do we do now, me old mate?'

Claire could only shrug.

'Hey!' The big Australian banged the table. 'Did you tell him about Jason?'

Claire looked defeated. 'No. I didn't bother. There really wasn't much point. He'd only have dismissed that as well.'

'The data we got from Coombes was shit-hot. I thought it was more significant than the chimp experiments. We'd have clinched it if the poor bugger hadn't died on us.'

Claire had to agree. They had been so near a breakthrough. Jason Coombes was a young serviceman who took a massive drugs overdose, and went into irreversible coma. His parents were both doctors, and when it was clear he would never recover, they asked for all support to be stopped. They wanted his kidneys used for transplantation, but he developed renal failure, which meant they would be of no use. Paul Sansome got to hear of the circumstances through a long-time colleague and confidant, whom he had met in the Royal Air Force when he did a short service commission soon after qualifying. His friend was senior to him then, and had remained in the service and now reached the highest office of Principal Medical Officer to the Royal Air Force.

Air Vice Marshal Sir Richard Jacobs had kept in touch with his more junior colleague, and had followed his career with interest. Now he had a case that he knew might help Paul Sansome to achieve a breakthrough. Jason's parents agreed to allow the neurologist to carry out some investigations on their son, and he had therefore been transferred from the RAF Hospital at Wroughton to the Research Institute in Bristol. The purpose of the tests was to see if even in deep coma the brain would register sound. Playing tapes of familiar music or voices seemed empirically to be of value in rousing patients from deeply unconscious states, but there was no proof the comatose person's brain could respond to such stimuli. The recoveries were possibly coincidental. Dr Sansome wanted to find out. Using the same three-electrode probe technique through laser-drilled holes in Jason's cranium, they were able to trace the auditory pathway from the cochlea, the hearing organ in the inner ear, via the auditory nerve to the brain stem and on to the cortex in the temporal lobe. Detectable signals were found all the way along the route, right through to the cortex.

Dr Sansome took this to indicate that it was possible that a deeply comatose patient could not only hear sounds, but interpret them. The next step was to see where the response to the sounds went from there. Claire well remembered the day of the culmination of that effort. She was working with Ted on a study of computer analysis when Paul Sansome rushed in.

'Claire! Ted! I want you to look at this!'

He was holding what seemed to be miles of computer print-out. He clumsily cleared an area of work surface and spread out some of the paper. 'Here!' He pointed to an area of tracing that was circled in red. They hardly had time to look before he pulled out some more of the print-out. 'And here!' Another red-ringed area. 'And —'

'Hold it a minute, Paul.' Ted was laughing. 'We haven't got a bloody clue what you're trying to show us.'

'Come on, man! You designed this technique.'

Ted knew that only too well. The print-outs were computerised analyses of EEG records that he had worked on for the chimp experiments. They were nothing like the EEG tracing themselves. What Paul was showing them was the 'cleaned-up' version, with any identifiable recurring patterns enhanced. 'Where did you get these? I thought we'd finished analysing the monkey data?'

'These are from Jason!'

Claire began to look more closely at the highlighted areas. 'What have you been doing?'

The neurologist could not suppress his excitement or pleasure. 'Shot in the dark, really. I positioned another set of probes in Jason's brain into the area we were investigating in the chimp project, and made a sound. Here.' He pointed to a marker. 'The top trace is from the subcortical fibres in the temporal lobe where we got most auditory response.' He pointed to a pattern of spikes in the trace. 'Look. Message received.'

Ted nodded, now concentrating intently. 'Next trace —' Paul indicated the middle of the three on the paper '— is from the area we called the thought centre in the monkey brain. See that?' He sounded triumphant as he pointed to another complex wave pattern.

'I certainly do!' Ted was sounding excited now. 'Jeez! The time lag looks like it's a response to the sound!'

Claire was thinking and looking ahead. 'This bottom trace shows another response here — after another few milliseconds' delay. What's that?'

'What indeed! That —' Paul could hardly contain himself '— is the output from a third set of probes focused on the connecting pathway to the speech centre! Remember we talked about there possibly being one or more efferent pathways — ones going out — from the thought centre. I think that's one of them!'

Food, drink, love and life were all forgotten for the next few hours, as their world contracted to focus on analysing this new information. Ted was now the key figure, and he had an idea which drove him to a frenzy of activity. In the monkey experiments, they had been able to identify certain signals as being specific to a particular response. Ted was now applying the same technique to the traces Paul had obtained from Jason. He had got his ideas initially from the computer analysis of voice prints, now used in security systems and forensic science. He had to make a series of adjustments to the program to accommodate the differing signal amplitudes and frequencies. Claire prepared the data for inputting, and Paul mostly paced up and down.

Claire could see the Australian was getting more and more agitated. It was now past eight o'clock and starting to get dark. She thought perhaps his concentration was wavering through hunger, until he looked at her with a fever of excitement in his eyes.

'Get Paul.' She rushed to fetch him from the next room.

'OK — I've checked and double-checked this, and I still can't believe it.' He tapped at the computer keyboard he had been hunched over for so many hours, and a wave pattern came up on the screen. 'That's the input pattern — from the auditory nerve, that is, the sound.' He worked at the keys again, and a second wave-form appeared below the first. 'That's the thought centre trace. Now look at this!' Ted's fingers flew over the keyboard again, and the two traces were merged one above the other. They matched almost perfectly. '*Voilà!*'

'Yes, that's good,' said Paul, 'but it's no more than I would have expected. How does it compare on the other traces?'

'In a mo, Paul.' As he spoke, Ted demonstrated alternative, varying patterns of wave-forms. 'These are clearly different from the first one I showed you. These too.' More traces were displayed. 'So I take it you were making different sounds?'

'I was. Actually, I used words.'

'I thought so. Now look. I'll swear that this —' his fingers typed quickly '— and this —' more keyboard work '— and this — are the same word. Did you use one more than once?'

'Well, as a matter of fact, I did, I —'

Ted couldn't wait for him to finish. 'This is the really top stuff. After most of the other sounds, there is no output response from the thought centre. But after each of these there *is* an output signal.'

Claire could see what Ted was getting at. 'It's just as if the thought centre was making its own response. As if Jason's brain was actually *replying* to what was said!'

'That's it!' Ted almost shouted. 'And it's the same pattern every time!' The keys were tapped in a frenzy now. 'Here's the output pattern . . . and here's the input. They don't *quite* match. But I'd swear they represent an identical sound.'

Claire was struggling to comprehend the implication behind Ted's explanation. 'You mean the word Paul spoke and the reply from Jason's brain were the *same*? How could that make sense?'

'Depends what was said.' Ted turned to the neurologist. 'What exactly *was* the word you used several times, Paul?'

Dr Sansome had gone pale. He looked from one to the other, licked his lips. 'I only used one word more than once.'

'Well come on!' Ted urged. 'What was it?'

Paul looked at them both. 'It was — *Hello*!'

CHAPTER 5

The interview with the police officer from the CID did little to reassure Sister Yeates. When her daughter turned up safely with her grandmother, she could see the policeman assessing the threat to such a vulnerable small child.

'It's not the work of a crank, is it?' They were sitting on a torn sofa amongst the wreckage in her lounge, and she waved her hand around at the debris surrounding them.

'I'm afraid not, Mrs Yeates.' Detective Sergeant Clothier was untidily dressed and rather overweight, but his manner was brisk, efficient, and to the point. 'I don't want to sound alarmist, but this is not the result of some yobbos breaking in and having their idea of fun. Too extensive, too systematic.'

'But why?' She was trying to hold back the tears.

'That's what we have to find out. And that's the question you can help us answer.'

'I've told you already! I have absolutely *no idea*.'

The officer had asked a great many questions. He had gone over her past life, her associates, friends, asked her about membership of political parties, unions, had she ever been an activist for or against anything, been in trouble with the law, her job? There was nothing. Her life had been relatively smooth and uneventful, until the time of her divorce. That was a very stressful time, but she had survived.

'Was there animosity between you and your former husband?'

'I just can't imagine him doing something like this. Or understand why he would. We didn't exactly part the best of friends, but there were no threats of violence, and he seemed to accept my having care and control of Lucinda as inevitable.'

'Money worries?'

'I don't think so. He has a good job — works for IBM. He pays some maintenance for Lucinda. Not much for me, because I'm working. He married again soon after the divorce.' She gave a wry grin. 'To another nurse. She has a good job, I believe, so they've probably got a decent income.'

'Have you seen him recently?'

'We used to meet regularly, for him to see Lucinda. But that's been getting less and less since he moved to IBM headquarters in Hampshire. Long way to come.'

'And the last time?'
'Was about two months ago.'
'How was he then?'
'Same as usual, I think.'
'Thanks, Mrs Yeates. We'll check up on it, anyway.'
'It's not him, I'm sure. I almost wish it was.'
'What makes you say that?'
'Because then I'd know who to fear. As it is, I'm terrified and I don't know what of.'
'We'll keep a close eye on you, don't worry.'
'On Lucinda, I hope you mean.'
'Your daughter will be closely watched, of course.' He stood up. 'Where will you be staying tonight? I don't advise you to stay here. It'll be some time before the scenes of crime officers finish with this lot.'
'I'll go to my mother's place. It's only small, but it'll be all right for a few nights, while I get this mess . . .' She couldn't finish.
'Like I said, don't worry.'
Joanne looked up and gave him a smile that tried to indicate that she took comfort from his reassurance. But inside she felt only fear and dread.

* * *

At the meeting with Ted, Claire decided she would go along with Porthenoy's limited scheme. At least it would get her in to see Paul, and perhaps she could do enough to convince the neurosurgeon that her motives were not purely selfish.

She arrived at Paul's bedside in Side Room 3 just after nine in the morning. She had to wait while the nurses finished turning him and changed his catheter, which had become blocked in the night. She sat with Sister Yeates in the ward office. Previously chatty and with a ready smile, today she seemed withdrawn and did not appear to want to talk. She was quite relieved when a pretty student nurse came to say they had finished.

'Nurse Marvaine will take you along to Side Room 3,' said the sister, standing.

Claire looked across at the girl as she helped her carry some things along the corridor. 'I hope I didn't rush you this morning.'

Cherry Marvaine gave the researcher a cheerful smile. 'No problem. We'd nearly finished, anyway.' She looked down at the hold-all she was carrying. 'What's all this stuff?'

'I'm going to try and do something about Dr Sansome's coma. There's something I want to put to the test, but all this is just stuff to try and stimulate his memory, see if there's any reaction at all.'

The young nurse was full of enthusiasm. 'Oh, I'm so pleased. Although he's had super nursing and everything, no one seems to be showing any — well — sort of *personal* concern for him.' She pulled a face and half-whispered, 'Especially his wife.'

They entered the room, and set the bags down.

'Thank you, Cherry.' Claire read the first name on her identification badge. 'I'll sort it out now.'

'You're welcome. Give me a shout if you need a hand with anything.'

Claire smiled her gratitude, then set about arranging the things she had brought with her. She unpacked a tape-recorder and a selection of cassettes, some books, and a newspaper, then sat herself on a high stool next to the bed where she could see the patient clearly.

God, you look thin, she thought, studying the pale face, the features relaxed as if in sleep. She almost jumped as his eyes slowly opened. She expected him to turn to her with a look of recognition, and had to tell herself that this was a part of the 'chronic vegetative state' she had read about. If he was in a 'wake cycle' he might, just might, be more receptive to her attempts at communication. Well, better get started, she told herself. Through her mind went all the anecdotes, media reports, news bulletins she had read that involved family members whose loved one had recovered from coma.

'We spoke to him as if he was awake.'

'We knew we had to make her know we were there. We hugged her, kissed her, talked to her all the time.'

'Touching and talking. That's what we did. I knew he'd come back to us.'

There were countless examples. So why not try it? She cleared her throat and, feeling more than a little foolish, began her mission.

'Good morning, Paul. This is Claire Donaldson speaking.'

* * *

She spent two hours with him that day. She played music, of all kinds. She wasn't really sure what he liked, and she was damned if she was going to ask that bitch of a wife who had all but abandoned him. She read aloud about current affairs, and talked about the little she and Ted had been doing since his accident. There was no response.

The next day she took a portable television/video, and played tapes of programmes on science and nature of the kind that she had heard him talk about, and a recording of a short presentation they had made when they were trying to get more funds for their project. It was strange, seeing him there on the screen, erudite and animated, fit-looking. Such a contrast with the empty shell that lay on the bed at her side, thin, immobile, hooked up to feeding tubes and drainage bags. She wept silently, as if afraid he might hear her.

* * *

On the fourth day she was beginning to wonder how long she could keep this up. She had tried all she could. She had high hopes for one of her ideas — a tape of Ski Sunday. She thought the music, the talk of skiing, the association with the scene of his accident, might help. It didn't. She sat there in silence. He was probably too far into the vegetative state now to respond to any of this, she realised. She resolved to go on for a week before she gave up. But what, she thought, can I talk about now? She went over all they had done together, the hopes they had shared about a fantastic breakthrough in the field of clinical neurophysiology.

'Good morning, Paul,' she began, 'Do you remember that afternoon when you brought Jason Coombes' EEG tracings into the lab, and we stayed for hours while Ted analysed them?' She talked on, almost to herself, savouring the moment again.

She didn't notice at first. It was the change in respiratory rhythm that attracted her attention. She stopped and looked at him. He lay there, silent, breathing regularly.

She shrugged. Must have imagined it. She went on with her account of that exciting day, this time watching out of the corner of her eye.

'It was when Ted asked you if you used one word more than once that I went all goose-bumps. You said you had used a word several times, and —'

There it was again. A definite change in breathing! A pause, two short breaths, now gradually settling into rhythm again. Claire felt her pulse racing. What was she saying that was doing this? Was there a key phrase? She spoke the same sentence again.

'You said you had used a word —'

Paul's respirations changed again. Claire felt a chill down her spine. She hesitated a moment, then spoke a single syllable:

'Word.'

The breathing slowed, speeded up.

Why she said what she did next, she was not sure. Perhaps it was just another attempt to make contact. She suddenly realised she had not said it before. Maybe that was a little extraordinary — but she'd always greeted him with, 'Good morning.'

Now, her voice wavering slightly, she spoke questioningly, tentatively.

'Hello?'

Her whole skin tingled as she watched. Paul Sansome's breathing stopped altogether.

CHAPTER 6

The lift was crowded, and Joanne Yeates was tired. Her constant worry about her daughter's safety, trying to clean up the house, the hassle with the insurance company, were all taking their toll. Her mother didn't help much either. Of course, she wouldn't manage to keep on working without her help with Lucinda, but her mother was so thoughtless in the way she went on about the vandalism of her home and the accompanying threats. She was constantly speculating about what it meant, and had come up with a series of possible, and impossible, and downright ludicrous explanations clearly based on things she had read in the tabloid press. She seemed almost disappointed that, following Joanne's insistence on refusing interviews, she was not splashed all over the newspapers herself.

Although the hospital had flexible visiting hours, there often seemed to be a great influx just after two, and Joanne was caught up in it now. God, if she already felt this tired, how would she feel when she got home after work?

She was squashed in the crowded lift, afraid she would not be able to get out as it reached the third floor. She pushed her way forward, and felt a painful scratch on her left thigh. She thought she must have caught herself on a buckle or umbrella, but did not pause until she was well clear of the doors. She rubbed herself as she walked away from the lift, and felt wetness. When she looked at her hand, she saw blood. For a moment she was stunned. There seemed so much for what was surely only a scratch.

She looked back at the lift. The doors were just closing on the throng inside. Her mind struggled with the situation. Could someone in there have . . . ?

She thought for a moment of giving chase up the stairs, but dismissed it. She felt blood run down her leg, wanted to stop the bleeding. She hurried along to the staff toilet, stopping at the CSSD store to grab a dressing pack. Once locked in a cubicle she examined herself carefully. There was a dark stain on her uniform dress, but the material showed only a small slit. She lifted her dress carefully. Her tights were ruined where the fine threads, stretched over her upper thigh under tension, had pulled apart and left a ragged hole.

In the centre of the hole was a neat cut, angulated in the middle so the two parts of the incision were almost at right angles. Overcoming a vague faintness, she opened the dressing pack, pressed some gauze on the wound to stem the flow of blood, then looked more closely. It didn't look too deep. She pulled the edges apart carefully. Globules of yellow fat glistened amongst the red rivulets. She hurriedly pressed the dressing against her leg again, and sat on the lavatory seat while the nausea and weakness passed.

Not down to the muscle, anyway, she reassured herself. Reaching over to keep the pressure on with her right hand, she then used her left to reach down and mop up the blood that had run farther down, almost to her ankle. She felt better once the whole scene looked less gory. She debated with herself what to do next. It really needed stitching, but that would mean going down to Casualty, waiting around for God knew how long, answering questions, filling in an accident report form . . . No, she couldn't face it. Steri-strips would do; always some of those on the ward. She took off her one-size tights, reversed them, put them on again. They held the dressing nicely in place over the wound. She left the lavatory, picked up a pack of steri-strips, another dressing pack, and a role of Micropore, then returned to her temporary sanctuary, all without drawing attention to herself. Once there, she pulled down her tights and exposed the wound again. It was bleeding much less now. She peeled the first of the thin strips of adhesive tape from the backing paper, dried the skin, and held the edges together as best she could. She stuck the strip across the wound. Soon she had four strips straddling each arm of the cut. The edges were held quite neatly together. Some blood oozed between the strips, but she knew the dressing would cope with that. She applied two layers of gauze, and taped it in place with the Micropore. She pulled on her tights, left the cubicle, and at the wash-basin tried to sponge some of the blood from her dress. Not too bad, she assured herself. If anyone asks me I'll say I spilt a blood sample.

It didn't really occur to her at the time why she was being so secretive. When she thought about it later, she knew it was some subconscious concern that it had something to do with the events at her house and the threats to her daughter.

She didn't really have time after that to think much about her injury, except for the slowly developing ache under the dressing, or the sharper pain if she leaned on a bed, or if a patient she was helping brushed against it.

She got back to her mother's house late, exhausted, and wishing she were in her own home. There, she could have just made sure her daughter was fed, and planted her in front of the television. Then she could have flopped down on the sofa, closed her eyes, and let the tension unwind. Here, she had to face her mother's inquisition of the day's events, listen to her latest theories about the threats, and look as normal as possible. Otherwise there would be more fussing and clucking, more smothering.

Joanne felt guilty about such thoughts, knowing her mother would do anything to help, but at the same time she almost resented the intrusion into her life. She sighed deeply as she opened the front door.

'You're late!' was her mother's fatuously obvious greeting from the kitchen, almost accusing in its tone.

'Hi, Mum. Sorry. It's been a difficult day. How's Lucinda?'

'Fine, fine. Watching some cartoon rubbish on the telly as usual.'

Joanne went into the living-room and looked down fondly at her daughter. She lay on her stomach, kicking her legs back and forth, elbows bent and chin propped up on her hands. It occurred to Joanne that it was a scene a thousand mothers must see every day. But such simple sights took on a new significance when there was a palpable threat to your child's carefree existence.

Lucinda was watching a video of a cartoon she had seen a dozen times before, but which still held her interest enough that she had not heard her mother approach. Joanne sat in a chair and watched for a few more moments before speaking.

'Lucinda. I'm home.'

The child took one hand away from her chin and twisted round.

'Mummy! You're back!' There was a cackle of laughter from the television, and her attention went straight back to the screen.

'Aren't you going to tell me what you did today?'

With a sigh of reluctance, the little girl reached automatically for the pause button on the remote control and stopped the video. She hauled herself up, and came and leaned on her mother's knees.

'We did paintin' an' cuttin' things an' Domnick Bersford hit me an' Mary the one with the nose spilled her drink on the floor,' she said in one breath, then folded her arms and pressed her lips firmly together to indicate that she had finished.

Joanne managed to keep her display of amusement down to a gentle smile. 'Anything else?'

'Nope.' Lucinda tossed her hair. ''Cept that Mrs Lock got cross when James wouldn't wash his hands when he went to the lavat'ry.' She screwed her nose up, knowing her display of distaste at such behaviour would win her mother's approval.

'Naughty James.'

'Yes.' With a child's agile mind she abruptly changed the subject. 'When are we going to get a new kitten?'

Lucinda had been devastated by the death of their pet cat. Joanne shuddered at the memory, but covered it by moving to give her child a hug. 'Soon, dear. Not just yet.' She couldn't face the extra stress and responsibility of house-training another pet. When things were more settled, she'd promised.

Lucinda looked up with eyes wide. 'Mummy?'

Joanne prepared for a desperate plea. 'Yes, dear?'

'Can I finish watching the 'toon now?'

Joanne laughed gently and relinquished her brief hold on her daughter's attention. 'Go on, then!' Lucinda scampered back to the television and her mother got up and went into the hall.

She called into the kitchen. 'Mum! I'm just going up to change.'

Her mother came into the hallway. Looking conspiratorial, she held out a pink envelope.

'This came for you. No stamp. Must have been by hand.'

Joanne looked at it absently, then her attention riveted. The writing seemed familiar: *To Sister.*

Where had she seen that before?

Her mother nudged her.

'Well? Aren't you going to open it?'

Reluctantly, Joanne did so. She opened the page, managing to keep it from her mother's eyes.

There was no address, no date, no greeting, no signature. Just three lines, written in pencil:

I said no fuzz, remember?
I carved her name with pride.
Next time I'll carve her.

With a tremendous effort Joanne kept the shock out of her face. Nevertheless her mother detected something.

'What is it? Bad news? Who's it from?'

'It's nothing, Mum. Honestly. Just a note about playgroup.'

Without waiting to see if her explanation was accepted, she hurried up the stairs, calling back as she did so, 'Must go to the loo.'

For the second time that day Joanne used a lavatory as a sanctuary. She sat on the toilet in the bathroom for a while before she could bring herself to re-read the note, dreading its menace, its threat, trying to interpret the meaning. 'Carved her name . . .' she whispered to her self. 'Her name . . .'

She gasped, jumped up, lifted her dress, pulled down her damaged tights, hastily pulled back the dressing, and looked down at the injury again. One arm of the angled cut *was* longer than the other. But what . . . ? She picked up a hand mirror and looked at the reflection. Now it was obvious. She froze, panic threatening to overwhelm her. There was no doubt about it. The cut was in the shape of the letter 'L'.

'L' for Lucinda.

CHAPTER 7

'What do you mean, he just stopped breathing?'

Claire sipped her beer and looked round the crowded pub, as if afraid someone might be listening to their conversation.

'I mean what I say, you bozo. He just lay there, not taking a breath. I could see the carotid pulse in his neck clearly — he's so damn thin — so I knew he was still alive. Then his face started to go a sort of dusky red, then dark blue. I thought he was going to die. I thought his heart would pack up at any minute. I called the nurse, and just as she came in, he sort of shuddered, took a huge great gasping breath, and started breathing regularly. After a minute or so his colour was back to normal.'

Ted looked grim. 'Well if he didn't have irreversible brain damage before that, he will have now.'

'I don't think so. Although it seemed an eternity, it wasn't anything like three minutes before he started to breathe again. But I agree it can't have done him any good.'

'Did you try again — see if you could reproduce the effect?'

'Don't be stupid! I thought I'd killed him once. I wasn't going to try again.'

'But we can't just leave it at that, for Christ's sake! Not if you're sure it *was* in response to your saying hello.'

'I'm sure as I can be. It was really weird.'

Ted drank deeply, looked thoughtful. 'Look, I've been thinking. He must have had someone say "Hello" in earshot before that, even if it wasn't directed at him.'

'I know. I've asked myself that question too. I can only speculate about why he hasn't reacted before. I think he needed to be primed.'

'You make him sound like a bloody grenade.'

Claire smiled. 'Well, it is a rather explosive situation.'

'Could blow up in our faces.' Ted chuckled.

'We're sitting on a powder keg.'

Ted saw their laughter was attracting attention. 'OK, no more bum bomb jokes.'

That set them off again, and they stifled their giggles as best they could. As they sobered, Claire looked directly at the Australian.

'You know, we're making fun of this, but it could really be something terribly important.'

Ted's face became serious. 'I know.'

They were both silent for a moment, sipped their beer.

Ted sat back. 'So what about this "Hello" business?'

'What I was going to say, before you went off on your grenade tack, was that he was ready to respond. We know it's possible for people in a coma to register sounds in their brain, and I'd been talking about the tests we'd done with Jason Coombes. The moment when we identified the word traces on the computerised EEG interpreter must have been one of the most exciting of Paul's professional life. We kept talking about the key word, and when I used the word "word" —' she paused, gave a short laugh '— confusing isn't it? That's when I noticed a change in his breathing.'

Ted nodded his understanding. 'So the scene was set. You created a background, used an important word, and then hit him with the real key word from that evening, which was "Hello". Makes sense to me — as far as any of this makes sense.'

Claire emptied her glass. 'So what do we do now?'

'Risky or not, little Sheila, we've got to try it again.'

⋆ ⋆ ⋆

'Come in!' Gerard Porthenoy sat behind his desk, displaying, Claire noticed, another flamboyant waistcoat. The neurosurgeon gestured towards two chairs, and she and Ted sat down.

'I can give you ten minutes,' Porthenoy announced without preamble, looked at his watch, and repeated, 'ten minutes.'

'Christ, you make it sound like an audience with the bloody Pope!'

Porthenoy drew back with an expression of distaste. 'I beg your pardon?'

'Don't mind him.' Claire tried to sound soothing. She'd warned Ted they would have to suffer the man's arrogant patronising if they wanted to get anywhere. 'It's just his Australian sense of humour.'

'Well, it's not mine, so let's just get on with it, shall we? What do you want?'

Claire did most of the talking, telling the consultant about the events of the previous day, Paul's reaction, and their desire to investigate further. Porthenoy listened intently.

When she had finished, he looked pointedly at his watch.

'Sounds quite fantastic,' was his brief response.

Claire's heart sank. 'But it's true,' she said plaintively.

'I can't believe it. Can't believe it.'

'You mean you're not interested in our even trying any further?'

'I'll be interested if you can demonstrate it to me.'

'Of course.' Claire moved forward. 'That's what I want. To try again. And I'll be much happier if you are there, because it really frightened me last time.'

The consultant preened himself gently at this small flattery. 'Very well, my girl.' He put on some half-glasses and ran his finger down the following day's entries in his desk diary. 'Two o'clock. Sharp. Meet at Sansome's bedside. Good day to you both.'

Outside Ted was seething. 'Patronising bastard. "*Very well, my girl!*" Who the blazes does he think he is?'

No slight could dampen Claire's enthusiasm. 'Don't let the pompous old fart worry you. Just pray that I can make Paul do it again.'

* * *

Ted and Claire, feeling nervous and excited, were waiting in Sister Yeates' office. Claire glanced anxiously at the wall clock as she had done several times already.

'Joanne?' Claire had been here often enough now to be on first name terms.

Sister Yeates looked up from the cardex she was filling in. 'Don't worry. He's often late. I'm sure he won't have forgotten.'

Claire considered the nurse carefully. She seemed tired, pale. She usually looked so smart, but now she had a slightly unkempt look about her. She'd noticed the change over the past few days.

'Joanne, I don't mean to be nosey, but — are you all right?'

The sister looked up sharply. 'What do you mean?'

Claire realised she had struck home. 'I'm sorry, I'm not trying to pry. But you look, well, under strain.'

Joanne Yeates made a feeble attempt at a smile. 'I'm all right, really.'

Ted joined in then, blunt as usual. 'You don't bloody look it to me, mate.'

'Ted!' Claire admonished him.

Joanne produced a more genuine smile. 'It's all right. I must admit I'm a bit worried about one or two things.' She drew a deep breath.

She wanted to share her troubles with someone, someone she could trust, someone who wouldn't overdramatise like her mother. She wanted to share the burden, to ask if she was doing all she could to protect her child. This intelligent girl and her bluff Australian friend seemed sensible people, and she'd really got to like Claire, and reckoned her concern for Paul Sansome was genuine. Oh, well, here goes, she thought.

'It's my daughter. Someone has been making —'

The door burst open and Porthenoy strode in. 'Right let's get on with it. Bit behind schedule, I'm afraid. Bit behind.' Without waiting for a response, he turned and went to Paul Sansome's room.

No apology for being late, Ted noted grimly. We're obviously meant to be thankful to the gods that the Great Man deigned to grace us with his presence at all.

As Claire entered Side Room 3, Porthenoy was stationed on the far side of the bed, impatient for the demonstration to begin.

Sister Yeates and Ted filed in behind her, and moved to stand at the foot of the bed. Claire pulled up a chair and sat next to Paul. She reached out and took his hand, then looked plaintively up at the neurosurgeon.

'Look, I can't do this in a hurry, you know. If I rush it too much, it may not work, and then you'll think —'

'It's all right, young woman,' Porthenoy interrupted, holding up his hands and taking a step backwards. 'I won't rush you.' He glanced at his watch. 'I've got fifteen minutes. Long enough for you?'

Ted could not restrain himself. 'Ripper. You've been promoted, Claire. Congratulations.'

She looked up at him. 'Sorry?'

'From *My girl* to *Young woman.*'

Porthenoy looked across sharply. 'What was that?'

'Please!' Claire pleaded, looking from one to the other. 'I'd like to get on with this.'

'Sorry, chum,' Ted said to no one in particular. Joanne suppressed a smile.

Claire moved to make herself comfortable, then spoke in a soothing, gentle voice, her lips close to the comatose man's ear.

'Good afternoon, Paul.' She paused, feeling self-conscious doing this in front of an audience. Try and forget them, she urged herself. 'I want to talk just like we did yesterday. About the time you discovered the exciting changes on Jason Coombes' EEG tracing.' She tried to search for the same sequence of events she had used before. She spoke slowly and carefully, trying to cut herself off from the resonance of impatience that she was picking up from across the room.

After five minutes, she was reaching the crucial part. 'Do you remember Ted asking you about the words you'd been using?' She waited a moment. There was no change in Paul's breathing. 'The words, Paul,' she repeated. 'Ted asked you whether you used one of the words more than once.'

Claire was looking at the patient's face, but heard Sister Yeates gasp. Something had happened!

'Try again, Claire.' Ted spoke softly, as if afraid to break the spell. 'Use it in the singular.'

Claire nodded her acknowledgement without moving round. 'What was the word, Paul? What was the word we all got so excited about?' She glanced down at his chest, aware of the others all straining forward. His chest moved rhythmically, up, down, up, down.

'The word, Paul.' Up, down, up — up — he was holding his breath! Then out — two short breaths — then regular again. She looked triumphantly at Porthenoy, who seemed to be trying hard to look unimpressed.

Ted had moved much closer. 'Now try the big one,' he prompted.

Claire swallowed, her mouth dry. 'Hello, Paul.' Everyone in the room was still, even Porthenoy bending closer and concentrating hard. The man in the bed breathed on, unchanged.

'Hello, Paul.' Claire spoke more loudly. Nothing.

Disappointment began to seep into her stomach like a cramp. 'Just the one word,' Ted whispered.

Claire tried to use the same inflection as she had done the first time. 'Hello?'

Porthenoy straightened up, losing interest.

'Look!' It was Sister Yeates who shouted. They all turned to her. She was pointing at the foot of the bed. Under the covers something was moving! Claire's scalp crawled.

The neurosurgeon moved to the bedside, and as he went to pull back the blanket, the movement increased, spreading up the bed. Paul Sansome's left leg was trembling violently, now his arm, now his head. Porthenoy threw off the blankets. The back was arched, the whole skeletal frame going rigid, the face showing a ghastly rictus smile.

Claire and Ted drew back involuntarily.

'He's going into status. Get some IV diazepam and phenytoin. Quickly!'

Sister Yeates was back in the room within 20 seconds. Claire was staring horrified as the naked figure began to subside from its bizarre rigid posture. She relaxed slightly, but then flinched back as Paul's body jerked again into a prolonged spasm. The nurse helped Porthenoy draw drugs up into two syringes, the first being injected quickly via the drip tubing, the second more slowly. Within 30 seconds, the jerks and spasms began to subside, the breathing became deep and regular.

'He'll be OK now,' Porthenoy announced to Claire and Ted. 'Sister, put some diazepam into the next bottle of dextrose and run it slowly over six hours. That should stop any more trouble.'

Claire looked at the consultant. 'Did — did I do that?'

'Can't say for sure. Could be coincidence, but he's never had any seizures before. Something triggered it, though.'

'So what do we do now, mister?' Ted wanted a decision, not more hedging.

Porthenoy looked at his watch, something he did a hell of a lot, thought Ted. 'Have to think about it, old chap. No time now. No time.' He went to the door. 'We'll meet again tomorrow. My office. Nine a.m.'

'Old chap my arse!' Ted said to the closed door.

Claire didn't hear this exchange. Her head was in her arms, leaning on the bed, her sobs helping the tension to drain away.

CHAPTER 8

Christine Sansome walked briskly down Atherton Road, heels clipping the pavement, hips swinging, aware of the frequent favourable glances she received. She was in no mood to appreciate the fact that she still provoked interest in men, however. Her mind was on the forthcoming interview with her solicitor, and her eyes were looking out for the offices of Caskett, Barque and Trefoil. She had corresponded with them often enough, but never actually visited the premises. Things were too complicated, now. She needed to talk.

She sat impatiently in the waiting-room for ten minutes before the receptionist called her.

'Mr Barker will see you now, Mrs Sansome.'

'Mr Barker? I thought I was going to see one of the senior partners.'

'Oh, you are, Mrs Sansome.'

'Then what about the others?'

'What others, Mrs Sansome?' The girl looked worried.

'Caskett, Barque and Trefoil, of course.'

The girl relaxed, smiled. 'Oh, no, they're long since retired. I think perhaps dead, even. Mr Barker is the senior partner now.'

'All right, I'll see him, then.'

Another receptionist snorted a suppressed laugh and, struggling with her own expression, the girl showed Christine Sansome up the stairs and into a chaotic-looking office. David Barker was in his late forties, bearded, a little overweight, and looked tired. 'Come in, come in, Mrs Sansome.' He went to offer her a seat, saw they were all piled high with papers and files. 'I'll just move some of these . . .' He cleared a chair by putting some files on the floor so that his visitor could sit. He went behind his desk, and moved another pile of files aside so they could see each other across the surface.

'Now then . . .' He reached for the phone, spoke into it. 'Miss Totter, would you bring us some coffee, please?' He shuffled some more papers before looking up at the woman opposite, and smiled benignly. 'Now what can we do for you, Mrs Sansome?'

She sat back, crossing her legs and allowing her skirt to ride above her knee, then planting her hands firmly in her lap. She looked directly at the solicitor.

'You know the circumstances of my present situation.'

'I believe so, yes, from our telephone conversations and correspondence. Most unfortunate.'

'Unfortunate is hardly the word,' Christine Sansome replied tartly. 'My husband is lying brain dead in hospital and likely to stay that way for God knows how long, and I'm stuck in limbo without a bean.'

Barker blinked rapidly several times, delaying while he framed a diplomatic reply. He frowned with concern. 'Surely that is not quite the case, Mrs Sansome. Of course, I cannot comment on the tragic circumstances of your husband, or how long he may remain in his — er — his unfortunate state. But I imagine that he is still receiving his salary from the District Health Authority.'

'Huh!' Her expression showed her derision. 'Yes he is, thank God. But he earned nearly as much again from his private work, and that has dried up completely.'

Barker looked surprised. 'And are you not able to manage on his current income?'

'No, I bloody well can't. We've got a sodding great mortgage on the house, and another loan paying for all the fancy equipment he insisted on having for his private rooms. There's hardly enough left for me to live on.'

'Surely there's some insurance?'

She spoke to the solicitor as if he were a stupid child. 'Of course there is. But that's no damn good to me unless he actually dies, is it?'

'No, no, my dear.' Barker raised his hands defensively. 'I mean insurance against loss of earnings in the event of illness, or to pay for the mortgage and loan repayments in such circumstances.'

'Ha! He didn't think of that, did he? The only things he's got pay up if he's dead. That's all.'

Barker looked genuinely worried. 'Oh, dear. I'm not at all sure how I can help. It seems to me as if you really need a financial adviser rather than a solicitor.'

'I've tried that. They advised me to use my savings and move to a smaller place. Why should I put up with some grotty little estate house with no pool and no privacy? I like it where I am.'

Barker tried to conceal his increasing dislike of the woman's selfish manner. 'I'm sorry to hear of your predicament, Mrs Sansome, but I really don't see how I can help.'

'You can answer some questions for me.'

'Well, of course, I'll try.'

At that moment a woman, presumably Miss Totter, brought in the coffee. Christine Sansome pointedly waited until the secretary had left and closed the door before continuing.

'I wish to be granted power of attorney over my husband's affairs.'

'Oh, I see.' Barker looked slightly embarrassed. 'I'm afraid that is not possible, Mrs Sansome.'

'Not possible? Why not? I'm his wife. I need to be free to manage his — our — affairs.'

'Power of attorney can only be granted by the person whose affairs are to be dealt with. Your husband is not in a position to grant such power. It is not an appropriate or feasible remedy in such a case, I regret to say.'

Christine Sansome stood up and turned away, biting her lower lip with an angry expression of frustration. She looked out of the window a moment before turning to address Barker again.

'All right, then. I want you to tell me if I can divorce my husband.'

The solicitor was barely able to conceal his shock at the question. He turned his face away and shook his head. 'I'm not sure that would be a very appropriate move in the circumstances. The poor man is hardly —'

'I'm paying you to give me advice, not a moral lecture.'

Barker looked very unhappy. 'I don't know that I'm really in a position to —'

'Can you answer my questions or not? If not, then I'll go elsewhere.'

Barker sighed, took a long sip of his coffee, and composed his thoughts.

'Divorce is a very complicated issue in these circumstances, Mrs Sansome, and certainly isn't an easy option. Someone would have to be appointed as a guardian *ad litem* for your husband, and in any event it would not be possible for five years.'

'Five years!' Christine Sansome moved to her chair and sat down. 'But — but — he's just lying there, useless! Why should I have to wait five years?'

'Because, Mrs Sansome,' the solicitor replied, unable to hide a grim satisfaction, 'that is the law. Mutual consent is needed to end a marriage any earlier. Dr Sansome is not in a position to be able to give that consent.' He looked up at her. 'And in any case, I'm not sure how divorce would help your situation. Your husband would be awarded at least fifty per cent of the assets, including the house, which with its large mortgage would almost certainly have to be sold.'

'Oh come on! I can't believe that. Surely the judge would give me the lion's share, leave me with the house to live in? What the hell good is it to Paul?'

'I think, Mrs Sansome,' said Barker, his exasperation beginning to show, 'that the judge would consider the future needs of your husband. There would need to be a contingency in case he recovers. He may need care for a long time. Circumstances may arise where it would no longer be appropriate for him to be in an NHS hospital. Private care of such an intensive nature is very expensive indeed.'

Christine Sansome could not hide her annoyance. 'For God's sake! What good will some fancy private home do him?'

Barker looked at her and forced himself to give her a smile. 'Well if that were not possible, might I suggest that you may care to look after him yourself?'

She looked away. 'Oh, very funny,' she muttered.

Barker stood up. 'I don't think there is much point in us continuing this conversation, Mrs Sansome.'

Paul's wife stayed resolutely in her chair. 'One more thing, Mr Barker. Can I not apply to the Court of Protection? Then I can arrange our affairs in any way I like.' She looked up and gave him a challenging smile.

* * *

Ted was waiting outside the door of Claire's flat when she got back from the meeting with Porthenoy. 'Well? What did the old buffer say?'

Claire ignored the question until they were both inside. She went straight to the kitchen and filled the kettle, plugging it in before finally turning to Ted.

'Do you want the good news or the bad news?'

'Jeez! Make it the good.'

'He said he'd thought about it, and he'd let us go ahead — with one proviso.'

'Magic! What's the proviso?'

'That we get permission *and* funding from the Clifton Neurological Research Institute.'

Ted looked relieved. 'That should be no problem. They've already said we can use up the rest of Paul's budget allocated for the year. That should be enough.' He looked eager. 'When can we start?'

'That's the bad news. After we get Mrs Sansome's permission.'

'Oh, ratshit! From what Sister Yeates was telling you, I can't see her agreeing to anything that might actually *help* her old man.'

'No.' Claire sat down at the kitchen table and rested her chin on her hands. 'Nor can I.'

Ted pulled out a chair, turned it round, and sat, cradling the back. 'Did he say when he'd be able to get hold of her?'

'Funny thing, that. He seemed terribly keen all of a sudden. Didn't look at his watch once, or call me *my dear*. In fact —'

The cordless phone on the kitchen wall trilled out its interruption. Claire answered, looked at Ted and mouthed, 'It's him.'

Ted leaned forward, trying to work out what was happening from one end of the conversation. It was obvious a decision had been made, and equally obvious that Claire was pleased. She put the phone down.

'Well, come on!' Ted urged.

'She's agreed!'

'Beaut. Did Porthenoy have any trouble bringing her round?'

'No, far from it. Porthenoy said something quite extraordinary. He said Mrs Sansome told him we could do what we liked to her husband. She said that with any luck we'll kill him.'

CHAPTER 9

The next morning Claire was in Paul Sansome's hospital room by eight-thirty. She'd brought a suitcase full of equipment with her from the research laboratory. Sister Yeates helped her move in a table big enough to carry all the computer equipment, and rearranged the room so that Paul's day-to-day care could continue uninterrupted.

Ted arrived about half an hour later, also laden with equipment. Claire was bent over her case, looking for a mains lead. Her colleague waited, admiring the view, and did not speak until she straightened up.

'G'day, Claire. How's it goin'?'

'Oh, thank goodness you're here. I'm getting really mixed up over all this wiring.'

'No sweat.'

They worked together for most of the morning, Ted setting up his computer equipment and Claire her EEG machine. The compact modern equipment did not take up a lot of space. The room allocated to Paul Sansome was actually intended for two beds, and was laid out like a small ward. Their paraphernalia used up most of the area where the second bed would be. They had to stop a few times, while the patient received necessary attention, being turned, washed, drip feeds changed, catheter bags emptied, drugs administered.

Just before they were about to leave for lunch, Porthenoy called in on them. He surveyed the array of complex instrumentation.

'My word, we have been busy.' He looked under the tables at the mass of wiring and cables. 'God, that looks like spaghetti junction. Is it safe?'

'Safer than a nun's knickers,' Ted assured him.

Porthenoy ignored the crudity and addressed Claire.

'When do you think you'll require the implantation of the electrodes?'

This was a job that the neurosurgeon would have to do himself. Claire had thought originally that was one reason why he had not wanted her to carry out the special tests on Paul. Whether it was relevant or not, the consultant now seemed only too willing to help.

'We'll need to test this stuff this afternoon.' She waved vaguely at all the electronics. 'But once it's all checked out, if there are no snags, then we'll be all set.'

'Splendid.' Porthenoy smiled at her. 'Then I'll schedule him for theatre at the end of my list tomorrow morning. I take it you have the special probes and mounting devices available?'

'Yes, we have. Two sets are ready and waiting, sealed and sterilised.' When she, Paul and Ted had done the work with Jason Coombes, they had used specially designed fine wire electrodes, with fixing and adjusting devices, based on the chimp experiments. Several sets were made, as at the time they had hoped to be doing more work with Paul. Now, ironically, he was to be the recipient of the probes.

Porthenoy cleared his throat, and looked slightly embarrassed.

'I'd like you to be in theatre with me, please, Miss Donaldson. It's clearly essential that the things are placed with pinpoint accuracy, and you probably know better than I about their exact location.'

It was Claire's turn to smile. 'I'd love to be there. Thank you.'

'Till tomorrow, then.' He swung round on his heel, leaving the smell of expensive aftershave hanging in the air.

'Strewth! Wonders never cease.' Ted snorted with derisive laughter. 'He's actually admitted that you, a mere woman, might know more than him about something.'

'There wasn't much gallantry there, I can assure you. He wouldn't have a clue where to put the electrodes. We have all the X-rays and CT scans from the Coombes case, but now that Paul can't tell us, I'm the only one who knows the precise depths and angulations required. And he knows it.'

'So why did you look so bloody pleased when he asked you? I'd have said, too right I'll be there, mate, just try it without me.'

'I only want to keep on the right side of him, that's all.'

'I give up. Let's go round the pub. I'm so bloody hungry I could eat the crutch out of a low-flying duck.'

* * *

The tests that afternoon went smoothly. There were one or two problems, but nothing Ted couldn't sort out. Not only did he know all there was about programming, he was a very good electronics engineer.

There was a simple problem with the EEG machine, some interference which Claire couldn't get rid of. Some more screened cable and a secondary earth cured that. Otherwise it was all straightforward, made easier by the fact that Paul was out of the way some of the time. He was taken down to the Radiology Department where he had up-to-date X-rays, CT scans and Magnetic Resonance Imaging carried out, all necessary to ensure precise location of the electrodes the following day.

By five they were finished. Tired but full of anticipation, they left the hospital, agreeing to meet later for an Indian meal.

* * *

Claire was up early, partly because she felt she could not lie in bed with the excitement of the day to come, and partly because she wanted to clear up the flat before she left. Ted had come back with her last night after their curry, and they'd had a few beers and eaten biscuits and cheese. Her sitting-room looked a mess.

She was rather surprised that Ted hadn't tried anything. Perhaps I'm losing my allure, she joked with herself. Or maybe — just maybe — he's respecting me more. The responsibility of working together like this, on equal terms . . .

She smiled to herself. Who am I kidding? He's as randy as ever. Just tired, more like!

The operation was not scheduled until late morning, but she had plenty to occupy her at the hospital. She left the house at eight-fifteen.

By a quarter to nine she was knocking on the door to Sister Yeates' office.

'All right if I go in?'

'Of course. Nurse Marvaine is in there doing his obs. You can ask her to help if you need anything.'

'Thanks.' Claire walked briskly down the corridor to Side Room 3. She felt a warm glow of excitement. Things were going better at last. Co-operation from the nice ward sister, Porthenoy acting human, Ted behaving less neanderthal; and she was getting the chance to help Paul and do some incredible research.

The nurse was standing by the bed, just taking off a blood pressure cuff, and recognised Claire from her earlier visits. The activities in this room had generated a lot of interest amongst the ward staff.

'Good morning, Miss Donaldson.'

'Hello, Cherry. And it's Claire. Sorry if I'm disturbing you.'

The nurse started to fold up the cuff to replace it in the machine. 'No trouble. I've nearly finished.'

Claire was impatient to get her equipment checked out, but the nurse was standing between the bed and the tables of machinery, and she could not get past to switch it on. 'Sorry to be a nuisance, but could you just reach behind you and put the power on for me?'

'Of course.' Cherry Marvaine turned round and surveyed the array before her. 'Which one is it?'

'The one on your far left.'

The nurse reached out and touched a large grey box sporting chromium bars and a multiplicity of dials and switches. 'This one?'

'No, those are the filters. It's on the big computer.'

The student nurse moved her hand. 'Here?'

'That's it. The switch is round the back. On the left. I don't know why they put them in such silly places.'

Cherry reached round, feeling for the switch. She frowned. 'Can't find it.'

'Never mind,' said Claire, 'You come out and I'll do it.'

The girl's face brightened. 'It's OK, I've got it.'

There was a click. Nurse Marvaine's head jerked back, teeth bared, eyes showing the whites. Claire jumped back in horror as she watched the girl's whole body go into spasm, muscles jerking erratically, hideous gagging sounds coming from her throat. Claire thought she was re-living the nightmare of Paul having his epileptic fit, and moved back to the door to call for help. But something was different! The nurse was transfixed, not falling, her hand still behind the machine.

My God! She's being electrocuted! The thought exploded into Claire's mind, and instinctively she moved to save the girl. She jumped forward, grasped the jerking, outstretched, clawing hand — and felt the shock travel into her body.

Claire's own hand went into spasm, she could not let go. She was briefly aware of a painful rhythmic throbbing in her head, then felt herself falling, falling, a multicoloured spinning kaleidoscope illuminating her journey into oblivion.

* * *

There was a strange smell. What was it? And something hard — hard under her face, pressing against her cheek. She opened her eyes, saw she was lying on the floor. The smell — stronger now, like burning meat. And a faint sizzling noise, as if something were cooking, as if . . .

Nausea swept over her with the memory of the nurse jerking helplessly, her hand still behind the machine. Claire started to move, tried to raise her head. Suddenly, complete silence, the sizzling had stopped. Then a faint movement, material rustling? There was a rushing dark shadow, and as Claire instinctively closed her eyes she heard and felt a thump which caused her to open them again immediately. She would always regret that simple action, never forget what she saw: Cherry Marvaine's contorted face, lying only inches from her own. The teeth were bared, and the eyes . . . She had never seen eyes opened so wide, so filled with terror, yet empty and unseeing.

Claire's shocked system could take no more. She slipped back into darkness.

CHAPTER 10

Claire gradually became aware of an ache. Not an ordinary pain in one part of her body, but an all-pervading sensation that seemed to involve every limb, every muscle. She tried to move, heard a groan, realised it was her own voice. Someone picked up her hand, and she tried to pull away, recollection of her last waking memory returning. The hand gripped tighter, and she jerked her arm, snatched it away. The nightmare of being unable to release her grip from the dying girl set off a wave of panic.

'Claire! It's all right. It's me.'

She turned her throbbing head towards the sound and slowly opened her eyes. Ted was leaning over her, concern on his face. Behind him, Sister Yeates looked on anxiously.

'Ted?'

'That's me. Your old Australian deadhead.' He gently stroked her arm. 'You're OK, honey, you're OK.'

Claire tried to sit up, and her neck and back rewarded her with a jag of pain. She cried out, flopped back on the pillows, and tried to look round the room.

'What — what happened to Cherry?' She forced herself to ask, even though the blank staring eyes she would never forget had already given her the answer.

Ted and Sister Yeates exchanged glances. Ted took Claire's hand. This time she did not try to withdraw. He spoke softly.

'She's dead, I'm afraid.'

Claire could not speak, just closed her eyes, releasing some latent tears.

'You tried to save her, I know. Crazy bastard. Nearly killed yourself, too.'

Claire forced her eyes open again. 'I — I didn't think — just wanted to get her away —'

'Not a very sensible thing to do, eh?'

'She was dying, Ted!' Claire tried to choke back her sobs.

Ted spoke softly. 'I know, I know. Silly thing for me to say. I'm just upset for you — I wouldn't want anything to happen to you, old girl.'

There was a silence, and Joanne Yeates moved forward. 'It was very brave of you. You probably only survived because you fell away from poor Cherry, and that broke your grip.'

Claire sniffed, and the sister produced a tissue. Claire accepted it gratefully. 'How is it she died and I didn't?'

Ted spoke authoritatively. 'For one thing, she was getting the shock through her much longer than you. And it's a fact that some people are much more susceptible to the effects of electric shock than others. What would kill one person wouldn't bother another at all.' He hesitated. 'There was nothing more you could have done, Claire.'

She looked at Ted, tried to smile, but her sense of loss for the dead girl was too great. She hardly knew her, but Cherry Marvaine seemed so nice a person, didn't deserve to die. 'Such a waste,' she said, then reached out and held on to Ted and shed her tears.

Sister Yeates withdrew discreetly, and left the two of them alone.

Slowly Claire's crying subsided, and she pulled away.

'Sorry about that. I suppose you think I'm a feeble English female.'

'No way. I know you're not the sort to spit the dummy. You're tough as a dingo's dick.'

This time Claire did manage a smile. 'You certainly know how to flatter a lady.'

Ted laughed. 'Can't help it. 'Sa natural trait in us smoothie antipodeans.'

Claire's smile faded slowly, and Ted felt he knew what was coming when she looked at him, a puzzled frown forming on her brow.

'Ted?'

His heart sank. How was he going to handle this one?

'What went wrong? I mean, with the equipment? I've switched it on hundreds of times, and I've never felt —' She shuddered.

Ted wiped his hand over his face and thought about it. Is there any point in hiding it from her? She'll know sooner or later. Shit! She's gonna feel bad all over again!

Claire easily read the signs. 'What is it, Ted? Please tell me.'

The big man took a deep breath. 'There was a fault in the wiring.'

'What sort of a fault?' Claire looked puzzled.

'The earth and live wires had been changed over. When it was switched on, the whole chassis became live.'

He watched Claire's expression change as she absorbed this information. 'What do you mean, changed over? You mean someone *did* that?'

Ted nodded sombrely.

'Deliberately?'

'It was no accident.'

Claire's hand went to her mouth. 'My God!' Her eyes met Ted's, and she saw no reassurance, no denial. 'Someone tried to kill me!'

* * *

Despite the death of Cherry Marvaine and Claire's narrow escape, Porthenoy wanted to go ahead with the operation on Paul Sansome. He came to see Claire as soon as he heard she was recovering. Ted was still with her. It was now about 10.30.

Porthenoy put on a sort of oily charm which Claire supposed represented his best bedside manner. It made her feel rather uncomfortable, and his sexist patronising was much in evidence.

He was dressed in a green theatre gown and cap. He patted her thigh through the bedclothes. 'So sorry to hear about our little tragedy,' he said with exaggerated concern in his voice.

Little tragedy! Christ! Ted could hardly hold back his anger at the way an innocent girl's life was being dismissed. Claire looked at him, as if to say, I know what you're thinking, but please keep your mouth shut. With an effort, he did.

Porthenoy continued, unaware of the signals flashing past him. 'I was hoping I could still do the procedure on Dr Sansome at the end of my list this morning. I won't have an opportunity again for some time. Lot of commitments, you see. Lot of commitments.'

Claire had almost forgotten about the scheduled operation. She felt desperate about the nurse's death, already guilt clouding her thinking as she told herself that Cherry would still be alive if she hadn't insisted on working on Paul Sansome. Her head ached, she felt lousy. The last thing she wanted to consider was the need to concentrate on a complex medico-scientific problem.

'I really don't think —' She looked worriedly at Ted for support.

'Poor girl's been through hell, Mr Portlenoy. Can't you give her a break?'

'It's *Porthenoy*, Mr Parkes, and I'm afraid my schedule does not allow any flexibility in the matter.'

'You mean,' said Ted bluntly, 'that either you do the business now, or you'll bugger off and leave us in the shit.'

Porthenoy tried a jolly laugh and failed pathetically. 'Well, I wouldn't put it quite like that . . .'

'But that's what it comes down to?' Ted looked from the consultant to Claire.

'Yes, yes — I'm afraid so. As I said, my commitments are such that —'

'Yeah, yeah, we heard you.' Ted didn't want to push Claire, but knew how much the project meant to her — and to him, he realised. He really didn't want to let this opportunity go by. 'What do you think, Claire? It's gotta be up to you. If you don't think you want to face it . . .'

Claire sighed deeply. 'It doesn't look as if I have much choice.' She looked at Porthenoy, his face a mask of forced concern. Even so she could detect the impatience behind his eyes. 'I don't suppose you can do it without me there.'

If it hurt him to admit it, the neurosurgeon managed to suppress the feeling. 'No, dear girl, I can't — as you well know. Placing these things in exactly the right spot is critical, and it is you, not I, who are familiar with the relevant topography.'

'How long have I got? I'll need to look at the latest CT scans and MRI pictures.'

'I've got an exploratory to do on a possible acoustic neuroma. Looks pretty straightforward. Shall we say an hour and a half?'

Claire closed her eyes. Ted moved over and took her hand.

'Think you can make it, gal?'

'I'll try.'

* * *

Ted was surprised by Claire's performance. Overcoming her aching muscles and ignoring her thudding headache, with a tremendous effort of will she had forced herself to concentrate on the problems of the surgery. Gradually she became engrossed in events. In the theatre she was decisive and positive. Even Porthenoy was clearly impressed, and after an initial skirmish of wills he followed Claire's directions attentively. Claire's involvement initially was with the siting of the electrode mounts, but once that was decided, the next part was all Porthenoy, and Ted had to admire his dexterity.

This was the first time the Australian had witnessed an operation, and he found it a harrowing experience. Dr Sansome's head was completely shaved, and when Porthenoy made the first incisions into the exposed scalp, Ted had to look away. Maybe I'm not as tough as I think, he wondered.

Then there was the drilling, and the sizzling of diathermy and laser. The smell of singeing flesh troubled him, but not as much as when Porthenoy started to screw the electrode mounts into place. The small stainless steel cylinders were designed to hold the ultra-fine probes in their precise locations, and were finely adjustable. They had to be fixed rigidly to the skull to hold their position exactly, which meant firm attachment to the skull itself. It looked to Ted as if Porthenoy was screwing them halfway into Sansome's brain, and he felt close to retching.

That done, a rigid steel wire cradle was attached to the skull. This was to enable head movement to be limited, and thus reduce the chance of the electrodes being disturbed.

Now it was Claire's turn again, as they threaded hairlike test electrodes into place, using X-ray scanning and EEG tracings to check position. At last Claire was satisfied that they were near enough. The fine tuning could be done later, with Dr Sansome back in his room, the computer to help them, and no pressure on their time.

Porthenoy pulled off his gloves and mask as he left the theatre. Ted felt he owed him something. 'Thanks, mate. That was very impressive.'

The consultant waved a hand. 'Straightforward enough.'

Claire came across to them as her patient was wheeled into recovery. 'Thanks for your time, Mr Porthenoy. We really appreciate it.'

He nodded slowly, momentarily closing his eyes and smiling, as if the accolade was no more than his due. Then he surprised them both. 'You were damn good, young woman, damn good. Good luck with the tests, eh?'

He swept out of the theatre, leaving Claire and Ted to exchange astonished glances.

CHAPTER 11

'How can you be certain the equipment was tampered with overnight?' Detective Sergeant Clothier asked Claire.

The CID officer sat on the edge of his seat, notebook on his knee. Bent forward as he was, his prominent lower stomach seemed almost to rest on his thighs. Ted lounged on the sofa with a beer, while Claire stood by the window.

'I've told you that already. I checked it all over the previous afternoon. Ted was with me. We left about five. I switched the machine off myself. If it had been got at, I would have been electrocuted then, instead of that poor girl . . .' Claire choked off the sentence.

'Yes, miss, I'm sorry. And after that?'

Claire sighed. She was getting weary of going over the same ground that she had already covered at the police station the previous afternoon. 'We both left the hospital, and we met again about half-past eight. At the Tandoori Palace in Eastern Road. We left there about eleven, came back here for a beer, and Ted — Mr Parkes — left soon after midnight.'

'He — er — didn't stay the night, then?'

Claire was indignant. 'No, he didn't!' Ted grinned.

'This is all confidential, miss. I'm not just being nosey about your private life.'

'He did *not* stay the night. If he had, I'd have told you.'

The policeman was disappointed. 'Pity.'

'I beg your pardon?'

'Sorry, Miss Donaldson. No offence. It's just that it would clear up the matter of Mr Parkes' movements that night.'

'Give him an alibi, you mean?'

'Yes.'

'But he doesn't need an alibi. You're not trying to say that he messed about with the wiring?'

Ted sat up straight. 'I should bloody well hope not!'

'No, no, I'm not saying anything of the sort. But as we've heard, Mr Parkes says he went straight home, and didn't see anyone until he returned to the hospital in the morning.'

'That's not exactly unusual for someone who lives on his tod, Sergeant,' Ted said with thinly disguised sarcasm.

'No, sir, it isn't.' Sergeant Clothier consulted his notebook. 'You said you looked at the wiring after the electrocution incident.'

'Too right.'

'And you said it was done by someone who knew what they were doing?'

'Look, you don't need to be an electrical genius to know that if you connect the positive to the earth it could be bad for someone's health. But getting the cover off the computer to gain access to the rear panel is not so simple. It was taken off and put back again very carefully so it didn't look as if it had been disturbed. It was very cunning. The switch is plastic, so no danger there. But the mounting screws and baseplate are metal, and our murderer made sure they were live.'

'Yes, I see.' The sergeant made a note. 'How long do you think it would take to do that?'

Ted thought for a moment. 'Dunno for sure. I reckon ten, fifteen minutes, tops. If you knew what you were doing.'

Claire had not really considered the practicality of setting up the attempt on her life before. She moved away from the window and sat down. 'Sergeant Clothier, did you ask how often Mr Sansome is checked on during the night?'

'Good question, miss. As I understand it, about every 15 to 20 minutes. But it's not a rigid schedule.'

'If something was going on somewhere else, you mean, he might be left longer?'

'I suppose so. I'm probably less familiar with hospital routine than you are.'

Claire thought again, spoke slowly. 'But it wouldn't be easy — I mean to go in at night and not be seen, get into the room and work for a quarter of an hour undisturbed.'

'No, Miss Donaldson. Although there is a difference between not being seen, and not being noticed.'

Claire was only momentarily puzzled. 'Oh, you mean if it was someone familiar to the staff, to the hospital . . .'

'Exactly.'

Ted had been listening closely to the discussion, and saw a flaw. 'But surely you've questioned all the staff who were on duty that night? Asked them about all the people they saw? Especially anyone who wasn't usually around at night.'

'We have indeed, sir. Everyone, that is, except one.'

Ted frowned. 'And who is that?'

'Cherry Marvaine.'

Claire looked across at Ted, then at the policeman. 'But of course not! She's dead! How could she —?'

'If you'll let me explain, miss. Student Nurse Marvaine was a kindly girl, it seems. She'd done a swop to help out one of her friends, just for that night, for the night duty. Some pop concert in London, I think it was for. She was also working that morning, but was off at noon. So she stayed on, going to go straight to bed after, I suppose.'

Ted concentrated. 'So it could have been *she* who saw someone in Paul's — Dr Sansome's — room, but didn't know what was going on?'

'It's a possibility, sir.'

Claire looked worried. 'I don't suppose — it couldn't have been that Cherry was *meant* to be the victim? Because she saw who was there?'

'No, that doesn't work.' Ted dismissed the idea immediately. 'There's no way someone could be sure she would be the victim. You — or me — must have been the intended coffin fodder.'

Clothier nodded. 'I'd agree with you there, sir.'

Claire bit her lower lip, released it. 'Of course, we both use the stuff, were planning to work together . . . Oh, Ted!'

He shrugged dismissively. 'No worries, Claire. Maybe they were just trying to frighten us off.'

'But why?'

'Search me.'

The sergeant looked inquiringly at them both. '*Why* is a most pertinent question.'

Claire shook her head. 'I have absolutely no idea.'

'Me neither.'

Clothier shifted his bulk and suddenly changed tack. 'Mr Parkes, you're quite sure no one else can corroborate your story as to your whereabouts last night?'

'It's not a story, mate, and no there isn't.'

'Were there any lights on in nearby flats? Anyone who might have been awake, heard you come in?'

'I don't bloody know. Why don't you ask them?'

The policeman gave him a polite smile. 'Yes sir, I think we will have to do that.'

Ted was getting fed up with the inquisition. 'Look, have you checked the gear out for fingerprints and all that stuff?'

'Indeed we have.'

'So — any luck?'

'So far only three sets of prints have been identified. Miss Donaldson's, your own, and Nurse Marvaine's. And a lot of smudges.'

'He could've worn gloves.'

'That is a possibility we have considered.' The policeman smiled politely again, and Ted scowled, covering his annoyance by swigging from his can of beer.

The sergeant heaved himself up. 'I don't think I need to trouble you any more at present. I appreciate your co-operation.'

Claire showed him to the door.

'Hey!' Ted called after him. 'Aren't you going to tell me not to leave town?'

The policeman's response was a frosty smile, then he turned and left.

'Ted!' Claire admonished him. 'There's no point in antagonising him. He's only doing his job.'

'Bloody Ds. Can't he see that if I had anything to do with it I'd be off like a bride's nightie?'

Claire laughed. 'Perhaps he thinks a clever man would stay around and stick it out.'

'Just a minute! You don't think I had anything to do with it?'

Claire was never more sure of anything. Ted's undemanding support these last few days was causing her to revise her opinion of him. She went and sat beside him on the sofa and gave him a chaste kiss. 'Not you.'

Ted picked up her hand. Claire expected a joke, or a sexual advance. She got neither. Ted looked at her with his pale blue eyes and murmured softly, 'Thanks.'

* * *

Sergeant Clothier sat in his car outside Claire's flat for a few minutes. Something was worrying him, and that something was the connection that had prompted his superintendent to get him to look into this case. Someone had apparently tried to kill Claire Donaldson. Or had they? It seemed too much of a coincidence. He'd been investigating threats made to someone else — someone who was a sister on the very same ward. Surely there had to be a connection, he thought. If there was one, he couldn't make it. He started the car and drove off.

* * *

Joanne Yeates had the morning off. Thankfully, her mother had offered to do the shopping, so she had a little peace, the place to herself. There never seemed to be time for her to do any thinking, her mother seemed to have a knack of always intruding. If she was quiet for more than a few moments, she was asked if there was something wrong, was she all right? Poor Mum! I wish I didn't resent her so much. I know it's just her way. Joanne tried to push away the guilt and concentrate on her latest concern.

The death of the girl on her ward had been a terrible shock. Suddenly her life seemed filled with violence, and she could not suppress the fear that she was connected with this latest horror. The thought would not go away that the electrocution was somehow meant for her. After the last warning until now she had not had any more contact with the police, although it had been impossible to avoid it after what happened to Cherry Marvaine. My tormentor would realise that, surely? she tried to convince herself. And what is it he, or she, wants? She shook her head in desperation, unable to understand. She thought about the dreadful message on the wall written in the blood of her dead cat, and shuddered. *Unless you help me.* What did it mean? She had racked her brains about it. No one had asked her for help, she had refused no one's assistance. Was the demand still to come?

Her fingers found their way to the wound on her thigh, touched it lightly. It was healing well, no infection. She wished her mind would heal as quickly. She was so tired. Sleep had not been coming easily recently, she was physically and mentally exhausted. She lay back in the comfortable chair and closed her eyes, hoping for the escape of sleep, praying for freedom from her nightmare.

* * *

The figure moved nearer to the window where the light was better, and read the headline of the local paper again.

STUDENT NURSE ELECTROCUTED IN HOSPITAL

A snarl contorted the face and a stream of poisonous abuse poured out.

'Stupid bitch. Why did the little whore have to get her interfering fingers into this? Serves the bastard little cow right!'

The paper was screwed into a ball and flung into a corner. If anyone had been listening they would have heard an angry growl change into a gentle chuckle and then swell into squealing laughter. Slowly the amusement faded, and the eyes looked round for the photographs, seeking solace from this setback.

They were in the dressing-table, under a pile of underwear. Hands sifted through them, looking for the favourites, found them, the children, the naked children . . .

Lying back on the bed, the eyes began to scan the images, and the expression changed to one of sly contentment. Almost without conscious guidance, a hand went down to add to the pleasure.

CHAPTER 12

It was not until after the weekend that Claire felt ready to resume the investigations with Paul Sansome. Even then, on that Monday morning, re-entering Side Room 3 promoted symptoms of acute anxiety. Her pulse rate and breathing slowly settled, however, as she and Ted set about checking all the instruments and their connections. Ted had a complex circuit tester that could determine if the equipment was correctly wired, and even when that was done all the accessible plugs and connections were visibly checked.

Ted had asked the police to search the room and check it for bugs, and they had even had a technician from the anaesthetics department check the oxygen delivery system.

'If he has another of those fits and we need to give him oxygen, I don't want cyanide gas coming out of those pipes,' he joked with the technician, who assured him that all was in order.

Claire was aware that Paul seemed somehow much quieter. His breathing was slower, the pupils more dilated, eye movements less frequent. She attributed this to the sedative effects of the phenytoin which he was being given via his intravenous fluids. This was to ensure there were no further convulsions such as the one Claire herself had appeared to precipitate when demonstrating Paul's reactions to Porthenoy.

It took most of the following day of testing by trial and error before she and Ted were certain that the superfine electrodes were in the right place in the brain. The devices Porthenoy had fixed to Dr Sansome's skull were set perfectly, but the exact location of the electrodes was critical to a fraction of a millimetre. It was vital to make sure they were in precisely the right part of the brain. Numerous X-rays were taken, and Claire used up metres of EEG paper.

Ted filtered the signals using his specially devised computer program. Finally he was satisfied he had a 'clean' record, and that the signals were emanating from the parts of the central nervous system that their earlier experiments with Jason Coombes had indicated: the subcortical fibres in the temporal lobe, the connecting pathway to the speech centre, and the association fibres of the mid-zone of the parietal lobe. This last was the area they had termed the 'thought centre'.

It was after seven before they agreed to call it a day.

'I'm bushed.' Ted pushed his chair away from the table holding the computer. 'Let's sign off.' He tapped the keyboard four times and the screen went blank.

'Good idea.' Claire was tired, hungry and hot. She said so.

Ted nodded his agreement. 'We've been at it for nearly ten hours non-stop.'

'Not quite non-stop,' Claire reminded him. 'We've had a fair few interruptions.'

Ted laughed. 'You can say that again!' Every fifteen to twenty minutes Paul needed attention from the nurses. He was turned, limbs were moved to prevent contractures, fluids balance was checked, catheter bags drained. Every time something happened, they had to stop for a while. Although Paul Sansome's head was kept still by the wire cradle, any muscle movement could produce artefacts on their delicate measuring instruments. 'Can't be helped, though, eh?'

Claire looked across at the big Australian. He had been working unstintingly with her all day, never complaining. She knew he was interested in the research, but it was not something he *had* to do. He hadn't tried to chat up the nurses, hadn't made one sexist remark all day. Perhaps he wasn't feeling well. Or maybe he wasn't such a bad guy after all. Steady, girl. Don't go all soft on him now, she warned herself. Still, she reasoned, feeding him tonight won't do any harm.

'How about coming back to my place? I'll make us something to eat.'

Claire was disappointed to see the familiar leer return. 'Sounds great. Only tucker on offer, is it?'

She looked heavenward in mock despair. 'Yes, Ted. Only tucker.'

'Well, never mind. Still sounds like a good deal to me. What d'you say we pick up some tinnies on the way?'

Claire cooked a simple meal, and they washed it down with the beer. Then, inevitably, they began talking about the work that lay ahead. They were both full of anticipation, hopeful, excited.

It was gone eleven when Claire noticed the time. They were sitting comfortably on the sofa, Ted's arm across her shoulder, their position suggesting the unconscious intimacy of a long-standing relationship. Claire smiled to herself. He's getting good. I didn't notice when he put that there.

'We've got a long day tomorrow. Time for bed.' She immediately regretted her choice of words, expecting Ted to interpret the statement as an invitation. She was not disappointed.

'That's just about the nicest thing you've ever said to me.' He smiled with his wicked schoolboy grin, and stroked her shoulder. For a moment she almost considered playing him along. A few caresses, strong arms holding her, it would be comforting, a pleasure she had not had in a long time, ever since . . .

The memory and pain of her broken engagement swept away her relaxed mood. Ted saw the change in her face.

'Hey! What happened? Just for a minute there, I thought — '

She lifted his hand up and over her head. 'Sorry, Ted. Too tired, too uncertain — '

'Too many memories of that bastard that left you in the clag still hanging around?'

She nodded slowly, sadly. 'Something like that.'

'I don't know how he could do it.'

Claire looked up sharply. 'Do what?'

'Leave you up the duff like that.'

Claire started to deny it, then her rising defiance collapsed. She spoke softly, looking down at her hands. 'How did you know I was pregnant?'

Ted was genuinely apologetic. 'Look, I'm sorry, Claire. I shouldn't have mentioned it.'

'How did you know?'

Ted shrugged. 'People talk, y'know.'

'I suppose they also told you I had an abortion.'

'No, as a matter of fact, they didn't. Just knew you lost it, that's all. Thought it was the shock.'

Claire was silent for a minute, then forced herself to face Ted, who was watching her with concern. He was surprised to see tears in her eyes.

'Do you think that was very wrong of me? Getting rid of a baby like that?'

'Does it really matter what I think?'

Claire looked at him, considered only briefly. 'Yes, it does matter.'

'Christ, woman!' Ted laughed awkwardly. 'You know me, the way I live. What right do I have to make any judgement of you?'

'I'd still like to know.'

'OK, for what it's worth. I reckon you did the right thing. You couldn't give the little sprog much on your own. And who knows, you might have resented it, being the offspring of the lousy dag that ditched you.'

Claire simply nodded.

'And if what you're really asking is do I think any the less of you, then the answer is — I still think you're a really great girl. Honest.'

'Thanks.'

'Any time.'

Claire's tears were drying on her cheeks and she ventured a small smile.

'Ted?'

'What is it, girl?' Ted spoke tenderly.

'What's a dag?'

Ted looked at her sombrely, the expression on his face grew more serious.

'Sheepshit,' he intoned.

They collapsed into each other's arms, laughing helplessly.

* * *

When Claire awoke the next morning, the Wednesday of the third week in May, she felt an eager excitement, keen to be at the hospital. She ate a hasty breakfast, then cleared away the beer cans. She paused as she lifted the lid to drop them in the waste bin, thinking of Ted. With a gentle sigh she dropped the cans and replaced the cover, symbolically putting the lid on her thoughts.

'Time to leave.' She spoke aloud to herself, briskly, and went for her car keys.

CHAPTER 13

'Ready to go?' Ted sat before his computer. Claire was sitting where she could reach the controls of the EEG machine, and could watch Ted's screen and the patient. She looked at the test trace from the electro-encephalogram, and then at Paul Sansome. He was lying still. Sister Yeates herself had helped the nurses to bathe him and change his gown, and had told Claire they could safely leave the patient undisturbed for at least half an hour.

She looked at the shaven head. It was like something from a science fiction movie, held in its stainless steel wire cradle. The three electrode focusing devices jutted out from the skull, two either side towards the back, one centrally towards the front. Fine coiled wire led to a junction box that connected them to the computer and the EEG machine. She noted that there was just the beginning of hair regrowth, except for the small circular areas she had prepared for the external EEG electrodes. Cables from these small adhesive pads went straight to the electro-encephalograph.

The headphones Dr Sansome wore looked incongruous. That had been Ted's idea. To exclude errors or misinterpretation from extraneous sound, he had set up a microphone and small amplifier, so that any speech could be transmitted direct to the headphones.

Paul Sansome lay quietly, as if waiting for something to happen. His eyes were open, staring unseeing at the ceiling.

Claire gave a little shiver. 'Ready.'

Ted saw her reaction. 'Don't worry. There are no thunderstorms forecast.'

'Thunderstorms?'

'You look as if you half expect a bolt of lightning to come through the window, go down the electrodes, and energise the Doc here to get up and walk.'

Claire gave an uncertain smile. 'You must admit that what we're doing is a bit spooky.'

'Cobblers. This is a scientific investigation.'

'I know. Sorry.'

'So — ready?'

Claire took a deep breath. 'As much as I ever will be.' She reached out and set the EEG machine running. Paper began to spill out onto the floor. Satisfied by what she saw, she turned it off again. Most of their data would come straight from the three implanted electrodes and go straight into the computer. Ted tapped at the keyboard, looked at the wave-form on the monitor, and nodded. 'Off you go.'

Claire had to swallow, her mouth was so dry. She massaged her salivary glands with her tongue until there was enough fluid to speak. She leaned forward to the small microphone on its stand in front of her.

'Hello, Paul.'

Ted spoke immediately. 'Just the one word to start with, remember?'

'Sorry.' Pause. 'Hello?'

Ted frowned. 'Something's wrong. I'm not getting any response.'

Claire reached across and checked the EEG print-out. 'This looks OK.'

'Try again.' Ted looked anxiously at the screen in front of him.

Claire leaned towards the microphone again. 'Hello?'

'Zilch. Not a dickie bird.'

Claire got up and looked over his shoulder. 'I don't understand. We were getting sound recognition signals from the auditory pathway and the association fibres yesterday.'

'Did you check the headphones this morning?'

'Yes. And the microphone was — Oh!'

Ted looked round, surprised to see amusement and not anxiety. 'What the hell's the matter with you?'

'I — er — forgot to switch the microphone on.'

'You drongo! I thought all our work had gone up in smoke at the first hurdle.'

'Sorry.' Claire sat down. 'Let's try again.' She flicked the small sliding switch on the body of the microphone, leaned forward, and spoke the familiar word once more.

'Hello?'

Ted's response was immediate. 'That's better. Auditory signals going in. Hold it one second.' He worked at the keyboard. 'Right!' He now had two wave-forms on the screen, one above the other. 'Again.'

'Hello?'

'Beaut. Afferent pathway to the thought centre is responding. Now then.' Once more his fingers tapped messages into the computer. Three traces were now displayed. 'That's the efferent pathway recording. If there's any response, that's where it'll be.'

Claire was feeling very nervous. It was at this point that Paul had stopped breathing the first time, and the second had the horrendous epileptic fit. She wiped her palms on her jeans, swallowed, tried to keep the tremor from her voice.

'Hello?'

'Again,' Ted commanded.

'Hello?'

'Nothing.' He typed in a series of commands. 'Let's run it again.'

Claire glanced at Paul Sansome's chest. His breathing pattern had not altered. 'Hello?'

'Bugger it!'

'What's the matter?' Claire stood up, came over to stand at his shoulder.

'There's something there, but it's very indistinct. Look.' He replayed the signals the computer had recorded. 'See.' He pointed in turn at the three wave-forms. 'The top one — sound in.'

Claire could see the irregular trace zigzagging across the upper part of the monitor.

'The middle one — signal received at the thought centre.' The signal traced an almost identical pattern in green phosphorescence.

'But here — look.'

Claire watched the lower trace as it wavered across the cathode ray tube. There was some irregularity towards the middle of its pathway, but the amplitude was small, the pattern nothing like those above it.

Claire felt relief and excitement. 'Don't panic, Ted. There *is* something there! It's just not coming through properly. One of the probes needs refocusing. It probably got accidentally disturbed overnight.'

Ted smiled up at her. 'Good on ya, Claire. Let's try it.'

She went over to Paul Sansome, and moved round to the back of his bed. The head of the bed had been removed, and it had been pulled away from the wall to allow easy access to his skull and its attachments. She made a fine adjustment on one of the micrometers holding the electrodes, then they repeated the whole process from the beginning.

'Better', announced Ted, looking at the much higher amplitude wave-form on the lowest trace. 'Another half a millimetre should do it.'

Claire made the adjustment, and they began again.

'Hello?'

'OK.'

'Hello?'

'Looks good.'

Claire hesitated. 'Hello?'

Ted stared at the screen. 'Say again.'

'Hello?'

'Jeesus! Come and look at this.'

Claire jumped up, staring at the screen, while Ted frantically instructed the computer to replay the findings.

The tracings flickered across the screen. Ted held the images steady, and there they were: the pattern produced by Claire's 'hello' going down the auditory nerve, being received by the thought centre — and then, after a delay of about a second, the response! An almost similar pattern!

'That's it! Just like we saw with Jason Coombes!' Claire almost whispered the words, excitement tingling through her.

'Looks like it. Longer delay in response, though.'

'Almost as if he's considering his reply.'

'Funny thing, though, Claire.' Ted looked thoughtful. 'Have you noticed a change in his breathing pattern?'

Claire had wondered about that too, had been watching carefully for any sign of a change in their patient's respirations, or any sign of another epileptic fit. There had been nothing. She had some ideas about it, though.

'I think it must be the phenytoin — the drug he's having to make sure he doesn't have any more seizures. It has a sedative effect. We don't even know how it works in detail. I reckon it's interfering with the reflex connections from the thought centre, so that anything emanating from there that would normally cause stress, and hence a change in breathing or the massive electrical discharge of a fit, is being blocked.'

Ted was impressed. 'Hey! That's pretty good.'

Claire looked modest. 'I *have* been giving it a lot of thought.'

'Well, let's not sit back on our laurels. Let's run it again. I want this to be fully reproducible. We've got a lot of sceptics to convince.'

Claire moved back to her seat and sat before the microphone. She drew in her breath, was about to speak, when Ted shouted.

'What the hell — !'

Claire looked across anxiously. 'Ted?'

'Did you touch the mike then?'

'No. Why?'

'Must have been an artefact. I just saw a discharge on the bottom trace.'

Claire frowned, shrugged. 'Shall I go again?'

'Yep! This time I want — *shit!* There it goes again!'

Claire left her chair to look. 'Run it back for me.'

Ted clattered the keys. 'Here it comes.' They watched in silence as the irregular pattern formed on the lower tracing. 'That was the first one.' More keyboard work. 'And that's the second.'

'My God!' Claire paled, felt her arms form goose-bumps. 'I'd swear that's no artefact.'

'But the patterns aren't like the one in response to your *hello*. See where it builds up and dies away, then builds up again.'

'Can you bring the two output traces together?'

'Good idea.' Ted's fingers flew over the keys. 'That should do it.' The screen cleared, to be replaced by only two tracings, one above the other. 'That one,' he pointed 'is after you said *hello*. And the bottom one is the spontaneous discharge I saw just now.'

'Quite different.'

They stared in silence at the flickering image. Ted finally broke the spell.

'One of us has to say it, however crazy it sounds.'

Claire licked her lips before she spoke. 'The second signal coming from the thought centre represents a different word.'

'Almost right. The trace has a double peak, right?'

'You mean it's two words?'

'I'm going to bring up our first output response. There. Now, look at the first peak again.'

Claire stared hard, holding her breath, letting it out in a rush. 'Christ! The first peaks are the same.'

'You see what he's doing? Without prompting, a two word response. The first one, hello, the second one . . .' Ted was sweating. 'I'm going to save this to disk before the bloody thing blows up on me.' He issued the commands, the hard disk softly squeaked its response, the screen cleared.

As they watched, the twin-peaked trace went across the screen again, unbidden.

Ted clenched his fist. 'He's said it again.'

Claire was shaken. 'Thought it again, you mean. But — how do we find out what the second word is?'

Ted wiped his face in his handkerchief. 'I don't know. We've got to—'

A student nurse put her head around the door. 'Sister Yeates wants to know if we can turn Dr Sansome again.'

Ted looked up sharply. 'No!' The girl looked startled. He tried a smile. 'Sorry, look, can you tell her we want just five more minutes.' The face disappeared, the door closed.

'OK.' Ted's face was creased in concentration. 'Go to the mike, say "Hello, Paul." Two words.'

Claire did as she was instructed. A twin-peaked wave pattern appeared on the top two tracings. After a longer interval than before, another double-peaked response flickered across the output section.

'OK.' Ted cleared the screen. 'Now say your own name.'

'My own — '

'Just do it!' Ted almost hissed at her, teeth clenched. She leaned forward, spoke into the microphone.

'Claire.'

'Again.'

'Claire.'

'Now come and look.' Ted carried on talking as he manipulated the pictures on the screen. 'Top trace — the input response to *Hello, Paul.* Second trace — output response from his thought centre. First peak equals *Hello.*' He paused, glanced at Claire, then went back to the screen. 'Now I'll just change the top trace — there. That's the input response to you saying your name.' He paused again. 'Now look at the second peak of the thought centre response.'

Claire did so, and caught her breath. Her eyes went back from the top trace to the lower, back again, double checking.

'But — but — my name and the second peak seem to be almost identical!'

'Yes. I think they are.' Ted turned to her. 'Which means . . . ?'

Claire felt light-headed. 'It means he knows we're here, knows who I am. He's saying, "Hello, Claire"!'

* * *

Ted looked across the table at her as he took a long swig from his beer. The pub was crowded, they had been lucky to find a small sanctuary away from the bar. He put down his dimple glass and grinned.

'Christ! I needed that. Something to steady my nerves.'

'Me too.' Claire was drinking gin and tonic. She had felt she needed something stronger than a beer.

'I still can't believe it.' Ted shook his head.

'We're a bit thin on proof, though.'

'I've got an idea about that.' He tried to look mysterious.

Claire smiled. 'Out with it then, Dr Frankenstein.'

'If this is genuine, we have the chance of communicating with a man in a deep coma.'

'You don't have to tell me that! But how?'

'We need to identify more word patterns.'

'But to do that we'd have to build up some sort of vocabulary.'

'Exactly,' the Australian agreed. 'And I'm surprised if you can't see how.'

'Using the input signals from known words, you mean?'

'Right. When you say a word, we get a pretty good idea what sort of pattern it produces from the efferent pathway in the association fibres. If the traces on "hello" and "Claire" are the real McCoy, then we know from what we have already that there are only marginal differences between the brain listening to the word and the thought of that word that presumably in a conscious person would produce speech.'

Claire understood, spoke urgently. 'So we go through a vocabulary, me speaking the words and you recording the input signals.'

'That's right. I store them all on computer, and teach the computer to recognise a particular wave-form as a word. Shouldn't be too difficult. Then we try and match up the output responses. We can construct a thesaurus, and I can easily get the computer to search it and print out suggestions.'

'A bit like a spelling checker on a word processor, you mean?'

'Dead right. Same principle.'

'How many words do you think we'll need to give us a chance of making any sense?'

Ted thought a moment. 'Well — I read the other day there's about half a million words in the English language.'

'Half a mil — don't be ridiculous, Ted!'

'All right, all right. But even in a small dictionary there are thirty thousand or more words.' He held up his hand to stop Claire's further protest. 'But we can whittle that down. We'll use a computerised thesaurus, go through the headwords, and just include the really common stuff. I should think a couple of thousand words should do it. Maybe three.'

‘Three thousand!’ Claire was daunted by the prospect. ‘It sounds a mammoth task.’

‘Mammoth, nar, elephantine, maybe. Couple of weeks, we’ll be home and hosed.’

CHAPTER 14

The two bags of groceries were heavy and the plastic handles, stretched by the weight of the contents, were cutting into her hands. Joanne Yeates always did her weekly shopping in Sainsbury's on a Friday, when they had late opening, even though it was so crowded. With her work schedule it was really the best time.

She climbed up the stairs to the third level of the multi-storey car park, and recalled her annoyance that when she'd arrived someone had pinched a space just inside the entrance from under her nose. She kept her head down as she climbed, it was almost a habit now to avoid looking at the vulgar graffiti that defaced the grimy concrete walls.

She turned left at the top of the litter-strewn stairs, then stopped. Suddenly she wasn't sure she was in the right place, it looked oddly unfamiliar. She stared hard for a moment, tutted in annoyance, and continued. She *was* in the right place, but the lights were out on this side. Although it was still dusk, the sky was overcast, and in here with the grey walls giving no reflection and the narrow strips between floor and ceiling admitting little light, it was quite dark.

She followed the line of cars until she came to her battered Ford Escort. She had driven into the space so that the boot was easily accessible. She put the bags down, using her leg to stop them falling over, while she unlocked the lid. She heaved the bags in with a barely audible grunt followed by a sigh of relief. One of her least favourite tasks had been completed yet again.

She slammed the boot lid shut, using considerable force. It would spring open if she didn't. She unlocked the car, and flopped down into the driver's seat. It was completely dark inside. Pulling the door shut wearily, she inserted the key into the ignition, then jiggled the steering wheel. She always had to do that to free the steering wheel lock. One of these days, she thought, I'll get the garage to fix it. She stopped trying to free the wheel. What's that smell? Vaguely familiar. Where the hell's that coming from?

She turned her head into the darkness, and was aware of a black shape exploding towards her from the well in front of the passenger seat. There was a grunt, a rustle of clothing, and Joanne Yeates felt a fierce pressure in the left side of her chest. Her heart felt as if it had stopped with the shock, her breathing seemed paralysed.

'Don't scream! Don't move!'

The commands were hissed at her, coming out of the dark. Joanne pulled away towards the door. The hard pain in her side followed. She was trying not to panic, groping for the door handle, when the voice spoke again.

'Just keep quite still. There's a gun in your ribs. I don't want to use it.'

The voice was like a soft growl, gruff, yet almost effeminate. And evil. Sister Yeates could almost feel the evil.

She tried to find her voice, could not disguise the shaking. She looked towards the vaguely discernible greyish blur that was all she could make out of her assailant's face, as her eyes got a little better adjusted to the dark. She was scared, but defiance was still in her.

'Get out of my car!'

The weapon was jabbed into her side, making her gasp. 'I give the orders around here!' The strange guttural voice came at her in the dark, words spoken so forcibly that she felt spittle on her face. She wiped it away, abhorrence and fear making her heave.

She waited for control over her reflexes. 'What – what do you want?'

'Don't worry, Sister *dear*. I'm not going to hurt you. Not if you just do as I ask.'

Joanne tried to move away to ease the pressure on her ribs, but she was already up against the door. She could no longer turn to reach the catch without giving away her movements. She tried to think of a way out. Blow the horn to attract attention? Damn! She remembered that she had not yet turned the stubborn ignition key. The horn wouldn't work. The lights! What about the lights? She couldn't switch on the headlights either – but the sidelights might show something, give her a chance. She reached forward slowly to the switch. Her sleeve made a faint rustle.

'What are you doing, bitch?' The voice came again, and almost at the same moment Joanne felt her hair grabbed, her head pulled back. The pressure in her side momentarily eased, then a fiery jolt of pain made her cry out. The gun had evidently been withdrawn a few inches to give it room to be rammed into her more forcibly.

Sister Yeates knew terror and shame at the same time. She was a resourceful woman, but she felt defeated and terribly frightened. Her bladder suddenly seemed full, and she knew that in a moment she might wet herself.

'Tell me what you want!' She virtually sobbed the words.

The strange, low voice seemed to suppress a laugh. 'I want you to examine this. Hold out your left hand, open, palm upwards.'

Joanne did so. Something touched her arm, and she instinctively pulled away.

'I'm not a leper.' Another half-snigger. 'I'm only going to hold your arm and guide it. I want you to identify something.'

Joanne steeled herself as the hand touched her again, moved down her forearm to her wrist, grasped it, directed her hand across the seat, into the blackness. She hesitated, tried to pull back. The grip tightened, there was another jab in her ribs.

'Now close your hand.' The command was reinforced by another lancing pain in her side.

She obeyed. Reluctantly, slowly, fearfully, she closed her hand, encountering a thick rod-like structure, slightly compressible. She stopped.

'Well?' A hint of amusement in the hateful, strangled tones. Another fierce prompt in her ribs.

Joanne moved her hand slightly, and the voice came out of the dark, softer, quieter.

'All *right*!'

Realisation and revulsion struck simultaneously. She whipped away from the erect penis as if her hand had been plunged in boiling water.

Again that half-chuckle. 'What's the matter? Don't you like it?'

'You bastard!' Joanne was breathing fast, too fast. She felt her head starting to spin, forced herself to slow her respirations down. Don't pass out! God knows what he'll do to you if you pass out!

The voice came at her again. 'So here's the big question. Do you think your little Lucinda would like it?'

This time Sister Yeates nearly did faint, had to fight for consciousness. 'Oh, God! Please. She's only four!' She realised, no shame this time, that she was crying.

'So young.' The voice dripped false sorrow. 'I don't know if she'd cope, you know.'

Joanne almost lost control. 'For God's sake, what do you want?'

Her assailant sensed the nearness of hysteria, changed from the taunting, cajoling tone to a business-like briskness.

'Now just listen to me, *Sister*, and I'll tell you how you can spare your little girl from a meeting with Percy here.' There was a pause. Another jab in the ribs.

'Are you listening?'

'Yes, yes, I'm listening. Please, don't —'

'Shut up! Just pay attention. It's very simple. All I want is to know everything that goes on in Side Room 3. I think you know what I'm talking about. Now you may speak.'

'Side Room — but there's just a man in a coma. There's nothing to tell.'

Joanne cried out as she was struck another cruel blow in the chest. Her ribs felt on fire, repeatedly jabbed in almost the same spot by the gun barrel.

'I don't want any discussion. Don't try to fool me. There are experiments going on there. Very interesting experiments. I've known about them for some time.' The voice went higher, seemed to change, then became gruff again. 'You want your little girl safe and sound. I want to know *everything* that goes on in Side Room 3.'

'But — but I don't know how, I —'

'I *will not accept* any excuses!' The voice trembled with a suppressed anger that the nurse could almost feel in the air. 'You will have to work out for yourself how to find what I need. You will also have to learn how to operate their computer, so you can copy data from its hard disk.'

'Hard disk? I don't know what you're talking about.' Joanne was pleading, desperate.

The half-chuckle was back. 'Well you're just going to have to find out, aren't you?'

'I can't, I don't *know* —' The jab in the ribs was almost as much as she could stand. She gasped, breath rasping, trying to get air into her lungs.

'You have no choice. Think of little Lucinda. The police won't be able to protect her 24 hours a day, you know. In fact, if you tell them about our little meeting, I can promise you — you'll find her split asunder within days.' The mock sorrow returned. 'Poor little girl.'

Joanne was sobbing, barely able to think straight, her chest wall agony.

'Do you hear me?'

Joanne nodded.

Another searing pain. She had forgotten her nod could not be seen. She could only manage two or three words at a time. 'Please, please stop . . . poking me . . . I can't . . . can't breathe.'

Her torturer waited in silence until the shuddering breaths became more even. 'All right. I'm waiting to hear it. Don't let me have to prompt you again.'

'I'll do my best. I promise. Please don't hurt Lucinda. Please, she's only four, she's—'

'That's enough. Just remember. Find out what's going on. Learn how to copy disks and extract information from the computer. We'll meet again, soon.' A guttural, sinister laugh followed. 'One more thing before I go. Something for you to remember me by.' She thought she heard the door open, tensed, expecting a blow to immobilise her before her assailant left. Instead, Joanne's hair was grabbed at the back, her head was pulled back. 'Now,' the voice hissed. 'struggle and I'll poke this barrel right through your chest wall.' The gun was jabbed at her again, in that same searingly tender spot, to emphasise the point. The direction of pull on her hair changed abruptly. She was caught unprepared, as her face was pushed over to the passenger seat, forced down.

'No!' As she opened her mouth to scream, something was forced into it, something hard, and cold. *Cold*? her mind asked, trying to tell her something was wrong, but her terror and disgust overwhelmed coherent thought. She gagged as the thrusting object reached the back of her throat. All reason seemed to leave her, all other thoughts, fear of death, fear for her daughter, were swept away. She could barely move her jaw, but she had one overpowering desire. In a frenzy of rage, she wanted only one thing. Revenge, regardless of the consequences. With all her strength, she bit her teeth together.

Her strong incisors sank in, came closer, met almost with a snap. Her head was freed, she pulled it back, spat out what was in her mouth. There was no scream, no salty metallic taste of blood, just a hoarse chuckle and the slamming of the car door. Joanne realised she was alone, and collapsed, sobbing, onto the empty seat, which was still warm from the evil presence that had occupied it moments before. She did not know how long she lay there, trying to regain some reason, some sanity. Eventually she gently pulled herself up, her injured side giving her a series of jags of severe pain.

Now she was upright, holding her side, wanting to drive away, get home, but wanting to look, to see . . .

She reached up and turned on the interior light, her eyes searching to her left, coming to rest on the dark phallic shape on the floor. She felt a surge of strange emotion, a mixture of utter revulsion and triumphant glee. But – something was odd, something not quite right . . .

She forced herself to reach down and pick up the object. It was a courgette.

CHAPTER 15

Ted and Claire had been compiling the computer vocabulary for three weeks now. On this particular day the Australian had been working hard for hours, trying to keep his concentration going during the frequent interruptions necessary for Paul Sansome's essential nursing care. Although it was only three-fifteen, he was getting tired and irritable and knew it was time to stop.

'I need a proper drink,' he announced suddenly, throwing his clip-board on the floor and standing up. 'My mouth's like an abo's armpit after all this cheap hospital coffee.' He stretched and yawned. 'Let's call it a day, and I'll buy you some grub and a schooner, eh? What d'you say?'

Claire was only too happy to agree. They seemed to be struggling now to find words that were likely to be useful for communicating with Paul, and that was good. After all the standard prepositions, common adjectives and adverbs, they had moved on to nouns, and now were working through the verbs, trying to separate the various tenses and make them identifiable. There were over three thousand five hundred words stored in the computer's memory. Not many compared with the thesaurus in a word processor, but for Ted's specially written complex program it was near the maximum. Each word had to be analysed from its wave-form, using Claire's voice input and the 'thought centre' input from the electrodes in Paul Sansome's brain. That way they hoped to identify the wave patterns that came *out* of his thought centre, and equate them with recognisable words, just as they believed they had done with 'Hello' and 'Claire'.

Testing it out was going to be an exciting time. Both of them felt they had done enough preparation and wanted to give it a try.

They started to tidy up their equipment, switch everything off. Joanne Yeates came in as they were about to leave.

'Packing up early today, then?' she asked pleasantly.

Claire smiled at her.

'Yes, we've had enough.' She was worried about the nurse, who looked drawn and tired, and seemed to be losing weight. She was certain she was troubled, and remembered how she had seemed to be on the point of talking about it one day in her office some weeks back. But the sister had not tried to confide in her since, despite ample opportunity.

'That's good. I didn't want to interrupt you again, but it's time for his obs. and the drip needs changing.'

Ted had noticed that the ward sister was doing a lot more of the coma victim's care now; also that she had become more talkative — at one point he had briefly entertained the thought that she was chatting him up. She was certainly more interested in their project, and seemed quite well informed about it, even asked about the computer a few times.

'We'll leave you in peace for a couple of days,' Ted told her. 'We've just about got everything we need now to go on to the next stage. I think we'll have a rest, plan things over the weekend, and come in again on Monday. So you'll have three whole days without us.'

Joanne Yeates tried to conceal her relief. That meant she could take some time off herself. These two had worked all hours, most weekends too, and she had been terrified to be away when they were working in case she missed some vital development. Another of those pink envelopes had been delivered last week. This time there was a little couplet to keep her on her toes.

Little L will go through hell
If you don't have news to tell

The recollection made her grimace.

'Are you all right?' Claire asked, stepping forward.

'Yes, yes, I'm fine. Bit of indigestion.' She tried to laugh it off.

'You look as if you could do with a rest yourself. I should take the weekend off, too, if you can.'

Joanne was touched by Claire's concern, and guilt-ridden by her own duplicity. She hated being forced to spy on these nice people who were only trying to help a man in a coma.

She forced a smile, but did not have to falsify her agreement. 'I think I will do just that.'

'See you, then.' Ted waved one big hand from the door, a carry-all full of his essential gear in the other. 'Coming, Claire?'

'Won't be a minute. Meet you in the car park.' Ted left, and Claire turned her attention to the nurse. 'Are you sure you're OK?'

'Just tired, that's all.'

'It's none of my business, but you look as if you're under a bit of strain.'

Joanne felt anger and gratitude at the same time. The conflicting emotions made her hesitate. She was angry because she didn't want to be questioned, loathed the deceit, but wanted to respond to the researcher's genuine concern. To give herself time, she sat down in Ted's chair. She tried to respond flippantly but her intonation betrayed her.

'You mean I'm not looking myself? Do I need a tonic? Am I getting enough sleep?'

Claire detected the note of bitterness. 'I'm sorry, I didn't mean to upset you, it's just that —'

'It's all right. It's nice of you to be interested. I've had a few worries, it's true, but it's nothing I can't cope with.' She made a tremendous effort to look bright, to dismiss the matter and allow a change of subject. 'Anyway, you don't want to hear about my minor woes. How's the project going?' She waved in the direction of the masses of equipment.

'Pretty well, really. We're quite excited about it.'

'So you'll be back on Monday?' Sister Yeates felt her despair filling her, promoted by thoughts of the monster who was forcing her to do this prying.

'Ted seems to think we'll be ready to go on to the next phase then.'

'He must be a clever man.'

Claire nodded. 'He certainly is that.'

'This program he's written, all these words you've been recording. What's it all for, exactly?' Joanne had tried asking Ted this question, but had not understood the answer. She was trying to build up a picture of what the two researchers were trying to achieve, and how they were doing it, but for her non-technological mind it was difficult to grasp. She had even taken to making notes, so that she could have some recorded facts to show her predatory tormentor, show him she had been trying, at least. Enough, she hoped, to protect her daughter.

Claire thought the nurse's interest was fully justifiable and quite natural. After all, they were working to try to help Paul Sansome. It was good that the senior nurse should be included in their project. She sat down again, and explained at some length about their aims and how far they had got.

Joanne Yeates felt dismay rising in her as Claire explained, simply and expertly, the detail of what was going on. She now had a clear picture of the project for the first time, realised it was something exceptional, an incredible advance in neuro-physiology, saw that it had a chance of success. At one point she had to suppress the desire to shout at Claire to go away, to stop telling her all this, all these things that she would have to pass on to an evil stranger in order to protect her child. But she didn't. The worry over her daughter was driving her insane, and this knowledge was the longed-for balm to soothe her feverish anxiety.

Claire finished her explanation by describing what they hoped to do the following week. Sister Yeates had been concentrating hard, but now, as Claire finished, she was looking away, seemed distant, her thoughts elsewhere.

'Sorry if I went on a bit. But I find it so exciting.'

The nurse jerked her head back towards Claire. 'Oh, no, I wasn't bored. You explained it so clearly, I can see exactly . . .' She shuddered. 'It's almost frightening. I was just thinking . . .' Suddenly the conflict of her inner turmoil, the deception, the worry, her new knowledge, all combined in a maelstrom of emotion she could not contain. She leaned forward onto the desk in front of her, hiding her face, and wept uncontrollably.

Claire was taken completely by surprise, did not know how to react. She got up, stood behind the distressed woman, then leaning forward, put her hands on the trembling shoulders.

'Is there anything I can do, Sister? Should I fetch someone?'

Joanne was feeling ashamed. She had never let herself give such a public display before. Already the floodwaters of her anguish were receding, the catharsis effected. She shook her head vigorously, sniffed, kept her head bowed as she searched for a tissue.

'No, please. Just give me a minute.'

Claire stood, feeling awkward, stroking the woman's shoulders, feeling the breathing return to normal. She stepped back as Joanne straightened up, and turned her reddened eyes towards her.

'God, I'm sorry. I've never done anything like that before.'

Claire looked at her, shocked at the contrast between the capable nurse and the woman now showing the weakness of ordinary mortals.

'Please, don't apologise. Did I say something that upset you?' She could not think what it might have been.

The sister's eyes were clearing, she was looking more composed. 'No, really, you mustn't think for a moment . . .' Lord, how am I going to explain this? she thought.

'I've noticed you've not been yourself lately.' Claire was perplexed. These were uncharted waters for her. 'Will it — will it help to talk about it?' She felt a self-conscious uncertainty, talking this way to a health professional whom she had seen display so much competence, dealing with situations Claire herself would have had no idea how to handle.

Sister Yeates recognised the hesitancy in Claire's inquiry, and wanted to try and resolve the situation. An element of truth would be the best way out, she decided.

'I *am* worried. About my daughter.'

'Your daughter?' Claire's stomach turned. What was she going to be told that could distress a mother so? Cancer? Leukaemia, perhaps?

'Yes. It's . . . family problems. I'm divorced. Her father – he's trying to upset her, turn her against me.' She'd read the words so often, they came easily to her now.

Claire had no experience in counselling anyone in such a situation, but she felt almost a sense of relief – for herself as well as for this caring nurse and mother – that the explanation did not involve serious illness.

'I'm sorry. I don't know what to say.'

'Just knowing someone is concerned is a great help,' said Joanne, making a good attempt at a reassuring smile. 'Don't worry, I'll get over it.'

'I didn't mean to be nosey — upset you or anything.'

'It's all right. Honestly.' The sister almost laughed. 'It'll be easier for both of us, now you know. It'll save you wondering. That's something.' She pointed to Paul Sansome's bedside locker. 'Do you think I could have one of those?'

Claire handed her the box of tissues. The door opened quickly and Ted put his head round. 'Hey, how much longer —?' He took in the scene quickly, Sister Yeates wiping tearful eyes, Claire standing near her, looking worried and uncomfortable. He just managed to control his blunt antipodean levity, suppressing a comment about how cheerful they both looked. He settled for the obvious banality.

'Something wrong?'

Claire gave him a 'leave us alone a minute' look, intercepted by Joanne Yeates. She stood up, and looked from one to the other. 'It's all right. Claire and I were just having a little chat.' She put her hand on the younger woman's arm in a gesture of gratitude. 'Just helping me get something off my chest.'

Ted once again had to stop himself voicing a rude sexist riposte. 'Er, shall I leave you two ladies a bit longer, then . . .?'

'No, please, I've held you up long enough already. Just a minor aberration.' She smiled at Claire. 'I'm sorry if I embarrassed you. I promise it won't happen again.'

'Don't be silly.' Claire hesitated. She knew what she wanted to say, but couldn't think beyond the trite and hackneyed phrases she had heard so often. She gave up the fight to be original. 'Joanne — if there's anything I can do . . . ?'

'Thanks for the offer, Claire. Now go on, start your weekend off — and I promise to do the same.'

Ted needed no further prompting. He took Claire's arm and marched her to the door. 'So long then, Sister. See you Monday.' Remembering her earlier distress, he added awkwardly, 'Hope everything works out.'

* * *

Joanne sat down and looked at Paul Sansome, desolation returning, but this time a controlled emotion. 'We're both alone, aren't we?' she said to the inert figure. 'Both with different problems. You can't communicate with anyone, and I daren't.'

Recalling all she had recently learnt, she watched her patient's breathing rhythm carefully. She could not suppress the urge to try it. She leaned forward, spoke questioningly.

'Hello, Paul?'

She tried again. There was no response.

Back in her office, she looked away from the mirror, finally satisfied that her appearance would pass muster. The pain was starting to come back in her abdomen, just below the inverted 'V' of her ribs below the breastbone. She noticed it was getting more frequent, especially after an upset. It felt as if a drop of acid had been poured on a raw spot in her stomach, which she knew was probably not far from the truth. She winced, and cursed under her breath, trying to ward off thoughts about an ulcer. She had no time to be ill, to be away from work, not now. Hoping no one would see her, or check the stock, she unlocked the medicines cupboard and took another four hundred milligrams of cemetidine.

* * *

Ted gave a loud and ungentlemanly belch.

Claire looked anxiously about her. 'I wish you wouldn't do that. Especially in public.' It was only seven, and the Indian restaurant was almost empty.

He grinned. 'Just letting them know I appreciate the grub.'

'God, that's just schoolboy stuff.'

Ted's grin widened. 'True enough. You ought to know my level by now.'

Claire shook her head in mock despair. 'You're hopeless.'

'Me? Nar!' His face suddenly looked more serious. 'Here, that nursing Sheila, Sister Bates —'

'Yeates.'

'Yeh — what was all that about, then?'

Claire told him, Ted listening attentively.

'Y'know, I've thought she's had something on her mind,' he said when she'd finished. 'Didn't think it was personal problems, though.'

'What makes you say that?'

Ted pondered. 'Well . . . it's just that her — her sort of attitude — to us and what we're doing — has changed.'

Claire gave him an amused look. 'This all sounds unusually subtle for my bone-headed little ex-convict.'

'Give it a go! I'm not *that* insensitive, you know.'

Claire wasn't sure if his apparent hurt was genuine. 'Well, go on, what had your super-tuned antennae picked up?'

Ted rebelled. 'You're not taking this seriously.'

'It's difficult to know when you *are* being serious half the time.'

'Yeh, OK. Point taken.'

Claire looked inquiringly. 'So?'

'Sounds a bit daft, now — but, well, when we started she was just all business and nursing efficiency, sweeping up around us as though we were just part of the furniture. But lately she's been asking me lots of questions, about the project, even the computer.' He sniggered. 'And it's obvious that what she knows about computers you could write on a wombat's willy.' He thought again a moment. Claire waited. 'It's as if she's been trying to learn something.'

Claire was defensive. 'Well what's wrong with that? She has good professional reasons to want to increase her knowledge about the care of coma victims.'

'That's what I thought. And you're probably right. But it's the change in her approach that I can't understand. She was quite indifferent to what we were doing to start with, but now . . . it's difficult to say what I mean. She seems to be sort of collecting information, rather than learning out of interest.'

'I'm not sure what you're trying to say, Ted. It sounds as if you almost think she's spying on us.'

He shrugged. 'That's just the feeling I get.'

Claire sat back, feeling indignation on behalf of the nurse with whom, after this afternoon, she felt a closer bond.

'Rubbish!'

Ted's serious face broke into a grin. 'I thought you'd say that.'

'Come on, Ted! What would she gain? Who would she be spying *for*?'

'All right, all right!' He held up his hands. 'I knew you girls would stick together.'

'I wish you wouldn't use these sexist expressions. We are *not* "us girls". You make it sound as if we're in the dorm discussing the next hockey match.'

Ted's blue eyes looked at her from under his bushy blond eyebrows. 'I'll bet you'd look great in a gymslip.'

Claire looked back, something stirring in her at the look in his eye and the innuendo in his voice. He read the signs, and reached under the table to put a hand on her thigh.

'Ted!' Claire admonished him, glancing round, trying to ignore the delicious frisson as he stroked upwards.

'Talking of gym,' he said, keeping his voice low, unsure just how far he could push, 'I don't suppose that you'd fancy a little work-out?'

Claire wavered. They'd been working hard, she'd welcome a diversion. Crass though he appeared in some respects, Ted was turning out to be a much better companion on this project than she had anticipated. The excitement that was already building in her pelvis, the relaxation she'd feel afterwards . . . and it had been a long time . . .

'Will you be excusing me, please, but can I be getting you anything else?' The smiling Indian waiter seemed to materialise beside her. She almost jumped back in her seat, felt Ted's hand slip away.

'No, not for me, thank you.' Her excitement died quickly. The interruption was timely. She knew she was not ready. Not yet, anyway.

CHAPTER 16

Detective Sergeant Clothier could see his inspector was impatient for him to get on with it, and for results. He knew he had little to offer.

Detective Inspector Howard looked at his watch again. He obviously had something more important on his mind. Clothier waited for the next question.

'Have you had the results from the calligraphist about the writing on the bedroom wall?'

'Yes, but not much help directly, I'm afraid, sir.'

The inspector looked up sharply. 'What's that supposed to mean?'

'All she came up with was that the writing seemed unusually neat, but didn't tell us much more. But she did put us on to a colleague, a psychologist who has an interest in the interpretation of writing.'

The senior officer was not impressed. 'Ha! A sort of shrink for writers?'

'No, sir. She's not a psychiatrist, more of an analyst.'

Inspector Howard sighed resignedly. 'So did this lady come up with anything useful?'

'It's not much, sir, but she did say this.' He looked down to read from the notebook he was holding.

> 'It is a truism that written threats such as these are almost by definition made by persons with a violent nature. The majority of such offenders are of low educational standard and may be of low intelligence. The use of colloquialisms is common, and they are often mis-spelled. The use of the words *fuzz* and *pussy* could be taken as examples of such colloquialisms, with the close linking of *pussy* and the child's name having a threatening sexual connotation familiar in the world of the uneducated.'

The portly sergeant paused to draw breath, and the inspector interrupted.

'Is there much more of this stuff, Clothier? There are only 20 words to talk about. Can we get to the point?'

'Yes, sir. There's not much more.' He turned back to his notes and read quickly.

> 'However, there are no mis-spellings, and the calligraphist draws attention to the relative neatness of the writing, itself unusual in

such examples. The construction of the short sentences is sound, with no grammatical errors. There is even an example of deliberate alliteration (*fuss* and *fuzz*). These findings taken together suggest the writer was not a typical uneducated criminal personality, but someone of above average intelligence trying to imitate criminal graffiti.'

Clothier glanced up, anxious to finish. 'She then goes on to say that — '

There was a knock, and the door to the office opened. A young constable put his head in. 'The car's here, sir.'

'Tell them I'll be right there.' The inspector stood up, and the constable withdrew. 'Thank you, Clothier.'

'I haven't quite finished, sir, if you've got just another minute.'

'I can see what she's getting at, Sergeant, and I accept it's useful. Not the usual criminal type, that's what your psychologist friend is saying.' He picked up his hat from the top of a filing cabinet. 'Have you got anything more from the nurse? Yeates, isn't it?'

'No, sir, I haven't. I went round yesterday. She said she had nothing more to say. A very nervous lady, that, sir. Almost seemed hostile, wanted me to go almost as soon as I arrived. I'd have thought she'd welcome the attention of the police.'

'Perhaps it's your manner, Sergeant.' The inspector put on his cap, and pointedly looked over the tubby untidy figure. 'Or your appearance.' He left Clothier alone in the office.

The sergeant looked down at his pad and shrugged. Oh, well, if he doesn't want to hear the most interesting bit . . .

He closed the notebook and headed for the canteen.

* * *

Christine Sansome turned away from the solicitor's desk and walked over to the window. 'I don't care if it is an expensive business, Mr Barker. I told you last time I was here. I want to go ahead and try to get a Court of Protection order.' She turned back to him. 'What the hell have you been doing in the past three weeks? I thought you'd called me here because you were ready to go.'

Barker wished, not for the first time, that he had the courage to tell this woman to go elsewhere for her legal advice. 'I can see you are disappointed, Mrs Sansome, but these things do take time.'

'I haven't *got* time, Mr Barker.' She made a great effort to stop shouting, clipping her words as she spoke through a barely opened mouth. 'I *must have control* of my husband's affairs.'

'But, Mrs Sansome, this is by no means a foolproof method of achieving that aim. As I have said, it could prove very expensive indeed. And you are already concerned about your pecuniary interests.'

'That's none of your business. I'll spend whatever I have to.'

'But in a way it *is* my business, Mrs Sansome. I have a professional duty to advise you if I feel your action is folly and could ruin you. And a duty to my partners, not to incur a large debt with no hope of recovery.'

'Ha! That's more like it.' She spoke with a sneer in her voice. 'Let me assure you, Mr Barker, that you'll get your money.' She changed abruptly, made an effort to appear businesslike. 'So tell, me, please. Your considered opinion. What are the chances of getting Court of Protection?'

The solicitor swallowed. 'First of all I think I must clear up some misconceptions I think you have about the function of the Court of Protection.'

'Oh. So now you're going to hide your incompetence behind a load of legal jargon, are you?'

David Barker closed his eyes momentarily, measuring his response. 'No, I am doing nothing of the sort. I just want you to understand the position fully. It may help you to accept that what you hope to achieve by this action may not be attainable.' He looked directly at her, anticipating a further angry reaction, but it was not forthcoming. He cleared his throat and continued.

'The Court of Protection is there, as the title suggests, to protect. And it is the incapacitated party that it is there to protect — not the interests of anyone else, however close their relationship, who may be adversely affected by that incapacity. Any action the Court may take will be designed to benefit the incapacitated person, not yourself.'

'It sounds as if I might as well not bother, then?'

'No, I wouldn't go so far as to say that. The Court's primary concern is with providing for the unfortunate victim, both now and in the future. But if there is a genuine need from a dependant, such as yourself, then the Court is empowered to make certain directions for the release of a proportion of the estate for such a purpose.'

'Well, that's me, surely. I have a need. I depend entirely on my husband.'

'We can try that approach, as I said.'

'Why doesn't the Court just hand over the reins to me and let me get on with it?'

Barker smiled indulgently. 'The Court may make you the receiver of the estate, but you will be bound by very strict restraints. You will be limited as to what assets you can dispose of, and will have to present annual audited accounts. I think that in a case such as this the Court will also appoint the Official Solicitor to represent your husband's interests, especially if you are looking to get the Court to award you a Gift — that is to say a capital sum — out of the estate.'

Christine Sansome looked downcast. The solicitor was surprised. He had expected anger rather than disappointment.

'It's not going to be easy, then?'

'That's what I've been trying to tell you,' he said gently. 'There is another problem in that your husband has not made a will. If he dies intestate you will not automatically receive his entire estate. There is something worth trying, however,' he hurried on. 'We can apply to the Court to make a statutory will, asking them to leave everything to you as the sole beneficiary.'

She raised her head, some of the defiance returning. 'Now that sounds more like it!'

'Please, Mrs Sansome, you must not expect too much.'

'But there is a chance?'

'I am advised — and getting that advice is what takes time, you understand — that there *is* a possibility such an application may meet with success.'

'I take it that's a *yes*.' Her sarcasm was undisguised.

'All right. There is a chance. It is small. Do not ask me to quantify it.'

'Good enough.' Christine Sansome sat down at the desk, placed her palms flat on the surface in front of her. 'What do we have to do first?'

'We have to file a Certificate of Family and Property with the Court. It is very detailed and will include many personal details, I'm afraid. Assets, insurances, income, details of your personal history —'

'What's my personal history got to do with them?'

'The Master of the Court needs to satisfy himself — or actually it's herself at the moment — that you are a fit and proper person to be appointed receiver.'

'All right. So what else?'

'We have to get a doctor's certificate, stating that your husband is mentally incapacitated, what his chances of recovery are, what his long-term needs may be.'

'Surely that won't be too difficult. Is that it?'

'A notice of the summons to the Court has to be served on the patient.'

'You must be joking! You mean some official has to go and give my husband a piece of paper to tell him what's going on, even if he's virtually brain dead?'

'It may seem a little incongruous, Mrs Sansome, but that is the procedure.' Barker gave a wry smile. 'It's quite true that in cases of dementia I have served summons and you might as well be giving them Magna Carta or the secrets of the H-bomb. But that's the way of things. I have heard of waivers in exceptional circumstances, but . . .'

'How long is all this legal hocus pocus going to take?'

'It's not hocus pocus, madam, it is all designed to protect the incapacitated from exploitation.' He just managed to stop himself adding 'from people like you'.

'You still haven't answered my question. How long?'

We have to get all the papers together. That'll take two or three weeks at least. Then from lodging the papers to the hearing — about six to eight weeks, I'd say.'

Christine Sansome gave a deep sigh of exasperation. 'Three

months — probably four, allowing for the legal dragging of feet and over-optimism.'

'There will be no dragging of feet on my part, I can assure you.'

She ignored the remark. 'You said a hearing. Where is this Court?'

'In London. But don't worry. Normally it is all done on paper. Personal representation is rarely required. And if it is, it's very informal. Sitting round a table, something like that.'

'And the Master — is that what you said? — is a woman?'

'That is correct.'

'Hmm. Think that'll work in my favour?'

Barker looked at the fashionably dressed, arrogant, selfish female before him, then pictured the present Master of the Court. They were light years apart. He suppressed a wry smile.

'No, I don't think it will help much.'

Mrs Sansome gave him a curious look, then pulled her chair nearer the desk.

'All right. Let's get on with it, then.'

* * *

Claire came awake, sweating, her breathing irregular. Sleep had not come easy to her the last two nights. Her dreams were mostly disturbed, a mixture of curious eroticism, making love with heavy faceless men, and of struggling with endless streams of computerised data. She had nightmares of rooms filling with listing paper spewing from printers, of EEG machines, the tracer needles waving in a frenzy of epileptiform activity, the traces passing through her hands faster and faster, demanding analysis. Just before she woke, as the pressure to interpret the irregular patterns became unbearable, she had looked up and seen a jerking body, a rictus smile, flesh falling from a pretty face, electric sparks surrounding the skull like a bizarre halo . . .

Her bedside clock-radio said it was six-fifteen. She decided to get up. Today they would start work in earnest. She wondered what they would find. Would Paul Sansome really 'talk' to them? And if he did, *what would he say*?

* * *

Ted was there already when she arrived at Side Room 3. So was Sister Yeates.

'Have a nice weekend?'

'Very relaxing, thank you.' The nurse hoped it didn't look as if she was lying. How could she relax? At any time she expected another visitation, another threat, another letter. 'So today is the big day?' She tried to make her inquiry light, as if she were not really interested.

Claire thought of the conversation with Ted on the Friday night, and glanced across at him. He was looking curiously at Joanne. She caught the unspoken exchange between the two, and was puzzled, then alarmed. Surely they didn't suspect her of prying, searching for information. She had been so careful, and yet the look they exchanged . . .

Claire moved to her and smiled. She had detected the anxiety that clouded the nurse's face. 'Was everything really all right at the weekend? With your daughter?'

Sister Yeates couldn't disguise her relief. 'Yes, really. I'm fine.' Yet again guilt and fear churned her emotions. Obviously Claire had told the big Australian about her 'family problems' and their exchange of glances was no more than sympathy. Careful, woman, she admonished herself silently, you mustn't get paranoid or you'll give yourself away.

Claire was talking again. '. . . today's the day, all right. This is when we hope to really make a breakthrough. You won't want to miss any of this.'

How right you are, thought Joanne Yeates miserably.

She stayed to watch while they set up and prepared to start. To the nurse it seemed an age before they were ready. She was getting agitated about being away from the office for so long. Already there had been two student nurses popping in to ask questions and getting disapproving glances from Ted Parkes.

At last they were ready, Claire before the microphone, the Australian at his computer. The nursing sister could feel the tension, the excitement in the room, felt herself getting caught up in it, realised she was holding her breath as Claire leaned forward to speak.

'Hello, Paul.' Claire paused, glanced over to Ted.

'First two traces OK. No response yet. Try again.'

'Hello, Paul.'

The keyboard clicked frantically. 'Beaut! Double peak response trace. Now . . .' He was typing again as he spoke. 'And the signal identification program says that's . . .' he drew out the words, pausing while the hard disk softly whirred '. . . Hello, Claire!'

He banged a fist into the palm of his hand in triumph. Claire clapped her hands several times in delight.

Sister Yeates wanted to share their exuberance, but knew that every advance, every discovery, put more weight on her burden, more importance on her mission.

'Ask if he can hear us,' instructed Ted.

Claire's mouth was dry. She massaged her salivary glands with her tongue, and leaned towards the microphone.

'Paul, can you hear me?'

Ted worked the keys furiously. 'Again!' he demanded.

'Can you hear me, Paul?'

Ted jumped up. 'Look! Look!' he stabbed his finger at the screen.

Claire and Sister Yeates moved over to see. On the screen was a message: *Probable interpretation of word.* Below it the cursor was flashing next to three letters.

They spelled 'Yes'.

CHAPTER 17

'This isn't going to be quite so easy as I thought.' Ted wiped his hand across his mouth and bent over the keyboard again.

'It's happened again?'

'Yes. It's worse than a crossword. Too many choices.'

They had been working for about an hour. At the start everything had gone well. Too well, Ted now realised. When Claire gave her usual greeting and got an immediate two-word response, he had thought it was all plain sailing. But the problem was, although they were getting potentially exciting and different responses, the computer program he had written was giving them too large a selection of words.

'It's the program, isn't it?' Claire asked tentatively.

'Yes. Bloody hell. I've made it too complex, I think that's the trouble. We seem to have no problem with one-word responses — which mean just Yes and No. But if he responds with anything else, it's throwing half the thesaurus at me!'

'Can't you cut it down?'

'Yeah. But it'll take a hell of a long time. I grafted on a standard word-processing thesaurus and spelling checker, and it's got much too much information compared to the three-and-a-half thousand words we put in.'

'Let's not give up yet, Ted. Try again. Something simple.'

He sighed. 'OK. Try "Are you in pain?".'

Claire moved nearer the mike and spoke the phrase.

Ted sat back. 'See? No problem.' The cursor winked by the word 'No'. 'Go for "What happened in Austria?".'

Claire looked across at him. 'Don't be daft, Ted. Are you expecting miracles, or something?'

'No, I just want to illustrate the problem to you.'

Claire paused.

'Go on. Say it.'

'Paul, what happened to you in Austria?'

Ted's fingers worked, then he pushed away from the screen again.

'Now watch.'

Claire went to look. The cursor blinked by 'I'. Ted moved the cursor to *Next word* on the on-screen menu and pressed return. Three columns of words filled the screen, divided up into verbs, marked (v), nouns, marked (n), and a short list of opposites or antitheses, indicated by (ant). There were 31 words. Claire studied the display.

(v)		
1 A • ache	desire-(n)	• reject
B • aspire	5 • ambition	
C • long	• aspiration	9 • dislike
D • wish	• longing	• aversion
E • yearn	• want	• generosity
	• yearning	
2 F • covet		
G • crave	6 • appetite	
H • need	• craving	
I • want	• lust	
	• obsession	
3 J • choose	• passion	
K • prefer		
	7 avarice	
4 L • ask	• greed	
M • request		
N • urge	desire-(ant)	
	8 • spurn	

Replace Word; 2 View Doc; 3 Look Up Word; 4 Clear Column: 0

'I see what you mean. I suppose the next word could be *want*.'

'Or *ask*.'

'Or *choose* or *urge*. Yes, I take your point.'

Ted asked for *Next Word* again, and they studied the list together.

(v)		
1 A • abet	help-(n)	
B • aid		
C • assist	5 • assistance	
D • serve	• relief	
	• service	
2 E • extricate	• succour	
F • rescue		
G • save	6 labourers	
	workers	
3 H • ease		
I • expedite	help-(ant)	
J • facilitate	7 • hinder	
	• ensnare	
4 K • ameliorate	• worsen	
L • better		
M • improve	8 • hindrance	

Replace Word; 2 View Doc; 3 Look Up Word; 4 Clear Column: 0

Claire frowned. 'It could be *I urge assistance.*'

'Or *I need relief.* Or *I want rescue*, any number of things.'

He pressed *Next Word* twice more and got more long lists. Finally he got the message *End of series.*

'Quite honestly, all we learned from that is that there was probably a five-word sentence, the first word of which is "I". As for the rest, we could make it mean almost whatever we liked by choosing from the lists.' He looked despondent. 'It's bloody useless.'

Claire felt for her colleague. He'd worked so hard, but to feel he had failed was ridiculous.

'Buck up, man! We should be high as kites with what we've done already. Even knowing the responses are more than one word is fantastic news! We mustn't be too impatient.'

'Trouble is,' Ted grumbled, 'I've tried to be too bloody clever. Tried to run before I could walk. I'll have to take out the thesaurus and just get it to give us its best guess, straight from the wave patterns.'

'Will that take long?'

'A few days, at least.'

Claire was silent for a moment. 'OK — you'll just have to get on with it. But there's still a lot we can do today.'

'How do you mean?'

'Well, we can get "Yes" and "No" answers, can't we? We can learn a lot from that.'

'I don't know. I ought to get straight on and start rewriting the program.'

'Don't be so stubborn, Ted!' Claire was getting angry with him, his self-centred defeatism. What was wrong with the man? 'Please. For me. There's so much to learn, so much I want to try. Please?'

Claire knew she had won, could see the interest, the excitement, slowly return to his eyes. 'Right, you old cheese. You've bullied me into it.' He settled himself in front of the computer. 'Ask away.'

Claire took up her position and was about to speak when the door opened. Sister Yeates put her head into the room. 'How's it going?'

Claire looked up. 'A few teething problems. We're going to have to go back to the drawing-board for a few days before we can get any complex responses. We're just going to try a few simple questions for now.'

'Can I stay?'

The nurse picked up that exchange of glances between the researcher and her partner again. There was a pause. Claire spoke first.

'OK. Come on in and see what we get.'

'Ready now?' Ted was poised over the keyboard.

Claire nodded, and spoke slowly and clearly into the microphone.

'Paul. Do you know where you are?'

Ted tapped the keys. 'He says "No".'

'You're in hospital. In the Bristol General Neurological Unit.'

'No response to that,' said Ted.

'It wasn't a question,' Claire pointed out. She turned back to the microphone. 'Did you understand where you are?'

'He says "Yes".'

Claire breathed excitedly, almost to herself, 'This is fantastic!' She leaned towards the mike again.

'We have used our experiments on Jason Coombes to communicate with you. Do you understand?'

Ted looked up. 'There's a "Yes" at the beginning, then a whole lot of undecipherable signals.'

Claire nodded. 'He's probably trying to qualify his answers, and we can only pick up "Yes" or "No".'

'We ought to tell him that.'

'Of course! Stupid of me.' She turned back to the microphone. 'Paul. We can only understand "Yes" and "No". You will have to limit your answers to that for now.' She paused.

'No response yet.' Ted did not look up.

'Paul, do you understand we can only pick up "Yes" or "No"?'

'He says "Yes".'

Her eyes shining with excitement, Claire looked across at Ted who was shaking his head in disbelief. 'This is amazing. Simply amazing. Let's try some more.'

Sister Yeates looked on with a mixture of fear and awe as Claire continued with her questioning, Ted relaying the response each time.

'Can you remember what happened to you?'

'Yes.'

'You know you are in a coma?'

'No.'

Claire swallowed and looked anxiously at Ted. She switched the microphone off. 'God, Ted. He doesn't know! What can I say? If I tell him he seems to be in an irreversible coma it may cause more damage to his mental state.'

Ted thought a moment. 'I think we'd better ignore that response for now. Ask him something else about the accident.'

Claire swallowed, tried hard to keep her voice steady. 'Paul, can you remember the accident?'

'Yes.' Ted looked up. 'He's trying to say something else again.'

'Paul, we can only understand "Yes" or "No". Do you understand?'

'Yes.'

Before Claire could ask another question, Ted interrupted. 'It's very unusual to remember events around the time of a severe concussion, isn't it?' He looked inquiringly at Joanne Yeates, who was standing as discreetly as she could in the background. The nurse was reluctant to be drawn into the situation, but couldn't see how she could refuse.

'Yes, that would be very unusual,' she agreed.

Claire spoke into the mike again.

'Paul. Can you remember right up to the time of your accident?'

'Yes.'

'Did you fall on –'

'Wait. He's giving us something else.' Ted tapped the keys. 'Christ! Look at this!'

Claire went to look at the screen, Joanne Yeates behind her. Claire gasped.

'God!'

They watched mesmerised as a seemingly never ending stream of words filled the screen:

No No No No No No No No No No No No No No No No No No
No No No No No No No No No No No No No No No No No No
No No No No No No No No No No No No No No No No No No
No No No No No No No No No No No No No No No No No No
No No No No No No No No No No No No No No No No No No
No No No No No No No No No No No No No No No No No No
No No No No No No No No No No No No No No No No No No
No No No No No No No No No No No No No No No No No No
No No No No No No No No No No No No No No No No No No

CHAPTER 18

'So!' Porthenoy leaned back in his chair, displaying another of his multicoloured waistcoats. This one looked like a montage of autumn leaves. 'What did you learn yesterday?'

Claire and Ted looked at each other. They had been virtually summoned to the neurosurgeon's office this morning by a phone call from Porthenoy's secretary.

Neither of them had been planning to come in to the hospital today. After the excitement of the previous morning, Claire wanted time to think carefully about a systematic approach to her questioning with the 'Yes-No' limitation, and Ted wanted to plan the rewrite of his program.

They both started to speak together, stopped, and then Ted made a bowing gesture for Claire to continue.

'We made some progress. We're definitely getting a response from Dr Sansome, but it's the interpretation of the response that's proving difficult.'

Porthenoy seemed to be trying hard not to look smug. 'I must say that doesn't surprise me. Doesn't surprise me.'

Ted snorted, and seemed about to say something, when Claire continued.

'We can't at the moment decipher anything other than positive and negative responses. But that in itself is a very exciting breakthrough indeed.'

Porthenoy leaned forward, startled. 'Are you saying that he can in effect answer "Yes" or "No" to your questions?'

Ted could not suppress his pleasure at Porthenoy's reaction. 'Got it in one, sport. Whatcha think of that, eh?'

'Well — I — I'm astounded, frankly.' As if to temper his enthusiasm, he added, 'If it's true, of course.'

'Well, good on yer!' Ted turned to Claire. 'He actually admits he's impressed. Maybe he isn't such a galah after all.'

'All right, Ted!'

'Don't worry, Miss Donaldson, I'm getting used to him.' He nodded slowly and swivelled his chair. 'And I freely admit that if what you say is verifiable, I am indeed impressed. A truly remarkable breakthrough. Remarkable.'

'Thank you,' said Claire, trying to sound as gracious as possible.

'Let me get this straight,' Porthenoy continued. 'I want to be quite clear in my own mind. You can ask Dr Sansome a question, and interpret a response which is definable with your electronic gadgetry as "Yes" or "No".'

'That's right,' Ted assured him confidently.

'How do you know it's not just a random response? Assuming first of all that Dr Sansome understands the questions, how do you know he means the answers?'

'Christ, mate,' Ted sounded exasperated. 'How do you know whether anyone means what they say?'

'Just a minute, Ted, I know what Mr Porthenoy is getting at. We are picking up signals that we *say* are "Yes" and "No", but how do we know they are not just random responses to our stimulation?'

'But we've checked the wave-forms against the input signals. We *know* what they mean. There's nothing random about them at all.'

'Exactly.' Claire looked at the man opposite. 'Does that answer your question?'

'It tells me that the electrical signals you are picking up probably represent the two words in question. But there could be some internal artefact, some loop system, in the man's damaged brain that is just reprocessing your input signal and pushing it out again. Not an original thought at all, in fact.'

Ted looked away in frustration. Claire compressed her lips firmly while she considered her reply. How could they convince him?

'Look, if only you'd been there! We asked a number of questions, and even asked if he understood we could only interpret positive and negative responses. His answers were entirely appropriate. If it was all at random it would have been obvious.' She frowned. 'There were *some* strange reactions, though.'

'Such as?' Porthenoy raised his eyebrows.

'Well, when we asked him about the accident, he seemed to keep saying "No" over and over again and again. Dozens of times.'

'Most curious. Why would he do that?'

Claire shrugged. 'I have no idea. We also got another curious response. I asked Paul if he could remember what happened to him, and he said "Yes". That is, the computer interpreted the signal as "Yes".' She glanced at Ted, who seemed to be warning her, but she carried on. 'Then I asked him if he knew he was in a coma, and he said "No".' She paused. 'I'd like your advice on that. We thought it best not to risk further mental trauma by telling him what state he was really in.'

Porthenoy seemed about to laugh, then changed his mind. 'I'm sorry. I was thinking that the poor man could hardly have any greater mental trauma than his present state, but I see what you mean. We are in unknown territory here. For the time being I must assume that you really *are* in communication with a deeply comatose patient, and we must tread carefully.' He looked thoughtful. 'I'm no psychiatrist. Perhaps we should get an opinion from one.'

Ted couldn't hide his prejudices. 'I don't think that'd help. The shrinks can't figure out what's going on in a conscious person's mind half the time, let alone a bloke who's completely laid out.'

Claire was astonished by Porthenoy's response.

'For once I feel we share a common opinion.' He smiled benignly at the Australian. 'But I am concerned that we do not precipitate another crisis such as the one where Dr Sansome went into that unremitting epileptic fit.'

'There's been no sign of that on the EEG,' Claire hastened to reassure him.

'But he is having phenytoin in his drip. That might suppress any EEG signs of distress.'

'There haven't been any signs of breathing disturbances, either.'

'That's encouraging, I agree. But I think it might be an idea to run an electrocardiograph monitor — or at least put him on a 'scope — while you're testing. A sudden rapid tachycardia — that's a rapid heart rate —' he directed his explanation of the term at Ted ' — would suggest undue stress. Less marked degrees of change in heart rate would be interesting if they correlated with particular questions or responses.'

Claire could see the wisdom of this suggestion. It might help protect Paul against undue stress, and at the same time provide them with another indicator of the genuineness of his responses.

'I understand, Mr Porthenoy. It sounds like a good idea.'

'How generous of you to say so.' The sarcasm was barely disguised.

Claire avoided Ted's eye. 'We'll set that up before our next session.'

'And when might that be? Just in case I can find the time to get along?'

Claire hesitated, and Ted spoke up. 'To be honest, we're not sure. Obviously, we're itching to ask more questions. But I need to rewrite my program, which'll take a few days at least. If you like, we'll ring your secretary to let you know when we're going to have another go.'

'Thank you.' The consultant looked from one to the other. 'This is all very interesting. Very interesting indeed.' He smiled his best this-is-the-end-of-the-consultation smile. 'And now if you'll excuse me . . .'

As soon as they got out into the corridor, Ted exploded as silently as he could.

'What a bullshitting bastard!' He imitated the neurosurgeon's upper class English accent. ' "*How generous of you to say so*".' He shook his head. 'Christ, do me a favour. This guy can't be for real!'

'Quiet, you idiot!' Claire admonished him. 'Just tell me this, you moron. You called him a galah. What in God's name is that?'

Ted looked at her sharply, suddenly serious. 'Ah yes.' He took her arm and guided her further down the corridor. 'A galah is a sort of silly multicoloured parrot that hangs upside-down from a branch and makes raucous noises.'

They stumbled down the steps and out into the rain, giggling helplessly.

* * *

Joanne Yeates crouched in the bushes, blinked raindrops out of her eyes, looked at her watch and shivered. The pink envelope had come in the post that morning. It had a Bristol postmark. Like before, it was written in pencil, with nothing but the message on the page of cheap notepaper. She had read it so many times she could still recall every word.

On ONE sheet of A4 write all you know of the situation in Side Room 3. Obtain a bottle of red Côte du Rhone wine from Sainsbury's, empty it and dry it thoroughly. Fold the paper firmly and insert it in the empty bottle. Do not attempt to re-cork the bottle. At two o'clock this afternoon take the bottle to the Texaco service station on the A639 near junction 19 of the M5. There is a bus stop 100 yards up the road on the same side. Behind it is a grass bank. Place the bottle on this bank, neck facing down the slope, with the label showing, and leave immediately. Make sure you are not seen. Do this exactly in every detail. Remember, no fuss, no fuzz, or there will be no Lucinda.

Joanne had done everything just as she was instructed. She had thought carefully about each step as she carried it out. The bottle had to be red wine as the glass was dark and would not show the message inside. The Sainsbury's label and the type of wine would identify the bottle if there were others. Placing it neck down with no stopper would indicate that it was empty, and less likely to be picked up casually. She realised more and more that she was dealing here with someone who was clever and calculating, probably very intelligent, and not some bizarre crank or pretty criminal — a realisation which made her all the more alarmed.

She was scared already that she had overstepped the mark by taking up her hiding-place across the road. She had tried to be clever about it, in case she was watched dropping off her message. She had delivered the bottle exactly as instructed, climbed back in her Escort, and left. She had parked it in a lay-by about three-quarters of a mile up the road, changed her coat from a bright red one to a black one, and put on a grey headscarf. Then she had walked back, gone into a field opposite the garage, and crept along the hedge until she was opposite the bus-stop. The bottle was still there when she got back. She had been away 13 minutes. She reckoned the bottle would not be collected for at least another hour.

Joanne looked at her watch. Forty-five minutes had now passed. She had cramp in her left leg, and she tried to shift her position slowly to ease it. She was soaked to the skin. Damn this rain, she cursed silently.

She reminded herself that there was of course only one reason why she was taking this chance: to try and identify her tormentor. If she could only see the face of this monster who was threatening her child, it might make it a little easier — a face to look out for in the crowd.

It might even be someone she came into regular contact with, and then — perhaps then she could risk telling the police.

★ ★ ★

It had been almost three hours now. Two buses had come along, picked up two passengers and dropped three. None of them had shown any interest in the bottle. She didn't think she could stand it much longer, and her mother would be getting alarmed. The older woman was so jumpy, still so full of fanciful theories, that Joanne would not have put it past her to call the police and report her missing. She had told her mother carefully before she went out not to worry if she was late, but even so . . .

A car drew up in the bus-stop lay-by. Her pulse speeded up and her muscle pains and cold were temporarily forgotten. A big man got out, hunched under a large raincoat. She caught her breath. He was climbing the bank! He passed by the bottle, went to the hedge, and — Joanne slumped back. He was emptying his bladder.

She looked at her watch again. She would stick it out for ten more minutes. As she changed her position, water ran down her back, and she shivered again. The man scurried back to his car and drove away. The bottle was still there.

Someone was walking up the road from the service station. She wiped the rain away from her eyes and squinted. It looked like a tramp, with a plastic mac tied with string, a balaclava with a dirty, wide-brimmed hat worn over it, a dark face barely visible beneath. He slouched along, carrying a bundle wrapped in a tattered oilskin which was tied up with an old webbing belt. He shuffled to a halt beside the bus-stop. Joanne wanted nothing more than to go home, but thought she'd better wait till this person left the scene.

Water dripped from her nose and down her chin. Christ, won't it ever stop? The tramp was looking round, moving away from the bus-stop. Hell, what's he doing? He's . . . Joanne had to stop herself shouting to him as he stepped onto the grass and picked up the bottle. He held it up as if to try and drink from it, then seemed to make as if to throw it away. Changing his mind, he carried the bottle back to the lay-by and dropped it in the litter-bin attached to the bus-stop post.

Damn! Joanne cursed to herself. That's all I need. A tramp who wants to keep Britain tidy!

She was debating what to do when a bus pulled in. The tramp got on, and she was left alone with only the rain to break the silence. She knew she had to put the bottle back where it was. If whoever sent the message couldn't find it . . .

She eased herself to a standing position, and had to wait for a few moments whilst the circulation came back, fiery pins and needles in her left foot causing her to wince in pain. She hobbled the first few steps before she was able to walk properly. Back to the gate, across the road. She hurried to the bus-stop, looking anxiously about her. What if he came to collect it now? There was nothing else she could do. She went to the waste-bin, took out the bottle, and went to place it back on the bank. She held it up to the grey sky and squinted through the dark glass, to make sure the message was still in place.

She froze, dropped the bottle, and put both hands to her mouth. The bottle was empty! Her mind racing, she rushed back to the waste-bin, frantically throwing out the contents a piece at a time. There was no message! Leaving the rubbish strewn about the lay-by, she ran back to her car, gasping for air between the sobs.

CHAPTER 19

Ted had been shut in his room with his computer for three days now, trying to make the program simplify the interpretation of the signals they were getting from Paul Sansome's brain. This morning Claire had a few hours to herself for the first time in ages. She decided to go shopping — not just for essentials, but to look at some fashions, try on some shoes, perhaps get a new summer outfit. She enjoyed clothes, but did not really earn enough money to indulge her taste, which was, she was told, very good.

She had gone to the city centre by bus. Parking was such a hassle, she rarely took the car anywhere these days unless she was sure of having somewhere to leave it.

Four hours later the bus dropped her off a few hundred yards from her flat. She was empty-handed. She had seen several outfits she liked, but they were all too expensive. She had enjoyed her trip, but all she wanted now was to get home and make herself a cup of tea.

The day was hot. It was now the first week in July, and the temperatures were in the high eighties. People were talking about the greenhouse effect again. She reached the sanctuary of the shade of her front door and was looking for her key, when she heard a cultured female voice call her name.

'Miss Donaldson?'

Claire turned. She had barely noticed the Mercedes parked across the road, but now a woman was getting out and calling her name again as she closed the door.

'Yes, that's me.' She stopped and turned as the tall, elegantly dressed woman hurried across to her, pushing her glossy black hair away from her eyes.

'May I talk to you for a moment?' She looked at Claire's puzzled expression, then held out her hand. 'I'm sorry. We haven't met before, have we? I'm Christine Sansome.'

Claire could not hide her surprise. She had heard a lot about this woman, Ted had met her several times, and she had heard stories from the ward staff about her attitude to Dr Sansome. Despite working with her husband so closely, however, she had never seen his wife. She realised she was staring, ignoring the offered hand. She took it automatically, and they exchanged the briefest of handshakes. 'I — I'm sorry, I don't mean to be rude. You've caught me rather on the hop, I'm afraid.'

'I'm sorry, too. But there's something important I want to discuss with you.'

Claire felt an inner warning. She wished Ted was here.

'How — how did you find me?'

The doctor's wife laughed gaily, dismissively. 'Oh, that was easy. But when I arrived, you weren't in, so I thought I'd wait in the car for a bit. The air-conditioning makes it quite a pleasant place to while away a little time.' She glanced at Claire to see if her superiority was having an effect.

Claire felt herself bristle. 'What exactly is it you want to talk to me about?'

'It's about my husband.' She paused, looked directly into Claire's eyes, forced a smile. 'May we go inside? I do feel so awfully uncomfortable standing here on the pavement.'

Claire was aware of the woman's impeccably cut suit, her jewellery, her perfume, her expertly coiffured hair, and standing there in her own simple sun-dress and no make-up could not fight off the feeling of being at a disadvantage. She wanted to tell her to go away, but didn't know how to do it without being rude. 'Are you sure it can't wait? If it's about your husband, I'd really like my colleague to be here.'

Christine Sansome tried to sound sweet and reasonable. 'It's better not to have that coarse Australian around, don't you think?'

Claire felt anger. Six weeks ago she would probably have laughed and agreed with anyone who made such a remark, but now she felt the urge to defend Ted Parkes.

'He's not coarse, and in this matter his involvement is important.'

'Oh, I'm sorry. I didn't realise you were sweethearts.' Mrs Sansome smirked. 'It's all right.' She changed her expression to another of her sickly-sweet smiles and looked down on Claire through half-closed lids. 'I'm not after any of your dark little secrets. Just some simple facts concerning my husband, which therefore, as his wife, also concern me.' She blew away some strands of hair that were sticking to her face. Sweat was beginning to bead on her upper lip. 'May we go inside? Please?'

Claire sighed and looked for her key, opened the door, and gestured to Christine to precede her up the stairs. She followed the expensively covered hips as they swung their way upwards, then lifted her gaze to see that Mrs Sansome was critically assessing the cheap carpet and the none-too-clean walls. On the landing she turned to Claire for guidance, and it seemed to the younger woman that her guest was barely able to disguise her disdain for these plebeian surroundings.

Claire produced another key, and opened the front door to her flat. She felt more anger, knowing the state of the place, in disarray after her lazy breakfast. After all, this was a day off, and she had not worried about making sure the flat was tidy before she left, as was her habit on working days. She took Mrs Sansome into the small sitting-room, and excused herself. Glancing back she saw her visitor appraising the room with feigned detachment.

Dammit! Why should I care what she thinks about it? Who am I trying to impress? Claire sat on the bed, changed her shoes for some comfortable sandals, then paused for a moment to collect her thoughts.

What does the woman want? Should I ring Ted and tell him that she's here? She dismissed that. She knew the idea had merit, but the phone was in the sitting-room. Just have to play it by ear. Keep cool, girl. She sighed. Oh, well, let's get it over.

She got up, put her head in the lounge. Christine Sansome was sitting uncomfortably on the edge of the settee, as if it might soil her suit if she relaxed in it.

'Would you like — ?' Claire almost bit her tongue. She was about to offer a cup of tea. Damned if I will. The sooner she gets out of here the better. I can wait for mine. 'Er, would you mind just waiting a moment?' She didn't wait for a reply, but went into the kitchen and as quietly as possible poured herself a glass of cold milk from the fridge and drank it. Satisfied that she had scored a small if rather childish point, she returned to the sitting-room, sat down opposite Mrs Sansome, and went straight to it.

'What is it you think I can help you with?'

The lack of pleasantries and preliminary small talk did not bother Christine. She had to suppress a smile. I certainly won't open with 'Nice place you've got here', she thought. Instead she said aloud, 'At the suggestion of my solicitor, I've just been to see Paul's doctor. I believe you know Gerard. Mr Porthenoy, I expect you know him as.'

Is the woman deliberately trying to be offensive, or is she always like this? Claire wondered.

'Mr Parkes and I are working with Mr Porthenoy.'

'Mr Parkes?' Her visitor raised her eyebrows, then lowered them as she answered her own question, her words laced with distaste. 'Ah yes. The Australian.'

Claire was stung into a response she immediately regretted. 'Do you have something against Australians?'

Again the sickly-sweet smile. 'Oh, no. Only the loud-mouthed ones with one thought in their heads and nothing below the belt to back it up.'

Claire stood up, her face reddening. 'Ted Parkes is a very intelligent man. If you've only come here to insult him, then I suggest you leave now.'

Christine Sansome did not move. 'There's no need to be so sensitive. I do apologise, I didn't realise your taste in men was so . . . undiscriminating.'

Claire could not believe her ears. 'Undiscriminating! What the hell do you mean by that?'

The doctor's wife refused to be rattled. 'Nothing. Nothing at all.'

She patted the seat next to her. 'Come along, settle down and we'll start again.'

'You patronising bitch! This is my house, and I'll decide when and where I sit!'

Mrs Sansome shook her head, tutted, and sighed. 'Oh dear, oh dear. Such an attitude. Never mind, I forgive you. I'll put it down to Mr Parkes' influence.'

'Get out!' Claire pointed at the door, could not stop herself from shouting, knowing even as she raised her voice that losing her temper was only conceding a victory to this hateful woman. With a great effort she tried to keep her voice more even. 'For someone who came here wanting information, you've got a damn funny way of getting co-operation.'

'I don't feel the need to waste time and effort on meaningless pleading and cajoling. The information I want is mine by right. Dr Sansome is my husband. If you don't co-operate with me now, you and your antipodean friend will find yourselves the subject of a subpoena. You'll be in court, where you will be directed by a judge to answer my questions.'

Claire hesitated, fatally. Surely this was an empty threat, but . . . Could she be hauled before a court to reveal facts about this woman's husband? She was trying to formulate a reply, when Mrs Sansome produced another of her insincere smiles.

'I see you are giving the matter some thought. It will be so much easier just to answer a couple of questions now, than to go through all that unpleasantness later.' She smiled again.

Claire felt she wanted to slap the grin from the woman's face, but a voice was telling her it would be better at least to find out what she wanted. Whatever would Ted say if he found himself in court because she couldn't keep her temper with this despicable female?

Trying not to sound too cowed, she asked, 'If you tell me exactly what it is you want information about, I may be able to decide if I can help you.'

'How gracious of you.'

Claire clenched her jaw and her knuckles, but fought down another outburst. Christine Sansome swished one elegant knee over the other, clasped them both with her hands, and tossed her hair.

'As I was saying earlier, my solicitor suggested I go and see Gerard — Mr Porthenoy, that is — about my husband's state of health and his prospects of recovery. The reasons for this need not concern you. Gerard told me that the experiments I gave you and the Australian permission to carry out have resulted in your communicating in some way with my husband.'

'They're not experiments as such.'

'Whatever you choose to call them, it is the almost unbelievable fact that you have communicated with Paul — Dr Sansome — that interests me.'

If Porthenoy's told her, there's no point in denying it, Claire considered.

'It's in the very earliest stages. It's true we do seem to have made some simple contact with Paul's thoughts.' She used his first name, sensing the familiarity would annoy his wife. She immediately regretted it, as a cold fear entered her. 'It's an incredible breakthrough. You're not going to try and stop us, are you?'

Christine Sansome enjoyed holding the researcher in suspense, savouring her power. She kept her face serious until the last moment, then relaxed into a condescending smile. 'On the contrary. I want you to pursue this vigorously. When you are ready, I shall want some specific questions answered. I understand from Gerard you have further work to do before comprehensive communication is possible.' She tipped her head back and looked down her nose. 'How soon will you be able to conduct a rational conversation with him?'

Claire was earnest in her truthfulness. 'I honestly don't know. Ted is having to rewrite the computer program now. That'll take days, even weeks if it still isn't right when we try it. And it isn't as simple as you make it sound. Paul can't talk. We are analysing minute electrical currents that seem to arise in response to our sound input, and trying to interpret them as words.'

Mrs Sansome's brow furrowed. 'But it *is* true. You *will* be able to communicate with him?'

'Yes. I'm sure we will.' Claire could not suppress the question. 'What will you want to ask him?'

'My dear child, as I said before, that is no concern of yours. Your function is to get this communication system working. Then I'll tell you what I want to know.' She uncrossed her legs and rose carefully from the sofa, brushing and smoothing her skirt as if she had sat in something unpleasant. Claire felt her anger rising again, but knew that if she and Ted were to pursue their incredible journey into the workings of Paul Sansome's brain, they would need the co-operation of this obnoxious person. She compressed her lips.

'All right. We'll let you know when we get to the necessary stage of advancement.'

'You can report to Gerard Porthenoy. He'll tell me when it's time.' She turned and left. Claire stood shaking with a mixture of suppressed rage and palpable humiliation, then flopped into a chair and beat on the arms with her fists. Slowly the anger settled, and although he had made her swear not to interrupt him, she knew she had to speak to Ted.

By the time he answered the telephone, Christine Sansome was easing herself into the cool comfort of the Mercedes, convinced that whatever her husband's responses might be, she could turn them to her advantage in her quest to be appointed receiver by the Court of Protection.

CHAPTER 20

Ted grinned and put down his pint.

'You really called her a patronising bitch?'

Claire tried to look contrite, but failed miserably.

'Yes, I'm afraid I did.'

'And the little darlin' didn't try to put your eyes out?'

Claire lifted her chin and looked mock-serious. 'No. She said she would forgive me.'

Ted grinned. 'The patronising bitch.'

'Exactly.' They both laughed. The couple at the next table in the pub looked round.

Claire leaned forward. 'Tell me something, kind sir.'

'I'm at your disposal, ma'am.'

'Why was she so anti you?' She smiled mischievously. 'I mean, fancy calling you a loud-mouthed Australian with one thought in your head. That doesn't sound like you at all,' she mocked.

Ted laughed. 'Absolutely right.'

Claire looked at him sideways. 'And nothing below the belt to back it up. That sounds like a serious allegation. And intriguing.'

'Is that what the little witch said?'

'Word for word, as I recall.'

Ted swore under his breath.

Claire looked puzzled. 'I get the distinct impression you two have crossed swords before.'

Ted nodded slowly and rubbed his left ear ruminatively. 'It was at an Open Evening at the Research Institute — before you joined us. It was something to do with getting more funds, putting on a show for the providers of the loot. It was a best bib and tucker job. I'd knocked back a few quick ones. Then I thought I'd do me stuff and have a chat to the boss's wife.'

'And?'

'She was all over Paul's Air Vice Marshal friend — Sir Richard something.'

'Jacobs.'

'Yeah, that's the one. I mean, can you imagine, a Sir and all that. She was really laying it on. I thought I'd be a good fellow male and rescue the poor bugger.' He laughed.

'So what happened?'

Ted shrugged. 'After I got the Air Marshal off the hook, I started off with me usual chat, trying a bit of the old charm. Nothing much, just thought I was doing me cocktail party bit.'

'Go on.'

'At first she was angry — annoyed I'd broken her thread with the Air Force big noise. But then she did a one hundred and eighty degree turn, and took me completely by surprise.' He chuckled briefly at the recollection. 'And that takes a bit of doing with me where women are concerned.'

'You make it sound as if she propositioned you!'

Ted looked at Claire. 'Right on the button. She did. Told me I looked like a handsome sort of chap and how would I like to come round for a kinky bonk one afternoon.'

Claire's eyes widened, her mouth open. 'You're kidding!'

'Nope.'

Claire studied Ted closely. He didn't look as if he were boasting, making it up. 'But she didn't come right out with it. Using words like that as well. She can't have.'

'Honest injun. Those were her very words. Kinky and bonk.'

'Was she drunk?'

Ted looked at her impishly. 'Are you implying that a woman has to be drunk before she will consider going to bed with me?'

Claire grinned back. 'Probably.'

'Well, she wasn't. Not that I could tell. I thought she was a raving nympho. If you ask me, she bangs like a dunny door in a gale. Any case, there was no way I was going to shit on my own doorstep, and besides I prefer to take the initiative in such matters.'

'So you turned her down?'

'Flat as a fart.'

'Ted, your language is getting worse.' She gave him a mock-severe look. 'But . . . I'm beginning to see the light.'

'Is that a cue for a song?'

Claire looked amused. 'Very funny. No, you've explained Mrs Prim and Proper I'm-the-doctor's-wife Sansome's displeasure with Mr Edward Parkes.' She cupped her chin in her hand. 'I take it she was not enamoured of you by your refusal?'

'That's one way of putting it, I suppose. She really took umbrage, asked me who I thought I was, gave me the ex-convict routine. I told her she was a silly cow.'

Claire could just picture the scene. 'I can imagine she was not too happy with that response.'

'She wasn't either. She was ropable. Told me she was going straight to her husband and get me the arse.'

'Sorry?'

'Y'know — the sack.'

'She obviously didn't succeed.'

'Nope. Funny, that. D'you know, he never even mentioned it, later on. Mind you, I kept me head down for a bit after that.'

'I wish I'd been there to see her face when you called her a silly cow.'

'I'll try and give you a demonstration. Next time we meet up with her.'

'Don't you dare!' There was a genuine tinge of panic in her voice. She knew he was quite capable of carrying out that particular offer. Ted gave her a reassuring grin, and they sipped their drinks in silence for a while.

As the animation dropped away from Ted's face, the muscles slackened, and he looked drawn and anxious, somehow vulnerable. I hope he's all right, Claire thought, and realised that she felt a genuine concern for this 'coarse Australian'. His hand lay on the table. She reached out and covered it with hers.

'You look tired.'

He took a deep breath, put down his drink, and wiped his free hand across his face.

'Yeah.'

'Isn't the programming going too well?'

'You could say that. A right bugger's muddle.'

'What's the problem?' She noticed he hadn't withdrawn his hand. She squeezed it. 'Tell me.'

Ted drained his glass, set it down, and took her hand in both of his. 'It's this bloody thesaurus. I was so damned confident it would work that I integrated it into the vocabulary you and I made up from Paul's responses. Straight onto the hard disk. I didn't just tack it on. I built it in.' He shook his head. 'To get it out I've got to go through the whole program line by bloody line.'

'So how long is that going to take?'

'A bloody sight longer that two or three days, that's for sure. More like two or three weeks.'

'Oh, no!' Claire had a sudden thought, and brightened. 'Surely you kept a copy of the vocabulary we made of Paul's output responses on a floppy disk?'

He nodded. 'I did. And if I could use it I would. It would be much quicker to work from scratch.'

'Why can't you use it?'

'The back-up disk is corrupted. Can't unscramble it even with Norton Utilities. I'd say it's been near a powerful electro-magnetic field.'

'How could that happen?'

'Well, if I left it on top of the monitor it might affect it. But I've never had that trouble before.' He looked at her, the lines deepening on his face. 'If I didn't know better, I'd say it had been done deliberately.'

* * *

Joanne Yates could see the pink square on the hall carpet from halfway down the stairs, and felt sick. Thank God her mother hadn't seen it first. She rushed to pick it up. Her legs were trembling. She sat on the stairs, tore open the now familiar coloured envelope, and read the message.

Not bad for a first attempt. But you'll have to do better if you want this happy state of affairs to continue. You should have a little breathing space. Use it to learn how to copy data onto disk from the computer in Side Room 3. Bye for now.

Somehow she'd hoped that once she had provided some information it would be sufficient for her tormentor, and she'd be left alone. She could see now how stupid that was. He wanted more, and would go on wanting more.

'God, what a mess!' She spoke softly to herself, and dropped her head onto her knees. After a moment her shoulders started to shake.

She jumped as she felt the touch on the back of her head, then relaxed as a familiar little hand snaked round her neck. The small voice sounded anxious.

'What's the matter, Mummy?'

* * *

The figure closed the drawer containing the pink notepaper, picked up the sheet of white A4 paper taken from the bottle and read it again. It started to shake its head violently, at first murmuring quietly, then building up to a crescendo, chanting out the same words over and over.

'Not enough! Not enough! Not enough! Not enough!'

A fit of coughing interrupted the chant. Spittle flew in all directions, some landing on Joanne Yeates' message. Seeing the mess smearing the paper seemed to cause a sudden cessation in the coughing. A grimace spread over the face. The head bent a little as the paper was brought closer, closer until the nose was only an inch away. The figure took in a deep breath, let out a guttural growl, slowly rising in intensity, until it was a full-blown howl of rage. Fists raised in the air held the paper, then tore it savagely, crushed the remaining scraps.

When all energy was spent, the breath dissipated, there was only enough strength for a hissed echo of the earlier chant.

'*Not enough!*'

CHAPTER 21

Sister Yeates made sure all her staff were busy elsewhere on the ward. She had volunteered to take care of Dr Sansome's observations herself. She often did this anyway, treated him with special tenderness, spent time doing things she would normally delegate. She worked as quickly as she could, marking the charts, changing the nutrient drip feed, emptying the urine bag attached to the catheter, checking the ripple mattress, then settling him down, smoothing the sheets, straightening his arms, flexing and stroking his fingers soothingly.

She stood and looked down at her special patient for a long moment, mistiness in her eyes. Abruptly she remembered her mission, and with her breathing made more rapid by tension, took a 3.5″ floppy disk in its firm plastic case from her pocket. She was glad the ports on Ted's computer were for the smaller, easily concealed type.

She switched on the computer, and waited while it made various announcements on the screen she did not understand. Then came the request: _Enter Password._

She'd seen Ted do this and heard him say the name. She did not think he took the security of his computer very seriously. She had to be careful, because the letters did not appear on the screen. She typed with one finger, slowly:

S-I-D-E-R-O-O-M

She pressed _Enter_, and held her breath. A brief delay, then there was the letter C, a colon, a back-slash, and a little arrow with the cursor winking beside it. She had gone through the next steps so many times in her mind, read the instructions over and over. She started to type: _C:\> copy *.* :A_

The disk drive operating light flashed, went out, the machine whirred briefly, then the message, _File creation error — 0 file(s) copied_, appeared below her entry. The nurse looked anxiously over her shoulder, felt the sweat of nervousness break out.

She tried again. She had forgotten the colon should be after the drive letter, not before. She typed again, carefully: _C:\> copy *.* A:_

The disk light came on, stayed on, and a series of intermittent squeaks and whirrs came from the drive. Joanne looked round again. The screen was scrolling down a list of file names as it copied them. They seemed to be endless. If someone came in now, she would have no idea how to stop it, had no explanation ready. She broke out in another sweat. As she looked back at the screen, the list of files stopped flowing, and the disk drive fell silent. Thank God! she thought. It's finished. Her relief instantly turned to dismay when she looked more closely at the monitor. There was another message: *No further files copied. Insufficient disk space.*

Oh no! She almost spoke aloud. What does that mean? I haven't got a big enough disk? That can't be it, surely. She knew she dared not risk any more time, was aware that for now she was defeated. Trying to stop her hand trembling, she removed the disk and switched off the machine.

You'll just have to go home, sort it out from that computer book, and try again tomorrow. It'll be all right, she assured herself, and left the room.

But when tomorrow came, it was anything *but* all right.

* * *

'I'm sure this is a good idea.' Claire put down her briefcase and watched Ted checking the equipment.

She was still trying to convince Ted — and perhaps herself as well — that they should try and get more information from Paul Sansome while they had the chance, even if they could only extract it through positive and negative responses. Ted had been reluctant at first. He wanted to get on with rewriting the program that they hoped would enable them to get more detailed responses from the unconscious doctor.

'The trouble is,' she had urged, 'we don't know for sure how long Paul's present state will last. He could deteriorate, die even. Patients like him can do that. Porthenoy may withdraw his consent. The research committee might stop our money. Mrs Sansome might turn even more nasty. She's very unpredictable. Any of those things could happen while you rewrite the program. Then our chance could be gone for ever.'

Ted had listened; thought about it; and agreed.

He looked up from the computer.

'It's OK, you can relax. I'm not going to change my mind.'

Claire smiled at him. 'Good. I know you don't like to have your direction determined by a lady . . .'

'Who says you're a lady?'

'Bloody cheek! Let's get on with it.'

They busied themselves setting up all the equipment, adjusted the electrodes that probed into the depths of Dr Sansome's brain, tested the circuits, ran the EEG.

'Oh.' Joanne Yeates put her head round the door of Side Room 3. 'Hello. I didn't think you'd be back for a few days yet.'

She tried to conceal her disappointment. She knew of the problems with the computer program, and thought it would give her some respite. She would have a good excuse not to be pressurised to give more information, and she could work on learning how to extract data from the computer as her blackmailer demanded.

'Hi, Sister. Yes, we're back.' Ted nodded at Claire. 'Blame the old slave-driver here. Keeps me at it. Hard yakka, it is.'

'Take no notice,' said Claire, giving Joanne a welcoming smile. 'We might have been away three weeks, but we thought we'd better get what data we could now. In case there were any unexpected developments.'

'Oh. I see.'

Claire looked up, saw the anxiety there. 'Everything all right, Joanne?'

'What? Yes, I'm OK.'

Claire was not convinced, and was about to press the nurse more closely, when Ted shouted.

'Ah ha! Gotcher!'

'Ted!' she admonished. 'This is a sick room.'

'Sorry.' He spoke quietly, but urgently, jabbing his finger at the computer screen. 'Come and look at this.'

Claire came over to look at the monitor. 'What is it?'

'There! Look! Someone's been at my program!'

Joanne Yeates felt her stomach churn, and reached out to the wall. She knew she must look pale, hoped the others wouldn't turn and see her.

Claire peered closer. 'What does this mean?'

Ted rubbed his hands almost gleefully. 'When we started getting all this important data and I tried the thesaurus program, it occurred to me that what with all the funny goings-on with that poor girl getting killed, someone might try and mess about with my computer.'

'So?' prompted Claire.

Ted looked smug. 'So I wrote a little security program that would tell me if anyone tried to run it in my absence. And they have.'

Claire looked worried. 'When?'

He pointed to the screen and read the message. 'Program last activated 1835 hours on Sunday 3rd July.'

Neither of them heard Joanne Yeates gasp, as Claire drew in a sharp breath herself. 'That was last night!'

Ted grinned. 'Correct! You win a major prize.'

'You don't look very worried about it.'

'True. That's 'cos I'm a clever bloke, see. They couldn't actually run the program, not without everything being connected up. So the only thing they could do would be to copy it. But not being as thick as certain people believe, I'd fixed it so they would just get a mess.' He looked proud. 'I changed the File Allocation Table.'

'I'll take your word for it.' Claire looked relieved. 'So they haven't got away with anything?'

'No chance.'

'And what's there is not corrupted?'

Ted hit a series of keys and waited. 'Nope. Looks all right. Besides, after that last back-up disk got messed up, I made two extra copies and kept them separate. Even if all this was wiped off, we'd be OK.'

'Well, that's good news anyway. But surely the question is . . .' She hesitated.

'What bastard has been poking around inside my machine?' Ted finished for her.

The sound of the door closing made them both turn round. Sister Yeates had gone. Ted shrugged his shoulders and exchanged a puzzled frown with Claire.

* * *

'Ready?'

Claire adjusted the headphones, leaned forward and moved the microphone a little nearer. 'Ready.'

'I want to go back to the point where we got that stream of "No, No, No's." It's obvious there's something significant about the questions you were asking.'

Claire looked at the transcript beside the mike. 'We were asking about the accident.'

'That's it.' Ted looked over the instrumentation once more. 'Let's go. Remember to establish the parameters first.'

Claire switched on the microphone, paused briefly, then spoke.

'Hello, Paul.'

Ted relayed the response. 'That's good. There's the signal for his "Hello". And something else. I think we'd decided it was probably your name.'

Claire shivered slightly. The thrill of their incredible breakthrough was slightly tempered by increasing familiarity, but it still seemed uncanny, unnatural somehow.

'Paul, we can only understand "Yes" or "No". You must restrict your answers to that. Have you got that?'

'He says "Yes" .'

'Do you know who I am?'

'Yes.'

'Ted is here too. Do you understand that?'

'Yes.'

'Are you in pain?'

'No.'

'Do you remember what we were talking about last time?'

'No.'

'We were talking about your accident. Do you understand?'

Instead of just relaying the responses, Ted turned to Claire, looking excited. 'That started with a "Yes" and then a stream of signals I can't interpret.'

Claire covered the mike with her hand. 'So there's something about this he's very worked up about. He can't seem to restrict himself to Yes and No when we talk about it.' She uncovered the mike again.

Ted shook his head sadly. 'It must be bloody frustrating for him, especially as there must be so much he wants to say, questions to ask.'

Claire reached out and touched the comatose man's hand and stroked it. 'Poor Paul.'

Ted chuckled softly. 'He says "No".'

Claire gave a wan smile, sat herself up straight and addressed the microphone directly.

'We want to ask about the accident, Paul. Do you understand?'

'No. He says "No".'

Claire creased her brow, trying to frame the question a different way.

'We want to talk to you about your head injury. Do you understand?'

'Yes.'

'About your accident.'

'No.'

Claire shook her head in frustration. She looked across at Ted, hoping for inspiration. 'He understands we want to talk about his head injury, but not his accident. I don't get it.'

'Christ!' Ted was staring at the screen. 'That's produced about ten "Yes's".'

Claire stared at Ted, then at the doctor, adjusted her position and spoke again. 'Paul. You want to talk about your head injury, but not your accident?'

'Yes.'

Claire clenched her teeth. 'This is so frustrating. I want to ask him why, but he can't tell me.'

'We need that bloody thesaurus program, that's why. We'll have to give this up, and I'll have to just work my balls off for the next three weeks.'

'Come on, Ted, where's your stamina? We've hardly started yet. Let me think a moment.' She got up and walked over to Paul, looked down at him. 'You understand head injury, but not accident. Can that be right?' She thought he couldn't hear her because of the headphones, but the microphone was still switched on and was obviously very sensitive.

'He says "Yes".'

Claire turned abruptly. 'God! Why?'

'Yes.'

Claire sat down before the microphone again. 'Head injury should equal accident, but you don't agree?'

'No.'

Claire glanced up at Ted, leaned forward eagerly. 'You mean head injury does not equal accident?'

'Yes.' Ted licked his lips, said, 'Keep going, girl.'

'Christ, am I being dense, or what?' Claire muttered. She closed her eyes, breathed deeply, opened them again. 'Paul. Head injury and accident are not the same?'

'No.'

Her eyes opened wide as the thought struck her. 'You mean your head injury was not an accident?'

'Jackpot!' Ted almost jumped up in his excitement. 'That's about 15 "Yes's"!'

'Paul, let's get this quite clear. You are saying that your head injury was not an accident?'

'Two "Yes's"!' Ted looked over to Claire, urging her on.

'Someone did it to you on purpose?'

'Yes.'

'God.' She whispered the word under her breath. 'Paul, listen carefully. If you are certain you understand the question, I want you to show me by answering "Yes" three times.' She swallowed, glanced at Ted. 'Paul. Did someone try to kill you?'

Ted looked directly at Claire before he relayed the response. 'His answer is "Yes, Yes, Yes".'

CHAPTER 22

Claire felt sick. The man lying before them was a victim of attempted murder. She looked across at Ted.

'God, Ted, what are we going to do?'

He shook his head. 'Jeez. I dunno.' He stood up and walked over to the bed. 'Christ! What a turn-up.'

'Perhaps we should tell the police?'

'Yeah. I thought of that.'

'So — why don't we?'

Ted scratched his head. 'I want to think this out a bit first. I mean, it's not actual evidence.'

'You mean you don't believe it, don't trust our techniques?'

'Course I do. But what have we got to show anybody?'

They were both silent for a moment. Ted came to a decision. 'Look, let's just pack up, go and work out where we go from here.' He tapped his skull. 'There's so many thoughts whizzing around in here, I'm getting a headache.'

Claire smiled grimly. 'I know what you mean. Like does Paul know who it was, and can we get him to tell us?'

'Right!' He started to shut down the machines. 'We might want to make an early start in the morning. Go and check with Joanne that it'll be OK, while I pack up here.'

Claire hesitated only a moment. 'All right.' She went down the corridor to the office. Joanne was behind the desk, but before Claire could speak the phone rang.

Joanne flicked her hair away from her ear with a deft movement, put the receiver to it, and leaned back in her chair.

'Sister Yeates.'

Claire indicated she would wait outside, but the nurse waved her to a chair. She listened to the voice on the phone, then smiled.

'Oh, hello, Mum.'

Claire relaxed. It was not business. She started to look around the office, but her attention was caught by a difference in the nurse's posture. She watched in horrified fascination as Joanne's face changed before her eyes. Her pupils dilated, her jaw went slack, and all colour drained away to leave her skin looking like soft putty. She could hardly speak.

'Oh, Mum, no!'

Claire wasn't sure whether to stay or go. She could see her friend was in great distress, wanted to help, but didn't want to pry.

Joanne was licking her lips, trying to speak. 'Have — have you called the police?'

The reply made Joanne close her eyes, sigh, and bite her lower lip. 'Oh, Mum!'

Claire could just hear the electronic gabble from the earpiece. Her mother must be shouting, she realised.

'All right, Mum, I'll come home. Right now.'

Joanne slowly replaced the hand-set. If Claire had not been with her at that moment, she would have left immediately, would never have told anyone, and things might have worked out very differently. But Claire Donaldson was there, someone she could talk to and trust; and by God, she needed someone like that right now.

She looked up at the researcher, who was almost as pale as she, anticipating the evident disaster. The nurse tried hard to keep her voice steady. 'It's Lucinda. My daughter. She's missing.'

'Oh, God!' Claire didn't know what else to say, moved over to the sister, and put her arm on her shoulder. 'What's happened?'

Joanne told her everything. Right from the beginning. It just poured out, wouldn't stop, even though her brain was saying *Home! You must go home*! Another part of her psyche was demanding to unburden itself of all the suppressed pressures, the horror, the threats, the guilt, the lies. Now, with Lucinda missing, covering up didn't seem to matter any more; she had lost her game of deceit and untruths. Claire sat and listened, mesmerised, her overwhelming emotion that of sympathy for the other woman's plight. She felt no anger or resentment at the spying Joanne had been attempting. Claire knew, felt sure, that she would have done the same, more even, to try and shield from harm a son or daughter. She understood intuitively that a mother's instinct to protect her young was one of the most powerful forces in nature.

At last Joanne stopped her flow, looked at Claire through her tears, and put out a hand to touch her arm.

'I'm sorry.'

Claire felt like laughing and crying at the same time. 'Sorry? You're trying to say sorry? Good God, woman, what for?' She stood up. 'Come on. I'll get Ted, then we'll go and find Lucinda.' She hurried out.

Joanne felt a wash of relief momentarily dilute her fear. Someone was sharing the burden. She composed herself enough to call the duty senior nursing officer, saying she had an urgent personal problem, and arranged cover for the ward. By the time she had done that, Claire had returned with Ted, still hastily explaining as she came into the office.

'. . . and I'll tell you the rest later. But first let's take Joanne home and get something organised.' She turned to the nurse. 'Do you mind if the police are involved now?'

She shrugged. 'My mother's already done that.' She shook her head.

'Anyway, I don't see what difference it makes if he's got her.' Her face took on the distorted expression of someone desperately trying to hold back a flood of tears and distress. 'Oh, God, please let her be all right!'

Ted and Claire stood, silent and awkward for a moment, while Joanne's shoulders shook with silent sobs. The Australian decided some action was required. 'You're in no state to drive, Joanne. Claire'll run you home. I'll follow. Then when we've got the police organised, we'll think about where to start looking ourselves.'

⋆ ⋆ ⋆

'I just knew something like this would happen!'

Mrs Bristowe, Joanne's mother, ignored the presence of her daughter's two companions and launched herself into a self-centred monologue.

'I knew it. I always said after that trouble at your house, the cat and everything. My own grand-daughter! I'm in such a state, I don't know how I'll manage. My palpitations have been coming back already. The doctor said I shouldn't get worked up about things.' She looked at the two unfamiliar faces watching her. 'It's my heart,' she said, 'I've got tablets.' She stopped, as if everything had been explained, and looked at Joanne.

Claire was astonished. She had thought mother and daughter would fall into each other's arms for mutual consolation and strength at such a moment, but Mrs Bristowe seemed to have no intention of offering such solace. They were all still standing awkwardly in the hall.

'Can we go on in?' Claire asked tentatively.

Joanne squared her shoulders. 'Yes, I'm sorry, come into the front room.'

They all sat down except Ted, who moved slowly about, unconsciously taking the initiative.

'Tell us what happened, Mrs Bristowe.'

She looked at Joanne as if seeking permission to speak, then began.

'I took her to playgroup this afternoon like you said. I left her with Mrs Simes. I mean, how was I to know something like this would happen? What's happening to her? You hear so much, kids being raped, murdered —'

'Yes, of course, you weren't to know.' Ted glanced at Joanne to see what effect these less than encouraging speculations were having. The nurse seemed unmoved. He directed himself to Mrs Bristowe. 'And when did you find out Lucinda was missing?'

'When I went to pick her up. I — I was only a minute or so late.' She looked across at her daughter, expecting disapproval. 'I only stopped off for my magazine. They always wait.'

'Was there no one there when you got to the playgroup?'

'Oh, yes, course there was. Always is. They'd never leave a child there alone if the Mum hadn't turned up.' She paused. 'Mrs Simes had gone, though. She'd taken a group round to the library, came back with them, and then left again. So Mrs What's-her-name said.' She turned to Joanne. 'You know, the one with the blonde hair, her assistant.'

'Mrs Harrison.' Joanne was impassive.

'Yes, that's her. Well, she thought Lucinda was still inside. I went in, couldn't see her nowhere. Her coat wasn't on her peg, neither. I went out to Mrs What's-her-name again, and we both looked.' Her face twisted. 'Not a sign.'

'Was Lucinda one of the ones who went to the library?'

Mrs Bristowe sniffed. 'Yes. But she came back. Mrs What's — Harrison — saw her. And she remembered Mrs Simes saying, 'All present and correct,' like she always does when they're checking on who's there. I've heard her say it myself. I reckon she must've been in the army or something because she often —'

Ted interrupted the flow. 'Have you been able to speak to Mrs Simes yet?'

'No. She went off. Probably home by now.'

He turned to Joanne. 'Have you got her phone number?'

Mrs Bristowe spoke again, a hint of triumph with defiance. 'Tried it. No reply.'

Ted pondered a moment. 'Did you wait long at the playgroup?'

'No. No, as soon as I realised Lucinda was missing, I —' She bit her lip and turned her head away.

'When did you phone the police?'

'Soon as I got back, of course. I took one of my pills, first, in case my heart —'

Ted interrupted again. 'How did you leave it with Mrs Harrison?'

'She said she'd wait there to hear if Lucinda's turned up. Terrible worried, she was. Worried about her job, I shouldn't wonder.' She wrung her hands. 'If anything's happened to that little girl . . .'

Claire leaned forward, tried to speak soothingly. 'I don't think we should jump to the conclusion that anything has happened to her. Not yet.'

Mrs Bristowe looked at her, affronted. 'You mark my words, something bad's happening. You didn't see our Joanne's house after that maniac had finished with it! The poor pussycat gutted, blood on the walls.' She clutched her left breast with her hand. 'God knows what someone like that is capable of.'

Joanne turned away, fighting down an outburst that threatened to make her lose control completely.

'Mrs Bristowe, please,' Claire urged. 'Saying things like that won't help. Think of Joanne. We must be positive.'

'Huh! The only positive thing about this is —'

A firm knock on the door stopped her in her tracks, but only momentarily. 'That'll be the police. Oh God, what've they found?'

They all rose, but Ted was quickest. 'You stay here. I'll go.' He went into the hall and closed the door after him. Claire went over to Joanne and put her arm round her shoulder. Mrs Bristowe started to talk about her heart again.

They all turned as the door opened. Joanne reacted first, stepping forward as she spoke.

'Oh! Mrs Simes! Have you heard anything about —?'

The woman smiled, stepped aside, and Lucinda ran into her mother's arms.

★ ★ ★

Joanne couldn't stop the tears flowing, even though she was almost laughing with joy.

'You look funny, Mummy.' Lucinda extricated herself from her mother's arms and took a step back. 'You said you're all right, but you're crying.' The child looked at her accusingly, disapprovingly. 'Mummies don't cry.'

Claire moved over and knelt by the little girl and put her arm round her waist. 'Sometimes Mummies do. When they're upset.'

'Why is my Mummy upset?' She looked round. 'Everybody looks upset.'

Claire laughed gently and gave the girl a small hug. She didn't want to say anything that would unsettle Lucinda, who was obviously disturbed at being surrounded by four emotionally charged adults and one puzzled playgroup leader.

'There's nothing to worry about, honestly. It's just that —'

'Nothing to worry about?' Mrs Bristowe moved forward. 'Nothing to worry about? Here we are thinking the child has been kidnapped, and you say there's nothing to worry about?'

Ted went to move between grandmother and grandchild, trying to smile at Lucinda as he directed his speech to Joanne's mother.

'Please, Mrs Bristowe. As far as Lucinda's concerned, there *is* nothing to worry about. We don't want to let her get too bothered about things, do we?'

Mrs Bristowe turned away, displeased at the intervention. Mrs Simes' puzzlement turned to consternation. 'Kidnapped? What do you mean — you don't think —?'

Ted took her arm. 'Come with me and I'll explain.' He led the protesting woman from the lounge and into the hall, closing the door carefully behind him.

'I — I was only gone a few minutes. I had no idea —'

'It's all right, it's not your fault. Just tell me what happened.'

'Nothing *happened*. I came back from the library and realised Lucinda had left her coat. I went back for it and Lucinda came with me — to help me identify it. We were only gone a few minutes. I thought Mrs Bristowe would wait. But when we got back she had gone. I told Mrs Harrison to go, and that I would drop Lucinda off at her home.'

'It looks as if Mrs Bristowe was a bit hasty in rushing off and jumping to conclusions. But why did it take you so long to turn up here?'

Mrs Simes looked awkward. 'I had to meet my nephew at the bus station. I was afraid if I came straight here I might miss him. He's only twelve, and he was travelling alone. I promised his mother I'd meet him.' She looked down at the floor, then pleadingly at Ted. 'Of course, the bloody thing was late. I just had to wait.'

Ted could see the woman was getting herself worked up. 'It's OK now, you don't have —'

'I had no idea it would cause so much trouble. I thought I was being helpful.'

'You weren't to know, Mrs Simes. In any other household your actions would have been appreciated for what they were. But here, I'm afraid we've been kind of screwed up about Lucinda's safety.' He went on to explain, briefly and without too much drama, the background to Joanne's and Mrs Bristowe's fears.

Mrs Simes shook her head. 'I see. Oh dear, oh dear. And of course they naturally concluded that the child had been abducted. How awful for them.'

'It's all right now. Honest. No worries.'

'Do you think I should —?' she gestured towards the closed door.

Ted considered briefly. 'No. Leave it be. I'll explain.' He moved to the front door, opened it.

'I'm so sorry. Tell Mrs Yeates I'm so sorry.'

As the playgroup leader left a police car pulled up. Ted let the officers in, and there was much all-round relief, some of it rather forced and hearty from the policemen, that all was now well. Claire hoped Joanne would tell them everything she had told her, but instead the nurse just apologised for the trouble the incident had caused. No trouble at all, better safe than sorry, she was assured. The policemen's delight at not having a case of child abduction on their hands was evident. Once again, Ted acted as butler and showed them out.

As he came back into the room, Lucinda looked round, noting the absence of her playgroup teacher for the first time.

'Has Mrs Simes gone?'

'Yes, dear, some time ago,' Joanne said gently, smoothing her daughter's head with her hand.

Lucinda looked up, eyes wide. 'Mummy?'

'Yes, dear?'

'What's kidnapping?'

CHAPTER 23

'Why are we sitting all funny like this, Granny?' Lucinda and her grandmother were crouched in the back of Ted's car, two small suitcases beside them.

'We're pretending to hide.'

Ted approved. He thought the old lady was playing along well for once.

'Why are we hiding?'

Ted thought he'd help out. He glanced over his shoulder briefly. 'We're just having a game. To see if I can drive you to the station without anyone seeing you.'

'Why?'

'Just for fun. Don't you think it's fun?'

'Not much. I wish Mummy was coming.'

Her grandmother stroked her hair. 'I know, dear. She'll come along too as soon as she can.' She tried to ease her uncomfortable position. 'And just think what fun you'll have playing with Piers and Stephanie.'

Ted concentrated on the rear-view mirror. He wasn't quite sure how to check if they were being followed, and tried to remember what he had read in books and seen on television. He slowed as they approached some traffic lights, then accelerated through as they changed to red. The car behind stopped, the following traffic held up. Good one, that, he thought. Next he did a complete circuit round a block before continuing on his way. The cars behind kept changing. He came to a big roundabout on the A38 into Bristol and went round it twice before continuing on into the city centre. He began to feel more confident that their departure had not been observed by anyone who might have an interest in Lucinda's whereabouts.

They had soon decided that the safest thing was for Lucinda to go with her grandmother to Cheltenham. It was no great distance away, just over forty miles from Bishopsworth, but they hoped it was far enough.

Joanne's sister lived there with her husband and two children, a boy of eight and a girl of six. He ran a small business making industrial air-conditioning units, and their house was large, so that accommodation would be no problem. Joanne had been unsure how much to tell her sister, so had kept it brief. She was worried, too, that she might be putting them in danger. But when Ted proposed his plan for them to go in his car, and make sure they were not followed, she felt a little easier.

'Whoever's out there will never know she's gone, let alone where she is,' Ted had reassured her, and the relief at knowing that her daughter would be safe overcame her own desire to stay as close to Lucinda as possible.

Ted drove along York Road, over the River Avon via Bath Bridge, and into Temple Mead Station. He had been carefully studying the road behind for some time, and was sure they were in the clear. He dropped Lucinda and her grandmother and arranged to meet them by the ticket office when he had parked the car.

Fifteen minutes later he was helping a rather uncertain little girl and a nervous old lady to settle in their seats, then waved them goodbye as the train pulled out. It's a funny old life, he thought. A few hours ago I'd never even met these two, and here I am fussing around them like an old hen. He returned to his car, smiling to himself.

* * *

'You were really terrific. D'you know that?'

Claire came up behind Ted as he stood in her kitchen pouring a beer. She gave him a hug, and he could feel the warmth of her against his back.

'Steady! I'll spill the old amber nectar here if you're not careful.'

Claire pulled away and perched on the edge of the table.

'I mean it, Ted. It's true. You were *so* helpful, getting everything organised. And you didn't swear once, or use any of your disgusting Aussie slang. Quite a revelation.'

Ted didn't seem very pleased by this unsolicited testimonial.

'Come on, woman, I'm not completely insensitive.' He sipped his beer, and wiped his mouth with the back of his hand. 'I know how to behave when I have to.'

'Oops, sorry.' Claire grinned. 'You *are* sensitive.' She stroked her straw-coloured hair away from her eyes, which were twinkling with gentle amusement. 'But you *were* good with Lucinda. Do you like children?'

'Ankle-biters? They're all right, I suppose. Haven't thought much about it.' He drank more deeply from his glass and gestured with it towards Claire. 'Want one?'

'Why not? I reckon we've both earned a drink today.'

'Yep.' He popped a can and poured. 'Fancy Joanne keeping all that to herself. You notice she still didn't tell the police the whole story?'

'She's scared. So would I be.'

'Reckon.' He drank again. 'What sort of evil bastard would play a shitty game like that? He must be shingle short.'

Claire nodded. 'Psychopathic, I should think.' She drained her glass.

'Christ! That was quick. Another?'

'Perhaps I will. It's been quite an eventful few hours. All that business with Lucinda — and what Paul told us.'

Ted poured them both another drink. 'I'd just been thinking about that myself. I was like a stunned mullet when those three "Yes's" came up on the screen.'

Claire shivered involuntarily as another thought occurred to her. 'Ted?'

He looked at her, saw her pale. 'Hey, what's up?'

'Suppose Paul is still — well, still in danger?'

'You mean someone might try and finish him off? Christ almighty, don't you think that's a bit much?'

'It's possible, isn't it?'

'Well, I guess it is. But surely, they'd have tried something by now if they were going to. Besides, his attacker probably reckons he's as good as dead.'

'That depends, surely.'

'On what?'

'Well, for example, if it was something to do with inheritance. He'd need to be actually dead.'

'You *have* been thinking about this.'

'Or —' Claire hesitated. 'Or if they knew we could communicate with him. Reveal who had tried to kill him. Or why.'

Ted drank deeply. 'That's a very good point, my girl. Very good indeed.

'So?'

'So we keep as quiet as possible about it for now, I reckon. No point in alerting the police if we've no evidence, and risking publicity for what we're doing. We've just got to solve this communication problem.' He drained his glass, and without asking Claire poured two more beers.

She looked at her glass, then at Ted.

'If I don't eat soon, I won't be able to think at all, let alone straight. Let me get something.'

'Sounds like a good idea. I'll go out to the off-licence and get some wine. What's on the menu? Spag bog, wasn't it?'

Claire laughed, the beer dissolving some of her earlier fears. 'Something like that.'

Ted grinned. 'So a fine claret to go with it, then, I think, modom.

'That'll do nicely.'

* * *

Two hours later later found them sitting on the sofa, halfway through a second bottle of wine. They had discussed the question of communication with Paul at some length. They were both more relaxed, the horrifying implications of their recent discovery tempered by the alcohol.

Ted, who had consumed more than his fair share of the wine, waved an arm expansively. 'Any other ideas you want to toss around?'

'Well — we need a short cut. To be able to interpret a few words that will give us the information.'

'But being able to interpret a few words — that won't give us a name.'

'That's it. Names are the problem.' Claire sat up as she got an idea. 'We can find out easily if it's male or female. Yes or no will tell us that.'

'Very good,' Ted agreed. 'That narrows it down from five billion to two-and-a-half.'

Claire snorted her derision. 'Idiot. We're not dealing with the population of the world.'

'How do you know?' He gave a silly grin.

'Surely it's bound to be one of Paul's associates, someone he knows. *That* narrows it down a bit.'

'I suppose so.' Ted poured himself another glass of wine. 'Look, we could make a list of the output responses to a whole list of names, everyone we can think of, however stupid or unlikely. Then ask him to say who tried to kill him, and compare all the responses to see if Paul's matches up.'

Claire looked excited. 'That's a good idea! Logical despite the wine.'

'We'll start tomorrow.'

'Right.' She lay back, feeling suddenly very tired. She let her head rest on Ted's shoulder. He picked up her hand and stroked it.

'Are you still feeling logical?'

Claire feigned a groan. 'You don't want me to do some more thinking?'

'Not exactly. I was just thinking that if your higher centres are all still functioning normally, then it's no good me trying to seduce you.'

Claire glanced up at him, then away, smiling.

'No good at all, I'm afraid.' She started to giggle.

Ted sounded hurt. 'I didn't know I was *that* funny.'

Claire moved away so she could look at him. 'My, there's that sensitivity again. You don't like a lady mocking you.'

Ted shrugged. 'I'm not worried.'

'Yes, you are.' She put a hand on his arm. 'I'm *not* mocking you. I was laughing at the situation. You see, even if I *did* want to — how do you so quaintly put it? — have a naughty with you, I can't.' She looked at him quizzically. 'Understand?'

'Oh.' Ted was taken aback momentarily, and joked to cover his embarrassment. 'Bloody hell! All that wine wasted.'

Claire smiled at him. 'You men are so funny. All macho and bravado, giving the girls the come-on. But hint at a natural female phenomenon like a period, and you go all blushing and awkward.'

' "You men",' Ted quoted. 'Have you known many men like me?'

'In the biblical sense, do you mean?'

Ted laughed. 'In any sense.'

Claire looked thoughtful and lay back against Ted's shoulder. 'No. Only the one, to be honest. My fiancé. And you know all about him. After that, I've been, well, pretty wary.'

Ted felt he wanted to protect her. He put his arm round her shoulder. She did not resist.

'I can understand that. Explains a lot.'

'You mean because I didn't find you so irresistible that I was able to stop myself leaping into bed with you on that enchanted evening when our eyes met across a crowded room?'

'God, you can be cruel!'

Claire lay back against him again. 'What about you?'

'You've lost me there for a minute.'

'Women I have known. That sort of thing. You asked me just now about men.'

'Oh. Well, after listening to you, makes me feel a bit of a shit.'

''Cos you've left a few women around who've got their fingers burnt, like me?'

'Yes, something like that.'

'Perhaps you flatter yourself.'

Ted cheered up at that. 'Yeah. Maybe I do. Maybe I'm not such a bastard after all.'

Claire stroked Ted's thigh, and almost whispered. 'Ted?'

He felt a stirring. 'What is it, my English rose?'

She put on a mock accent. 'This Sheila's fair tuckered out, me old sport, me old cobber.'

Ted suppressed a laugh. 'They don't use those expressions in Australia any more. Only in Earl's Court.'

'Oh. Never mind, the sentiment's the same.' She sat up and smiled innocently at him. 'I'm going to bed. Alone.'

Ted felt his stirring melt away. 'Just teasing me, eh?' He slapped a hand on his knee. 'Shucks. Missed out again.' He stood up, wavered, sat down again. 'Whoops! Never thought I was a one-pot screamer.'

'You've had three beers and well over a bottle of wine.'

'Jeez. And I never even noticed. Hell! I'll get done for DD.'

'Taxi for you, then, my boy.'

'I spent my last change down the off-licence. Lousy investment, too.'

Claire sighed with resignation. 'How much is the fare?'

Ted scratched his head. ''Bout a fiver, I reckon.'

She went to the kitchen, rummaged in her purse, then returned to find Ted standing more steadily. 'I've only got three pounds.'

'Aw, bugger it. I'll drive.'

'Oh, no you won't. Not like that. It's crazy to risk it.' She looked heavenward. 'Forgive me, Lord, for I know not what I do.' She turned a stern look on Ted. 'You can stay the night. On the sofa.'

Ted went unsteadily down on one knee. 'Oh, fair maiden, such munificence, such generosity. How can I ever repay you?'

Claire laughed. 'Just keep out of my underwear.'

'It really wouldn't suit me.'

'Idiot!' She went to get some blankets, then left Ted to make up his bed while she made a hot drink. By the time she came back he was asleep, breathing noisily. She smiled down at him, then went into her bedroom.

* * *

Ted woke and cursed silently at the numbness in his left leg. His mouth felt foul, and his bladder was demanding relief. He sat up in the darkness and pressed the light on his watch. It was a quarter to three. He rose carefully, massaging his leg, and made his way to the bathroom. On the way back he passed Claire's bedroom door. It was just ajar. Aha! he thought, she must have looked in to check up on me. He pushed it slightly and peered in. The room was surprisingly bright. The thin curtains were diffusing yellowish light from outside. Must be a street lamp near the window, he decided. He took two paces into the room. Claire was asleep on the far side of a double bed. He moved closer. She lay on her back, the bedclothes across her chest, the swell of one breast showing clearly, the darkness around her nipple just discernible, like a rising sun above the edge of the sheet. He felt the stirring return. Just a look, he told himself as he moved to the edge of the bed. He imagined how warm and cosy it would be under those sheets, the soft skin, the smoothness of her curves . . . He felt himself harden.

Her breathing was soft and even. She's sound asleep. Go on, just lie there a moment. She'll never know. He pulled back the sheet, slowly, slowly. Her left breast became fully exposed. Quite small. Pointed. Exciting. Ted's mouth went dry. Very gently he sat on the bed and eased his legs under the covers. He lay on his back next to Claire, not daring to move. His distended organ ached. Claire turned slightly towards him, and touched his arm. He drew it away as if burnt. He began to sweat. Fear of discovery suddenly became the overwhelming emotion. What if she woke? Would she scream rape, call the police? His tumescence subsided. This no longer seemed such a fun idea. He rolled very softly out onto the floor, then crept from the room and back to the sofa.

As Ted went through the door, Claire turned towards it and watched it close. Her heart was racing, but was it from fear or excitement? Did she feel violated or flattered; or rejected? She turned over the other way and tried to go back to sleep, but two sensations dominated, telling her the answer. They were emptiness; and frustration.

CHAPTER 24

David Barker leaned forward over the intercom, scratched his beard, and groaned.

'God! Why did I ever get myself involved with this bloody woman?' he asked his secretary.

'Shall I tell her you're not available?' the tinny voice asked from the loudspeaker.

'No, no, no, no.' He said the words so quickly they ran into each other. 'Can't do that, Might as well get it over with now. Send her in.'

The solicitor cleared a small space on his desk and checked that the chair opposite was not encumbered with files. He was about to sit down again when Christine Sansome walked in. He straightened up and shook her hand before escorting her to her seat, and as he did so tried hard not to stare. Whatever's she up to? he asked himself as he took in her very short skirt, patterned black stockings, and low-cut silk blouse which was so thin there was no doubt she was bra-less beneath it.

When they were seated on opposite sides of the desk, he cleared his throat and tried not to look at her nipples.

'What brings you back so soon?'

'So soon?' Christine Sansome frowned. 'It's nearly a fortnight. I thought you might have some news.'

David Barker sat back, trying to disguise his relief. 'Oh, I see. If it's a progress report you wanted, then I could have saved you the trouble of a visit and brought you up to date over the phone.'

'Well, I'm here now. So how *are* things going?' She crossed her legs ostentatiously.

'Not much progress so far, I'm afraid. We're still waiting to file the Certificate of Family and Property with the Court of Protection.'

'Why?'

'The reason, Mrs Sansome, is that you haven't given us sufficient information to complete the forms.'

'I filled them in and sent them back ages ago.'

'But with insufficient detail, I'm afraid. We wrote you a letter last week explaining where the deficiencies lay.'

She looked at him with a mixture of defiance and aggression. 'I-I can't have seen it. I'm not always at home these days.'

The solicitor could have sworn she coloured slightly and looked embarrassed, the first time he'd noticed any sign of a crack in her arrogant façade. 'Well, the fact remains,' he said, forcing himself not to glance at her *décolletage*, 'that we need more personal details and some references from you before we can proceed.'

The doctor's wife licked her lips. 'I really don't see the need for all that.'

'I'm sure that in your case there *is* no need, Mrs Sansome. But it is a requirement of the Court, and if we provide inadequate information at this stage, the documentation will only be returned to us with further unwanted delay.'

She sighed her displeasure and tutted. 'The letter's at home, you said?'

'That is correct.' What's she playing at? Barker smiled at her as he wondered. Does she want the Court of Protection order or not?

'There is something else I wanted to discuss with you.'

The solicitor stroked his beard then placed his hands together. 'I'll do my best.'

'You know I told you about the experiments — tests, rather — that were being done on my husband to try to communicate with him?'

'It sounded so incredible, I could hardly forget.'

'Well as you suggested, I went to discuss it with the researcher who is running the project. She seemed reluctant to be co-operative. I could make her tell me what she has found out, couldn't I? Get her into court with a subpoena?'

'Your tone suggests to me that you have already threatened such action.'

'I hinted at it, yes.'

'I did advise a gentle approach, you know. Co-operation would be so much better.'

'The little bitch was so superior. As if it were her private little business.'

Barker winced at the outburst. 'There is the matter of medical confidentiality, as I reminded you. Even between husband and wife.'

'But she's not the doctor. Mr Porthenoy is.'

'Ah, yes, Mr Porthenoy, glad you mentioned him. Have you got the Medical Certificate from him yet?'

'I've asked. He said he would do it.' She breathed deeply and deliberately. The solicitor concentrated on looking at her eyes.

'Then I'm sure he will oblige.'

'You still haven't answered my question. Can I make the research woman divulge what she gets from Paul?'

'I honestly don't know. I think I shall have to seek counsel's opinion.'

She stood up. 'More expense, I suppose. And more delays.'

'I'll be quite frank with you, Mrs Sansome,' Barker said as he too rose. 'You are being much too impatient. The way ahead is not as straightforward as you may like to think, and some delay will be inevitable.' She was about to protest when he held up his hand. 'And you can best help me by getting those personal details and references as soon as possible.'

He braced himself for another tirade. Instead she seemed to change, chameleon-like, and gave him a wide smile. 'I'll attend to it right away.'

The solicitor stood by the door and ushered her out. She turned on the landing, stood momentarily in fashion-model stance, one hand on hip, one knee bent forward.

'I'll be in touch,' she said brightly, then trotted off down the hall, hips swinging.

David Barker became aware that Miss Totter, his secretary, was at his elbow.

'Mutton dressed as lamb,' she said disapprovingly.

'I can't agree. A wolf in wolf's clothing, I'd say.'

'Huh! Quite a madam, isn't she?'

'Indeed she is.' He took out a handkerchief and wiped his forehead. 'She's a strange lady. One minute all angry and distant, the next all seductive.'

'Nymphomaniac, probably.'

'Now there's a thought.'

'I beg your pardon?'

'I just have the feeling there's something in her background she doesn't want me to know about.'

CHAPTER 25

Paul Sansome lay quietly, eyes open, breathing regularly, headphones in place. Ted and Claire had wired up the electrodes and were ready to go.

'You're sure you've checked everything?' Claire asked. Ever since the electrocution of poor Nurse Marvaine, she was almost obsessional about the electrical checks.

'Relax. Everything's fine.'

Claire had spent the whole of the previous day reading a list to Dr Sansome of the names of everyone they could think of who might have the slightest relationship to him, while Ted recorded the input responses from the thought centre. The idea was that the computer would compare them with any output responses that the patient might generate himself on direct questioning.

'Let's go, then.' Claire took up her now familiar position before the microphone. Her hand shook a little as she reached out and switched it on.

'Hello, Paul.'

Ted hesitated only briefly. 'He says hello. . . . and the second trace matches with Claire.' They had included both their own names in the list.

'Paul, I want to talk to you about your accident.'

'Several "No's", like last time.'

'It's all right, Paul. We know you've told us it was not an accident. I'll call it your injury. Do you understand?'

'That's a "Yes".'

'You understand that you have suffered a head injury which has left you in this condition?'

'Yes.'

'And you must confine your responses to "Yes" and "No"?'

'Yes.'

'Last time we asked you if you knew who was responsible for your injury.'

'Yes.'

'And we asked you to say the name of that person.' She hesitated. 'Paul, do you know who was responsible for your injury?'

'Yes.'

Claire looked at Ted, and could not control an involuntary shiver.

'Go on,' Ted urged. 'You can't stop now.'

Claire nodded, swallowed. 'Paul, this is important. We have made a list of names. It might contain the name of your attacker. We might be able to identify it from your thought patterns. Do you understand?'

'Yes.'

'Paul, I'm going to ask you the name of your attacker. When I ask you I want you to say it. Not "Yes" or "No", but the name. Do you understand?'

'Yes.'

'To make quite sure you understand, I want you to say "Yes" twice.'

Ted changed his position slightly. 'That's it. "Yes" twice.'

Claire breathed in slowly, held it for a moment. 'Paul what is the name of your attacker?' She looked over towards Ted expectantly, knowing the computer would be searching the list for a pattern that matched up.

'There's a response of some sort,' Ted reported. They could hear the hard disk squeaking and whimpering softly as it made countless comparisons.

Ted banged the desk gently with his fist. 'Shit! It says *Not found.*'

'Hang on!' Claire sounded excited. 'Except for us, we only put in surnames, didn't we? To keep it simple.'

'Right.'

'So if Paul said a Christian name as well, it might confuse the computer.'

'It's possible.'

She turned back to the microphone. 'Paul. I want you to say the name of your attacker again, but only his surname. Do you understand?'

'Yes.'

'Paul, give me the name.'

'It's searching.'

Claire watched, hope fading as the disk drive stopped. Ted shook his head. 'No good. Nothing again.'

Claire spoke directly to the man on the bed. 'Oh, Paul, why can't you tell us?'

'That got a response! Searching now.'

Claire switched off the mike, got up and went to look at the screen. The cursor winked by the word *Searching*.

With a final flourish, the drive stopped whirring, and pronounced: *Word identified: Ted.*

Claire could not believe it. 'We'll clear this up right away,' she said, going back to the microphone and switching it on. 'Paul, do you mean Ted Parkes is your attacker?'

'Phew. That's a relief. He says "No".'

Claire didn't look up. 'Paul, someone else, not Ted, was your attacker?'

'Yes.' Ted beckoned her over. 'You'd better come and look, so you know I'm not cheating.'

Claire smiled at him. 'Ted, I trust you.'

'I still want you to look.'

She came and looked briefly at the screen, nodded, then went back and turned the mike off. She sat on the edge of the table.

'I wonder why he mentioned your name.'

'Beats me. He might have been trying to say I knew the name. Or that there's some connection between me and his attacker.'

'Or that you're at risk from the same person!'

'Hmm. Don't like the sound of that idea.'

'Look, why don't we try this another way? Using "Yes—No"?'

'Go on.'

'Give me the print-out of the list and I'll show you.'

Ted did so, and she settled before the mike and flicked the switch.

'Paul, I'm going to read you a list of names. I want you to tell me after each one if that was your attacker. Do you understand?'

There was a long pause before Ted reported that the response was 'Yes'. Claire repeated the question. She wanted to be sure. This time the positive came much more quickly.

'All right.' She smoothed the list on the table. 'One at a time, Paul, with a response after each.'

She began to read from the list, which was in alphabetical order. All the people had been involved in the research project in some way, or were known to be acquaintances. They knew they were short on his personal friends, but had decided not to involve his wife at this stage in order to get more.

Ted sat before the monitor, intoning 'No' at regular intervals. He felt tension rising as they got over halfway through the alphabet.

'James North.'

'No.'

'Edward Parkes.'

'No.'

'Margaret Partridge.'

'No.'

'Gerard Porthenoy.'

Ted glanced at Claire. 'No.'

'Maurice Richardson.'

'No.'

'Christine Sansome.'

There was a long pause. At last Ted said, 'No.'

'Kenneth Trenchard.'

'No.'

They were soon at the end. Claire read the last name.

'Joanne Yeates.'

'No.'

Ted blew out his cheeks and pushed his chair away from the table. 'That's it, then. Confirms it. It's nobody we know.'

'Looks like it.' Claire's head hung down.

Ted came and put his arm on her shoulder. 'Cheer up. We'll think of something.'

Claire was hesitant. 'Look, Ted, I expect you've had enough for one day, but — I've had another idea. It's long-winded, but I'd like to try it before we pack up.'

'Oh.'

'You don't want to?'

'Forgive my lack of enthusiasm. I'm exhausted, emotionally and physically. I was just day-dreaming of a nice cool schooner.'

Claire covered his hand. 'You poor thing! Tell you what, I'll make a start, and then you can see if you want to try it now or leave it.'

Ted blew out his cheeks and pressed his fingers over his eyes. 'OK – just for you.' He looked at her wearily. 'Let's have a go.' He settled before his computer once more.

'Right,' said Claire, her hand on the microphone switch, 'I'll read out the letters of the alphabet and you tell me the response.' She threw the switch. 'Paul, we're going to try and spell the name of your attacker. I'm going to go through the letters of the alphabet and you stop me when I get to the first letter. Do you understand?'

'He understands.'

'OK, let's go.' She paused. 'A.'

'Bingo. He says "Yes".'

'Oh. Do you think he might have misunderstood?'

'Well — ask him.'

'Paul, is the first letter of your attacker's name A?'

'He still says "Yes".'

Claire looked sceptical. 'Right. Let's try for the second letter.' She went slowly. 'A, B, C, D . . .'

She got nearly halfway through the alphabet before Ted called out to her to stop. 'It looks like L.'

'Paul. Is the second letter of your attacker's name L?'

'He says "Yes".'

She wrote it down next to the A. Her excitement began to mount. She started again. The next letter was G. She pulled a face, looked at Ted. 'A-L-G. What sort of a name is that?'

Ted tried to relieve his tension with a smile. 'Surely he didn't know anyone called Algernon?'

The next letter made Claire wonder if they were on the right lines after all. It was an H. Her adrenaline level and her hope were dropping fast.

'This doesn't look like a name at all to me. A-L-G-H?'

Ted's tiredness was falling away. 'Come on, Claire, keep going. We don't know what we've got yet.'

She started off through the alphabet again, sounding a little weary. 'A, B, C, D. . . .'

At the ninth run through the alphabet Ted reported no response.

Claire spoke into the mike. 'Paul, do we have all the letters?'

'Yes.'

'You have given me all the letters that spell the name of your attacker?'

'Yes.'

'In the correct order?'

'Yes.'

'Thank you, Paul.' Claire switched off the microphone and leaned back in her chair, wiping both eyes with her fingers.

'Oh boy! All that for this.'

Ted came over to study the piece of paper. Pencilled on it were eight letters:

ALGHRAID

CHAPTER 26

Joanne Yeates wondered how Lucinda was getting on. She had spoken to her on the phone earlier that day, as she had done every day since her daughter had gone to Cheltenham. The child had sounded happy enough, her sister was obviously trying to give her a good time. Her mother didn't sound so happy, though. She never did get on as well with her younger daughter as she did with Joanne.

She looked at her watch. Seven-forty-five. Nearly time to go. She had agreed to work a late shift to help out the senior nursing officer, who was having trouble with her staff rota. She stood up, smoothed her uniform. I'll just go and check Paul once more, she decided. Pushing open her office door, she stepped into the corridor, and stopped, frowning. She was sure there was a movement down the corridor. Unless she had imagined it, someone had just gone into Side Room 3.

Joanne felt a shiver of apprehension, her skin prickled. Silly woman, she told herself. Probably one of the students being keen. Even so, she approached the door carefully, quietly, and peered through the glass.

She had difficulty suppressing an audible gasp. *Porthenoy*! What the devil is *he* doing here at this hour? She watched as the consultant bent over the bed, then straightened and looked quickly round the room. He looks furtive, Joanne thought, then stepped back and chastised herself. Don't be stupid, it's his patient in there, he can come and go whenever he pleases. She didn't want to surprise him, so she raised her hand to knock before she entered the room.

Her hand stopped an inch from the door, and she involuntarily ducked back. Porthenoy had moved over to the computer equipment and turned it on. Joanne could see the small green light flickering as the program loaded, then she looked on in astonishment as the doctor took several floppy disks from the voluminous pocket of his white coat, and inserted one into the disk drive.

What the hell's he doing? The nurse could not decide what to do. She glanced up and down the corridor to see if anyone was watching her looking through the side room door. It was empty. She looked back into the room. Now he was tapping at the keys. She could not see what was on the screen.

She felt she should go in and confront him, but did not dare. He was the consultant, she the nurse. What right did she have, what business was it of hers, if the senior neurosurgeon in charge of the case chose to visit his patient? But to take something from Ted's files? OK, he *had* authorised the research, but was the information his to take? The irony of it all struck her: here she was wanting to protect Ted and Claire's discoveries when only days ago she had been trying to do the very same thing as Porthenoy. Despite her tension she gave a grim smile. Her resolve hardened. She *had* to do *something*! She glanced into the room again. He was changing disks. Obviously he'd filled one disk and was about to fill another. Silently she hurried back to her office, picked up the phone, and dialled Ted Parkes' home number. There was no reply. She let the phone ring as long as she dared, then tried calling Claire.

She was about to put the phone down when Claire answered, and she quickly told her what she had seen. She heard Claire cup the mouthpiece and talk to someone else. She recognised Ted Parkes' muffled voice. Claire came back on the line.

'We'll be with you as soon as we can. Try and keep an eye on him, and if he comes out, see if he leaves the hospital.'

'I'll try,'

There was a brief pause. '. . . And, Joanne.'

'Yes?'

'Thanks.'

Joanne tried to keep a discreet watch on the side room from the door of her office. She knew it would take Ted and Claire a good ten minutes to get here. Surely Porthenoy would be long gone by then.

She kept glancing at her watch. Six minutes had passed. She had just looked out of her office again when Porthenoy appeared. He stepped backwards into the corridor, and Joanne had time to duck out of sight. She didn't think he would come past her office if he didn't want to be seen, so she quickly peeped out again. She was just in time to see him disappear through the double doors at the far end of the corridor.

Now she was in a dilemma. She shouldn't abandon her post, but she desperately wanted to see where he was going. She heard a banging in the sluice a few doors away, rushed over to it and found a staff nurse tidying up.

'Will you man the office for five minutes?' She asked, and left without further explanation.

She ran down past Side Room 3 and into the hallway at the end of the corridor. Porthenoy was jabbing impatiently at the lift button. He turned and saw her. Joanne decided to keep going, and went past him, trying to look relaxed. He nodded curtly in recognition, and she tried to respond with a smile that she hoped did not seem too contrived. Endeavouring to look purposeful, she carried on through the hall and into the corridor opposite. When the doors had closed behind her, she turned and peered through the glass. Porthenoy was getting into the lift. As soon as the doors closed she hurried over and watched the indicator lights. He was going up! With luck he would still be in the hospital when Ted and Claire arrived.

She hurried back to her office, and dismissed the staff nurse, thanking her warmly. Another minute, and a breathless Ted arrived, closely followed by Claire, also breathing hard and looking flushed.

'Where is he?' Ted held onto the door frame, trying to get his breath.

'It's all right, he's gone up to the sixth floor.'

'What's up there?'

'The Postgraduate Centre — and the library.'

'Is there a computer up there?'

'I — don't know. I should think so.'

Claire mopped sweat from her face. 'Are you sure he took data from the computer?'

Hastily, Joanne repeated what she had seen.

'Sounds certain that's what he was after. Let's go!'

Claire hurried after Ted as he turned away. 'Have you thought what we're going to do if we catch up with him?'

Ted looked at her without breaking his stride. 'Do? What do you mean, do?'

'Well, what are you going to say? That we've been tipped off he's been stealing our data, and would he please hand it all back?'

Ted jabbed at the lift button impatiently. 'Something like that.'

'And if he denies it, what then? Pick him up and shake him and see what falls out?'

Ted poked the lift button again viciously. 'Come on, you bugger!'

'Well?' Claire insisted.

Ted raised his voice angrily. 'I don't know what I'm going to fucking do! I haven't caught the bastard yet!'

'Ted, please. Don't shout. Remember this is a hospital.'

'Sorry.' He cursed under his breath. 'Come *on*!' he ground out. The lift arrived, the doors opened. 'Thank Christ!' They got into the empty car. Impatiently Ted pressed the button for the sixth floor.

'Ted?' Claire was getting increasingly anxious about the prospect of the forthcoming confrontation.

The doors began to close. 'What's worrying you now?' He pressed the button repeatedly. 'Jeez, this lift's slower'n a constipated sloth.'

'Why are we so worried about this? You said anyone who tried to copy the data would end up with a disk full of gobbledygook.'

'Come on, Claire. I can't just pretend this didn't happen! I want to nail the bastard.'

'But he's the one who authorises the research. If you go off half-cocked at him and he withdraws permission, we're finished! We'll never complete the project, or find out who tried to murder Paul.'

The lift was slowing for the sixth floor. Ted chewed his bottom lip, and Claire pressed on.

'It might be better to pretend we didn't know.' She had a thought that she knew was unworthy, but said it anyway. 'It might even be a useful lever. We could bring it up if he gets difficult.'

The doors opened, and as they stepped out Ted grinned at her appreciatively. 'You crafty bitser! And I thought you were a nice girl.'

'Ted, please!' She followed him through the double doors to the right of the lift. They found themselves in a corridor. Signs on the wall pointed in opposite directions. POSTGRADUATE CENTRE one way, LIBRARY the other.

'Which way, d'you reckon?'

Claire shrugged. 'I don't know. The library, first, I think. I'm sure there'll be a computer in there.' Ted strode off to the right. Claire rushed to catch up. 'Just let's think about this.' She held his arm, but Ted ignored her. When he reached the doors to the library, he looked through the clear glass panel first, then nodded.

'There he is.' He spoke in a hoarse whisper. 'Back towards us, table on the far left.'

He stepped away so that Claire could see. 'I wonder what he's doing.' She too spoke in a whisper.

'Christ, how the hell do I know?'

'He's not using the computer.'

'So he hasn't found out he's got a load of crap yet.' Ted rubbed his chin. 'Maybe you're right, y'know.'

'About what?'

'About not confronting him. I'd sure as hell like to know what he's going to do with those disks.'

Claire sighed with relief. 'How do we do that?'

'Follow him from here. C'mon, let's go and wait where we can see his car.'

Claire found one apprehension was replaced by another. The prospect of a punch-up was out, a car chase was in! She swore, almost involuntarily. 'Bloody hell.'

Ted smiled as the lift doors opened. 'Definitely not a nice girl.'

* * *

They had waited only ten minutes when Porthenoy came out to his car. Ted followed the dark blue BMW from the hospital car park at what he hoped was a safe distance. Porthenoy turned into Redcliffe Way, over Temple Bridge and into Bond Street. Here Ted fully expected him to continue round the city centre ring road, but instead the car turned into Newfoundland Street. They were heading towards St Paul's, not one of the most salubrious areas.

Claire voiced his thoughts. 'I wonder why he's going down here?'

'Search me. At least he's not going to the motorway.' Ted was concerned that if they found themselves on the M32, the new BMW would leave Ted's ageing vehicle behind.

After only a few hundred yards, Porthenoy took a left fork into Newfoundland Road, then left again into St Theresa Street. The brake lights came on ahead, and Ted pulled in to the side, fifty yards back.

They could see a figure get out of the car and hurry into a building opposite.

'Wait here, and keep the doors locked until I get back,' Ted commanded. Claire did as she was told, and sat tense and anxious. Her pulse speeded up when she saw a group of four youths approach, laughing and swearing loudly, but they paid her no attention. She glanced at her watch. Nearly nine o'clock. Soon be getting dark, she realised. She closed her eyes momentarily in relief as Ted reappeared from behind the parked vehicles up ahead. She released the lock as he approached.

'Well?'

'It's a funny sort of pub he's gone into. Called the Horse's Hoof. Lot of biker types, crummy décor. Not the sort of place he'd feel comfortable in, I reckon.'

'Perhaps he's meeting someone there — to sell them the data, perhaps.'

'Looking at the clientele, if he sells them the rubbish he's got he'll end up stiffer than a donkey's dong.'

'What'll we do now?'

'Wait, I suppose.'

'But shouldn't we try and see who he's dealing with?'

'What do you suggest? That I put on my instant disguise, go into the bar, and hope he won't recognise me?'

Claire tried to smile. 'No. Sorry.' She looked up and down the road. Another group of tough-looking young men were approaching. 'Ted, I don't like it here.'

'Not your average friendly neighbourhood, is it?'

'Not exactly. Near here is where they had all the rioting one hot summer a few years back.'

'We'll give him a few more minutes, and then we'll — ' He reached for the keys, fired the engine. 'There he is.'

Claire leaned over to look. 'There's someone with him!'

'Well, well. Lookee here.' Porthenoy crossed the road, his arm round the shoulders of a dark-skinned man with black hair. It was too far away to recognise him, but he seemed smartly dressed. Porthenoy went round the BMW and opened the door for his new companion, then returned to the driver's side, got in, and drove away.

'The essence of politeness,' Ted commented.

'I wonder where they're going now?'

'Home, I reckon. D'you know where Porthenoy lives?'

Claire shook her head. 'I don't know his address. But I think he has his private practice in Clifton. He might live there, too.'

'That seems to be where we're heading.'

Ted concentrated on his driving, trying to keep back but not get left at any lights. They went over the famous suspension bridge over the Avon Gorge, and into an area of elegant streets and large houses. Porthenoy signalled well in advance that he was turning into a gateway, so Ted had plenty of time to stop. As soon as the occupants of the BMW were out of sight, Ted opened his door.

'I'm coming too,' Claire scrambled out. She felt safe enough in this neighbourhood, and wanted to see for herself if she could get a close look at Porthenoy's companion. They ran the thirty yards to the start of some iron railings, behind which were some laurel bushes which mostly screened the large house beyond. Before they reached the double-gated entrance into which the car had driven, there was a gap which gave the two would-be spies a view of the driveway and the imposing front door. They could see a brass plate on the stonework.

'This must be his home and his private rooms.' said Claire softly.

Ted looked up and down the road. They did not seem to be attracting attention. Dusk was making them less obvious.

'Looks like it.'

The two men were still sitting in the car, talking.

'Perhaps he's just a patient.'

'Don't bet on it.'

Both front doors of the car opened together and the men got out. Porthenoy came round to the younger man and put his hand on his shoulder. Ted and Claire could hear laughter as the pair ascended the three steps to the front door. They obviously had no idea they were being watched, and must have thought they were effectively screened from the road. There could be only one explanation for their next action. Ted and Claire stared open-mouthed as the two men embraced each other and kissed passionately.

CHAPTER 27

'I just *knew* he was a bloody shirt-lifter!' Ted thumped the steering wheel to emphasise his certainty. 'I just knew it!'

'All right, Ted. So Porthenoy's a homosexual. But where does that get us? We still don't know why he's trying to steal your computer program, or who he's getting it for.'

Ted looked about him. It was nearly dark now as they sat in his car round the corner from Porthenoy's house.

'True. But it sure as hell gives me a way of finding out.'

'How's that?'

'Like you suggested earlier in the hospital. Certain items of knowledge can be used as a little leverage.'

Claire looked alarmed. 'You don't mean blackmail him!'

'Well, not exactly. I don't mean send anonymous letters in the post demanding money, nothing like that.'

'What, then?'

'We just go and ask him what the hell he thinks he's doing. And if he won't tell us, then we'll find it difficult not to mention in conversation with various people that he has certain proclivities.'

'Ted, that *is* blackmail.'

'No, it isn't. We'll be telling the truth. He's the one who's been stealing.'

'It's morally wrong.'

'I can live with it. Ends justify the means, and all that.'

'But don't you think — if we try it — he'll try and stop us from working with Paul?'

Ted bit his lower lip. 'I suppose he might. But I don't think so — he'd know we'd let the cat out of the bag for sure, then.'

'He might call our bluff.'

Ted was set on his course. He *wanted* to confront the man, see the expression on his face. 'I don't think so.'

Claire was silent for a while, going through the problem in her mind. A question occurred to her.

'Ted, I think Porthenoy was the one who was threatening Joanne.'

Ted looked at her. 'Yeah. Could be!'

'It all fits. When her daughter disappeared, and he lost his power over her, he had to try and get the information for himself.'

Ted nodded. 'Makes sense. And shows even more what a bastard he is — messing up her house, threatening a child.'

'There's something not quite right about it, though. I can't see Porthenoy going into a house and smashing things up, torturing an animal. He seems far too — well, cultured for that.'

'I don't suppose he would have done it himself. He's got plenty of money. He'd have paid someone to do it for him.'

Claire could only agree. 'You're right. He's even more hateful than I thought. Poor Joanne, what she's been through.'

'So don't you think he deserves to have the squeeze put on him just a little? He's a menace to society. We'd be doing everyone a favour if we exposed him.'

'Yes, I can see that. So why don't we do just that?'

'What d'you mean?'

'Well, expose him. Go to the police. Let them find out why he's stolen our stuff. Tell them about his homosexuality.'

Ted turned and looked at her, his expression serious. 'That wouldn't get us anywhere. First of all, there's nothing illegal about his homosexual activities as far as we know. That bloke he was with certainly wasn't under age. It might damage his reputation, but the police just wouldn't be interested.'

'What about the disks? We have a witness — Joanne saw him.'

'But how far would that get us? There'd be a huge legal wrangle about ownership of the material, whether it's ours, or belongs to the Clifton Research Institute, or even the Department of Health — and he'd hire a fancy lawyer to argue he had a right to see it, anyway. There'd be a lot of hot air and we'd be left with bugger all.'

They sat glumly in the dark for a minute, before Ted went on. 'And don't forget he's a clever bastard. We've no proof about the connection with Joanne. He won't have left piles of pink notepaper everywhere. There'll be no fingerprints on the letters, and he'll have used an HB pencil from Woolworth's. Forget the police.'

Claire put her head on Ted's shoulder. 'Oh, dear. I hate to say it, but I think you're right.'

Ted put his arm around her. 'That's my girl!'

* * *

When Ted rang Porthenoy's secretary the next morning she answered at the first ring. Ted introduced himself and said he wanted to see her boss immediately.

'I'm sorry, Mr Parkes. Mr Porthenoy is in the hospital for only half an hour this morning, and will have no time for appointments.'

'What time is he coming?'

'Well, it makes no difference, Mr — '

'Just tell me what time.'

The secretary tutted. 'It's ten o'clock, but I'm afraid it's no use you —'

Ted put the phone down and grinned at Claire. 'I've just made us an appointment.'

* * *

They waited in the corridor outside the secretary's office. Ted thought there was no point in alerting her to their presence, she might contact Porthenoy and head him off. Claire was nervous, mouth dry, heart racing. She wanted to go to the lavatory, even though she'd been only fifteen minutes before. She never liked confrontations, and this promised to be a major one. She had thought about letting Ted go alone, but had decided she might be needed to curb his exuberance. She didn't want any more trouble than was necessary.

Ted stopped pacing, straightened up. 'Here he comes!'

Porthenoy appeared at the end of the corridor, striding purposefully, alone. He recognised the little deputation as he approached.

'Good morning Miss Donaldson, Mr Parkes.' He gave them a manufactured smile. 'Mrs Chambers told me there was a small problem you wanted to discuss.'

'Too right there is. May we go into your office?'

'I'm awfully sorry, old chap, but I just don't have time this morning.' He put his hand on the office door. 'If you'll just see my secretary, she'll fix you up with —'

'We want to see you *now*, Mr Porthenoy.'

'Please, Mr Parkes. I'm a very busy man. Your problem will have to wait.'

'It won't wait!' Ted's anger was rising to match Porthenoy's. He glanced behind the consultant and saw a group of doctors and nurses approaching. 'And I don't think you'll want what I have to say shouted out to all and sundry in the corridor.'

Porthenoy glared at the Australian, his lips working as he tried to overcome his annoyance and form a coherent response. Ted lost patience. He pushed past him into the outer office and, ignoring Mrs Chambers' protests, went straight into the neurologist's inner sanctum.

Porthenoy followed, spluttering his objections, Claire close behind. His secretary stood in the doorway.

'Shall I call security, Mr Porthenoy?'

The consultant looked from Ted to his indignant secretary and back again. He was showing the first signs of uncertainty. He had no idea what this was about, but was beginning to guess that it had to be serious to provoke Ted Parkes into this sort of behaviour.

'No, no, it's all right, Mrs Chambers. I — I'll just see them for a minute.' He licked his lips. 'You'd better ring the UGM and tell him I'll be a couple of minutes late.'

The woman went out, closing the door with more than necessary force. Porthenoy went behind his desk, face reddening, veins bulging in his neck. He spread his hands on the desk and leaned forward.

'Now you'd better tell me what the hell you mean by this insolent intrusion!'

'And I think you'd better calm down and listen carefully, *sport*.' Ted spat out the last word, full of menace.

The two researchers watched as Porthenoy, the senior consultant unaccustomed to such impudence, struggled to control his inner rage at being confronted in this manner in his own office.

He sat down. 'So.' He made an attempt at composure, but his shaking hands gave him away. 'You'd better sit down and tell me what this unseemly behaviour is all about.'

'I prefer to stand, thanks. It's about the theft of data from my computer in Paul Sansome's room.'

'I don't know what you're talking about.'

The lie was so pathetic that Ted laughed.

'Ha! You arrogant bastard. You were seen loading the disks into my computer.'

'And when was this alleged episode supposed to have happened?' Sweat was visible on his upper lip.

'Last night, at ten minutes to eight precisely.'

'And just who is making this allegation?'

'I don't think that need concern you just now.'

Good for you, Ted, thought Claire, no need to get Joanne into trouble if we can help it.

'That bloody Yeates woman, I suppose.'

Claire's heart sank. What a nasty man this was. All her inhibitions about confronting him were gone. Without thinking, she said, 'Sister Yeates is a damn good nurse and a very nice person. She deserves better than to be threatened by you!'

Porthenoy was taken aback by this new attack. 'Threatened? I've never threatened the woman!'

Ted held up his hand to Claire. 'Let's leave that for a minute.' He turned back to Porthenoy. 'Let's discuss these disks, shall we?'

Porthenoy seemed to accept defeat. 'All right. I was just going to borrow the data. It's all very, very interesting. I wanted to look at it, in peace and quiet, at home. On my own computer.'

'*Borrow* it?' Ted's tone was derisive.

'Well, it doesn't belong to you, anyway. It belongs to the Clifton Neurological Research Institute. They gave me permission.'

'*I've* got the copyright on that material. And anyway, I don't believe you. If they gave you permission, why the secrecy?'

'I didn't want to bother you.'

'Up you for the rent! What d'you think, I'm a shingle short or something?'

Porthenoy tried to look superior. 'I really think I would prefer you to use the Queen's English.'

Ted moved forward a step, fist clenched. Claire reached out towards him. 'Come on, Ted. Take no notice.'

'I'll go the bastard, I swear it!'

'I cannot tolerate threats of physical violence. I've given you my explanation, and that's an end to the matter. Now you'd better leave.' Porthenoy made an attempt to sound authoritative.

'I bet you don't want any physical violence. I bet you get enough with your homo friends at the Horse's Hoof.'

Porthenoy paled. 'What did you say?'

'That one hit the spot, then, eh? You've gone as white as a monk's bum.'

Porthenoy jumped up, trembling with rage. 'That's libel. I shall sue you for every penny you've got!'

'You won't, mate. Because we saw Daddy kissing Santa Claus on the steps of his front porch last night. And anyway, it's slander.'

The consultant slumped into his chair, breathing heavily. He worked his fingers constantly, hands together, now apart. His voice was flat.

'What do you want from me?'

Claire stepped forward. 'We only want to know why you wanted the computer disks, and what you're going to do with them.'

Porthenoy tried a weak attempt at defiance. 'I've told you.'

'Bollocks!' Ted thrust his face over the desk. 'That's ratshit!'

The consultant was defiant. 'It's the truth.'

'And so is the fact that you go on assignations to gay bars and pick up strange men.'

Porthenoy looked up. 'Al- Albert is not a strange man. I do not pick up strange men.'

'But you don't deny that's where your proclivities lie?'

'It's not illegal.' Porthenoy avoided Ted's eye, then seemed to decide to be less defensive, looked at Ted almost with defiance. 'It's my right. It's my choice.'

'Too right! But I wonder how it would go down with the old private practice clientele? Or with your colleagues? Or the hospital administrator?'

Porthenoy sat up. 'Are you threatening to blackmail me?'

'Who said anything about blackmail? Passing true remarks in casual conversation isn't blackmail.'

Porthenoy stood up, paced back and forth once, then delivered a speech which sounded almost rehearsed.

'All right. I'm a homosexual. Always have been. Only married for respectability, my career. Even had a son, more's the pity. Poor devil's just like me. When my wife died, I thought, why be lonely for the rest of your life? So, I —' He paused, looked them both in the eye in turn. 'Well, I can live with the consequences. It's my life.' He paused for breath. 'And as for the disks, you have no case there, I'm sure. I don't think you do own the copyright. It belongs to your paymasters, the Neurological Research Institute. I think you'd better examine the small print on your contract.'

'You're bluffing.'

Porthenoy's composure was returning. 'It'll cost you an awful lot of money in legal fees to find out.'

'Bastard!' Ted muttered, and turned away.

'So I'd like you to leave.'

Claire's heart sank. She felt she knew what was coming. Porthenoy seemed to detect her dismay, and allowed himself a smug smile.

'That's right. I mean leave the room, the hospital, everything. On your way out you can take your personal belongings from Side Room 3, but please be good enough to leave all the equipment.'

Ted exploded. 'You can't bloody well do that!'

'You leave me no option. You propose to denounce me to the world, and I have no doubt you will do so whether you believe you have my full co-operation or not.'

Claire held onto Ted's arm. 'Ted, I did try to warn you.'

He pulled away. 'But he can't just — just —'

'But I can, Mr Parkes.' He smiled ingratiatingly. 'You see, my dear chap, I have long anticipated this scenario. I'm only surprised that it has not come sooner. It's a severe blow to me, I admit, but not, I think, a mortal one. I long ago resolved to ride it out if I was ever, ah, exposed. Under no circumstances will I be under any threat or coercion.'

Claire moved in front of Ted. 'But the project! How can you throw away everything we've done? And Paul! What about Paul? We're just beginning to get through to him. We may be able to help him!'

'I'm sure we shall find some capable people to carry on your work. With the help of the computer data I have, Dr Sansome's own research papers which his wife will give me access to, and everything you have so expertly set up, we shall proceed.'

Ted's voice was low, but charged with fury. 'You may think you can stop us having contact with your patient, you stuck-up bastard, but you can't tell the Research Institute what to do.'

Porthenoy smiled ingratiatingly. 'There, I think, Mr Parkes, you will find you are wrong.'

Claire sent a look of near-panic to Ted. 'What do you mean?'

'I mean that the chairman of the Research Grants Committee is a close friend. A very close friend, if you get my meaning.'

Ted slammed the desk with his hand. 'Are you trying to tell me — ?'

The door from the outer office opened and the secretary entered. 'Do you need any help, Mr Porthenoy?'

'No, it's all right, thank you, Mrs Chambers.'

'I'm sorry, it's just that all this shouting, and banging, and . . .' she trailed off.

'Everything is under control, *thank* you.'

Ted didn't wait for her to leave. 'Are you trying to tell me that the chairman and you are — are —'

'I have said nothing. You are the one trying to draw an inference.

But the fact remains, you will get no more funding from the Clifton Research Institute. Of that you can be certain.'

'You bastard!' Ted growled the words venomously.

Porthenoy had the upper hand now and was enjoying it.

'Mr Parkes, your vocabulary would seem to be as extensive as your antipodean charm.'

Claire was certain at that moment that Ted was going to hit Porthenoy. He advanced on the desk. The consultant tried to face him out, but flinched as Ted drew back his arm swiftly, fist clenched. He stood threateningly for a moment, then dropped his arm and, turning, stormed from the office. Claire contemplated pleading further with Porthenoy, thought better of it, and raced after Ted. As she went through the outer office she got a curious glance from Mrs Chambers, but not as curious as the one she saw the secretary give in the direction of her boss. Claire felt a brief glimmer of grim satisfaction, but it was soon swamped by tears of frustration as she ran down the corridor.

CHAPTER 28

Ted sat down in front of the computer in Side Room 3, switched it on, and slammed a disk in.

'For God's sake be careful, Ted, you'll damage something!'

'So bloody what? Won't make much difference now.'

'What are you trying to do? Mr Porthenoy said we had to collect our things and go.'

'I don't give a pinch of goat shit for what that bastard said.'

'But, Ted —'

'Look, Claire, we've got work to do here, and fast. This may be our last chance.' He put in another disk.

'Work? What do you mean?'

'This poor bugger —' he indicated Paul Sansome's still form '— knows a lot more than we've been able to get out of him yet. About his attacker, and God knows what else.'

'Well — well, yes, I know, but what if Porthenoy comes and finds we're here?'

'What do you think he can do? He can get us thrown out, sure, but nothing else. So what have we got to lose?'

Claire shrugged. 'Put that way — not a lot, I suppose. Except maybe our jobs.'

'If he's a bedfellow of the Research Committee chairman, we've probably lost them anyway.'

Claire sat gloomily. 'I think you're right.'

'Sure I'm right. It sticks out like a dog's balls.'

Despite herself, Claire could not suppress a smile. 'Porthenoy was right about something.'

'What's that?'

'Your vocabulary and your charm.'

Ted growled at her, then set to work.

* * *

In fifteen minutes they were ready to start. There had been no word from Porthenoy, and they had checked with Joanne, who was on duty. They told her only that they had fallen out with the consultant, and wanted to try and get some work done quickly for fear he would stop them. They did not elaborate, more to save time than anything.

All the while they were preparing, Claire expected the door to fly open and Porthenoy to charge in. But nothing happened, and she gradually became more absorbed in what they were doing.

'Microphone ready?' Ted asked.

'Ready,' said Claire. 'Headphones in place, standing by.'

'OK — after you've made contact, we'll have to work as fast as possible. We'll have to go for "Yes-No" again because there may not be time to keep going through the alphabet to spell something.'

'What do you want me to ask?'

'You'll have to take whatever direction you think is best. But let's start with questions about his attacker — like does he know him well, do *we* know him, is he still around? I don't know, play it by ear.' He looked at his watch, then at the door. 'Come on, let's go.'

Claire pushed the hair back from her face. 'It's all such a rush.'

'I know, I know. I'd rather have planned this more carefully, too, but we've no choice now. He might be here any minute.'

Claire switched the microphone on and leaned forward.

'Paul, this is Claire. Can you hear me?'

'Shit! Lousy signal.'

'Last time it was the posterior electrode that needed advancing about a millimetre.'

'Good girl! I remember.' He left his position in front of the monitor and went behind the bed. He made a fine adjustment to one of the probes, then settled again at his keyboard. 'Try again.'

'Paul, this is Claire. Can you hear me?'

'Well done. He says "Yes".'

'We want to talk to you again. We want you to answer "Yes" or "No".'

'Christ! He says "No".'

'Paul, do you understand?'

'Yes.'

'I want you to answer "Yes" or "No".'

'He still says "No" to that one.'

Claire looked anxiously across at the unconscious figure, then addressed the microphone again. 'Paul, don't you want to talk to us?'

'He says "Yes". Thank Christ.'

'But you don't want to say "Yes" or "No".'

'No.' He says "No" again! What's he playing at?'

Claire looked across at Ted. 'I wonder if it's because he wants to try and spell something — like we did yesterday?'

'Maybe. I dunno. Jeez, all this is wasting so much time. I wish — just a minute! There's a load of "Yes's".'

'So he *does* want to spell something.'

'Looks like it. "Yes" again.'

'Paul, do you want us to go through the alphabet like we did before? And you'll stop us with "Yes" when we reach the right letter?'

'Yes.' Ted sighed. 'We'll have to go for it, sod it! It'll take so bloody long.'

This time Claire looked anxiously from her watch to the door.

'Paul, is the first letter A?'

'No.'

'B?'

'No.'

'C?'

'No.'

'D?'

'Yes. That's a "Yes".'

'Second letter, Paul. Is it A?'

'Bingo! He says "Yes".'

'Third letter. Is it A?'

'No.'

'B?'

'No.'

As she went on through the alphabet Claire knew what the word was even before it was finished. She switched off the microphone and shivered. 'Did you follow that?' she asked Ted.

'I reckon I did.'

Claire looked down at the paper in front of her on which she had written the word.

DANGER

Ted was thoughtful. 'That's all very well, but danger from where? And who is in danger — us? Or him?' He pointed at Paul.

'Or maybe it's Joanne. Suppose the person behind all this has been in here. Would Paul know? Could he overhear conversation?'

'I think he could. But if it's one person, who isn't in the habit of talking to himself, I don't think Paul would know anything about it.'

'We've just got to try some more while we have the chance.' She went back to the microphone.

'All right, I'm ready.'

'Paul. *Please* answer yes or no. Is it me who's in danger?'

'Yes.'

Claire looked at Ted, eyes wide.

'It might not only be you. Ask him.'

'Paul. Is Ted in danger?'

'Yes.'

She licked her lips. 'Are you in danger?'

'Yes.'

'Joanne Yeates, the sister on the ward. Is she in danger?'

'Yes.'

Ted was shaking his head. 'I just don't know what to make of this.'

Claire spoke again. 'Paul, we want you to tell us more.'

'Yes.' Ted looked round. 'And then some more stuff I can't interpret.'

'He seems to do that when he wants to spell something.' She leaned forward again. 'Paul, do you want to spell something?'

'He says "Yes". Damn this slowness. We could be thrown out of here any minute.'

'Can't be helped.' She addressed the microphone. 'Paul, tell us more. I'm going through the alphabet again.' She paused. 'A'.

'No.'

'B.'

'No.'

They got as far as T before they got a positive response. Nine frustrating minutes later they had four words:

THEY KNOW SAVE ME

Claire frowned. 'Does that mean everybody knows something except him?'

Ted came over and looked at it, took the pencil, and put in a full stop between *know* and *save*. 'I think it means that. "They know. Save me".'

'This is driving me crazy. We're in danger. Paul wants us to save him.' Claire tapped her fingers on the table. 'And who are "They"?' She sent Ted back to his computer before putting the next question. 'Is Mr Porthenoy the man who is the danger?'

' "No." Bugger me, he says "No".'

'Paul, is it to do with the word you gave me yesterday?'

'I think that was a "Yes", but then a lot of other stuff.'

'Paul, is it to do with the word you spelled to me yesterday? A-L-G-H-R-A-I-D?'

'Yes.'

Ted and Claire exchanged perplexed glances, and then in frustration Claire asked a question she was to regret.

'Oh, Paul, what can we do?'

'Christ, you've done it now, Claire. The signal's gone haywire!'

'Oh, my God!' Claire looked at Paul. His breathing was becoming shallow, more rapid, his colour changing. 'Something's happening! I think he's going to have another fit! Go and get Joanne! Quick!'

Ted stood stock still for a moment, eyes wide, fascinated by the sudden animation of their patient.

'Ted!'

He dashed out of the door.

Claire went to the bedside and tried to soothe Paul with touch and gentle words, but his breathing became more irregular and the muscles in his face began to twitch. She looked across at the monitor which Ted had been sitting at moments before. A storm of electrical signals flashed again and again across the screen, ever more irregular, the amplitude higher and higher. Paul's back started to arch.

Joanne Yeates ran into the room, Ted close behind. She looked at the distorted face, the arched back, the skin now a dusky hue.

'He's going into status epilepticus again. Mind out the way.'

Claire stood back. Joanne looked at the two drip feed bottles. She turned to Claire. 'Have either of you touched these?'

They both shook their heads in denial. 'This one's got the anti-epileptic drug in it. It's almost stopped!' She opened the tap fully for a few seconds, allowing the liquid to run rapidly into the vein. Paul's legs were beginning to move in sudden jerks. Ted thought he might have to hold them down, and moved to the foot of the bed. As he did so, the doctor's body began to relax. Slowly, the arch of the back settled, the facial muscles slackened, and the colour returned. His breathing became slow and deep. The sister reduced the flow of intravenous fluid to a steady drip, about two a second.

'Has he come out of it?' Claire looked anxiously at Paul's face.

'I think so. Looks like we just got him in time. I can't understand why that drip was running so slow. I'm sure I checked it earlier this morning.'

'Is that what sparked off the fit?' Ted asked.

'Difficult to be sure.' Joanne busied herself at the bed as she talked, wiping the sweat tenderly from the doctor's brow, straightening the sheets. 'It would make him more susceptible to a fit, but I don't think it was off long enough to actually trigger one.'

'Claire had just asked him a pretty powerful question, and he seemed to get very agitated straight after. Could that have done it?'

Claire was upset. 'Oh, Ted, you're not trying to blame me for what happened?'

'No, of course not, you did nothing knowingly. But you did ask him a direct question that he couldn't answer. It must have been one hell of a frustration to him.'

'You mean just by saying, "Paul, what can we do?" '

'Exactly. If he knew what we *should* do, but couldn't tell us . . .'

Claire turned to Joanne. 'Could something like that have done it?'

'I can't honestly tell you. It's not a situation I've ever come across before. But emotional stress *could* precipitate a seizure, I'm sure.'

'Oh, dear.' Claire went to the microphone and switched it on. 'Paul, if you can hear me, I'm sorry.'

Ted went to the screen. 'He can hear you all right. That's a "Yes".'

Claire smiled. 'That's a quick recovery!'

'Who knows how the brain reacts when it's in that state?' said Joanne. 'Mind you, poor man, he should have a stinking headache.'

Claire leaned towards the mike. 'Paul, have you got a headache?'

'Yes,' from Ted.

The sister nodded. 'Ask him if he feels sleepy.'

Ted snorted. 'Don't be daft. He's asleep all the bloody time.'

'To us he is always *unconscious*, yes, but we know coma patients do exhibit a sort of sleep-wakefulness cycle, clinically and on EEG — you ought to know that.'

Claire looked excited. 'She's right, Ted. That's a very good point.' She spoke to the microphone again. 'Paul, do you feel sleepy?'

'Yes.'

'Do you have times when you are unable to hear? When you are asleep?'

'Yes.' Ted looked up. 'This is fantastic!'

'It's also taking up time,' Claire warned. 'I want to ask him something else. I want to know what sort of danger we're all in.'

'Danger? We're *all* in?' Joanne looked acutely anxious. 'What danger?'

'Paul started this morning by telling us we were in danger. Me, Ted — and you. And himself. But we don't know what sort of danger, or who from.'

Joanne put her hands to her cheeks. 'My God! Can't we find out?'

'That's what we're trying to do.' Claire swallowed. 'Paul. I'm going to go through the alphabet again. How much danger are we in?'

They all watched, spell-bound, horrified, as the letters emerged. Claire was writing the last one down when they heard a shout from the corridor.

'That's Porthenoy!' Joanne headed for the door.

'Oh, Christ! Try and stall him a minute, will you?'

'Do my best!' she called as the door closed behind her.

Claire stuffed the piece of paper in her pocket. 'What'll we do?'

'Stop him coming in until I've finished.' He was working at the keyboard, waiting impatiently for each process to finish. He took a floppy disk from the drive, put three more in his pocket, then tapped the keys again. There was more shouting, louder now, from the corridor.

'You've got to stop him, Claire. I've not finished!'

Claire had no idea what to do. She ran over to the door and put her foot and shoulder against it, just as an enraged Porthenoy arrived at the other side. He banged on the glass. Claire was afraid it would break.

'Another ten seconds!' Ted called.

Porthenoy pushed hard. Claire's shoes could not grip on the polished floor; slowly the door opened. Claire gave up, and Porthenoy stormed in.

'I thought I told you to get out of this hospital!' he roared.

Ted gave him an amazingly relaxed smile. 'Just going, matey, just going.' He hoisted his hold-all, and beckoned to Claire, who was cowering behind the door. 'Come on, my girl. We'll take our leave.' He pushed past Porthenoy, who made no attempt to stop him. Claire followed, almost running. Joanne was in the corridor, and motioned them to go on without saying anything to her.

Neither of them spoke until they were in the car park.

'Bloody hell! What a morning.' Claire felt weak.

'You can say that again. What were you doing there when Porthenoy was coming?'

They reached the car. Ted opened the door, but did not get in. 'Well, first thing, in anticipation of a hasty departure, I copied all the important stuff on the hard disk onto these floppies.'

'So what did you do at the end?'

He grinned. 'I wiped the whole bloody hard disk as clean as a whistle!'

'So Porthenoy hasn't got anything?'

'Absolutely sweet FA.'

'The disks he's got are corrupted, and the main computer's blank?'

'One hundred per cent.'

Claire grinned back. 'He won't be pleased.'

'Madder than a hornet that's stung itself in the arse.'

They got in the car, and Ted started the engine. Claire put on her seat belt, let her head drop back against the head-rest, and closed her eyes. She smoothed her dress, and felt the screwed-up paper in her pocket. Her eyes came open and she sat upright. The excitement of their hasty departure and the triumph over Porthenoy drained away in seconds. She withdrew the crumpled sheet, smoothed it out on her thigh. Ted had let off the handbrake and was about to ease the car forward when he noticed what Claire was doing. He re-applied the brake and put the gear in neutral.

They both looked down at the paper in silence, this time taking in the full implications. In answer to Claire's question about how much danger they were in, Paul had answered with one word:

DEATH

CHAPTER 29

The day that dawned seventy-two hours after Claire and Ted were excluded from the hospital was a day of disasters.

Claire got her letter only minutes before Ted. She opened the envelope whilst walking about the kitchen eating her breakfast — a piece of toast. She stopped chewing as she saw the letter-heading:

Clifton Neurological Research Institute

She wiped her sticky fingers absently, held the paper in both hands, and sat down to read.

Dear Miss Donaldson,

I am writing to you on behalf of the Research Grants Committee to thank you for all the excellent work you have done for the Institute over the past three years. Your work with Dr Paul Sansome, our unfortunate Senior Researcher, has been of particular importance.

However, it is Dr Sansome's continuing incapacity that has led to the writing of this letter. Having taken advice from the appropriate medical authorities, it seems most improbable that Dr Sansome will ever recover. We have had consultations recently with Regional and Government Finance departments, and regretfully we now consider it impossible to justify further funding for Dr Sansome's 'Deep Probe Electro-encephalography in Severe Unconscious States' project.

Sadly, therefore, we must disband his loyal research team, effective immediately. As the laboratory facility at the Institute has already been closed, there is no point in you working out your notice. The termination of your contract is thereby effective immediately, and you will be paid one month's salary in lieu of notice.

I must ask you not to have any further contact with the Hospital or Dr Sansome. Please will you return any research papers, equipment, or computer programs relevant to this project to the Institute, whose property they remain according to the terms of your contract.

If the Institute publishes any papers connected with your work in any scientific journals, you will of course be given appropriate acknowledgement.

The Committee and myself would like to thank you for your good work on our behalf, and wish you well in your next appointment. We will be pleased to provide any prospective employer with an excellent reference.

Yours sincerely,
Miles Longden, MBE
Chairman, Research Grants Committee

Tears came to Claire's eyes, whether from anger or despair she could not have said. A jumble of thoughts went through her mind. She had just lost the best, the most rewarding job she had ever had. She had no idea what she would do now. She wouldn't be able to live for long on a month's income. How could she forget everything she and Ted had done these last few weeks? Could they possibly continue? Not if they had to hand back every scrap of knowledge they had gleaned. Was it a try-on that all their data belonged to the Institute?

Anger became the dominant emotion then, as she cursed Porthenoy with every unladylike expletive she could think of. That disgusting bastard was behind this, she was certain. All that sanctimonious crap about her good work, how sad Longden was to break up the team, and all that bullshit about money. She knew that, following the last review, their project was funded until the end of the year.

She thought of Paul, lying there in his other world. What would happen to him? Whatever sanity he had would probably leave him, she felt certain. After months of silence, he had been able to communicate with the world he knew. If his self, his soul, his inner being, whatever it was in there that they had been talking to, was suddenly shut off again in a world of silence and darkness, surely his spirit would break. She could only imagine that madness would ensue. Perhaps that happened to all those who were in prolonged coma. Those who were spoken to, touched, cared for lovingly, had a thread to hang on to. Their research had shown that unconscious people could 'hear'. But if no one tried, or if their carers gave up, lost heart, so that the nursing became routine, carried out in silence, then perhaps some form of inner madness overwhelmed the victim, and all hope of establishing contact, and hence regaining consciousness, was lost. As she thought of the tortured despair Paul would suffer if he were abandoned now, she broke down and wept, slumped forward over the table.

Her sobs were beginning to subside when the phone rang. She blew her nose hurriedly on a piece of kitchen paper and answered it. She knew it would be Ted.

'So,' Ted observed as soon as she spoke, 'you've had a letter from our dear Chairman as well.'

Claire almost managed a laugh. 'Is it that obvious I've been crying?'

''Fraid so. But why the tears? I'd have thought a bit of waspish rage would have been more in your line. I can tell you, I'm absolutely doing my block over that pillow-biter Porthenoy. He's behind all this!'

'I'm angry, too, but I was thinking about poor Paul. His mind will go insane, Ted, I know it! After just making contact with us, to be shut off altogether. Imagine what it'll do to him!'

Ted heard the catch in her voice. 'Easy up, girl. I know what you mean, I'd thought much the same thing. So let's channel all the energies these emotions are making into doing something about it.'

'Come on, Ted! What the hell *can* we do about it?'

'I don't know. But come over here, and we'll start talking.'

Grateful to be given a lead in some direction, Claire readily agreed. 'I'll have a shower and come straight round.'

After putting the phone down, she went into the lounge, pulled back the curtains, moved on into her bedroom and dropped her towelling robe onto the bed, then walked naked into the bathroom and pulled down the blind.

As if reacting to a signal, a man across the street started towards her front door.

* * *

Joanne Yeates got her letter a few minutes later.

The night before she had been able to suppress no longer the desire to see her daughter. She had gone by taxi to the station, watching carefully from the back window all the way to see if there was anyone behind. Even the taxi-driver had noticed, and had asked if she was worried about being followed.

She went by train to Cheltenham, and at the other end walked around for a while; then, when she was sure she was alone, she phoned her sister from a call-box to come and pick her up. Lucinda was overjoyed at the surprise visit, and even her mother seemed happier.

Now, back in Bristol, as she walked up the road to the house, Joanne thought of last night, when she had tucked Lucinda in. Her sister's home was a good size, comfortably furnished, and Lucinda had a room to herself. Her cousins were making a noise in the bathroom, and Joanne heard her sister's voice shouting up the stairs to quieten them.

'How are you getting on with Piers and Stephanie?' she asked Lucinda.

'Stephanie's six,' her daughter replied, a tinge of awe in her voice.

'And do you like playing with her?'

'Yes. She lets me play with her dolls. She goes to school.' It was obvious Lucinda was proud to know someone who was old enough for full-time education. 'She lets me play with her dolls when she's at school.'

'And what about Piers?'

Lucinda wrinkled her nose and pulled a face. 'He's a boy.'

Joanne laughed gently. 'But doesn't he play with you?'

'Not much. He won't let me have his soldier things, 'cos of the batt-trees.' She thought for a moment. 'He plays with Granny, though.'

'Auntie Karen's nice, isn't she?'

Her daughter's face glowed with pleasure. 'Ooh, yes. She lets me do lots of things, an' takes me out, an' we play on the swings, an' — an' — lots of things.'

Joanne felt a pang of guilt. She never seemed to have enough time for things like that, working as she did. And she knew her sister took genuine pleasure in Lucinda's presence. Karen missed having her own daughter around during the day. She'd half-jokingly told Joanne that it was worth putting up with their mother to have Lucinda around for a while.

'Mummy, you're looking sad.' Lucinda had caught the wistful expression on her mother's face, and her tone was accusing.

'Oh, sorry, dear. I'm not sad, really.'

'I'm not sad either. I'm happy cos you've come.'

Joanne hugged her daughter tenderly, gratefully, and kissed her good-night.

* * *

It was with such warm thoughts in her mind that Joanne let herself into her mother's house, having arrived back on the early train from Cheltenham. She had to be at work by twelve. She picked up the newspaper from the floor, and a collection of junk mail. She put them on the work-surface in the kitchen and went through them. Two slim catalogues in plastic covers offering the chance to win large sums of money and a new car in response to her order, a computer-printed envelope covered in writing that told her she was one of the few lucky people in Avon to be in the final stage of a prize draw, and — her stomach turned over and her mouth went dry — a pink envelope.

She sat and looked at it for some time, debating whether to open it, or just burn it, unread. She had promised herself that once her daughter was safe, she would ignore any further attempts at communication from this deranged person. But she could not bring herself to ignore the contents. Eventually she picked up a knife, and with a trembling hand slit open the envelope.

There were only three words, written large in pencil.

FAREWELL, MY LOVELY

Joanne felt sick. What in God's name did it mean? Could she dare hope it meant that they were giving up, that she would hear no more? Now that the research with poor Dr Sansome had come to an abrupt end, perhaps her tormentor knew there would be nothing to offer. She could hardly force herself to entertain the thought that it might refer to her daughter. It would be impossible, with her safe and sound, constantly attended by her sister forty miles away. *No, it couldn't be that. Not Lucinda. Not now.*

Joanne felt overcome with a desperate weariness. She hid the letter with the others in the bottom drawer of the chest in her bedroom, and slowly got herself ready for work. She groaned inwardly as she remembered her old Escort was at the garage, having its MOT. She would have to get a move on now, it took much longer to get to the hospital by bus.

* * *

Claire came out of the shower and dried hurriedly, powdered herself and, leaving a trail of white footprints, went into the bedroom. She put on her pants, fastened her bra, and sat on the edge of the bed to put on her tights. She'd got one leg in, and had just started on the other, when she heard her front door bang open. 'Is that you, Ted?' she called, unconcerned. He must have decided to come here, she thought, then remembered she was certain she'd locked the door after she'd gone down to the front hall for her mail.

She became alarmed when she heard footsteps in the kitchen.

'Who's that?'

She hastened to get the other leg in her tights, but her foot caught halfway down. She stood up to hobble to the bedroom door to look, when a figure appeared. The man's appearance nearly made her heart stop. He was dressed ordinarily enough in denim wind-cheater and jeans; it was his face that shocked her so much she couldn't move. All she could see were his eyes — small and round, looking out through rough slits cut in a woollen mask. No mouth, no nose, just featureless grey.

She tried to back away, unable to cry out, to speak. Hindered by her tights, she fell back against the bed. The man crossed the room and was on top of her in a moment. Claire found her voice, screamed, and in her terror produced enough force to roll her assailant off.

She yelled at him as loud as her lungs would allow. 'Get away from me, you bastard!'

There was a muffled chuckle. 'Fuck you, ducky!' His arm swung out in front of him, and she nearly froze as she recognised a Stanley knife in his hand. He slashed at the air threateningly, braced with legs apart. The muffled voice came again. 'I've got a little remodelling job to do on you, honey.'

Claire knew she couldn't run whilst her foot was stuck in her tights. She managed to stand on the loose leg, holding it down while she pulled her foot out. Although one leg of her tights hung loosely, at least her feet were free. Seeing the man straddled before her, she sized up his vulnerability in an instant, and aimed a kick at his crotch.

Her blow was right on target, but the material of his trousers, held taut by his stance, prevented a really devastating blow.

'You little bitch!' the man said hoarsely as he staggered back, swearing, doubled up. Claire tried to run past him, but he was too quick for her. He straightened up, and pushed her square in the chest with the flat of his hand, sending her back towards the bed. As she recoiled from the push, his fingers closed around the front of her bra in the 'V' between the cups. The material tore and fell away. The man hesitated a moment, and Claire knew he was gaping at her exposed breasts from behind his mask.

'Right!' The growling voice from behind the mask sounded full of menace. 'Now I'm gonna have a little fun!'

Claire crossed her arms over her chest to cover her breasts, and at the same time edged backwards around the side of the bed. The man jumped nearer, and raised his knife. She saw it flashing down towards the left side of her face. She raised her arm to deflect the blow, and felt an ice-like sensation on her forearm as if she had been slashed by a frozen whip. Almost instantly it was followed by a warm feeling, and as her assailant danced away she turned her arm to see a gaping wound from which her blood was pouring freely. She was paralysed at the sight. Her sadistic attacker laughed, then calmly moved in again. Before she could react he drew the blade down from high above her head, and kept it moving down in a swift arc. She tried to jerk away, but too late. She felt the knife strike her cheek-bone as it opened up the left side of her face, on down, not touching her neck, but then encountering the white skin of her left breast. The flesh opened, exposing yellow fat which quickly suffused with red. She heard more laughter, but as her brain registered the devastation inflicted on her body, she crumpled to the floor beside the bed, barely conscious.

Her befuddled mind was still trying to force her to think about survival. Hardly aware of what she was doing, she tried to work herself backwards over the carpet, aiming for the safety of the bathroom. There was a dark shadow, and then she felt a weight on top of her, a smell of stale sweat and cigarettes. She tried to struggle as she felt a hand roughly groping towards her groin, fumbling at her pants. She gave vent to one last desperate scream, and thought at first she had imagined an answering shout from the kitchen.

Her would-be rapist hesitated a moment, then the shout came again, nearer. There were grunts and curses, and the weight was lifted from her. *Ted! It had to be Ted!*

The man was standing over her now, and the greyness of her vision began to clear. She started to scramble to her feet, and her eyes focused on two men! Her heart nearly stopped; they were dressed alike, both with the grey, featureless masks. *Two of them*! Her mind could barely register. She tried to think, but all her body would do was crawl back into the corner, hunching like a foetus for protection, only aware of the two pairs of eyes boring into her. Her overstimulated brain was desperately trying to reason. Should she give in, choose compliant rape rather than death? Or would they kill her anyway? Would it be better to fight and die in the attempt? Her ragged breathing was making whimpering sounds, obscuring the muttering she heard from across the room. What were they planning now? She tried to hold her breath.

'Stupid bastard! They said we was only meant to scare her! Christ, look at all that fucking blood! Is she gonna die?'

'Fucking bitch kicked me in the bollocks!'

'Come on, we've done here.'

'Sodding killjoy, you are!'

'Come on!'

Slowly the men backed out of her bedroom, and moments later she heard the front door slam. Claire could not believe it. She was alone.

She lay there for several minutes, too terrified to move. She was afraid they were playing with her. She felt warm stickiness – it seemed to be everywhere – and knew she was still bleeding. Her brain was clearing now. She had escaped rape and brutality, but she was badly injured. Had she survived these horrors only to bleed to death here in the corner of her bedroom? She forced herself to sit up, then pulled herself up onto the edge of the bed. The sight of the blood, on the floor, her body, on everything she touched, caused her almost to pass out again. She crawled over the bed, reached for the phone, took off the handset and placed it with the mouthpiece near her, as she clumsily dialled. Her head swimming, she managed to speak a few words, then she lost consciousness, sprawled across the bed.

Ted found her there ten minutes later.

* * *

Joanne came down from the top deck of the double-decker bus and stood on the swaying platform. Fifty yards round the corner was the stop nearest to the hospital. She tried to clear her mind of the pink envelope and its message; she needed to concentrate on another day at work. The bus lurched, and she grabbed for a hand-hold. Once steady, she had to let go again to move forward and make room for another passenger who had come down the stairs behind her onto the now crowded platform. She was briefly aware of a smell, not unpleasant in itself, but somehow associated with an unpleasant memory.

Only another twenty yards. She forgot about the smell as she concentrated on keeping her balance. She staggered slightly as the bus started to slow. She moved nearer the edge, and as she did so she felt something touch her leg. She looked down and saw the crook of an old-fashioned umbrella handle. It seemed to be around her ankle. She was starting to turn to see who owned the umbrella, when she was pushed in the back and at the same time the umbrella was jerked backwards, preventing her stepping forward to break her fall. She toppled forward, the road came up to meet her, and the back of her head struck the ground. She felt pain, but did not lose consciousness. She was aware of tumbling over, and caught a glimpse of the green and chrome of the huge truck before it went over her head.

CHAPTER 30

Detective Inspector Howard drummed his fingers impatiently on the desk as he waited for his junior officer to come in. He stood up, intending to go and see what was causing the delay, when there was a knock at the door.

'Come!'

Sergeant Clothier entered, breathing rather heavily.

The inspector's greeting was terse. 'What kept you?'

'Sorry, sir. I was in the canteen.'

'Christ, filling your face again?'

Clothier clenched his jaw. What the hell's the matter with the man lately? he wondered, not for the first time in recent weeks. 'Sorry, sir. Didn't have a chance for lunch earlier.'

The inspector went straight to the point. 'This business with the nursing sister — Joanne Yeates — and the threats to her child.' He picked up a file from his desk and waved it at Clothier. 'She's cropped up again. RTA.'

Clothier stepped forward, genuine concern on his face. 'She's had an accident?'

Howard nodded. 'Fell from a bus into the path of a lorry.'

'Christ! Badly hurt?'

'Miraculously, no. She went between the wheels. Shock, cuts and bruises.'

'So what's the angle? Where do I come in?'

'She was interviewed at Casualty by one of the traffic boys. She swears she was pushed.'

'Pushed?'

'Yes, sergeant, you've got it.' Howard made no attempt to conceal his sarcasm. He picked up the top sheet from the file. 'I quote: "Someone hooked an umbrella handle round my leg and pushed me in the back. I fell right into the path of the lorry." And no, she has no idea who it was. In fact, at first she said she'd just tripped and lost her balance. But a good samaritan passenger who came in with her in the ambulance piped up and said he thought she looked as if someone had given her a shove. Apparently she broke down then, and came up with the umbrella story.'

Sergeant Clothier nodded his head. 'I'll go and talk to her. Is she still at the hospital?'

'No. Went home soon after the cuts were dressed.' The inspector put the sheet of paper down and picked up another. 'I thought I'd asked you to keep an eye on the Yeates investigation.'

'That's right, sir.'

'So how did you miss this?' He shook the paper in the sergeant's direction. 'In the canteen again?'

'Miss what, sir?' Clothier began to sweat slightly.

'This report from an area beat officer. Call-out to Mrs Yeates' mother's house nearly two weeks ago. Apparently the mother thought her grand-daughter had been abducted. Turned out it was a false alarm. The child was simply back late from her playgroup.'

'She must have been worried, sir. She didn't strike me as one to panic.'

'Maybe so. But I think you ought to look at this carefully. The report says that a Miss Donaldson and a Mr Parkes were at the house.'

Clothier frowned for a moment. 'The researchers from the hospital. The death of that nurse — the one that was electrocuted.'

The inspector looked at a paper on the desk. 'Cherry Marvaine.' He sighed. 'Do I have to do *all* your work for you, Clothier?'

The sergeant was feeling distinctly uncomfortable. 'Sorry, sir?'

'Shall I spell it out for you? There's obviously a connection here. Go and find out what it's all about, dammit!' He picked up the folder and threw it down on the edge of the desk near his junior. 'Now!'

Clothier grabbed the folder and made for the door. 'I'll look into it right away, sir.'

'Yes, you do that. Interview all three of them. And any witnesses to the bus incident.' He drew in a breath. 'And, Clothier.'

'Yes, sir?'

'Spend a little less time in the canteen and more doing something to get your weight down, will you?'

Sergeant Clothier went out, closing the door a little more forcefully than necessary.

* * *

Joanne Yeates took so long to answer the door, the policeman was beginning to think she was not in. He introduced himself, showed his warrant card. She looked awful, standing there in a housecoat, pale, nasty oozing red graze on her left cheek, swollen lip, a bandage on her left wrist.

'Yes, Sergeant, I remember you. But I've already spoken to the officers who came to Casualty.'

'I'm sorry. My inspector asked me if I could follow up one or two things. If you feel up to it, that is. I could always come back later.'

Joanne sighed wearily. 'It's all right. Let's get it over.'

Clothier went over the events of the last few days. Joanne told him about taking her daughter to Cheltenham, and visiting her the previous day. She didn't tell him about the pink envelope — she couldn't really explain why, even to herself. She thought, mainly, that she would show herself to be deceitful, not trusting the police, if she owned up to the threatening letters now, or told about her escapade to try and identify her tormentor.

Joanne repeated what she had told the police officers about her fall. She was frightened now, and increasingly certain her fall was no accident.

'Did you get a look at the person responsible?'

'Not really. I was just looking round to see who was holding the umbrella when I was pushed. Then I was falling. I caught a glimpse — but there were a lot of people. There's no way I could be sure.'

'Have a go at a description for me, eh?' Clothier coaxed.

Joanne frowned in concentration. 'Really, I — no, it's no good, I'd just be guessing.'

Clothier gave up on that and went on to ask about the 'abduction' of her daughter, and casually asked how it was that Ted Parkes and Claire Donaldson were there. Joanne told mostly the truth. They had become friendly, working with Dr Sansome, and she had confided in them when she thought her daughter was missing. They had simply come back with her to try and help.

Clothier concluded his questioning, and then thought he should follow up on the man who had accompanied Joanne to the hospital. He asked her if he could use the phone. He rang his station to get the name and address, so that he could go there next — after he'd had a bite to eat, he promised himself. He waited while someone went to look it up. The desk sergeant came on the line.

'Jonathan?'

'Yes, what is it, Mike?'

'I think you'd better come back in. Another passenger on the Yeates incident bus has just come in. I think you ought to talk to him.'

'I'm on my way.' He abandoned thoughts of food, thanked Joanne profusely for her co-operation, hoped she would soon be feeling better, and set off back to the station.

* * *

The man apologised for not coming to the police immediately. Something about an important meeting. As a witness he was observant, quick-witted, resourceful. You don't often get one of these, Clothier thought, as he took rapid notes.

'So you're certain that the lady was pushed off the bus?'

'I couldn't believe what I had just observed.' The man was well-spoken, dressed in suit and waistcoat. Something to do with insurance, Clothier remembered, but obviously not the house-to-house type.

'You say you were standing on the stairs?'

'Yes, I couldn't come all the way down, the platform was too crowded. I just happened to be looking in the right direction.' He smiled wryly. 'An attractive dark-haired woman, it was. She placed her hand full in the poor lady's back, and gave a shove. All hell let loose then. Someone screamed, the lorry's brakes were squealing, passengers were shouting. The driver didn't stop right away, naturally, didn't know what was going on. But when someone attracted his attention, the bus stopped, the woman jumped off, and —' he laughed diffidently '— I followed. Don't know why, really. There was already a group of people around the lorry, not much I could do there. Thought she must be dead.' He laughed again. 'Reckoned I'd just witnessed a murder, y'know!'

'You've done very well indeed, so far, sir. I take it you tried to follow the lady?'

'Yes, I did. Probably a silly thing to do, but . . .'

'You got a good look at her, did you, sir?'

'Well, yes, I did, actually. It was when she got into a taxi. I shouted out. You know, Hey! Stop! — that sort of thing. Felt a bit of a fool, actually. She was only, what, 20 feet away. She slammed the door and the driver took off.'

'You'd be able to identify her again, would you? In a line-up?'

'An identification parade? Oh, undoubtedly.'

'What sort of car was it, sir? A regular taxi? Minicab?'

'Oh, it was a regular taxi. But I've no idea what sort of car. Not very good on cars.'

'Oh.' Clothier accepted the disappointment. It had been going too well. 'Nothing else to help us, then, sir?'

'Oh, yes. I took the registration number down, naturally.'

Naturally, the sergeant thought. 'Wrote it down, sir?'

His star witness handed him a piece of paper.

Clothier copied down the number. 'And how about a detailed description of the lady herself?' His stomach rumbled, but he continued writing.

While the desk staff were locating the taxi firm from the registration number, he managed a quick trip to the canteen. When he came back, the address and phone number of the taxi driver were waiting.

* * *

'And this is the address you took the lady in question to?'

''S'right, mate. Classy bit of stuff. What's she done, then?'

'Just a routine inquiry at the moment, sir.'

'Garn. Pull t'other one. Drop 'er knicks job, is it? High class tart, is she?'

Clothier ignored the question. 'You've been very helpful, Mr — er —'

'Jenkins. No problem. Wish you could tell me wot it's all about, though.'

'All in good time, Mr Jenkins. Thanks again.' Clothier left, smiling. Have to tell the boys about that one. The latest definition of a prostitute: a 'drop 'er knicks job'.

* * *

The detective sergeant went over to the patrol car. There were no CID cars immediately available. The driver turned to him as he climbed in.

'Where we going, then, chum?'

'Hopefully, to nick a woman for attempted murder.'

'Oh-ho! Big stuff, eh?'

Clothier settled back, fastened the seat belt. 'Could be.'

'Got 'er cold, 'ave you?'

'Have to see. We're going to bring her in, ask a few questions. See what we get.' And then get the insurance broker to identify her, he added to himself.

They drove to a part of Bristol he did not know well, beyond Clifton. Smart houses, pre-war mostly, but big and comfortable. He had expected something run-down, sleazy. That was his policeman's prejudice showing, he told himself. Just because it was an inquiry into attempted murder, it didn't mean everyone involved had to be from the inner city.

The house was impressive. Clothier rang the bell, heard deep, soft chimes from somewhere inside. He saw a curtain move in the bay window to the right of the door, then moments later a shadow approaching behind the frosted glass panelling. When the door opened, he knew beyond doubt it was the woman the insurance broker had described. She cocked a questioning eyebrow at him.

'Excuse me, madam, I'm Sergeant Clothier, CID.' He held up his warrant card. 'I'd like to have a word with you, if I may.'

The woman paled, a hand went to her mouth. 'It's not my husband, is it?'

The sergeant was puzzled. 'Your husband, madam? No, I'm not aware of —'

'He's in hospital, you see. I thought — well never mind. I suppose you'd better come in.'

'Well, thank you. But — I'm sorry, could you give me your name?'

'Why yes, Sergeant.' She smiled her best smile. 'I'm Mrs Christine Sansome.'

CHAPTER 31

Ted looked down at Claire, unable to suppress the lump in his throat. The doctors here at Bristol General Infirmary had done a marvellous job, no doubt about that. He could not have imagined the gory mess being repaired so well. There was no dressing, just a thin transparent film, so he could see the extent of the wound clearly. Christ, the size of it! How was she going to feel when she saw herself? Despite the excellence of the repair, surely there would be a scar? And her face looked somehow a little lop-sided.

The cut ran from just below her right eye to level with her mouth. He didn't know how the medics had done it, but there were no stitches he could see holding the edges of the cut so perfectly together. At each end of the cut a short length of very fine blue nylon was taped to the skin. He supposed this thread was holding the wound closed with some sort of internal stitching. He reached out his hand to caress her cheek.

'I wouldn't touch her, Mr Parkes. Let her sleep.' The doctor came in to the cubicle. 'She's pretty heavily sedated, but I don't think we should risk waking her just yet.'

'Looks like you've done a great job, Doc.'

'Thank you.'

'But — but what sort of a scar will it leave?'

'Frankly, it's difficult to say at this stage. Some people heal with scars that are much less noticeable than others. She has an appendicectomy scar that looks as if it healed very nicely, so she's got a good chance of this doing very well.'

'Thank God for that.'

'There is another problem, though.'

Ted looked quickly from Claire to the doctor. 'What's that?'

'The knife cut through her facial nerve. That's a small but important nerve that works the muscles on the side of the face. That's why her face looks a little asymmetrical. When she smiles, it'll look much more noticeable, I'm afraid.'

'Can't you patch it up?'

'We have done our best. It was a very clean cut, and we've identified the ends of the nerve and sewn them together.'

'So it should be OK, then?'

'It may be. Nerve regeneration is a very unpredictable business. You hardly ever get a perfect result. And we won't know for months, nerves regrow very slowly.'

'Poor kid.' Ted was silent for a moment. 'What about the other damage?'

'The arm was nasty — right into the muscles — but no major nerves or blood vessels were severed. We had to use interrupted sutures on the skin — lot of tension there. So it won't be as neat a job as the face, but it'll be OK.'

'And what about — ' Ted felt strangely embarrassed. 'What about the — her — ?' he indicated his own left chest.

'The breast? That was quite easy to repair, thankfully. We put a subcuticular skin closure there, like the one on her face. I reckon she won't mind going topless again some day.' The doctor gave a weak smile at his attempt to lighten the mood.

Ted clenched his fists by his sides. 'I'll make some bastard pay for this.'

'Best left to the police, don't you think?'

'That's a matter of opinion. Have they spoken to her yet?'

'Just briefly, before she went to theatre.'

'She was so scared, Doc. When she came round, before the ambulance arrived — she thought I was one of them. Screamed and screamed. Then when she realised it was me — nearly went hysterical all over again.'

'It won't be easy for her to get over it.'

Ted allowed himself a proud smile. 'She's a tough one, this.'

'You're obviously very fond of her.'

Ted nodded slowly, not replying for a moment, not trusting his voice to be steady. At last he looked the doctor in the eye. 'Yeah, Doc. I reckon you could say that.'

'Why don't you go home for a bit? Get something to eat. I don't think she'll be round for a couple of hours or more.'

'I want to be here when she wakes up.'

'If you're back by — let's say one-thirty — I'm sure you'll be in time.'

Ted debated with himself, wiped his face with his hand. He could use a drink. And he ought to go back to his flat, anyway. He wasn't even sure if he'd locked up, he'd left in such a hurry.

'OK, I think I will. And hey, Doc?'

The doctor angled his head as if the better to receive the forthcoming statement. 'Mr Parkes?'

'Thanks for the chat.'

'My pleasure. Wish I had more time for people in situations like this.' As if to emphasise the point, his pager started an insistent bleeping. He shrugged his shoulders. 'Here we go again.'

Left alone, Ted touched Claire's good cheek, very, very gently. Just, he told himself, to let her know he was there. Then he left for home.

* * *

'Really, Mrs Sansome, it's no good denying it was you on that bus. You've just been identified in a parade.' Sergeant Clothier was amazed at the woman's cool arrogance.

'The man must be mistaken.'

'Mistaken or not, I cannot ignore his identification.'

'It's no crime to be on a bus.'

'No, madam. But the witness says that he saw you push a lady into the path of a lorry. She was nearly killed. That could be attempted murder.'

'But she *wasn't* killed?'

Clothier could tell she was interested. 'No. In fact, she got away with little more than a few scratches.' He watched the woman's reaction carefully. Was there a trace of disappointment?

'Lucky for her. So what's all the fuss about?'

'The fuss is about the fact that she *could* be dead.'

Christine Sansome pursed her lips in a gesture of impatience. 'Isn't Mr Barker here yet?'

'Mr Barker?'

'My solicitor. You did send for him, didn't you?'

'Well, not personally, Mrs Sansome, but I asked someone at the front desk to do it.'

'Am I going to be charged?'

'I shall have to consult my superiors about that, madam.'

'I have influential friends, you know.' She studied the overweight officer with deliberate scorn. 'You could be out of a job over this.'

Clothier was unruffled. 'I'll take my chances.'

Christine Sansome turned to the wall and stamped her foot. 'Shit!'

The policewoman who was taking notes looked at Clothier. They both grinned.

* * *

David Barker hurried after his client, trying to keep up. 'It's no good being annoyed with *me*, Mrs Sansome. At least I've managed to get you out without charges being laid.'

Christine Sansome tossed her head. 'Great!' They walked on a few paces. 'Tell me, Mr Barker, what exactly does being released on police bail mean?'

'It means they're not sure that they have enough evidence to make a charge stick now, but they hope to by the time they've asked you to come back.'

'And will they?'

'What?'

'Make the charge stick?'

'They do have an independent witness.'

She stopped and turned so abruptly the solicitor almost bumped into her. 'You could have pulled some strings. Spoken to the Chief Superintendent or something.'

'Really, Mrs Sansome, one just doesn't *do* that sort of thing.'

'Huh!' She gave him a contemptuous look, and resumed her fast walk.

'Remember,' Barker called after her, 'Don't go away anywhere without telling me. We gave them our word.'

Mrs Sansome did not reply. She climbed into a waiting taxi, rudely jostling the previous occupants who were alighting.

The taxi driver turned slowly in his seat and observed dryly, 'In a hurry, are we madam?'

'Yes, we are.' She told him where she wanted to go.

His attitude changed at the implication that this was a medical emergency. The driver repeated the destination before speeding off. 'Bristol General Neuro Unit it is.'

* * *

Christine Sansome was getting angry with the senior nursing officer's secretary. 'How much longer am I going to be kept waiting?'

'I'm sorry, Mrs Sansome. She'll be here as soon as she's free.'

'Can't you try phoning her again?'

'I really can't do that. She's in a meeting with the UGM and the FHSA.'

'That's just double Dutch to me.'

The secretary sighed. 'That's the Unit General Manager, and the —'

'It really doesn't interest me what they mean. I only want —' The door of the office opened. 'Ah, at last.'

The secretary stood up hastily and moved between her impatient visitor and her boss. 'Mrs Creech, Mrs Sansome has been waiting to see you. Dr Sansome's wife. I told her it might not be convenient, but —'

Rosemary Creech was not the archetypal matron figure. She was thin, smartly dressed, almost elegant, and to Christine looked much too young to hold a senior position in a hospital. She smiled at her visitor. 'It's all right, Rachel, I'm sure I have a minute. How are you, Mrs Sansome? Was it something about your husband?'

'In a way, yes. Perhaps we could . . . ?' She indicated the nursing officer's office.

'Yes, of course, come on in.' Mrs Creech led the way into her inner sanctum. Christine Sansome followed, giving the secretary an imperious look as she swept by.

'Now, how can I help?' the nursing officer asked when they were seated either side of her desk.

'This is rather difficult for me, you understand. I don't like to complain.'

Rosemary Creech leaned forward anxiously. 'Complain? Oh, dear. About something in the hospital? Your husband's treatment?'

Christine Sansome took out a handkerchief and made a show of distress. 'I really don't want to make a fuss.'

'Please, Mrs Sansome. If there is something you are unhappy about, I'd like to know.'

'I — I'm not sure. Perhaps I should leave it.' She made to rise from her chair.

'Mrs Sansome, really, I think you must tell me what the problem is.'

'I don't want to get anyone into trouble.'

'You just tell me. I'll decide if anyone's in trouble.'

The doctor's wife made a show of pulling herself together, coming to a decision. 'Very well. If you insist. It concerns a member of your staff.'

'You'll have to tell me which one, Mrs Sansome.'

She drew in a breath, and hesitantly, almost reluctantly, appeared to make the decision to speak the name.

'It's the sister on my husband's ward. Joanne Yeates.'

* * *

Christine Sansome and the nursing officer spoke for fifteen minutes, the doctor's wife allowing details to be extracted from her bit by bit. Eventually Rosemary Creech sat back, her expression one of deep concern. 'This is a most serious matter, and I promise you we shall investigate it thoroughly. I will not tolerate such behaviour or attitudes in a member of my staff, and from what you've told me about her — her almost callous attitude to your husband's care! Well! You can rest assured I shall take it most seriously.'

'There is one thing . . .' Christine Sansome looked distraught.

'Tell me.'

'I shall feel very, er, awkward, if I — you know, visit my husband, and Sister Yeates is . . .'

'Don't worry. I have already decided that I shall suspend Sister Yeates from duty until this matter has been thoroughly investigated.'

'Oh, dear, the poor girl, I didn't want —'

'Nonsense.' The nursing officer was firm, indignant. 'I cannot have a patient in this hospital, or his wife, treated in this way by a member of my staff. You can rest assured, next time you visit your poor husband, you will not have to face Sister Yeates.'

Christine Sansome was effusive in her thanks, and left the office, head bowed and solemn. As she turned the corner to go to the lifts, her step developed a spring and she had to work hard to suppress a smile.

CHAPTER 32

Ted left his car and walked up the concrete stairs to his flat, his thoughts still back in the hospital, preoccupied with the vision of Claire looking so peaceful as she slept off the effects of the anaesthetic. His mind's eye was constantly drawn to the wound on her face, and his stomach churned at the thought of her reaction when she saw it.

He knew he would feel no differently about her. Increasingly in the last few weeks he had found himself looking forward to her company, and not just because he liked the look of her. After this — well, the feelings he was experiencing now he had never experienced to this extent before. He felt protective, fiercely so, but it wasn't just in a paternal, feeling-sorry-for-her way. He wanted nothing to hurt her, he felt he would give anything to save her from the shock and horror and fear of rejection that he sensed might come with her disfigurement.

He pushed his key in the lock, but the door opened before he could turn it. Damn, he thought, I didn't lock the bloody thing after all. He did not notice the splintered woodwork on the frame. He was already in the hall. He thought he heard a noise in his lounge. He didn't think much of it, but diverted from the kitchen just to take a look.

'What the fuck!' He tried to take in the devastation that greeted him. His eyes went first to the furniture. It was all ripped open, the guts of the upholstery spilling obscenely from gaping holes onto the floor which was strewn with debris. His eyes went across to the cabinet that held his prized record collection. He stepped further into the room to look beyond the ruined sofa. CDs and albums were strewn everywhere. The standard lamp had fallen, the shade crumpled as if it had been stamped on. Pictures from the wall lay around, glass smashed. An African carving lay with its head broken off. The drawers from an old wooden chest had been pulled out and emptied, and his hi-fi equipment looked as if it had been thrown against the wall. He looked around wildly, his brain reminding him he had heard a noise.

He went to his bedroom door. His head swam for a moment. The mattress had been ripped to pieces; springs, cloth, filling were everywhere. All the drawers had been tipped out, contents jumbled. And what was that smell? He moved to go and look in the bathroom, but stopped as his eye caught some marks on a torn sheet. Lines of wetness, haphazardly over the material, as if — someone's pissed on this! an inner voice shouted. He threw the sheet from him in disgust, and the cloth moved to reveal a small brown heap of faeces on the off-white of the deep-pile carpet.

'YOU BASTARDS!' Ted roared, head thrown back. He started to heave in great gulps of air, snorting like the enraged animal he was becoming. There was another sound, and it was unmistakably a laugh. From behind him! He whirled round, and just caught sight of a figure ducking into the other bedroom.

'YOU FUCKING BASTARD!' He ran across the hallway and burst into the room. The laughing man's smile vanished as he saw the fury that approached, although Ted was unaware of this, because of the mask. He looked at the lightly-built invader. His fists worked as he moved slowly forward.

'I'll teach you to shit on my carpet, you puny little bastard.' He ground out the words, menace dripping from every syllable. As the man backed away, his hand went to his pocket, and he drew out a Stanley knife. He held it out in front of him, waving it back and forth to ward off any attack. He started to wheel round so that he could get to the door.

The sight of the knife caused Ted to lose control completely. He knew he had the man who had slashed and disfigured Claire.

'YOU LITTLE FUCKER!' His voice roared through the flat. Whether it was the sight of Ted, spittle flying, face purple, eyes bulging, advancing on him that caused the knife-wielder to panic, or whether his strategy was just ill-judged, the result was the same. He threw the knife at Ted, and made a dash for the door. The knife hit Ted in the chest, but it had rotated as it flew, and fell harmlessly to the floor. Ted's reflexes were lightning-fast, his muscles supercharged with adrenaline. He dived and caught the man before he reached the door. His rage gave him such strength that he dragged the man upright, grabbed him by the neck, and proceeded to smash the intruder's head against the wall, getting more satisfaction with each blow.

'Geoff! He's gonna kill me!' The masked man managed a muffled terror-stricken entreaty, as Ted pulled him from the wall for a more forceful blow. He could not see the face to tell what damage he was doing, but he felt an animal satisfaction as he saw a red smudge appear on the wall, where blood had seeped through the mask from the macerated scalp beneath. Something penetrated from Ted's subconscious, telling him he could kill this creature. And in the same moment, he knew he *wanted* to kill him, maim him, mess up his face, break bones, cause him pain and anguish to make him suffer for what he had done to Claire. He let the body drop to the ground. The man was evidently still conscious; he moved his head slightly, groaned, hissed out a hoarse appeal.

'Please . . .'

Ted bared his teeth, nostril flared, and lifted his foot over the man's face. *That'll be a good start*, a sadistic voice deep inside his brain instructed. Smash his nose, spread it all over his face, cheekbones and jaw should break, too.

His foot started its descent, the immobilised man started to scream, and a kitchen stool caught Ted full across his back. He felt a rib break, his head strike the wall as he pitched forward, the breath go from his lungs and refuse to return. His victim started to wriggle from under him, but he felt paralysed. He was rolled over by the second man who had caught him from behind, and failed to protect himself as a boot struck him in the side of the head. Coloured lights, pain, a sense of rotation, all blended together and merged into darkness and insensibility.

* * *

His bed wasn't this hard, surely? He tried to move, and burning agony stabbed his back below his left shoulder-blade. Memory returned in a sickening surge. Ted lay still on the floor, now tasting the salty metal of his own blood on his lips, wondering if he dared try and move, if he *could* move. There was another wave of nausea. Had they done anything else to him as he lay unconscious? What mutilations might they have perpetrated in revenge? He lay a few seconds more, then tried to move again. This time the pain was bearable, and he slowly rolled over onto his back and opened his eyes. He lifted his throbbing head and tried to look down. There didn't seem to be any other damage.

Thank Christ! He eased himself into a sitting position, rubbed his neck, held his chest, and very carefully stood up, leaning against the wall as he did so.

He surveyed the chaos of his home, and the memory of those record albums spread on the floor came into his consciousness. Groaning loudly, he forced himself to walk, staggered into the lounge, then slowly fell to his knees amongst his treasured possessions.

Some had been thrown, some had slid to the ground from the sloping shelf. Some memory stirred, bringing a wry grin through the hurt. Claire had always criticised the shelf, said it wasn't straight. One of his few attempts at do-it-yourself. Well, it was done now, all right.

He turned back to his collection, found Leonard Cohen's 'Songs From a Room'. After a struggle, under an overturned and disembowelled armchair, he located Arlo Guthrie Junior's 'Alice's Restaurant.' He took a record from its sleeve, noted with satisfaction that it was undamaged, then felt inside the cover. He sighed with relief as he extracted two 3.5 inch floppy disks. Two more were in the other album sleeve. He nodded to himself in grim satisfaction. At least the bastards hadn't got what they must have come for.

He took some co-proxamol to ease the pain in his head and back, phoned the police, and then the hospital. It was just after one-thirty, and Claire was still asleep. The doc knows his stuff, he thought, and told the staff nurse that if Clare woke she was to be told that he had been held up and would be there soon. He replaced the phone. *Held up!* He tried to suppress a chuckle at the irony, but the pain broke through.

He tried to be patient when the police came. Give them their due, he realised, they were trying to be brief, and encouraged him to go to Casualty and get himself checked over. He must have gone very pale, because one of the young officers suddenly stopped his questioning, and announced he would take Ted to the hospital himself immediately. He made sure he was taken to Bristol General Infirmary. Claire was there, too.

* * *

It was over an hour before Ted was pronounced free of serious injury. He had a cracked ninth rib, at the back on the left, the doctor said. Skull X-ray was clear. But he had been concussed, unconscious for probably ten minutes or more. That meant he was at risk of post-concussion syndrome, and possible internal bleeding into the skull or brain. He should be observed in hospital at least overnight, he was informed. Ted declined.

'Can't do it, mate,' he told the doctor, 'Got too much to sort out. And I've got a patient upstairs to visit.' He tried to sound jocular.

'This is not really a matter for jokes, Mr Parkes. I am being serious about this.'

'And I'm being serious about not staying.'

'You'll have to sign a disclaimer. That you are discharging yourself from the hospital against medical advice.'

Ted had had enough. His head throbbed, and he wanted to get out of here and see Claire. 'Look, I don't wanna be rude, Doc, but stuff you. I'm leaving, I'm not signing anything, and I'll be back if my head starts to fall off.'

Ted expected the doctor to get angry. Instead, he just gave him a piece of paper. It was headed *Things to look out for after a head injury.* There followed a list of symptoms, such as excessive drowsiness, nausea and vomiting, visual disturbance, that he should report.

'Just tell a doctor if you get any of these.'

'Thanks, Doc.' He stood up a little too quickly, swayed a moment, then steadied himself. He set off determinedly for the lift.

* * *

Ted peeped through the curtain. He could see Claire propped up in bed, pale, the injured side of her face turned towards the pillow as if to hide it.

Well, here goes, he thought, and stepped in.

'Hello, beautiful.'

Claire turned towards him, recognition taking a few seconds. Her eyes showed her pleasure, and then a smile started. He tried to hide his shock at how crooked it was, only one side of her face working properly. Her wound creased, and pain from the injury made her wince. By the time Ted got to the side of the bed there were tears.

He sat down, carefully, trying not to show his own discomfort. He picked up her hand. 'Hey, steady on.'

'Oh, Ted.' She tried to blink back more tears. 'Beautiful I am not.'

Ted didn't know how to play this. 'Have they given you a mirror?'

'No.'

'Then I think they should. I reckon it's not half so bad as you might imagine.'

'I don't want to see it, thanks.'

'I'm going to get one.' He got up.

'What are you? An expert on Freud all of a sudden?' There was a sharp edge to her voice.

'Hey. Just trying to help.'

'Please, Ted. I don't want to look. Not yet.' She paused. 'They told me the facial nerve was cut, that I've got a crooked face.'

He sat down again. He didn't feel secure enough about his amateur psychology to force the issue. He felt awkward about what he wanted to say. 'You still look beautiful to me.'

'I didn't know I did before.'

'You've been growing on me.'

'What, like a wart?'

'That's better. Bit of the old fighting spirit.'

'Not much of that left, I'm afraid.'

'You'll be OK. The quack said he'd patched up your arm, no sweat, and your titty is as good as new.'

Claire attempted a grin. 'I just love your bedside manner, doctor.'

'I know you find my suave sophistication irresistible.'

Claire changed her position carefully. 'Could you pour me a glass of water, nurse?'

'That's a rapid demotion. Doctor to nurse in five seconds.' He stood up a little too quickly, his rib stabbed him, and he could barely suppress a cry of pain.

'What's the matter?'

'Nothing, nothing.' He poured the water. 'Here. Drink your medicine.'

She drank, passed the glass back, and watched Ted closely as he carefully resumed his seat.

'Come on, Ted. I'm not that daft. It was my face they damaged, not my brain.'

Ted held up his hands, tried to sound nonchalant. 'I had a couple of visitors. Same ones as you had, I should imagine. They ransacked my place. Bloody terrible mess. Just like yours.'

'Oh, Ted. And they've hurt you.'

'Just a little.'

'They were still there when you arrived?'

Ted told her how he'd gone from the hospital to find his flat devastated, and found the man with the Stanley knife, had lost his temper, and then been attacked from behind. 'Gave me a cracked rib and a headache.'

'Were you unconscious?'

'A little.'

'Shouldn't you be under observation?'

'The doc offered it to me. But I said I'd only stay in if they got me a bed in here with you. It was no deal.'

Claire smiled carefully. 'I wouldn't be much use in this state.'

'Nor me. This broken rib's rendered me harmless.'

Claire took his hand and looked at him directly. 'Maybe when I'm out of here. If you haven't changed your mind.' Her hand went up to her face.

Ted looked into her pale grey eyes, and felt an ache in his chest. 'You're a fantastic girl, d'you know that?'

They formed a silent tableau for several seconds, before Claire's expression turned to one of concern.

'What's the matter?' She had watched his face change from a detached serenity to a picture of worry.

'I'm not sure that I'm such a nice person to know. That bastard with the knife, I bloody near killed the little fucker.' He sounded more anxious than proud.

'It's no more than he deserved.'

'I don't think you understand. I *wanted* to kill him. For what he's done to you. And I reckon I would have killed him, too, if the other son of a bitch hadn't got me.'

Claire reached out with her good hand and stroked Ted's cheek. 'You're no murderer. I'd feel safe with you anywhere.'

Ted looked up, covered his embarrassment with a light-hearted reply. 'You're just saying that.'

'No, I'm not.'

'I didn't get the impression you felt safe before. You've chucked me out of your flat enough times!'

'I've changed my mind.' Somehow, despite the dishevelled hair, the pale face, the facial wound, to Ted she managed to look seductive.

He felt a warmth suffuse him, accompanied by a pleasurable swelling in his groin. 'You are going to get me into trouble, Miss Donaldson.'

'How's that?'

'If you don't stop this line of discussion, I'll be jumping into bed with you right now.'

'What about your bad back?'

'All right, I'll crawl in.'

They smiled at each other, his gentle, hers its new crooked shape.

'When you said I still looked beautiful, what were you comparing me with? The Mona Lisa?'

Ted's smile grew mischievous. 'No. I was thinking of a camel from the back of Bourke.'

'A camel? Charming!' Her eyes twinkled. 'Just a minute. Which end?'

'Hey! I wouldn't put you down. The front end, of course.'

The more they tried not to laugh, the more it hurt and the stranger they looked to each other, Ted trying to hold his back, Claire biting her lip to stop her face moving. Their eyes brimmed, and through the curious mixture of tears, pain and suppressed laughter, they recognised a deep mutual feeling.

CHAPTER 33

Sergeant Clothier adjusted his bulk in Claire's armchair. 'You must have some idea why these men should break into your flat and threaten you.' It was a week since Claire's attack, and she had been out of hospital two days.

'Mr Parkes and I have been talking about it.' She looked anxiously across at Ted, whose injured rib caused him to sit uncomfortably in a high-backed chair.

'It's pretty obvious that it's got to be something to do with the work we've been doing with Dr Sansome over at the Neurological Unit. I'm certain they were after my computer disks. All the data about our research are on them.'

'All of them? On just four floppy disks?'

'You can get 1.44 megabytes on each one. That's a total of 5.76 megabytes. And some of the files are compressed. That's one hell of a lot of information.'

'I'll take your word for it, Mr Parkes.' He raised his eyebrows. 'I presume they are somewhere quite safe now?'

Ted nodded. 'Safe deposit box.'

He nodded his approval. 'Good, good.'

Claire looked from one to the other.

'But why would they come here?' She waved her arm around her now restored flat. 'And why do so much damage to Ted's stuff?' Her mouth turned down with distaste at the memory, and she felt the muscles in her face pulling on her wound. The stitches had been removed only yesterday, and she instinctively put her right hand up to protect the area from undue strain. Her left arm was bandaged, but no longer in a sling.

The policeman paused briefly. 'I suppose they thought you might have copies, or that you were keeping them hidden for Mr Parkes. And they wanted to frighten you — you heard them say so. In Mr Parkes' case, well, perhaps they thought he might not be so easily frightened.'

'Too right. The bastards!'

'And so they made a real mess of his place, tried to make an impression on him that way. They weren't keeping a look-out, so it doesn't seem as if it was their intention to assault Mr Parkes. He just stumbled in on them, when they thought he was at the hospital.'

Claire was not convinced. 'But why did they want the disks? Why try to frighten us off?'

'To make sure you don't follow up your research on Dr Sansome. You've told me enough to get the gist of what you're doing there. Sounds pretty scary to me, communicating with someone who to all intents and purposes is no longer of this world. Sounds as if someone else finds it scary, too. But for another reason.'

'And what reason might that be?' Ted asked.

'You're not going to pretend you haven't thought of this already, now surely? That locked in Dr Sansome's brain is something important, so important that it has prompted someone to try and steal your data and put the frighteners on you.'

Ted had to agree. 'I've thought something along those lines. It fits with Joanne Yeates being blackmailed with threats to her daughter, too.'

The sergeant sat forward. 'What's this? She hasn't mentioned it to me.'

'No, I didn't think she had.' Ted looked at Claire. 'But I don't think she'd mind. I think we ought to tell you now.' Claire nodded her agreement, and Ted proceeded to tell Clothier all they knew about Joanne being coerced into trying to spy on them.

When Ted finished, the policeman sat back and drew in a slow, deep breath, then blew it out contemplatively. 'I can't see the connection right now, but it's too much of a coincidence.'

'What is?'

'Why, someone trying to kill Sister Yeates.'

'Kill Joanne?' Claire was horrified. This was the first she and Ted had heard of it.

'When? What the hell happened?' Ted winced as he moved a little too quickly. His cracked rib was still very painful.

'I'm sorry, I thought you must know. It was in the local paper.'

'We haven't had much time for local news. You might say our attention has been elsewhere.'

'Yes, quite, Mr Parkes. Strangely enough, or maybe not, it happened the same day that you two were done over.'

'Is she all right?' Claire asked anxiously.

'Miraculously, yes. Someone pushed her off a bus into the path of a bloody great artic, but she only got a few scratches.'

'God! Poor Joanne!'

'Indeed, miss. Unfortunate to be attacked, but very lucky, very lucky indeed to be alive.'

'Any idea who did it?' Ted leaned forward intently.

'Now this is curious. There was a witness, or so he claims. I certainly can't fault his story. But it seems so unlikely, I can hardly believe it. The witness says the person who pushed Mrs Yeates off the bus was a lady — Dr Sansome's wife, Christine, to be precise.'

Claire and Ted gaped at each other. Ted winced again as he moved.

'Christine Sansome? You mean *she* was seen pushing Joanne Yeates under a truck!'

'That is what the witness alleges.'

'Well, bugger me!'

* * *

As soon as the police officer had collected his signed statements and left, Claire phoned the Neurological Unit to speak to Joanne. She was put through to the ward.

'Could I speak to Mrs Yeates, please?'

'May I ask who is speaking?'

'Claire Donaldson. We've been doing some research on the ward. With Dr Sansome.'

'Oh, yes. I'm sorry, Miss Donaldson, but Sister Yeates has not been here all week. I'm afraid to say she's been suspended from duty.'

'Suspended? But — but why?'

'I'm afraid I really don't know much about it. There's going to be an inquiry. I'm not sure I should be talking about it at all.'

'But was there an accident? Some mistake?'

The nurse on the other end of the phone could not resist passing on the gossip. 'Rumour has it,' she said in a conspiratorial tone, 'that it was for ill-treating a patient.'

'Joanne? I don't believe it!'

'That's what they're saying.'

'The poor woman. The patient must be making it up.'

'That's rather difficult to tell. The patient is Dr Sansome.'

* * *

When there was no reply from Joanne's home number, that of her mother, or from her sister in Cheltenham, they decided to drive over and see if she was in but just not answering the phone. Ted eased himself behind the wheel, cursing and swearing at the small size of the vehicle.

'You know, it's got to be Porthenoy behind this. He got us pushed out, and I'll bet my dick to a bluebottle's balls that he got Joanne the heave-ho on some trumped-up charge.'

'I agree. It's all got to be a fabrication. I just can't imagine Joanne being cruel to anyone.'

Ted put the car in gear. Steering slightly erratically and awkwardly, he looked across at Claire. 'But where does the charming Christine Sansome come in? Trying to kill someone! I find that hard to believe, even of a crabby bitch like her.'

'I'm not so sure. Remember how, after saying no, she changed her mind about us doing the research on Paul? They both did an about-turn. Porthenoy was all agin one minute, and sweetness and light the next.'

'That's right. Ouch!' Ted couldn't stop himself giving a shout as a jag of pain caught him when the car's suspension failed to cushion a ramp in the road. 'Those two could be in this together.'

'But not sharing the same bed!'

'Ha! Who knows? Seems to me you can't tell these days. Who does what, with which, and to whom. It doesn't seem to matter any more.'

'Is that a cue for a song?'

'Sorry?'

'Golden oldie. Buddy Holly. "It Doesn't Matter Any More".'

'Before my time, little groupie.'

* * *

Joanne's house was deserted, and so was her mother's.

'We'll try her sister again as soon as we get back. Perhaps they had just gone out.'

Claire was right. When they tried again, a child's voice answered.

'Is that Piers?' Claire asked.

'No.' An indignant tone came into the voice. 'This is Stephanie.'

'Oh, sorry, Stephanie. Is Mummy in?'

There was no reply, but Claire heard the phone clatter, and then the little girl's voice in the distance calling shrilly, 'Mummeee! Mummeee!'

Claire waited, heard footsteps approaching.

'Karen Henstridge.'

'Oh, hello, Mrs Henstridge. This is Miss Donaldson. I'm a researcher from the Clifton Neurological Institute. I've been working with your sister. I expect she's mentioned me.'

There was a welcoming note in the response. 'Of course. It's Claire, isn't it? Joanne's talked about you a great deal.'

'I'm sorry to trouble you, but is Joanne there?'

'No, Claire, I'm afraid she isn't. She did come up here, straight away, after the accident. But she's gone to stay with Maudie.'

'We only just heard about the accident — and now we hear she's been suspended from the hospital. Is she all right?'

'She was very upset at first. I mean, who wouldn't be? Someone tries to push you under a bus, and then you get falsely accused . . .'

'But now she's gone somewhere else?'

'Yes. You probably know Joanne well enough by now. She's pretty tough. After a few days she seemed to settle — and then we got a call from Freda.'

'I'm sorry, Karen, but I don't understand. Maudie and Freda? Who are they?'

'Sorry, I didn't realise. Freda is an old friend of the family, a sort of adopted aunt. She lives in Yatton. It must be near you.'

Claire knew the small town well. 'Yes, it's only about ten miles away.'

'As close as that? Well, Freda used to keep an eye on an old relative of ours, Great Aunt Maude. We all call her Maudie. She never married, lives on her own in Kingston Seymour — that's a little village about two miles farther on, near the sea.'

Claire was beginning to regret she's asked about these people. All she wanted was to find Joanne.

'Are you still there?' Karen asked.

'Oh, sorry, yes. I'm listening.'

'Well Freda and Maudie were good friends, used to spend a lot of time together. But Freda got arthritis, and can't get about now — and Maudie — well, unfortunately she's getting senile. Mind you, she is 78.'

'And that's where Joanne has gone?'

'Yes. Freda got a call from someone in the village to say Maudie was ill. So Joanne's gone down to sort things out. She was always very fond of her.'

Quite a woman, this Joanne Yeates, thought Claire. All these troubles of her own, and she's off to look after an aged relative. 'We'd really like to talk to her, Karen. Is there a phone?'

'No, I'm afraid not. There was a lot of trouble at one time, Maudie started ringing everybody up at all hours of the day and night. In the end we thought it best to disconnect it.'

'Could you tell us the address?'

'Yes, it's Willowside, Yenston Lane, Kingston Seymour.'

'When did she go there, Karen?'

'Two days ago. She went down by train.'

'Do you think she'd mind if we turned up to see her?'

'I should think she'd be delighted. There's only Maudie there for company, and as I've told you, she's a bit batty.'

'Thanks, Karen. Oh, how's Lucinda?'

'Fine. Seems quite happy. Give Joanne my love if you do see her.'

'Will do. 'Bye, Karen.'

''Bye, Claire.'

* * *

Ted grumbled a bit about driving again with his painful rib.

'Come on. It's only about 12 miles from here, and it's a lovely warm day for a drive in the country. Tell you what, we'll have an *al fresco* pub lunch and a pint of beer on the way.'

Ted brightened perceptibly at that, and there was no mention of his painful rib for some time.

* * *

They drove over a narrow bridge across the M5 motorway and down into the village of Kingston Seymour — mostly stone-built houses lining the road. Claire asked at the village shop where Yenston Lane was. She was interrogated about her destination, and when the address was mentioned she observed the knowing looks exchanged between two local people who were already in the shop.

Willowside was something of a surprise. Claire was expecting this lonely spinster to be living in a little cottage or terraced house. But the building was large, sombre grey stone walls partly clad in ivy-framed multi-paned windows, which gave the building a pseudo-Georgian look. It was set back about thirty feet from the road, and separated from its nearest neighbour by at least fifty yards of copse. Opposite was an open field. Behind a low stone wall, the front garden boasted an elegant cedar, a copper beech and a horse chestnut. Together they contrived partly to screen the house from the lane.

They pulled onto the grass verge, to allow other vehicles to pass, and went through the old-fashioned iron gate. Ted looked around the neat garden as they walked along the flagstone path to the front door.

'She must have some help with this,' he commented. 'It's not in bad shape.'

Claire raised the iron knocker and let it drop. It made a hollow sound. After only a few seconds, Joanne appeared. She was dressed in jeans and a plaid shirt, had rubber gloves on her hands, and looked flushed. As she opened the door her expression changed from a frown to one of delight.

'Claire! Ted! How did you find me here?'

'Karen told us.'

'My God!' Joanne had just taken in Claire's appearance, her face, her bandaged arm. 'What's happened to you? Oh, you poor girl!' She moved forward to touch her friend. 'Your face. An accident? What happened?'

Claire had to smile. 'Whoa, steady! We'll tell you all about it. May we come in?'

'Of course, of course.' She tried to push a wisp of hair away with her wrist. 'I'm sorry I look such a mess. I've been trying to clean things up around here. Aunt Maudie's —'

Ted picked up on Joanne's hesitation. 'It's OK, we know,' he said, then added somewhat less than tactfully, 'Karen told us the old gal's a shingle short.'

Claire gave him a disapproving look as they moved into the hall, which was tall, dark and cool, with a flagstone floor softened only by a strip of coconut matting. The house smelt damp and musty, as if it refused to succumb to the warmth and sunshine outside.

'Come into the kitchen and I'll put the kettle on. I could do with a cup of tea myself.' As she preceded them she peeled off her rubber gloves and hung them on the side of a plastic bucket. She had evidently been washing out a small walk-in pantry.

'Where is your aunt, Joanne?'

'She's up in bed. Come on in.'

'Wow!' Claire entered the kitchen and looked round. 'It's like a time capsule in here!'

The room was large, with a window opposite which looked out onto the back garden, where there were more trees. Below the window was a yellow porcelain sink, only about six inches deep, supported on a column of bare brick at each end. Two standing pipes rose behind it, old brass taps hung over it. One of them was dripping.

Claire took in the old Welsh dresser, piled with an assortment of willow-patterned crockery, a battered solid fuel stove, and a table on which stood a small electric cooker. Against an adjacent wall stood an old kitchen cabinet, the flap down to provide a badly chipped enamel work-surface. She could see no refrigerator or washing machine.

Joanne noticed Claire and Ted taking in the surroundings. She talked as she filled the kettle from the dripping tap.

'Aunt Maudie — she's my great-aunt really, but that's what I call her — has lived here most of her life. This house belonged to her brother. He was killed in the last war, and he left the place to his sister. She's never had anything done to it since.'

'It's fascinating.' Claire shook her head in wonderment.

Ted gave a short laugh. 'I think it's bloody awful.'

'Come on, where's your sense of history?'

'Wiped out by my sense of smell.' He sniffed the damp air. 'Got a niff like an abo's armpit.'

They all turned at the sound of shuffling steps in the hall. Aunt Maudie came in.

'You're supposed to be in bed!' Joanne admonished.

The old lady took no notice, but moved unsteadily into the room, peering at the visitors. Barely five feet tall, she was dressed in a long, well-worn nightgown, with a baggy cardigan worn over the top. She had a round face topped by thin, wispy grey hair. Despite her deep wrinkles, her expression had an almost cherubic quality, emphasised as she suddenly smiled, revealing widely spaced, uneven teeth. She held up her bony hands, which were clad in fingerless gloves, and gave a squeal of delight. She tottered forward eagerly, embracing Ted and Claire in turn.

'I knew it was you!' she exclaimed in a querulous high voice. 'I knew you'd come.' She drew back from the startled couple and turned to Joanne. 'Look, dear. It's Victor and Nellie!'

* * *

Pieces of pink notepaper fell like confetti, thrown up in the air by the naked figure on the bed. It breathed rapidly, deeply, not only from the peal upon peal of unstable laughter, but from the exertions of the self-induced orgasm just achieved.

Dry lips were moistened with a delicate, flicking tongue. The slightly staring, darting eyes watched the last piece of paper float to the ground. A hand reached out and shakily poured a small tumbler full of vodka. The bottle clattered as it was set down clumsily on the glass-topped dressing-table. Half the contents of the tumbler were swallowed in one mouthful.

Suddenly the figure jumped up, and strutted before the full-length mirror, admiring the body, running hands over the firm flesh, the smooth contours.

The hungry eyes steadied themselves for a moment, locking with those in the reflection.

'It's no good her thinking she can escape me, now is it?' The speech was slightly slurred.

The figure in the mirror replied with a vigorous shake of the head.

'Hiding won't be enough. It's just a matter of time.' The head in the reflection nodded, a crooked, knowing, leering smile slowly spread. 'And then we know what we'll do, don't we?'

With head thrown back, another peal of laughter disintegrated into frustrated whimperings, as eager hands clawed through the pile of pornographic photographs, searching for the favourites, the children. Oh, yes, where was that angelic face? The little boy, the darling little boy with his hand on — on . . .

CHAPTER 34

It took a little while for Joanne to settle Aunt Maudie down again after her excitement. Claire and Ted waited in the kitchen. They could hear the occasional raised voice: Joanne was obviously being firm. They sipped the tea which Claire had made, using a kettle that stood, black and battered, on the solid fuel stove. It seemed to live there permanently, always full of hot water, well-lined with scale inside. While they waited they took a look round the ground floor. There were three rooms off the hall, apart from the kitchen. They went through the door opposite, into a drawing-room that was almost overwhelmed by the accumulation of possessions over many years. There were ornaments, pottery, figurines, plates, samplers, vases, and faded sepia photographs in silver frames. Almost all the available space on the ancient furniture and on the walls had been utilised. Two small occasional tables, and a pianola complete with elaborate candelabra, were covered with more treasures. The room was dominated, if that were possible amongst such a veritable museum of bygones, by two enormous oil paintings in ornate but dusty gilded frames. It was difficult to make out their subject-matter, so blackened by time had they become.

'I'd love to see those restored,' Claire commented.

'Yeah. Jesus wept! Just look at the stuff in here. I bet some of it's worth a penny or two.'

'I'm sure you're right — but I can't get Maudie to have any of it valued, let alone insured.'

They both turned, startled, at the sound of Joanne's voice. Claire felt embarrassed.

'I'm sorry. We didn't mean to be nosey.'

'Liar,' Ted said with a grin. 'We were being nosey. It's the sort of place that invites it.'

Joanne smiled her agreement. 'It's true. It's like Aladdin's cave in here. She's kept everything she ever bought or was given. There's another room, a bedroom upstairs, that's full of more stuff. Some of it's still wrapped in the original packing.'

'Has she settled down now?'

'Yes, I think she'll be quiet for a bit. I've given her a sedative the doctor prescribed to try and stop her wandering at night.'

They followed Joanne back into the kitchen.

'I hope you weren't bothered by her little outburst. She's convinced that you are Nellie and Victor, that's her sister and brother-in-law. They've both been dead for donkey's years. She wouldn't settle until I told her you'd stay.'

Ted could not hide a momentary look of alarm. Joanne laughed. 'It's all right. Next time you see her she'll think you're someone else. Her short-term memory is completely hopeless.' She smiled sadly. 'But if she starts to recall something from her childhood, well — the detail is amazingly accurate.'

Once they were settled round the table they began to exchange news, and it took nearly an hour and two more cups of tea to bring each other up to date with the events of the past week.

Ted stood up, paced, turned back to the two women.

'The fact is, we're all up shit creek. Which poses the question, what are we bloody well going to do about it?'

Joanne looked defeated, her shoulders slumped. 'I've just got to wait for the inquiry. I can't really do anything else.'

'What'll happen if it goes against you?' Claire asked.

The nurse shrugged. 'I don't know. I could always get a job somewhere else, I suppose. Well-qualified nurses are in short enough supply. Or . . .' She looked round the archaic kitchen.

'Or what?'

'Or I could just stay on here — especially if Aunt Maudie doesn't improve. Since she's had this chest infection her dementia has worsened. Although when she's had bronchitis before, it's usually improved again after treatment.'

'But you couldn't bring Lucinda to live *here*!'

'No, I'd have to sell my place in Bishopsworth and try to get somewhere in the village. I've thought about it before when Maudie's been ill. And there's a very good local school in Yatton.'

Ted frowned. 'But what would you do for money?'

'Before poor Maudie went completely do-lally, in one of her lucid moments when she could see what was happening, she gave me power of attorney over her affairs. Her solicitor says I could legitimately use her not inconsiderable resources to employ myself to look after her.'

'And if she dies?'

Joanne looked almost guilty. 'I believe I'm well provided for in her will.'

'So why don't you just wave two fingers at the bastards at the hospital and tell them to stuff their job?'

Joanne had to smile. 'Professional pride as much as anything. If I did that, they'd just assume I was guilty, anyway. Besides, contrary to popular belief about Health Service workers, I enjoy my job.'

'That bastard Porthenoy's got a lot to answer for. He's got to be behind all this.' Ted clenched his fists.

'I don't think he's the one behind my problems.'

'How's that?' The Australian came back to the table and resumed his seat.

'The senior nursing officer as good as told me that the complainant was Christine Sansome.'

'Christine -!' Ted banged the table, making the cups rattle in their saucers. 'Christine Sansome? But the miserable little tart tried to shove you under a truck!'

'Maybe. It wasn't I who saw her.'

'But if it was her,' Claire joined in, 'it might be her spiteful way of getting back at you, trying to discredit you. She might even claim that your mistreatment of her husband mitigates her own actions. And she must have known it would make life unpleasant for you, even if her charges were ultimately proved false.'

'That's more or less what I thought.' Joanne turned from Claire to Ted. 'But what about you? Porthenoy is certainly behind *your* troubles.'

Claire's eyes narrowed. 'We thought he might be behind the men who — who attacked me and Ted.'

'I'm sure of it,' said Ted firmly. 'I should reckon in that poofter's paradise where he hangs out there's someone desperate enough to carry out a little shake-down for a few quid and a sexual favour or two.'

Claire shuddered. 'Yeuk!'

Ted grinned at her. 'Well summed up, m'lud.'

Joanne glanced up at the grimy face of an old electric clock that hung by its wire to the wall. Ted's attention had been drawn to it earlier by the variable whirring sounds it made as the worn cogs turned.

'Look, I must go into the village and get some supplies. There isn't much food in the house, and as there's no fridge I have to keep stocking up with fresh food.'

Claire stood up. 'Yes, of course. You must have your hands full here, and we're just holding you up.'

'No, no, you're not really.' She looked down at her hands. 'You've no idea just how pleased I am to see you.' She hesitated. 'Since my husband — since we — well, I haven't really had any friends — proper friends, that is.' She looked up at them, tried a smile. Claire thought she was blinking back tears, and moved round the table.

'Joanne — just tell us. What can we do to help?'

She gave a short laugh. 'Difficult to say really. How about staying a bit longer, keeping me company?'

Claire looked round at Ted. 'We haven't got to go back to Bristol immediately, have we?'

'No problem to me. How about if we stayed until this evening?'

Claire detected a flicker of disappointment on the nurse's face.

'Is that too long?'

'No, no, don't be silly. I was — well, I thought perhaps . . .'

'We'll stay the night if you like.'

Joanne looked up. 'Oh, no, I couldn't ask – '

'What do you say, Ted?'

'I'm not bothered. As long as there's somewhere to put me head down.'

'Are you sure?' Joanne's concern was genuine.

'Course I'm sure.' Ted laughed. 'You ought to know me by now. I usually say what I think.'

Joanne's body seemed to relax, the lines in her face eased away. 'I would be grateful. I've been so frightened since — since — '

'It's OK, our pleasure. Mind you, we haven't brought any overnight stuff.'

'I can lend Claire a nightie. I haven't got anything that'll fit you, though.'

'That's OK, I usually sleep in the altogether anyhow.' He grinned. 'I'd better warn you. I'll look a bit bristly round the chops in the morning.'

Claire laughed. 'I expect we'll be able to face that.'

Ted stood up. 'Tell you what. Claire and I'll go and explore the culinary resources of the village, and we'll have a nice little dinner party tonight — the three of us and Maudie. What d'you say?'

Joanne looked pleased. 'Sounds great.' Her smile changed to a frown. 'Your car – '

'What about it?'

'When you get back, perhaps you'd better put it out of sight.'

Ted nodded. 'Yeah, sounds like sense.'

'There's a small barn at the side of the house. If you move some of the stuff around, you'll get it in there.'

'Will do.'

* * *

Claire and Ted's trip for provisions took them longer than they expected, as they decided to get a few basic necessities, toothbrushes, razor, make-up, as well as the food. Some items they needed were not available in the village shop, and they ended up going to Yatton. Meanwhile Joanne prepared the beds and set about cleaning up the rest of the house. Although the vicar and the district nurse tried to keep an eye on the old lady, Maudie declined all offers of home help, and lived in just two rooms, the kitchen and her own bedroom. The rest was dusty and dirty, and mouse droppings were everywhere. The beds seemed damp, so Joanne threw open the windows, moved the mattresses into the sun, and hung all the bed-linen and blankets outside to get an airing.

By evening she was exhausted. Claire volunteered to cook the dinner while Joanne settled her great-aunt upstairs and took her a specially prepared meal, the old lady having first come down to say goodnight to 'Victor and Nellie'. The dining-room was unusable so they ate in the kitchen. After the meal, Ted leaned back and surveyed the scatter of dishes and the empty wine bottle.

'That was first rate. My compliments to the chef.'

'Mine too. Thanks, Claire.' Joanne raised her glass. 'Here's to the pair of you.'

Ted raised his glass in turn. 'And to you, Joanne, and we mustn't forget Paul.'

Mention of Paul brought them back to their own predicament. Ted opened another bottle of wine, and they talked and talked until they were too tired to think. Eventually Joanne stretched, yawned, and announced that she was going to bed.

'I'm going to sleep in Maudie's room, in case she gets up in the night and tries to wander round. Ted, you're in the big front bedroom. I hope you're not allergic to feathers, because there's an old stuffed mattress on that bed. And Claire, you're in the little single room at the back. Is that all right?'

'Suits me,' said Ted. 'I used to pluck chickens back home, and they never even made me sneeze.'

'I tried to give the beds a good airing this afternoon, so I don't think they'll be damp.'

Ted laughed. 'All that grub and the booze, I think I'll sleep if it's dripping wet.'

Claire got up and started piling plates to take to the sink.

'The washing up can wait till the morning. You can help me tidy up then.'

Claire did not take much persuading. 'Good idea. Let's be really decadent.' They left the washing up, went upstairs together, and said their goodnights.

Ted stripped off, sank into the softness of the down mattress, and lay back in the centre of the iron-framed double bed. He heard the ancient cistern flush, the clank of the chain and the attached mechanism reverberating along the linoleum-covered hall. He closed his eyes and was asleep in minutes.

* * *

He wasn't sure what first made him aware that there was someone in the room. He didn't think he had heard a noise, but he was certain that someone was there. Perhaps the old woman's having a wander, he thought. He held his breath and listened. The door! It was being carefully, slowly, closed. He heard a rustle of clothing. It was being closed from the inside! And it was someone being stealthy, certainly not the actions of a confused old lady. Ted changed his position in the bed, moving his legs and freeing the covers on the side away from the door. He tensed, ready to roll off the bed and onto the floor if he was attacked. His pulse was racing, blood thumping in his ears. He heard a soft footstep, and prepared himself to make a move.

'Ted?'

'Jesus Christ! Claire!'

He reached out and fumbled for the cord switch on the bedside lamp. He found it, and the weak bare bulb lit the room dimly.

Claire stood halfway between the door and the bed, shivering in the short, thin nightie Joanne had lent her.

'Did I frighten you?'

'Not so you'd notice. I just about managed not to shit the bed.'

'Sorry.'

Ted sat up. 'What's the matter?'

Claire came and sat on the bed. The cold had made her nipples erect, showing prominently. Ted tried to be gentlemanly and not look.

'I — it's creepy in my room. The bed's damp and lumpy. I keep hearing noises. And the way the moonlight shines in, it's really spooky.'

Ted reached out and touched her arm. 'Feeling lonely, huh?'

Claire looked directly at him. 'Yes. Very.'

He felt the mass of goose-bumps. 'And cold?'

'Freezing.'

'What time is it?'

'Two-thirty.'

'It's a long time till morning.'

'Yes.' Claire shivered.

'I suppose I should be gallant and offer you this lovely cosy warm bed, while I crawl off into your ghostly dank pit.'

He couldn't tell the expression in her eyes in the feeble light, but he saw the smile playing on her lips. 'I don't think I want you to be that gallant.'

'In that case, dare I offer . . . ?' His voice tailed off, a husky catch to it, as he lifted the corner of the cover nearest to Claire. She needed no further encouragement. In a moment she was in bed beside Ted. The warmth of the feathers and Ted's body enfolded themselves deliciously about her. She snuggled closer, felt his arms go round her. Her breathing quickened and she pressed her pelvis against his, feeling him already firm. Ted ran a hand up her back, causing a tingling sensation that went through her whole body.

As if he felt it too, Ted asked her softly. 'Is this really happening?'

Claire moved her face away. She gave a mischievous grin and looked into his eyes. 'It feels real enough to me.' She wriggled against him, then remembered they were not alone in the house. 'What if Auntie Maudie comes in?'

Ted raised himself up a little. 'She'll have to wait her turn.'

Claire looked up at the shadowed face, her desire almost overwhelming. 'Ted, I don't want to wait any longer for mine.'

They sank into the soft down, arms wrapped tightly around each other, caressing, exploring, moving, until they shared a long explosive moment of passionate release.

Slowly Claire relaxed. She had been biting her lip to stop herself crying out. She sensed that at the moment of orgasm she had been so oblivious that she could well have made a sound. They lay there for some minutes, enveloped in mutual contentment, arms around each other. Claire gave a deep sigh.

'Did we make a noise?'

'I don't know, I wasn't listening.'

'I thought I heard something.'

'Well it wasn't the earth moving, but I swear the bed is two feet nearer the window.'

They both chuckled, the movement making them aware of the pleasure of their continuing physical contact.

'I ought to go back to my pit.' Claire didn't sound very enthusiastic.

'You ought. We don't want to offend the mistress of the establishment.'

'In a minute.'

'OK — in a minute.'

Ted reached out and switched off the light.

Claire sounded sleepy. 'Good, though, wasn't it?'

Ted found her mouth in the dark, kissed her gently.

'You could say that.'

* * *

Ted surfaced to the sound of the curtains being drawn and sunlight streaming in. He blinked, trying to focus on Joanne. 'I've brought you a cup of tea. Claire seems to be up already.'

Ted tried to sit up, wincing at the pain from his rib. He glanced down and realised that Claire was still in the bed beside him. Perhaps if she stayed still, hidden by blankets in the voluminous feather mattress . . .

Claire's dishevelled head appeared. 'What's going on? Where —?' She looked up at Ted, then at Joanne. 'Oh, my God!' She sat up, clutching the clothes to her chest. 'Oh, Joanne, I'm sorry!'

Joanne did not seem upset, more quietly amused. 'It's all right. If I'd known, I'd have put you both in here anyway.'

'But we're not — weren't — that is, in the night I —'

Joanne laughed. 'Don't worry about it. Here, share this cup of tea and tell me all about it at breakfast. It'll be ready in ten minutes.' She went out.

The new lovers turned and smiled at each other.

'You look pretty happy, Miss Donaldson.'

'You look quite content yourself, Mr Parkes. If a little unshaven.'

'I hope we haven't upset Joanne.'

'I don't think so. You heard what she said.'

'In that case . . .' Ted caressed her breast then ran his hand down over her stomach. Claire shivered in delight, but pulled away.

'No, not again. Not now, anyway.'

She rolled out of bed and stood up. Ted would have expected her to wrap herself modestly in a sheet, but she unselfconsciously walked, naked, across the room to pick up her discarded nightie, which she slipped on over her head. Ted watched, enjoying the view and the sensual feeling of arousal it provoked.

'Right.' Claire stood near the bed. 'We've got things to do. You can't just lie there.'

Before he could make a move, she grabbed the bedclothes and swiftly pulled them off onto the floor. He lay there naked, startled. She nodded at his erection, and grinned. 'That'll have to wait.'

She went out, leaving him to scramble hastily into his clothes.

CHAPTER 35

Claire had to shout upstairs twice before Ted came down for some breakfast. He stumbled into the kitchen, unshaven, and the two women looked at him with amusement.

'Something tire you out?' Claire asked with a smile.

'Me? No!' He grinned sheepishly. 'I've been thinking.'

'Thinking? What about?' Claire felt a knot of unwelcome anxiety, and glanced at Joanne. She thought he was going to say, 'About us.' She knew she wasn't ready for that.

'About Paul, and what to do next.'

Joanne called over from the solid fuel stove, where some bacon was cooking slowly and making a mouth-watering smell.

'Have something to eat first, and then we'll sit round the table and talk over coffee.'

Aunt Maudie had been catered for earlier by Joanne, who had been up since seven. It was now nine-thirty. Ted ate hungrily and in silence, then helped them clear the dishes.

'All right, Einstein,' said Claire as they finished washing up and sat down with mugs of coffee, 'What has the Australian Super-brain got on its tiny mind?'

'Well, if you're going to be sarcastic . . .' He gave a very good imitation of a petulant child.

Joanne laughed. 'Come on, no sulking. You've obviously been thinking about it all through breakfast. What's bothering you?'

Ted sipped the hot liquid. 'I've been going over it all, again and again. Everything that's happened to us lately. Someone has tried to blackmail Joanne, threatened her little girl. And now she's suspended from work.' He looked at Claire. 'We've both had our places done over, and been physically assaulted. And earlier, I'm convinced someone tried to kill one of us.'

Claire nodded, her face grim. 'Poor Nurse Marvaine, you mean?'

'Exactly. And what's the common denominator?'

'Surely it's all down to Porthenoy?'

'Is it? Don't forget it was Christine Sansome who tried to finish off Joanne.'

'We don't know that for sure. Even Sergeant Clothier wasn't convinced.'

'It's too much of a coincidence.'

'So you think she is the key to it all?'

'No! Can't you see what I'm getting at? The common factor in all this is Paul.'

Joanne agreed. 'Yes, I can see that, but surely it's not Paul himself, but the communication research, and the computer programs you've been developing. That's what these people seem to be after.'

'They may be. But why? Because of the research itself? Or because of what the research might reveal?'

Claire shook her head. 'We'll never know, now. Only Paul can tell us that.'

Ted banged the table. 'Exactly! I'm sure that he holds the answers. I reckon he could tell us what it's all about!'

'So what good does it do? Why are you getting so excited?' Joanne asked.

'And we'll never get back into the hospital again, Ted, you know that.' Claire got up and poured more coffee. 'Porthenoy's got the Research Institute sewn up. We won't get back on the ward. Ever.'

'Who says we've got to work in the hospital?'

Claire laughed dryly. 'What do you suggest? We hook him up to a modem and work from home?'

'Hmm. I hadn't thought of that. Clever girl.' He considered briefly. 'Wouldn't work, though. All Porthenoy would have to do is go in and pull the plug.'

'So what is going on in that ex-convict's skull of yours?'

'We can't work on him there. So we get him out and work on him somewhere else. Like here, for example.'

'What!' Joanne was aghast.

'Don't be bloody stupid.' Claire was derisive. 'Imagine it: "Excuse me, Sister, we're just taking this comatose patient out for a little stroll. We'll be back in a jiff." And then we dash off down the street with him as if we're in a bed race.'

'Now just a minute —'

'Anyway, we'd need all the gear, the EEG, the computer, all of it.'

'We'd take that too.'

Claire laughed again. 'This is getting more and more ridiculous. We'd be no more than common criminals, kidnapping a patient, stealing expensive equipment.'

Ted nodded. 'I've thought of that. I'm not sure we *would* be criminals. I'm sure you can only be convicted of theft if it is your intention to deprive someone of something permanently. We can make it quite clear we are only borrowing the stuff.'

Claire snorted.

Ted was undeterred. 'No, wait. As for kidnapping, no one could say we were taking Paul against his will. Because no one knows what that is. But if we can talk to him afterwards — you know, communicate, as only we can — he may actually agree. And if we could prove it, well . . .'

'Sounds pretty far-fetched to me.' Claire was unimpressed.

Joanne felt the same. 'And think of the hue and cry. We'd have half the police in the country looking for us.'

'True. But what if we do it secretly, and smuggle him here? Who's to know? There are no neighbours popping in all the time, no one can see into the house.' He turned to Joanne. 'Does anyone else know you're here?'

'Well, my sister does, and Freda. But apart from them, no.'

'And Aunt Maudie isn't going to tell anyone — and if she did, they wouldn't believe her.'

'Yes, I can see that side of it,' Joanne said thoughtfully. 'And I'm quite capable of looking after him. Provided we had enough IV fluids, drip sets and so on.'

Claire gave her a look of alarm. 'You're not even considering this crazy idea, are you?'

Ted sensed an ally. 'Look, what have we got to lose? We're out of a job, and so possibly is Joanne.'

'Yes, but we hope to get another one some time. And we won't if we're branded criminals. We'll none of us ever be let near a patient again.'

Ted's spirits sank. 'That's true. But I thought if we were successful, if we could follow the research through and publish . . .'

'You mean we'd end up as world-famous Nobel Prize winners.'

He looked up at Claire ruefully. 'Something like that.'

'I really can't see what we'd gain, Ted,' said Joanne. 'Surely now that we're out of the picture and can't get anything more from Paul anyway, we won't have any more threats or harassment. We're not a danger to anyone any more.'

Ted sighed. 'You're probably right. But it gets my goat that there's someone who's caused us all this trouble and is getting away with it.'

'I know,' Claire sympathised, 'but I think it's best left to the police.'

'But the police can't do what we can.'

'How do you mean?'

'Ask the man who probably knows the answer.'

* * *

Claire sat perched on the bed, keeping the old lady company for a while. Joanne had gone to the chemist's in Yatton for some supplies. Maudie still thought her visitor was her long-dead sister, Nellie. Her lined face was alive with pleasure. She reached out a thin arm from the armchair in which she was comfortably settled, and placed her hand on Claire's.

'I'm *so* pleased to see you, my dear.' The old lady withdrew her hand and hugged herself with excitement. 'Who'd have thought it? You coming all the way down from Scotland just to see me? And you with your bad arm.' She looked up, puzzlement furrowing her brow. 'Where's Victor?'

Claire was not sure how to handle the situation. Trying to persuade this charming old woman that she was not her sister had proved impossible. Now Claire didn't want to disappoint her, she seemed so pleased. But she felt guilty at being party to a deception, although Joanne's advice had been just to play along.

'He's downstairs. In the garden.'

'Oh, yes, your Victor, he always did like his garden. Roses. That's what he likes, isn't it? Roses.' She chuckled to herself. 'Do you remember that time he gave Mother a fright? He came in one day and said, "I've brought the doctor." ' Maudie tittered like a child, then chewed ruminatively. Claire waited. 'Mother went all of a dither. Her first thought was that someone was ill, and the second that she couldn't afford to pay him.' She looked at Claire as if expecting some response.

'I — I'm sorry, I don't understand.'

'Course you do.' The old lady gave a prompting nudge. 'You were *there*. Mind you, none of us knew there was a rose called "The Doctor". Victor had brought Mother a rose!'

She nodded to herself repeatedly, chuckling softly. Her head began to drop, her eyelids drooping. Suddenly she lifted them up, her expression anxious. 'You do remember, don't you, Nellie?'

Claire reached out and laid a hand on the scrawny arm. 'Yes, Maudie, I remember.'

The old lady smiled gently, closed her eyes, and was soon asleep.

* * *

Claire found Ted in the garden. She walked up behind him, hoping to surprise him, but he heard her and turned.

'Hello, Miss Donaldson.'

She moved towards him, and went into his arms, laid her head on his chest. 'Hello, Mr Parkes.' She gave him a hug.

Ted reached down and slowly ran his finger down Claire's healing cheek. 'I — I, er — keep thinking about last night.'

'So do I.' She glanced up at him with a smile, and sighed. 'Despite everything, I feel really good. Or am I kidding myself?'

'I wasn't kidding, if that's what you mean. I feel sort of —' He wasn't very good at this. 'Sort of —' He hesitated again. He'd never had occasion to profess sincere affection for a woman before.

Claire was looking at him expectantly when they heard the scream from the house.

Ted moved first. 'That's Joanne!' He started running, Claire followed, shouting. 'My God! What's the matter!'

As they got to the back door, Joanne burst into the garden. She seemed completely out of control, face twisted with anguish. Claire had a fleeting thought. Surely if it was the old lady, she wouldn't be so . . .

Ted held Joanne by the shoulders. 'Come on, girl, steady up. Whatever is it? What's happened?'

Joanne stood there, taking deep rasping breaths, trying to regain control.

'It's Lucinda. She's gone. Someone's taken her.'

* * *

It was some time before Joanne calmed enough to give them the full story. She sat at the kitchen table, Ted and Claire on either side.

'On — on my way back from the village, I went to the phone box to call Karen and speak to Lucinda. Karen was in a dreadful state, praying I would call. It had only just happened, the police hadn't even got there.' She took another tissue from the box on the table and blew her nose noisily.

'Was she quite sure?' Claire tried to sound reassuring. 'I mean, last time —'

Joanne sniffed, tried hard to hold herself in check. 'No, there's no mistake. Someone saw. They were on the swings. In the playground down the road. Piers and Lucinda. You can almost see it from the house.' She bit her lip. 'I've let them do it myself, when we've stayed before. It's such a quiet place. But somebody — somebody —'

Claire stood and leaned over her friend, waiting for her to be calm enough to continue. After a minute, Joanne gave Claire's hand a squeeze. 'I'm all right now.' She swallowed. 'Somebody saw what happened. Piers started shouting, and this old man walking his dog saw a figure — he wasn't sure if it was a man or a woman — carrying Lucinda off to a car. She was — she was crying.' Tears were streaming down Joanne's face, but she went on with her story. 'Poor Piers didn't know what to do. The old man tried to give chase, but — she was gone.'

* * *

Claire watched Joanne put some things into an overnight case.

'I've really got to go — go up to Karen's, speak to the police.'

'Of course you must. It's OK, honestly. I'm just thankful we were here. I'm quite happy to look after Maudie for a bit. I'm sure I'll manage, and she's such a lovely old soul.'

'I — I hope I won't be long. It depends — '

'Stop worrying about this end.'

There was a shout from downstairs. 'That'll be Ted back from the garage. Come on.'

They stood round the car. Ted had readily agreed to take Joanne straight up to Cheltenham, and had rushed off to get petrol while she was packing. He put her bag on the back seat. 'All set?'

'Ready.' Joanne embraced Claire briefly, then stood back with moist eyes. 'Thanks, Claire.'

'No problem. Go on, taxi's waiting.'

Ted eased himself behind the wheel carefully, closed the door, and wound down the window. Claire put her head in and gave him a kiss on the mouth. 'Take care.'

'Don't worry.' He looked from one woman to the other. 'This may not be the time to say it, but it's obvious this business isn't over yet. We just can't let things be.'

Joanne looked determined. 'I've been thinking the same thing.'

Ted's hand was on the steering wheel. Claire placed hers over it. 'And me.'

'If Lucinda doesn't turn up double quick, I think we've got to talk to Paul Sansome.'

CHAPTER 36

Claire rang Joanne that evening from the phone box in the village. Her friend was incoherent, distressed, barely able to hold back the tears. There had been no sign of Lucinda. The police had been at the house all day, there had been bulletins on the local radio, and an appeal on television earlier that evening.

So far, nothing. No leads, no clues.

The only good news for Claire was that Ted was on his way back. Although she had not experienced any problems with the old lady, she had not been looking forward to spending the night alone in the big, isolated house. She was not afraid of Aunt Maudie, but knew she was often more agitated at night, and wasn't sure how she would cope.

Ted arrived at a little after eight. Claire waited anxiously as he put the car back in the barn and closed the doors. Only then did he proceed to tell her, in more coherent fashion than Joanne had managed, about the events of the day. He had spoken to the police, and put them as fully in the picture about the threats to Joanne and her daughter as he could.

'Did you tell them the *whole* story?'

'Everything. I told them about Joanne's suspension, about our work and Porthenoy's rejection of us and the project. I even hinted heavily that the creep's a homo, wondered what they might make of it.'

'He won't be very pleased about *that*!'

'Too right he won't! Then that chap Clothier turned up to talk to us. Seems he's co-ordinating the investigation on Nurse Marvaine, the attacks on us and Joanne, Mrs Sansome's arrest.' Ted turned his head at an angle and nodded contemplatively. 'He looks a bit of a slob, that guy. But I think he's pretty shrewd.' He laughed, a harsh sound. 'Either that, or he conceals the fact he thinks we're nuts very well.'

Claire made a meal for Maudie, and took it up to her room. 'I'm sorry it's so late, Maudie. I'm not sure what you like, so I just made something simple. I hope you like it.'

The old lady looked at her quizzically. 'What *do* you mean, you don't know what I like? How long have you been coming here and cooking for me?'

'Well, we only came yesterday.'

'Don't try and play tricks with me, Joanne.' She sounded genuinely annoyed.

'But — but I'm not Joanne. I'm Clai — I mean, Nellie.'

Maudie looked shocked. 'Joanne! How could you! Nellie's been dead for years!'

Claire felt a shiver go up her spine. This was taking her out of her depth. Damp broke out on her brow. 'I — I'm sorry, Maudie. Won't you try and have something to eat now?'

'Very well. But no more nonsense, Joanne.' She canted her head and raised her wispy grey eyebrows. 'All right, dear?'

'Yes, all right. No more nonsense.' Claire turned to go, ashamed that she was in so much of a hurry to leave. She got to the door and opened it.

'Joanne!'

Claire was about to close the door when she realised that Maudie was addressing her. She paused, turned. 'Yes, Maudie?'

'Whatever made you mention Nellie after all these years?'

'I thought you — that is, I — I don't really know, Maudie. I'm sorry if I upset you.'

The old lady beamed. 'No, not at all. She'll be pleased she's been remembered after so long.' She raised a forkful of potato, put it in her mouth, and began chewing. Claire closed the door gently, shut her eyes, and sighed deeply.

Later, she helped the elderly woman into bed, afraid any moment that she would start to be difficult. But she seemed sleepy and compliant, and soon was settled back against her customary four pillows. Claire leaned over and patted her hand. 'Sleep well. See you in the morning.'

The old lady scrutinised her face with drowsy eyes. 'You'd better put some iodine on that cut.'

Claire touched the scar on her face and smiled. 'I'll try and find some.'

'Goodnight, Joanne.'

'Goodnight, Maudie.'

* * *

Two hours later, Ted and Claire climbed the stairs together. They went into Ted's bedroom. It was now the end of the first week in August, the day had been hot, and the night was a much warmer one than the last, when cold had been the excuse that drove Claire to Ted's room. Claire marvelled at the artlessness of it all. They undressed and got into bed, talking naturally, without any comment, as if they had been doing it for years. They lay on their sides, facing each other.

Claire reached out and stroked Ted's face. 'I keep thinking of Joanne and Lucinda.'

'Yeah. Me too. It's a bastard.'

'I — I don't think I want to — well —'

Ted smiled gently. 'I know what you mean, pretty one. Wouldn't have our minds on the job, eh?'

She snuggled in to him, grateful for his understanding. Her mind seemed to be whirling with thoughts, about Lucinda, old Maudie in the next room, Paul. She felt Ted's arm heavy on her shoulder, felt the warmth, felt relaxation, drifted into sleep . . .

* * *

The next three days were uneventful. Maudie behaved remarkably well, although Claire found herself being mistaken for several different people from the old lady's past, as well as Joanne. She got up once in the middle of the night, tried to go downstairs, slipped and fell near the bottom, her cry alerting them. Fortunately she did not hurt herself. But then they had to sit with her while she rambled unintelligibly for over an hour before falling asleep again.

When they went back to bed, they made love again, less cautious this time of their injuries, which were healing rapidly. Despite the tensions and the worries, Claire found that during this glorious interlude she was oblivious to everything but the joyous sensuality of their bodies.

They found they had plenty of time to talk — about their new-found relationship, about Lucinda, but mostly about Paul and their predicament. They went over it again and again, piece by piece. And got nowhere.

On the fourth day, Claire made her now regular call to Joanne from the village phone box in the early evening. Joanne announced, despite Claire's protestations that they were coping well with Maudie, that she was coming back to the house.

* * *

'There was nothing much more I could do there,' Joanne said, as they had coffee in the kitchen together the next morning. 'The fact is I *wanted* to return. There's been no progress in Cheltenham. The interest of everyone there seems to be fading already. I'm sure they think Lucinda is dead.'

Claire was shocked at this blunt pronouncement. 'Oh, Joanne, don't say that! I'm sure they —'

'Don't worry. That's their view, not mine. I'm her mother. I *know* she's still alive!' She spoke with a determined vehemence, staring from Ted to Claire and back as if daring them to contradict her.

'So — what do you want to do now, Joanne?' Ted asked tentatively.

'She's got to be somewhere. With somebody. The police don't seem to have a clue. Apart from the old man's description, no one seems to have seen anything suspicious. They've done a house-to-house through the whole area. She isn't there.'

'But what can we *do*?' Claire shrugged and turned her palms upwards.

Joanne looked at her directly. 'You know damn well what we must do. There's nothing else left. We don't know anything. The police don't know anything. There's only one person who might know *something.*'

Ted nodded. 'Paul.'

* * *

They talked, drew up plans, made notes, prepared a room, made phone calls in the village, went over it all again. It took two more days before they called a halt. At eleven o'clock on that second night, Ted threw down his pen and drank from the last can of beer.

'That's it. We've got to stop now. We've got a scheme that *may* work. But if we fiddle about with it any more, we'll all go off the boil. I say we go for it tomorrow — it's Sunday, and I reckon that's our best bet. There won't be many supervisors about, and Joanne checked the rota on the ward on the phone: in the afternoon there's no one senior who knows her. That's when we do it.'

Claire was unhappy. 'In broad daylight?'

'Christ, it'll look a bloody sight more suspicious if we try it at three o'clock in the morning. It's got to look routine, remember? And look at all the stuff we've got to get — enough for two weeks, we decided. If we go back for more, we'll be rumbled, for sure.'

The two women exchanged worried glances, but both nodded their agreement.

Ted raised his can. 'Then let's drink to it.'

Joanne reached out with her mug of hot chocolate, Claire touched with her wine glass. With this strange combination of drinks and containers, the toast was solemnly made. They spoke as one, uncannily speaking together as if they'd rehearsed the line.

'To Lucinda, Paul, and success.'

CHAPTER 37

Ted parked the Transit van in the hospital car park against a wall where he hoped it would be unobtrusive yet near the chosen ground-floor emergency exit. He had come into Bristol by train earlier in the day and hired the van from a previously identified back-street garage that didn't ask many questions, especially when paid in cash. He had used a false name, a simple disguise, and had done his best to copy a West Country accent. On the way back, he had collected all his computer disks that had survived the break-in.

'OK, girls,' he said, looking at the two women huddled in the back. 'Time to get started.' Joanne was in her uniform, Claire wore a skirt and blouse, Ted sweater and jeans.

'You'll be all right here?' Claire looked at the nurse anxiously.

'Of course! Have you got the list?'

Claire patted her pocket. 'In here.'

'And you know where to go for the coats?' Joanne leaned forward earnestly.

'Pretty sure. Good job we know the place well enough by now.'

Ted had another look round. There were not many people about, and no one was paying them any attention. He opened the door. 'Let's go.'

Claire climbed between the front seats, leaving Joanne sitting on the floor in the back, got out of the van, and closed the door. She and Ted then walked casually round to the main entrance, trying to talk to each other as they passed through the double glass doors. They avoided the eye of the man at the inquiry desk, wanting to give the impression of two people at home in this environment, who knew where they were going. On down a long corridor, direction signs every few yards, almost every inch of wall-space covered with health education and information posters of some sort or another. Then round the corner towards the main lifts, an algae-encrusted indoor pool on their left, below the still waters of which they could see a carpet of coins. Ted wondered irreverently how often the incumbent goldfish were brained by a well-intentioned donation of loose change.

Past the lifts, down the service stairs, they followed the signs to the laundry, concentrating on their route. Then they both saw it at the same time: a labelled doorway, with a large grey plastic bin on wheels outside. Ted went up to the bin and looked inside.

'This'll do!' Claire looked over his shoulder and pulled a face. The laundry-bin was full of red-stained green and white gowns. 'Must be the theatre one.' The door stood slightly ajar nearby. Ted nodded towards it. 'Maybe they're in there.'

Claire looked up and down the corridor. 'But supposing —?'

'Joanne said there wouldn't be anybody here on a Sunday afternoon.'

'Go on, then. I'll keep watch.'

Ted disappeared into the room. The hum of machinery and the heat in the basement made her edgy. She wouldn't hear approaching footsteps easily. Sweat got in her eyes, made them sting. She was about to go and urge Ted to hurry, when he emerged triumphant. 'Put it on, quick.'

Claire struggled into a crumpled brown linen coat, and Ted did the same.

'How do I look?' He tried to smooth out some of the creases.

It was a little small for him, but Claire did not want to hang about any longer. 'It'll do.' She tied a scarf round her hair, then moved closer to Ted, handed him one of the home-made name-tags that approximated to the type worn by the hospital porters. 'You do mine, I'll do yours.'

Duly labelled, they headed for the stairs, then Ted stopped and went back.

'Come *on*!' Claire called after him impatiently.

'Nearly forgot this.' He went to the bin holding the soiled theatre clothing, pushed it to the clothing store and quickly threw most of the contents inside. He left a few gowns in the bottom, pulled the door shut and set off after Claire, pushing the trolley.

'Solves our transport problem,' he said, and pressed the button for the elevator.

They stood in the lift with a tired-looking young nurse who stared at the floor the whole time. She got out on the second floor, they went on to the fourth. As they proceeded upwards alone, Claire gave Ted a list from her pocket, then held his arm.

'Supposing there's some sort of emergency and the theatre's teeming with people? They'll be after all the sort of stuff we want.'

'Could be more of a help than a hindrance.' Ted waited as the doors opened. 'Anyway, we're here. We'll just have to suck it and see.'

Claire tried to moisten her lips. 'I don't think I could suck anything, my mouth's so dry.'

Ted ignored her attempt at humour, and glanced down at the paper she had given him.

'Round to the right, past the double doors to the main operating theatre suite, then second on the left.' They started moving off, Ted pushing the linen-trolley, but before they turned the corner they could hear footsteps approaching. A young doctor, one of the weekend duty housemen, came into view. He looked exhausted, barely glanced at them as he passed. They rounded the bend, Ted counted off the doors, stopped.

'This should be the one.' He pointed to the cream-coloured door before them. Someone had written 'IVs' on it in felt-tip pen. Ted reached out and put his hand on the door. At the same time a bleeping noise started. They both jumped, afraid they had set off an alarm. Moments later the young doctor retraced his steps past them, cursing softly under his breath as he went to answer his pager.

Ted stepped inside the room. The light was already on. On one side were boxes upon boxes of various types of intravenous fluids, pre-sterilized in their plastic bags; on the other, labelled shelves stocked with packages of tubing, needles — it seemed the choice was overwhelming.

'See if you can get that thing inside.'

Claire just managed to pull the trolley in behind her, and closed the door. She looked at the bewildering array of medical supplies. 'What do we want?'

Ted consulted his list.

'This shelf here looks like the parenteral fluids. Yes — look, nutritional fluids on the top here. I'll start with the Vamin and the Intralipid. You get the Addamel and Solivito, and then chuck in a dozen giving sets — they're on the shelf by your left hand.'

He dragged out several boxes of various fluid preparations designed for intravenous feeding and placed them carefully in the bottom of the trolley. Claire dropped the boxes of needles, tubing, drip sets, and connectors on top, then Ted covered them with the few soiled garments he had left in the bin.

Claire opened the door, then jumped as Ted hissed, 'Wait!'

'What's the matter?'

'Nearly forgot the normal saline and the dextrose.' He grabbed some plastic bags containing clear liquid from a lower shelf, and dropped them in the bin, covering them carefully. 'All right. Take a peek.'

Claire looked out, stepped through the door, then beckoned. 'All clear.'

Ted pushed the cart, heavier now, before him, past the doors to the theatre complex, on towards the lift.

They heard the theatre doors open behind them, but did not look round.

'Excuse me!'

Claire looked across at Ted. She felt she wanted to leave everything, run for the emergency stairs. They both kept walking.

'Excuse me, just a minute, please.' The voice was female, authoritative.

Ted stopped, murmured to Claire, 'Let me do the talking.'

He turned and saw a gowned nurse standing in the theatre complex entrance, as if afraid to come fully out of her sanctum.

'Yes, you. Come here. Quickly, please.'

Ted pushed the trolley a few paces back the way they had come, then released it, stepping forward on his own. 'Is there a problem?' he asked, trying to disguise his Australian accent and keep his voice steady at the same time.

'I want you to go down to Casualty. We're trying to do an epidural here, and we've got a duff batch of needles. The anaesthetist says there'll be some in the Casualty Theatre. Go and get them, will you?'

Ted felt relieved but tense in the same moment. This nurse wasn't interested in the contents of their trolley, she merely wanted him to run an errand. He looked at her blankly.

She frowned. 'What's the matter? This is urgent!'

'Sorry.' He went back to the trolley, started to push it to the lifts.

'Leave that! Just go for the needles.'

'Where —?'

'Sister will tell you. Now go!'

Ted let go the laundry-bin and went to the lift.

The woman's voice followed him. 'Use the stairs. It'll be quicker.'

He touched his forelock in the only deferential gesture he could think of, feeling ridiculous. 'Yes, ma'am. Sorry.' To Claire, who was watching was dismay, he said, 'You take that. I'll see you near Side Room 3.' Then he fled down the stairs.

Claire looked back towards the theatre doors. The nurse had gone. She pressed the lift button, hand trembling, wanting to empty her bladder, wanting all this to be over. The lift doors opened, and she manoeuvred the trolley inside.

Once on the floor below, she felt incredibly conspicuous, standing in the corridor that led to the Neurological Unit and Paul Sansome. Several people went by, some looking lost and preoccupied — visitors, she thought. But others moved efficiently, purposefully, as if they belonged: various members of staff, of whom she was meant to be one. She was terrified someone would recognise her, ask her what she was doing, or that some other member of the portering staff would confront her.

It was so obvious she was just hanging around. She decided to push the trolley back to lift area, just to make it look as if she was doing something. Where the hell was Ted? She glanced at her watch. He'd been gone fifteen minutes now. Were they on to him? She expected any minute that someone would point her out: 'There she is! That's the one!' And it would be over almost before they had begun.

She reached the large lobby where the lifts were accommodated, and began to turn the trolley awkwardly to retrace her steps. The lift doors opened, she saw the big man in the brown coat approaching. *Ted!* She felt herself pale, her stomach turning, as she realised it was another porter. She tried desperately to look relaxed as he went by, giving her a curious glance. Closing her eyes, she breathed deeply as she heard the footsteps receding, but opened them again in near panic as she heard them stop, then return.

'Thought I was the only one on this floor today,' a voice said from behind her.

Claire's mouth was dry. She turned, hoping she did not look like the frightened rabbit she felt.

'I — I'm doing a special trip for theatre.' She nodded at the linen-trolley.

Her imagined colleague leaned forward and looked at the soiled gowns. 'Busy up there, are they?'

Claire remembered Ted's errand. 'They're doing an epidural. They've had some problems.'

The porter nodded knowingly. 'Typical.' He looked Claire up and down. 'Don't I know you from somewhere?' His expression became almost a leer. 'Pretty girl like you, I'm sure I'd remember.'

'I — I have worked here before.' Claire tried to take consolation from the fact that the make-up disguising her facial scar must be effective. Or else he isn't fussy, she told herself.

'Thought so. Maybe I'll see you in the canteen later, eh?' He assumed a relaxed pose, leaning forward, one arm resting on the bin.

Claire felt a desperation overwhelming her. This man was trying to chat her up, and Ted might appear at any minute. That would be much harder to explain.

'Yes, maybe later —'

A nursing sister came up to them, but ignored them and jabbed fiercely at a lift button. Claire's new acquaintance gave an annoyed scowl, took a step back, then turned on his heel. 'See you later,' he called over his shoulder, then hurried off. Claire set off blindly down the corridor in front of her, pushing the trolley with trembling hands and weak legs. God, I'll never survive this. Two close shaves and I can hardly stand. She heard the lift doors close, stopped her headlong rush. The lobby was clear. She turned the trolley, caught the uninterested eye of a student nurse who came out of an office, then made her way back towards the lifts. She heard footsteps on the emergency stairs as she passed them, fought down the desire to relinquish her burden and flee the hospital, and moved on. More footsteps approaching, a hand on her shoulder. *That man!*

'Claire! Stop a minute, will you!'

Claire turned, almost fell against Ted. 'Oh, thank God! I've been near to abandoning ship, waiting here.'

'Sorry. I just had to do that errand.'

'What took you so long?'

'Got lost. Then they couldn't find the bloody needles.'

'Why didn't you just sneak off, instead of leaving me here?' Claire knew her annoyance was unjustified, but her fright suppressed her reason.

'That would only have drawn attention. Besides, it was a genuine emergency. I didn't want to be responsible for someone being hurt because they thought equipment was on the way when it wasn't.'

'Sorry.' She laid a hand on his arm. 'I'm so scared, Ted. I don't know if I can carry this through.'

'Christ, don't get cold feet now.' He gripped her shoulder, making her wince. 'If you think of nothing else, think of Lucinda. This is for her.'

Claire nodded, fought back moistness from her vision. 'OK.' She looked about her. No one was paying attention. 'What now?'

'We wait for Joanne.' He looked at his wrist. 'She should be here any minute.'

'I feel so conspicuous hanging around here. I've already been chatted up by another porter.'

Ted looked at her in alarm. 'Did he rumble you?'

'I don't think so. A grim-looking senior nurse turned up and he scuttled off.'

They heard the lift doors open. A junior doctor came out and almost ran past them.

Claire began to have further doubts. The idea was that Joanne would come in her uniform, and commandeer a student nurse as an unwitting accomplice, one who would not know who she was and hence associate her with being suspended from duty. She had checked the duty rota for Paul's ward on the Neurological Unit, to find out when there would be no senior staff known to her on duty. There were none this Sunday afternoon, overall responsibility obviously having been delegated to a staff nurse on another ward in the unit. But it would only take one person in the know to challenge her . . .

'Follow me, please.' The familiar voice spoke authoritatively. Joanne walked briskly past them with barely a glance. She wore soft-soled shoes, her approach had been almost silent. They fell in behind her, Ted now pushing the trolley. They turned into the corridor that led to the Neurological Unit, and after only a few yards Joanne stopped and held open a door.

'In there.'

They all squeezed in, trolley first. Joanne looked pale, but seemed completely calm. Claire felt a rush of admiration for this woman. Under suspension from this very hospital, her child kidnapped, yet she was looking completely in control as they prepared to abduct a patient!

Joanne pointed to the shelves around her. 'The naso-gastric tube feeding equipment and special solutions are all here.' She reached in her pocket. 'Have you got the theatre gown?' She directed the question at Claire, who nodded. 'Put it on, and wear this.' She handed Claire a paper cap. 'Now you're a nurse. Ted, you're still a porter.'

'Right.'

'Load this thing with what we want, but spread it out in the bottom. There's a lot more to go in yet. Then go straight to Side Room 3. Take the trolley, and go in with Paul. Ted, you start dismantling the EEG machine. Claire, you can start packing the computer. If anyone asks, just say you're waiting for Sister. I hope I won't be long.'

'Good luck.' Claire almost whispered the words.

Joanne looked from one to the other, took a deep breath, compressed her lips, then let it out slowly through her nose. 'Thanks. See you in gaol.' The door closed behind her.

Claire abandoned her brown coat, tried not to look too closely at the blood-stains on the theatre gown she took from the bottom of the trolley. Ted tied the ribbons at back and neck, and she donned her cap. Ted scanned his list and then the shelves, putting small plastic bags of flexible tubing, catheters, large syringes, connectors, clamps into the bin.

'These are going to be the bastards,' he said to Claire as she came to help him. He was pointing to some large plastic bottles of liquid, shrink-wrapped onto cardboard trays. He turned his head to read the label. 'Osmolite. That's the stuff. Doesn't look much like food to me.'

Claire hefted one down. 'Christ! It's heavy. How many do we need?'

Ted looked at the paper again. 'How many in a pack?'

Claire counted. 'Twelve.'

'Three packs should do it.' He took two more from the shelves and placed them in the trolley. It was nearly half full now of the items they had acquired. He arranged them to make a little more space. He made a quick reference to the list. 'That's it. Let's go.'

Claire opened the door into the corridor, and Ted pulled the laundry trolley after them, its wheels squeaking in protest at the unaccustomed weight. They went past the ward office, where Claire quickly looked through the glass-panelled door and saw Joanne addressing two young nurses. She felt a slight easing of her tension now that they were at least temporarily on familiar territory. She opened the door and Ted pushed the trolley into Paul's room.

She thought he looked thinner, weaker. Could that be? It was only just over two weeks since they had last seen him. She went over to the bed. His eyes were open, unseeing, making the random movements she had become accustomed to. His breathing was regular. His naso-gastric tube was taped to the side of his face, the drip running slowly into his arm. The electrode fittings that Porthenoy had so skilfully attached were in place, and the stainless steel cradle still restricted his head movements. She turned and surveyed the complex equipment which Ted was already feverishly dismantling.

He looked up at her. 'At least the bloody stuff's still here.'

She hadn't even considered that it might have been removed. Perhaps Porthenoy was planning to get someone else to try and carry on their research, as he had threatened. Either that, or it had just been abandoned, and administrative apathy had allowed it to remain.

'Come on, girl. Park the hard disk, then start disconnecting the computer.'

Claire moved into action, switched on, waited an impatient few moments while the machine warmed up, issued the instructions that would make it safe to move the hard disk without damage, then switched off and began removing cables, coiling wires. It took only minutes before she was carefully placing the various components into their ersatz transportation — the monitor, the PC with its external hard disk and massive 196-megabyte memory, two spare removable hard disks, microphone and leads, headphones, the intricate cables that connected with the EEG machine. The trolley was three-quarters full now.

Meanwhile Ted was parking the disks on the portable EEG computer, folding down the liquid crystal screen, stowing the EEG cartridge safely so that it would not get too shaken up. They did not take up much morc of thc diminishing space.

'That'll have to do. Cover them with a blanket off the bed.'

Claire did as he suggested, trying to arrange the blanket so that it did not appear to be covering hard angular surfaces.

The door opened and they both whirled round guiltily.

Joanne came in. 'God, you'll have to do better than that. If anyone else saw your reaction then, they'd know you were up to no good without having to ask.'

'We'll try. We've got as much in as we can.' Ted nodded at the trolley. How are you doing?'

'All right, I think.' She patted her pocket. 'I've got a supply of Paul's drugs. And I've persuaded the two nurses that Paul has to go for an emergency scan. One of them will help me move him. I filled in a form and forged one of the doctor's signatures before I went into the office. That means they won't get suspicious at least until we're on the ground floor.'

'You don't think they'll be checking? Surely they'd been told another nurse was in charge?'

'Can't be sure, but they looked pretty much as though they accepted what I told them. As long as the staff nurse doesn't turn up in the next ten minutes.'

'They're getting the stretcher trolley?'

'Should be here any moment. Ted, you've got all that stuff in the laundry-bin, so you'd better make your trip now. You go with him, Claire, and I'll get Paul ready.'

'But I'm in my gown. I'll look funny going outside in this.'

Joanne wasn't to be diverted. 'Go as far as the exit. Ted'll have to make two trips from there.' She looked at them both. 'Go on!'

'Come on, then. Waggons roll.'

Claire tugged at the trolley. It was now heavy and overloaded. She had to jerk it to get it moving, and the little wheels protested loudly. 'God, I can hardly move the thing!'

Ted moved over to her. 'Let me help.'

Between them, they got it going, though the wheels seemed to make an attention-demanding squeal as they went back along the corridor and turned into the lift lobby.

'Remember,' Ted said quietly as they waited alone for the lift to arrive. 'Just act as if you belong, as if you know your purpose. I don't think we'll be challenged.'

They had trouble pushing the overloaded cart into the lift, and a young nurse who was going down helped drag it over the threshold.

'Whatever's in there?' she asked with a smile.

'Lot of wet stuff,' said Ted, trying to look jocular.

The laundry room was in the basement. They hoped no one would comment on the fact that they got out on the ground floor. No one did. They started to do some careful navigating. Through the medical out-patients, fortunately deserted on a Sunday, past the endoscopy suite.

'There's the sign to the Haematology Department. Joanne said we go left here, then —' He paused as they turned the corner. 'Yes, here it is, down this slope.'

They set off down the poorly-lit incline, the wheels on the cart increasing their noisy objection as they picked up speed.

'Christ!' Ted cried out in agony.

'What's the matter?'

'My rib. Must have . . . pulled something . . . trying to . . . hold back . . . all this weight.' He was fighting to help Claire slow the trolley. Claire leaned back to get more purchase, but she chose a particularly smooth patch on the polished floor. She sat down heavily, and her hands lost their grip. Ted was well in front of her now, slithering and sliding, desperate to hold on to the trolley and stay upright. She shouted a warning as she saw his legs go under him. The trolley charged on, dragging him behind it.

'Let it go!' she shouted, but he hung on. The trolley veered as it reached the bottom, crashed into the wall, Ted alongside. Claire watched in horror as the large grey container slowly fell over onto him.

'Aaaggh!' He yelled, at the same time trying to cut off the sound. Claire was certain it was only a matter of moments before someone came to check on all the noise. She struggled to her feet and scrambled down into the gloom at the bottom of the slope, and tried to right the cart which was pinning Ted to the floor across his lower chest.

She tugged, felt her back straining. Ted, white-faced and sweating, tried to push as she pulled. The EEG computer and a box of disks fell out onto the floor, then slowly the cart came upright. Ted lay panting, his face twisted, holding his side where his broken rib lanced him with fiery pain.

'Ted, you've got to get up.' She tried to pull his free arm. 'Someone'll come.'

'A minute. Must have a minute.'

'There's no time. Come *on*!'

Gasping with jags of pain, Ted got slowly to his feet, Claire helping. She looked up the slope. Miraculously, no one was coming to investigate. She looked about, almost shouted, triumphant. 'Look! There!'

The emergency exit was no more than yards away, just where Joanne had told them. She held Ted until he was leaning on the cart, stooped to replace the fallen box and computer, then went to the one-way exit, lifted the bar, and pushed. A sliver of light appeared, then the door jammed. She pushed harder. It moved another few inches, but stuck firm. She couldn't move it any farther.

'Oh, bloody hell!' She dropped her head. Surely it was all over, all this effort pointless.

'What's the matter?'

'Door's stuck.' She was shocked to hear her voice like a plaintive wail of anguish.

'Have a look. Most be something outside.'

Claire made herself bend down, squint through the crack, look under the door: Yes there is something, a piece of wood, under the door. If I can just get my hand through . . . She swore again as she forced her narrow wrist through the gap, scrabbled with her fingers, felt a nail break, scraped skin off on the concrete. Clamping her jaw, she forced her fingers under the wood, pushed, pulled, levered. Splinters went into her palm. The wound on her face pulled with the grimace of effort. She was getting frenzied, her thoughts irrational, lost her temper — Come on you bastard! Come on, why won't the fucking thing —?

Suddenly it was free, the wood came away, the door swung open. Claire found herself on her hands and knees looking up into the bright August sunshine that washed over her. It took a moment, squinting into the light, to confirm that the doors opened onto the car park. The van was not ten yards away.

Panting, she struggled to her feet. 'Keys! Give me the keys!'

Ted supported himself with one hand, fumbled in his pocket. 'Here.' He held them out.

Claire snatched them, and set off for the van. Going round the back, she opened the double doors. She looked in dismay at the 15-inch step up into the rear floor area. She almost stamped her foot in tearful frustration, swore aloud. Ted was meant to do this, how could they possibly lift that damn great trolley in here?

A car came into the car park, stopped nearby. Claire didn't even look, left the doors open, and set off for the emergency exit, noting with relief that an old lady and a younger couple, obviously visitors, were making their way from the car in the direction of the main entrance.

She slid back into the gloom through the narrow opening and, as her eyes adjusted, was surprised to find the runaway trolley next to the exit. Ted was clinging to it, his breathing seeming to echo along the dusty concrete passage-way. Still no one else in sight.

'You idiot, you shouldn't have tried to move it!'

'Thought I heard someone coming,' he gasped.

'Wait here,' Claire commanded, wondering fleetingly why she wasn't just weeping helplessly in despair instead of trying to rescue something from the débacle.

She heaved at the trolley, got it going, bumped the door open with her back, and pulled it towards the van. Thirty feet to go, twenty-five . . . Her arms ached, her back strained, she began to struggle with her breathing. Twenty . . . There was a rending sound from beneath the trolley. It canted at an angle, and refused to move. Claire bent down on one knee to look. One of the wheels had collapsed.

'Bugger it!' She slapped the tarmac with her palm, tears of frustration in her eyes. She stood up. She wanted to scream, grab everything in the trolley and throw it about her, kick it —

Almost schizophrenically, her mood changed in a second. She pulled off the blanket, picked up as much as she could carry, and hefted it to the van, placed the items in the back, the wound on her breast dragging. She turned for more — stopped, gaping, a sick feeling overwhelming her as the exit door swung open . . .

It was Ted, staggering across the intervening space. He reached the trolley.

'No time. Be here all day unloading that way.'

'Ted, don't be a fool! You look awful! Get in the van.'

'No!' It was as near a shout as he could manage, and Claire could see the anger in his face, shining, glittering in his eyes through the pain. 'Do as I say. Lift the front corner, where the wheel's gone.'

Claire wanted to argue, wanted to abandon everything, laughing and crying at her thought — We ought to get you to a hospital. The bitter irony was swept away by more pain from her back as she gripped the edge of the container and lifted with all her remaining strength. Ted, breath rasping, skin transparently pale, leaned and pushed with his shoulder. The bin stayed put. Claire relaxed, wanted to stop, slide to the ground, wait for — for what?

'Again! Come on, again!' Ted snarled the words, frightening Claire with their intensity. She heaved, Ted grunted, the trolley began to move.

'Keep it going,' he gasped, and slowly the trolley scraped across the intervening space. Only ten feet, five —

'That'll do!' Ted slid to a sitting position. Claire went round to him. He waved her away. 'No! Unload.'

She almost threw the contents of the container into the back of the van, ignoring the warning pains from her back as she had to bend deeper for the items at the bottom. Now just the intravenous fluids . . .

'There.' She panted noisily.

'Good girl.' Ted used the cart to haul himself upright. Claire rushed to him. 'Come on, in the van.'

'But Paul —'

'We'll have to manage without you. You're neither use nor ornament like this.'

Ted protested feebly as Claire helped him into the passenger seat, put the keys in the ignition, shut him in. He slumped back in the seat, face grey, breathing irregular. She turned back to the hospital, muttering under her breath like a litany. 'Don't die, Ted. Please don't die.'

She paused, about to turn back, drive him round the hundred yards or so to the Casualty Department and salvation. Thought of Joanne upstairs, waiting, Lucinda somewhere, where? Images of grotesque figures, threatening phallic symbols pointing at a frightened child . . .

Come on, woman, it's only a broken rib, only pain, he'll survive. She went through the doors into the semi-darkness, glanced back to the van, the slumped shape barely visible. But I love him! If anything happens . . .

She heard a noise, voices, somewhere at the top of the slope, just round the corner.

'But this isn't the way —' A young voice, uncertain.

'It's all right, one of the technicians is going to show me. You may return to the ward.'

Joanne! That was Joanne. How could she —?

Claire tried to smooth her gown, wiped her dust-streaked face on a sleeve, pushed at her sweat-soaked hair. God, what do I look like? She walked up the slope, turned the corner.

Joanne's astonishment at her sudden and dishevelled appearance was registered as little more than a flicker.

'Ah, there you are, at last.' She turned from the young nurse who grasped the far end of the stretcher trolley bearing the inert figure of Doctor Paul Sansome. A portable drip stand was clipped to the trolley. Claire saw a glistening drop fall in the drip chamber.

Businesslike, Joanne addressed her assistant. 'Now you may leave. Thank you for your help.'

'But, Sister, I don't understand. You said he was going for an emergency scan, and now —'

Joanne put on her severest look, made her voice sharp. 'Don't argue with me, young woman. I suggest you return to your duties on the ward immediately, before I feel obliged to inform the senior nursing officer of your insubordination.'

The girl was bowed but not broken. She knew something was wrong, something strange, but she was new, the sister was senior. And this poor man — there was nothing down this slope but storerooms, she knew for certain. The scanner wasn't even on the ground floor. And now this rather wild-haired woman in a bloody gown and tear-streaked face had arrived, to do what? Help take the patient where? She felt a fierce loyalty to the unconscious, helpless man on the trolley.

'You can say what you like.' She turned and almost ran away. 'I'm going to tell someone.'

Joanne turned to Claire. 'Come on! Quick!'

'What about her? Is she going to —?'

Joanna ignored her, pushed past. 'Get the other end.' Already the stretcher trolley was gaining momentum. Claire grabbed the handles at Paul's feet and helped guide it to the bottom of the slope.

'Where the hell is Ted? I thought —'

'He's hurt. His rib. Fell.'

'Is the stuff — ?'

'All in the van.'

They manoeuvred the trolley so it would go through the door. Joanne put her hand on the bar, looked up sharply. Claire heard the sound at the same moment. Feet running, a girl's voice, shouting, 'This way! Down here!'

Then the junior nurse, pointing, appeared with one of the security staff from the main entrance, face not visible but intentions clear as he set off down the slope, waving his arms.

'Hey! Where the bloody hell d'you think you're going?'

Joanne pushed through the doors, Claire stumbling after her.

'Hey! Stop!'

Claire knew it was no use now. They'd never even reach the van, let alone get Paul inside, before they were caught. She felt defeat overwhelm her. They must stop this madness, stop pushing this thing so pointlessly —

Her foot struck something, she looked down and saw the wood that had jammed the doors. *Jammed the doors!*

'Go on!' Claire shouted at Joanne, reached down, grabbed the wood, slammed the doors. Pressure from the other side, someone pushing. She lunged forward, wedged the piece of wood even as the doors came apart. The timber was wide, she'd stuck it in the middle. Amazingly, both doors were wedged, open barely an inch! She'd done it!

Her triumph was brief. The man inside had put his shoulder to the doors and pushed them open another few inches. A hand shot through the gap. Claire jumped away, but wasn't quick enough. An iron grip encircled her wrist.

A shout of triumph from inside. A roar of rage. 'Now get these doors open, before I —'

The next few moments became an unreal blur for Claire as powerful forces of fear and anger took her over. Acting on animal instinct, she bent down and sank her teeth into the exposed wrist, clamping her teeth till her jaw shook, tasting salt, hearing the scream, the grip released —

Now she was running, joining Joanne at the back of the van with the stretcher, climbing in, dragging at the poles, thank God he'd half-wasted away, so light, poor Paul. Lying him down on the equipment at an uncomfortable-looking angle, head lolling back, legs askew.

Bellows from the exit, doors holding, wedging tighter with every blow. Where was the next exit, was anyone else on their way? Joanne pulled the rear door shut, knelt by her patient, looked up.

'Drive, Claire, drive!'

She clambered over into the driver's seat, glanced at Ted, who looked worse than ever, but at least he was conscious, just . . .

The engine fired. She crunched the gears. Hastily, too hastily, fumbling for the seat adjustment, that's better, now she could depress the clutch pedal properly, first gear, turn —

The steering was heavy and her arms and back protested. She ignored them, concentrated on swinging the vehicle round, perilously close to those doors, still only partly open, a hand reaching through, scrabbling for the piece of wood, aware they were getting away, away —

'Don't drive too crazily. It'll attract attention.'

'But they'll be after us!' Claire shouted without looking back.

'We've got a good start. Bound to have. Don't hit anything, just drive — but not to the motorway, that'll be too obvious.'

'So where?'

'Cross the river at Bedminster Bridge, then we'll go through the back streets of Southville. When we get to Long Ashton we can use the lanes to get to Kingston Seymour.'

Claire tried to concentrate on her driving. She felt weak, trembling, damp all over, her hair, her back. She shivered, felt uncomfortable, looked down, saw a dark stain on the gown, realised at some point she must have wet herself. But it didn't matter, they were getting away, they were —

A police siren. 'God, they're here!' she shouted. The siren was to their left, louder now, the white car with its orange and blue stripe turning in front of them from a side road, tyres squealing. Before Claire could react, it was past, rushing away towards the hospital, the way they had just come.

Claire's pulse and breathing slowed a little. Traffic lights! *Damn!* She looked round. Joanne was trying to rearrange the mess in the rear, moving boxes, making her patient more comfortable. Ted's breathing was shallow, rapid, but he looked less pale. He raised his eyes to hers and mouthed at her.

'Well done, girl.'

The lights were green. The street looked normal. More confidently, she accelerated into the traffic. They were over the river now. She wiped each palm on her breast in turn, gripped the wheel with both hands, pointed the vehicle towards Aunt Maudie's and safety.

CHAPTER 38

It was Joanne's idea to abandon the van away from the village and ferry their cargo by means of Ted's car. It was broad daylight, the description of the van would surely be reported on the media and, isolated though the house was, it would be impossible to conceal their arrival from casual onlookers.

The only worrying factor was time. Paul seemed stable, now that he was flat on the floor with the equipment and supplies piled round him. The drip was still running, tied up to the side of the van, and Joanne had given him some extra phenytoin from the stock she had taken from the ward. She wanted to make sure this disturbance would not precipitate one of his epileptic fits.

It was Ted who was causing the women concern. He was still in great pain, and his breathing was becoming increasingly rapid and difficult. But curiously, instead of looking pale, his face seemed suffused, almost dusky. Joanne was worried: for some reason his lungs were not working properly, and his oxygenation was poor. But he remained conscious, and when they asked him if he could wait it out while they fetched his car, he said he could.

Just through the village of Claverham they pulled off into a blind track that led only to farming pastureland. They were out of sight of the lane from the village, and a small copse concealed them from surrounding farm buildings. Joanne knew the area well. They were still the other side of Yatton, but across the railway line she knew there was a track over Ken Moor to North End. From there it was only about a mile and a half to Kingston Seymour.

Although Claire did not want to leave Ted, it was obvious that Joanne should be the one to stay with the two men. She drew a sketch map for Claire to follow. Claire took off her theatre gown, threw it in the back of the van, and set off to follow the track across the moor. The walk was about three miles altogether, and it was over half an hour later that she walked into the lane where the house was. She was sweating in the warmth of the mid-August day, feeling increasingly agitated about the time she was taking. A picture of Ted's unhealthy look and ragged breathing kept intruding. She wanted to get straight into the car and drive off, but Joanne had asked her to check on Maudie. They had had no choice but to leave the poor old woman alone. She was getting stronger by the day and there was little concern now for her physical health, but since this latest illness her mental state did not seem to be improving. Joanne was afraid her aunt was not safe to be left on her own in the house.

Claire unlocked the front door and called out.

'Maudie!' The house seemed quite silent. She went along the hall and started up the stairs. 'Maudie! Where are you?' She strained her ears, but there was no response, no sound of movement.

Claire backed down two steps, still looking up. A sound behind her made her jump, and as she started to turn towards the source, she felt an agonising pain in her left shoulder. She lost her footing, fell on the stair, and slipped to the hall floor on her back. Her eyes were clenched shut with pain. She forced them open to see Maudie standing over her, grinning fiercely. Her scrawny arms were raised over her head, and she was shaking visibly. Claire could not focus properly, tears stung her eyes.

The old woman laughed. 'Ha! Got you that time!'

Claire started to rise. 'Maudie? What are you —?'

Almost too late, she saw what Maudie was holding aloft. It was the poker from the solid fuel stove in the kitchen, and it was rushing towards her as Maudie brought her arms down, as if she were chopping wood. Claire started to scream, then rolled away. The poker crashed into the stair beside her head. The old lady's grip was too feeble to hold on to it, and it clattered to the floor. Maudie stared at her intended victim, and as Claire tried to get up, the old woman shuffled away as fast as she could into the back of the house.

Claire stood up, trembling and weak. After all that had happened this afternoon, she had thought it would be plain sailing once they got this far. She heard a door slam as Maudie shut herself in the old scullery. Shouldn't she try to make contact, try to convince her she was not an intruder? She took three paces down the passage, then stopped, flesh creeping on her neck. A plaintive wail echoed from within the bare room and into the hall. Then there were mutterings, and a voice, childlike, crystal-clear, unwavering.

'I won't let them get you, Annie! I won't let them!'

Claire's skin prickled. It sounded like a young girl in there, not an old woman. She hesitated, then fled from the house, locked the door, and rushed to the barn. Once inside the car, she locked the door, and fumbled in her haste to get the key in the ignition. She glanced over her shoulder, half-expecting to see Maudie coming at her with some other weapon. The car started first time, she backed out into the road, and within minutes was pulling up beside the van.

They took Ted first, together with a boot-load of equipment, reluctantly leaving Paul unattended. Ted needed the help of both of them to get into and out of the car. Before they went into the house, Joanne went in alone to see what Maudie was doing. When Claire had related her tale of being attacked by the old lady, Joanne had listened in disbelief, until Claire showed her the spreading bruise on her shoulder, which was stiffening up and making her already aching back even more uncomfortable.

Joanne was back at the car in less than two minutes.

'Maudie's upstairs in her room, sitting by her bed. She seems quite normal now.'

Claire shivered involuntarily. She felt somehow guilty about accusing the frail old woman of such aggression, and the look Joanne gave her almost seemed disbelieving, as if she had exaggerated her experience. All she could say was, 'Good.'

They struggled to get Ted out of the car and up the stairs. They laid him on his bed, and his breathing immediately became worse, his colour darker.

'He's not getting enough oxygen! Sit him up!'

Hastily they dragged him upright, packed several pillows behind him, laid him back again, and watched with relief as his colour rapidly improved.

Claire looked at her friend. 'What's the matter with him, Joanne?'

'I'm not sure. It seems much more than just the pain of the broken rib.'

'Haven't you any idea?'

'I think the most likely thing is a pneumothorax — a punctured lung.'

'Oh, God!'

'I can't be sure, but he's not oxygenating well. The broken rib might have punctured his lung when the trolley fell on him.'

'Is it bad? Shouldn't we get him to a hospital?'

'I saw a lot when I was in the ICU. Some were drained off, but many small ones absorbed slowly without treatment.'

'So you think it's safe to wait?'

'For the present, yes. Anyway, we must get Paul first.'

Claire had been so worried about Ted she had forgotten about Paul, lying alone on the floor of the van. God knows what would happen if anyone found him there like that! she thought.

They went back, relieved to find the little hidden spot still deserted. They transferred Paul, almost dragging him into the back of the car, where he was partly folded across the seat. They piled the rest of their supplies alongside him, on the floor, and in the boot.

He looked unreal, hardly human, lying there, immobile, the stainless steel wire cage surrounding his lolling head, surrounded by boxes and bottles.

Claire clambered once more into the driver's seat of the van, and Joanne opened the gate that closed off the end of the lane from the pasture. The ground was hard, and Claire had no trouble driving the vehicle across a short stretch of grass and into the copse. She had gone about ten yards when the van lurched forward, nearly pitching her from the seat. The wheels spun. She didn't make much of an attempt to extricate it. She jumped out, saw one of the front wheels had dropped into a ditch. She ran back into the open, and looked back. From the gateway there was no sign of their transport. Only if someone came into the field would it be spotted. It would have to do.

Claire drove the car back to the house in silence. Joanne perched herself on the front seat, reaching into the back to hold Paul's head steady as they negotiated the winding lanes to safety.

Getting Paul upstairs was a nightmare. With Ted out of action, they struggled desperately to get him up without injuring him or themselves. They had to pause halfway, Paul lying at an acute angle on the stairs, head lolling forward on his chest. Claire suggested that they abandon the attempt, and bring the bed downstairs, but Joanne just laughed.

'Have you looked at the beds?' she asked. 'They're great cast-iron monstrosities. They'd be a damn sight heavier than he is!'

Finally, they succeeded. Maudie came out of her room to watch their efforts, but seemed quite normal, and made no comment. Claire felt uneasy, and tried unobtrusively to keep the old woman in view as much as possible. Once Paul was settled, Joanne fashioned a drip stand from a wire coat-hanger and a standard lamp she brought up from the drawing-room.

'Very professional,' said Claire, feelings of normality after the nightmare day beginning to return.

'One more thing. We must get a single bed of some sort in here. One of us will have to sleep in with him at night.'

At last the room was organised. Claire kept looking in on Ted. He seemed to be slipping into and out of sleep, but if anything his condition seemed improved now that he was resting.

The two women stood on the landing and looked at each other. Claire smiled at Joanne's dirty, dishevelled uniform.

'Do I look as much of a mess as you?'

'I hope you look worse!'

They laughed, for the first time that day. Joanne put an arm round Claire's shoulder. She winced.

'Sorry. Was that the one —?'

'Yes. She really frightened me, Joanne.'

'What was it she said, afterwards?'

'Something about Annie, and saving her.'

She shook her head. 'I don't understand it, really. But I do remember she used to call me Annie when I was very small.'

Claire shivered despite the warm evening. 'But her voice! It sounded just as if she were a child herself.'

'Some sort of regression, perhaps. I found her once walking about with no clothes on. She seemed to think she was a little girl then.'

Claire gave Joanne's arm a squeeze. 'Never mind. Let's go and have a bath. You first.'

Joanne accepted the offer gratefully. Five minutes later she was trying to let the stress of one of the most eventful days of her life ease away. She lay back in the deep, warm water, closed her eyes, but could not relax. Her heart ached and her thoughts raced. Lucinda! Where are you, Lucinda?

★ ★ ★

The child gaped as her abductor entered the bedroom and drew the curtains. She had been trying so hard to understand what was happening. This stranger had promised her everything she wanted, and so far had made a big fuss, given her ice-cream, sweets, bought her dolls and toys. But Lucinda was still unhappy. The person had said she was being looked after for her Mummy, who had had to go away. Lucinda was sure that was not true. She was certain her Mummy wouldn't just go away like that.

She had cried a lot at first, despite all the consoling she was given. She had refused food, but then she got so hungry, and she ate. That was when the stranger started doing funny things. In the evening, when it was bedtime. When she had a bath. When she was dried. It wasn't like with Mummy. Why did the person keep looking at her, at bits of her, touching her? Lucinda didn't like it, but was too frightened to say. Not that she had been hurt, or even shouted at. But there was something, something she didn't trust, didn't like . . .

And now this. This was really funny. No clothes on — well, a top, a gold top, but nothing on the bottom. Lucinda had seen her Mummy with no clothes on, lots of times. But only when she had been dressing, or changing, or having a bath. But walking around like this, all dressed up on top, but nothing underneath?

A chair was brought into the room. At first, Lucinda had been given a warm smile, but now the face was serious, intent. Lucinda sensed she was momentarily forgotten. She shrank back into the corner of the room, down behind the bed, hiding, but still watching, watching the activity from what she hoped was her place of safety.

What was happening now? Climbing onto the chair. A lovely silken cord, thick, purple, tassels, very pretty, undoing a plug, taking down the light fitting, carefully, slowly. Buttocks showing bare, bending over to lay the glass lampshades on the bed. Now the nice cord, looped both ends, the smaller loop going over the hook that held the lights.

Lucinda shifted her position, made a small noise, and instinctively ducked. She peeped again, slowly, then almost stood up, absorbed by the strange happenings. Over to a drawer, getting a funny little plastic thing on a piece of string, climbing up on the chair again, looping that over the hook as well, letting it hang next to the silken cord. And now? What was happening now? *Looking!* — the person was looking — for *her*, calling, bending, reaching over, pulling —

The figure frogmarched the complaining Lucinda to the wall opposite the bed, and stood her in front of the chair.

'Now be a good girl. Just stand there where I can see you.'

Lucinda tried to dart away as soon as she was released. A hand shot out and grabbed her arm. She felt pain, wanted to cry. The face was directly in front of hers, the words hissed in her face, forceful.

'I'm not going to hurt you. I just want you to *stand there!*' Lucinda stared as if uncomprehending. '*Do you understand?*'

Lucinda nodded, suddenly too frightened to speak.

'Good, good.' All soothing, all kindness, now. 'Just stand there like a good little girl. And watch. Watch me. And I'm going to watch you.'

Lucinda did as she was ordered, mesmerised. She was to remember what she was about to see for the rest of her life.

The figure turned, climbed onto the chair, turned to face Lucinda, gave her a smile, a smile of relish, delight, anticipation, glee. Gave a little wave. Lucinda did not respond. It doesn't matter now, nothing matters now, in a few minutes, no, less than that even, paradise, the breakthrough to paradise.

Head in the loop — mustn't call it a noose. A look down to check, knife in the belt, must have the safety net, you never know, even when it's measured so carefully.

Now, the bend of the knees, take the weight, the loop of purple silk constricting, the heady feeling. Here it comes, now, ease the chair away a little so there is more weight. Where's my little gratifier?

Unhook the string, find the button, push it, a buzz as it's turned on. Now, reaching down, a bit more — There! Aah! And where's the girl? Can I see her? — yes, she's watching, I can see her —

Vision bright, now pink, everything pink, at the edges a touch of grey. Mustn't go too far. Ooh, but the feelings, the glorious feelings, ripples of ecstasy, such ecstasy, it's so incredibly good . . . But no! It's too soon, no, not yet!

The legs lashed out as if to kick away the unwanted orgasm, struck something, the chair, it teetered. Now the body on the cord was starting to spin, reaching out with both feet to rescue the chair, a misjudgement, the wrong way, the chair toppled, fell, rolled over.

Only grey now, soaring ecstasy replaced in seconds by a plunge into terror, panic, nightmare. Darkness descending, rasping noises from the throat. The knife, where's the knife? Someone help me! . . . Please, someone, the knife — got it! Now, panic easing. Should be easy, a close call, all right now, I've got the knife . . .

CHAPTER 39

At first Claire thought the coughing and choking sounds were from her dream. She was fighting off a mysterious illness which was depriving her of movement, while all around her were familiar faces, all seemingly similarly afflicted. But in her dream she was lying on the floor of a moving vehicle, and slowly it penetrated that she was in a bed.

She sat upright, realising the sounds were coming from Ted, who lay propped up on his pillows beside her. She reached for the bedside lamp, knocked it over in the dark, jumped from the bed onto the cold bare floor and fumbled for the light switch by the door.

She took one look at Ted, blue in the face, choking, gasping, and opened the door to shout.

'Joanne!'

She was sleeping down the passage, in Paul's room. Claire glanced back at Ted. His eyes were staring, a grotesque look of pleading on his suffused face.

'*JOANNE*!' Claire screamed from the doorway, then rushed to the bedside. She had no idea what to do. Ted was desperately trying to breathe in, and every time he did so he seemed worse. She pulled down the sheets, looked at his chest. It seemed somehow distended, barrel-like, overinflated. She stood there, helpless, convinced she was watching him die.

Joanne almost ran in, tying a robe round her as she rushed to Ted's side.

'What's happening?'

'Don't know! I heard him choking — he can't seem to breathe properly.'

Joanne tried to assess Ted professionally, tried to force herself to look, for some sign, some clue . . .

'Joanne! You've got to do something! He can't breathe!'

Joanne suppressed panic. She was responsible for this man, there was no one else. If she couldn't do anything . . .

'All right, Claire, just a few seconds, let me look.'

'Shall I call an ambulance?'

Joanne hesitated. Would they get here in time? The nearest station was in Weston-super-Mare. And if they did? That would be it, they would be exposed, the hoped-for chance of locating Lucinda through Paul gone. But — she couldn't let him die, she couldn't —

'Joanne, *please!* Look — it's like he's trying to breathe in all the time, but can only breathe out! What's stopping him, Joanne?' Claire was crying now, sure it was too late.

That's it! Suddenly Joanne thought she knew what was wrong. The rib injury, the possible punctured lung, and now, with every breath worse, trying to breathe in, but the chest already overinflated.

She looked at Claire. 'Tension pneumothorax! That's it!'

'What? What's that?' Claire sounded hysterical.

Joanne ignored her, felt Ted's pulse. Rapid, weak, irregular. Skin dusky, damp with sweat, shock setting in. Which side was it? Left!

'Claire, go to Paul's room. Bring me a drip set, the biggest needles you can find, a syringe.' Claire fled from the room. Joanne shouted after her. 'And some scissors!'

Ted's eyes were closed now. She pinched him hard over his eye. He winced. Barely conscious, but rousable. There might still be time. *Hurry, Claire, hurry!* She lifted an eyelid. The pupils were still small. Good, no brain damage yet . . .

'Oh, no! Is he —?' Clare stopped in the doorway, arms full of packages, staring at Joanne releasing the eyelid, the lolling head, the stillness. Then a convulsive movement of Ted's chest seemed to re-start her, as if she'd had a stalled engine. She moved forward and dropped everything on the bed.

Joanne was thinking feverishly. She'd never done this, but had often assisted. She tried to think of the routine even as her hands tore open the box of a drip set, used the scissors to cut the tough plastic, looked for the syringe. Don't be stupid! You won't need a local anaesthetic. As for sterility, a few germs won't matter compared to — to death.

She felt down from Ted's left collar bone, counted two rib spaces, pushed hard to locate the ribs, made sure she was feeling the space between them, reached for the drip set.

'No!' Claire shouted as Joanne plunged the wide-bore needle straight into Ted's chest. She started to sob.

'Be quiet. *Please!*' Joanne put her ear near the end of the tubing. Nothing. She looked along the tube. There was a rubber cap protecting the end. She removed it, heard the hissing of air.

'That's it! It's working!'

'But — you're letting air out!'

'Got to!'

She felt his pulse again. No change, colour still awful, only the occasional gasped attempt at a breath. She looked at the tube. It was much narrower bore than the ones she'd seen used, and at the end — at the end it narrowed even further for the connection to the drip tubing. She picked up the scissors, cut through the tubing, leaving only a few inches protruding through the chest wall. She listened again. Better, more air, but still not enough, surely.

'Give me another drip set!'

Claire was staring at the needle embedded in Ted's chest. 'What?'

'Never mind!' Joanne reached over and grabbed another box, tore it open, this time cut the tubing short first, and plunged it in an inch to one side of the first. Ted moved slightly, made a faint groan of protest.

'You hurt him!' Claire's voiced was raised, protesting.

'Good! It's a good sign. There must be more oxygen getting through to his brain.'

She felt the pulse again. Surely a little stronger now. She listened over both tubes: air was rushing out. She watched his chest. A convulsive breath in, then pause, wait, was there? Yes, a slight movement of exhalation. The pressure in his chest was easing.

Joanne felt herself calming, felt relief, weakness as the adrenaline rush was spent. 'I think we've done it.'

Claire stood, tears streaming, biting her lower lip. She nodded to her friend. 'What's happening?'

Joanne held up her hand. She was monitoring the pulse still, watching the chest, now moving more regularly, and with each breath noted his colour improving slightly, pink rather than blue around his mouth. She touched his arm. The skin was drier, less clammy. From the tubes protruding from his chest, the hiss of air; she'd have to watch for that stopping, clamp them off.

'Joanne, what happened?'

Sitting on the bed, still holding Ted's wrist, she turned to Claire.

'He developed a tension pneumothorax. I released it.'

'What's that, for God's sake?'

'I thought he had a punctured lung, remember? Well usually, when the lung collapses the hole closes, and gradually the lung reflates. With a tension pneumothorax, the hole acts like a one-way valve. With each breath air is pumped into the space outside the lung, into the chest cavity, but it can't get out again.'

She looked away from Claire, back to her patient, who was now breathing much more normally. Shallow and rapid, but breathing. She thought she detected a flutter of the eyelids.

Claire caught the movement, too, and moved closer, touched his face tenderly. 'I still don't understand.'

'Pressure builds up inside the chest. It collapses the lung even more, then pushes against the heart, restricts the other lung, it keeps getting worse. He was trying to breathe in, but couldn't because of the pressure in his chest. I stuck those needles in to let out the trapped air. It wasn't in his lung — it was *outside* it.'

'What — what happens now?'

'I'll have to make it up, I'm afraid. I think that when no more air comes out, I should clamp off the tubes, and then I'll try and rig up a device to get the rest of the air out, and that will help reflate the lung.'

'You're a marvel, do you know that?' Claire eyes were shining. She bent forward and gave Joanne a hug.

'Marvel, nothing! She stabbed me in the bloody chest!'

The two women turned to look at Ted, who coughed, then tried a grin. 'Christ, look at you two. You'd think somebody had died!'

Joanne looked solemn. 'Somebody nearly did.' Then there were smiles, hugs and kisses. 'All very unprofessional,' Joanne joked as she left to check on Paul.

* * *

Ted sat up in bed and watched the bubbles coming from the end of the tube with each breath. Joanne's device was simple but effective. He only had one tube in now, a long one that went to a large jar of water on the floor by his bed, the end of the tube under the water. As he breathed in, the pressure in his chest rose, and air was pushed out of the end of the tube. When he breathed out, the pressure fell, but the air was prevented from returning by the water, which rose a few inches in the tube but did not admit any air. He was slowly reinflating his lung and, apart from the pain from the broken rib, was feeling better by the hour.

Joanne was downstairs in the kitchen. Claire had gone out for some supplies. He was amazed at the speed of his own recovery. He had enjoyed the breakfast brought him, and felt a renewed burst of energy. He was sure his lung must be almost fully expanded. And he was bored. It was only ten in the morning, but just lying there was frustrating.

Slowly, carefully, he sat on the edge of the bed, then stood up. A twinge from his rib, but nothing drastic. He bent down, picked up the tubing and the attached glass bottle, and took a few tentative steps towards the door.

'No trouble,' he spoke under his breath to himself. 'Let's go see Dr Paul.'

* * *

Claire returned from the village shop and went into the kitchen. Joanne looked round from the sink as she came in.

'Get everything?'

'Yes, all except the cheese.'

'Never mind. We'll manage without that.'

'Joanne?'

'What is it?'

'Are there any — well — strange men around here? I mean, ones who might follow you about?'

'Whyever do you ask?'

'I — I thought I was being followed.'

'There was talk of a community mental hostel in Yatton. Perhaps that would explain it.'

Claire shrugged. 'I probably imagined it anyway.'

Joanne made an upward movement with her head. 'I think you'd better go and see what his majesty is up to.'

'How's he doing?'

'Very well. Perhaps a bit too well.'

Claire headed for the stairs.

Ted heard Claire's return, and her voice talking to Joanne, but could not make out the words. He heard her go into his room, the shout of 'Ted!', the tone of mixed concern and anger, and knew he was in for a row.

'What the hell do you think you're doing?'

She stood in the doorway of Paul's room, hands on hips, lips compressed.

'Thought I might as well get started.' He cursed himself for sounding so sheepish.

'I can't turn my back for a minute.'

'You sound just like my mother.' He sounded annoyed, but his lips gave him away.

Claire did not respond to the twitch of a smile. 'You're supposed to be in bed!'

'No, I'm supposed to be getting ready to communicate with Paul. About who may have Lucinda. Remember?'

'Of course I remember! But surely you should —'

'Oh, come on, Claire. I feel fine.'

She came further into the room. 'Suppose that air in your lung goes into tension again?'

'It won't.' He gazed at her steadily, at her worried frown, knew she was genuinely concerned for him. 'I'm all right, really. I feel surprisingly well. And I'm really impressed by what you two have done already.' He surveyed the room again, the neat stacks of intravenous and naso-gastric feeds, the bed placed centrally in the room, headboard removed for access to the electrodes. 'Joanne's done a good job.'

'Marvellous.'

'But this is the best.' He waved at the equipment in front of him. 'You've reassembled the computers and the EEG machine. And by God, they work!'

Claire's anger seemed to have dissolved. 'Well, the computer certainly does. But the EEG machine — well, although it tests out all right, we won't really know until we connect up the internal electrodes. And heaven knows where they'll be. All that dragging the poor man around could easily have disturbed them.' She looked at Paul, gaunt, still, eyes closed, but breathing regularly. He had stubby hair now, regrowing after the shave when the electrodes were installed. But his chin was clean-shaven, smooth. Joanne had seen to that earlier.

Ted picked up his drainage bottle and stood up. 'Another hour or so's work, and we should be ready to start.'

'Please take it easy, Ted.'

'I'll be all right. We can't afford to wait.'

'You're right about that.' She came across the room, holding a newspaper, and dropped it on the computer.

Ted picked it up. The tabloid had a huge headline about a Government scandal. But below, also on the front page, was another prominent headline, and a photograph of Paul Sansome.

Ted looked up. 'Christ!' he read the headline again, and the story that followed.

COMA DOCTOR ABDUCTED FROM HOSPITAL

> Hospital security was breached yet again yesterday afternoon when one of the most audacious kidnappings of recent times took place at the Bristol General Neurological Unit. Dr Paul Sansome (39) was abducted by two women and a man, despite the efforts of a young nurse and a security officer who tried to stop them taking the unconscious patient away in a white Ford Transit van, believed to have been stolen.
>
> The Hospital General Manager would make no comment other than that there would be a full inquiry. The police revealed that they had not yet been able to contact Dr Sansome's wife, Christine, but would not speculate on the reasons for the abduction. Dr Sansome was
>
> *(cont'd p.3)*

Ted met Claire's anxious gaze. 'Too bloody right! We've really done it now!'

* * *

Sergeant Clothier knew this would be a wild goose chase. They had sent a constable round to the Sansomes' house yesterday afternoon, who had reported no reply; Clothier himself had telephoned twice this morning. But instead of getting off early this afternoon, here he was in suburban Bristol, hungry for his tea, because dear Inspector Howard had insisted. She'll be off somewhere, probably out of the country, despite her assurance that she would keep the police informed about her whereabouts, he grumbled to himself.

He took a pace back, looked over the extensive frontage of the secluded house. Curtains drawn in one room upstairs. None downstairs. Paper in the door and milk on the step. That's a bit odd. Probably doesn't mean anything, though. Strikes me as being careless about these things.

He sighed, and decided he'd better go round the back. The side gate didn't open properly, and he had to squeeze his bulk through it, cursing as he risked snagging his trousers. Once through, he followed the path into the large, tree-lined garden. He whistled under his breath. Didn't realise it was this big. Must have cost a bomb.

He went to the back door, which opened into a glass conservatory. He looked through the glass, at the few dried-up plants, the pile of old boots and shoes near the door into the house. It all looked very ordinary. He tried the door. It was open.

He stood by the back door proper, and hammered on it. Hammered again, shouted. Silence greeted him. He put his hands up to the glass that formed the upper panel of the door and peered in. He could see nothing untoward. She's done a bunk, sure as eggs is eggs.

He was fed up with this. Waste of time. Still looking through the glass panel, he pummelled the door impatiently. As he turned away in disgust, a movement caught his eye. Surely that was something, down at the end of the hall?

He peered again, holding his breath, straining for a noise. Nothing. But he'd seen something! A cat perhaps? No, much too big, it had looked like a person all right . . .

Alongside the door was a window, obviously an outside one before the conservatory was added. Inside he could see a kitchen work-top and sink. He looked at the window carefully. It seemed closed, but he was quite sure — the latch was not down. Should go back to the station, I suppose, get a warrant. But there's no alarm, this window's open, not forcing an entry, and anyway, I'm sure I did see something.

He put his fingers against the thin edge of the window and pulled. It opened a few inches, then the stay jammed on one of the stops. He reached in and released it, the window fell fully open. He thought he heard a noise, a scampering. He cocked his head, listened. Silence.

A little more apprehensive now, he struggled to haul himself up and through the window, then floundered awkwardly on the work-top until he could turn and lower himself to the floor. He was panting, even with that small exertion. It was at times like these that he *knew* he was too fat.

He stood in the spacious kitchen, oak-panelled, tiled. The house was still. Perhaps he was imagining things. He began to worry. Suppose Mrs Sansome turned up now? How would he explain himself?

He went into the hall, and called out. 'Mrs Sansome!' Too tentative. He called again. 'Hello! Mrs Sansome!' That scurrying sound again, faint, he couldn't locate it. The skin on his neck prickled slightly.

Don't be stupid, man! A quick search of the house, then out. He hurriedly went into all the ground floor rooms. They were neat, tidy, empty. He went up the stairs. If there was anything, it must be up here . . .

Funny smell. What was it? Not very pleasant, not like downstairs where there were flowers, lingering perfume. He reached the large landing. A door on the right, partly ajar. He checked the room. A single bed, a teddy bear on it, some toys on the floor. Funny that, they've no children. Visitors?

The next room was a bathroom, big, blue and pink, corner bath, lots of knobs on it, a jacuzzi?

That sound again! Up here somewhere! He went to the door opposite, pushed it open. The smell made him gag, but the sight brought a rush of bile to burn the back of his throat. He dived into the bathroom, retching, heaving, leaning over the basin until he was empty. He ran the tap to rinse his face and hands, knowing he shouldn't touch anything, *anything*, but not caring, only thinking, thinking of that thing hanging there . . .

Finally he won the battle for control, knew he would have to look again, go in there.

The body of Christine Sansome moved almost imperceptibly in the tiny draught of air caused by the door opening. In the light coming through the partly drawn curtains, he could see the tight gold lamé top she was wearing, incongruous, ridiculous, with her nudity below. On the floor a fallen chair, some small plastic device with a string on it, and a knife, on the carpet, smeared with blood. It was the blood that was making the smell, that he was trying to avoid looking at, the pool of blood that had poured down from those hideous wounds, then congealed. He forced himself to look again at the face. Blotched purple, eyes bulging, tongue almost black, protruding, the head slightly to one side, the silken cord pushing it over, the wounds . . .

Why wounds, when you were hanging yourself? Deep slashes, all to the same side — the right side — of the face and neck; some small, one near a staring eye, larger ones lower down, one yawning gash almost severing the cord buried deep in the discoloured flesh.

Clothier fought down another surge of bile as his eyes were drawn down the body, following the rivers and tributaries of gore over the gold cloth, onto the bare skin, some flowing over the buttocks, disappearing into the natal cleft, then out again, down the thighs, legs, toes, where it had congealed and now hung in lumpy strands. Some of them almost touched the dark pool that spread on the carpet directly beneath the body like a sanguineous slurry.

The scurrying sound brought Clothier back from his animal fascination with the slaughter, in a moment replaced the primeval curiosity with profound fear. He whirled round, half-expecting a mad axe-man to charge at him through the door.

But there was nothing. Once again he listened, hairs on his neck on end, alarm gripping, almost paralysing him. He crept to the door, his back against the architrave as he moved cautiously into the hall. No one there. Empty. He raced to the top of the stairs, looking round as he went, then down, fast, almost slipping, searching frantically for the phone. There!

This time he remembered, reached in his pocket for a handkerchief to hold the hand-set, stabbed at the buttons, waited impatiently for his desk sergeant to answer, all the while looking round, even as he spoke, asked for assistance, back-up team, ambulance. He replaced the phone carefully, and decided he would wait outside. The smell was stronger downstairs now that he'd let it out by opening the door, the door to the chamber of horrors.

Front or back? Which would be easier? He was moving back towards the kitchen when the sound came again. Louder this time. Definitely upstairs, definitely alive, something, someone, moving.

From where he stood he could not see the top of the stairs. Soft, almost gentle footsteps, coming down! He moved closer to the bannisters, where he would not be seen until whoever it was had passed him. He heard another sound, a tiny whimper, a sob, almost like a child — a child?

He stepped forward, saw the look of shock in the eyes, the recoil, the beginnings of the turn to flee, then some sort of recognition, running down the stairs, tiny hands gripping his neck, his hair, sobs shaking the small body.

Clothier spoke into the soft hair, gently, so gently. 'It's all right, Lucinda. It's all right now.'

Then he was crying with her, helplessly, thankfully, with wave after wave of relief — for the child, for himself, the macabre sacrifice upstairs temporarily forgotten.

CHAPTER 40

Ted was triumphant. He had succeeded in reloading all his data onto the hard disk of the computer, and after only minor adjustments to the placing of the electrodes, the quality of the signals he was getting from Paul matched any they ever got in the hospital.

'Ya-hoo!' He shrieked, first with joy, then a change of note as the sudden movement of his chest gave him a stab of pain. He bent over and clutched his side. Claire was up in an instant from her position at the microphone. 'Idiot! Are you all right?'

Ted slowly straightened and forced a grin. 'Yeah. Sorry. Too much enthusiasm.'

'You're sure it's working?'

'Positive. Look — input response to your "Hello, Paul", output response matches what we know represents "Hello, Claire." We're in business!'

Joanne was watching the activity, keeping an eye on both her male patients. 'Seems incredible this delicate equipment survived all that dashing about.'

Ted nodded his agreement. 'I've always said — devilish cunning, these Japanese.'

Claire bent over Paul, adjusted the headphones, then went back to the microphone. She looked at her watch. 'It's five o'clock. Let's try for an hour, then stop for something to eat.'

'Suits me.'

Claire leaned forward and switched on the microphone.

'Hello, Paul.'

Ted looked at the screen. 'He says "Hello".'

'We want you to answer "Yes" or "No". Do you understand?'

Ted relayed the answer. 'Yes.'

'Can you remember talking to us before?'

'Yes.'

'Do you know how long ago it was?'

'No.'

'Did you think we had forgotten you?'

'Yes.'

Claire, Ted and Joanne exchanged glances, their eyes moist. Claire closed the microphone.

Joanne broke the silence. 'I'm no psychologist, but do you think going along these rather emotional lines is a good idea?'

Ted scratched the back of his head. 'I'm no psychologist either, but if I were him I would think a bit of emotional contact coming out of all that darkness and silence would be a real tonic.'

'I agree,' said Claire. 'Even though it's impossible even to start to imagine what it's like for him. I think it's a wonder he hasn't gone insane.'

Joanne nodded. 'You're probably right.'

Claire switched on the microphone again. 'Paul, do you mind me asking you these questions?'

Ted looked up sharply, then frowned at the screen, waiting for the response. It was a long time coming. Finally, he reported, 'He says "No".'

Claire flicked her eyes at her two companions, leaned towards the mike again.

'Paul, we have a problem we think you might be able to help us with. Will you try?'

'Yes.'

'It concerns your nurse, Joanne Yeates. She has looked after you almost all the time since you have been in your coma. Do you understand?'

'Yes.'

Joanne gasped. Ted and Claire looked at her. She was very pale. Ted turned away from the computer. 'Are you all right.'

'Yes. Yes, honestly. Carry on, please.'

'Joanne has a daughter called Lucinda. She has been kidnapped.'

'Wait!' Ted commanded urgently. 'There's a stream of stuff here I don't understand.'

'I think that's what happens when he gets frustrated and can't express himself properly.'

Ted looked up. 'Was the mike open when you said that?'

'Yes, why?'

'He's answered you. He says "Yes".'

Claire turned off the mike and looked sadly at the unconscious man. 'Poor Paul. It must be terrible to have to communicate in such a simple fashion.'

'But better than not communicating at all, surely?'

Claire settled again. 'Perhaps we'd better ask him to spell out his response. It'll take a lot longer, but we've got all evening.' She switched on the microphone.

Joanne cocked her head. 'Is that a car?'

They all listened, and heard a vehicle stop outside the house.

Ted spoke first. 'I think we've got visitors.'

Joanne quickly ran down the passage and looked out of the window at the end of the landing. She turned back immediately. 'It's a police car!'

'Oh, God! Shall we hide?' Claire's voice was high.

'There's no time. I'll try and stall them.'

As she hurried down the stairs there was a knock on the front door. Claire and Ted crouched on the landing where they could listen, unseen.

'Mrs Yeates?'

'Yes.' She sounded cautious.

'It's about your daughter, Lucinda. She's been found.'

Claire and Ted gripped each other's hands tightly. Joanne hesitated. 'Found? Is she — is —?'

'She's fine, Mrs Yeates. Safe and well. Not a mark on her.'

Joanne's instinct was to run and shout to her friends and share her joy — but she had little difficulty transferring her relief and gratitude onto the young constable standing beaming before her. She gripped him tightly in her arms as the tears flowed.

'Oh, thank you, thank God, thank you!'

The young policeman stood rigid, uncertain, but delighted. 'Er — would you like to come with me to Bristol, Mrs Yeates? Your daughter is having a check-up at the children's hospital. Just to make sure everything's OK.'

'Oh, yes, yes please!' She drew away, knowing she was grinning foolishly, tear-stained, but not caring. Once again she had to repress the urge to shout to Ted and Claire. The logic in her mind pushed its way through the emotions. 'I'll just go upstairs and get some things.'

She turned and rushed up the stairs. As she came Claire and Ted retreated to the back room where Paul lay. There they hugged each other, shed more tears, all in a strange whispered dance of relief and happiness. Claire had left the microphone on, and while the unseeing eyes of Paul Sansome roamed over the scene, the inner depths of his mind heard and digested the news.

* * *

Claire and Ted sat at one end of the kitchen table, Maudie at the other. Ted had his chest drain out now. Joanne had removed it rather hastily before she left, but he seemed none the worse, and was glad to be free of the tubing and the bottle.

Maudie was watching them like a timid bird.

'More tea, Maudie?'

'No thank you, Nellie.' Claire had been Nellie since they returned with Paul. 'Don't you think you and Victor should be going now?'

'Not until Joanne gets back, Maudie. That probably won't be until tomorrow.'

'Tomorrow. Oh, dear.'

'What's the matter?'

'Tomorrow's Sunday. I have to go to matins. I won't be able to prepare any lunch for you.'

Ted looked reassuringly at her. 'It's Tuesday tomorrow, not Sunday.'

Maudie gave him smile of relief. 'Are you sure?'

Claire spoke encouragingly. 'Quite sure, Maudie. So don't worry about it.'

The old lady seemed content to accept her error. 'That's all right, then.' She looked from one to the other, clearly wanting to say something more.

'What is it, Maudie?' Claire prompted.

'Who is that gentleman asleep upstairs in Bertie's old room?'

This was the first time Maudie had spoken of Paul to either of them. They had no idea what Joanne had told her, and were completely taken aback by the directness and clarity of her question.

Claire looked at Ted for inspiration, but got none. 'He's — he's a very close friend of Joanne and — and us. He's been very ill.'

Maudie gave a pleased, understanding smile, as if one of life's great mysteries had been revealed to her. 'Ah, I see. He's here to convalesce, take the air.'

'Um, yes. You could say that.'

The old lady stood up.

'I'll go and tend to him myself. I make a very good nurse, you know.' She moved towards the door.

Claire tried not to appear too alarmed. 'Oh, no, I — I think he's sleeping now. I think he should be left quietly for the time being.'

Maudie looked disappointed. 'Oh. Very well. Perhaps later.' She went into the hall, and Claire followed. She wanted to make sure the old lady didn't go to see Paul, but she went into the drawing-room and sat down, gazing out of the window.

Claire returned to Ted. 'Poor old thing. She looked really pleased there for a moment, at the prospect of nursing somebody.'

'Yep. It's a shame. The old girl's got too many kangaroos in her top paddock.'

'Ted! Don't be unkind.'

'I'm not. I think she's great. But she really doesn't know if she's Arthur or Martha.'

'That's why I didn't want her practising her nursing skills on Paul.'

'We've got to decide what we're going to do there.'

'About Paul, you mean?'

'S'right.'

Claire sighed. 'All that hell we went through. The trouble we're in. You damn near died. And all for nothing.'

'Maybe not.'

'How d'you mean?'

'Well, we're in the shit with Paul here, there's no two ways about that, is there?'

Claire shook her head gloomily. 'Because we can't claim in our defence that we succeeded in locating Lucinda by what we did.'

'Right.' Ted pointed his index finger. 'That would have protected us from the full force of the law, for sure.'

'So? What do you suggest? We take him back in the dead of night and leave him outside the hospital with a note saying, "Whoops, sorry"?'

Ted had to grin. 'That's not such a bad idea. I'll remember that for later.'

'Later?' Claire looked anxious.

'Look, we've been to Bullamakanka and back to be able to spend some time working with Paul again, so let's do it anyway. We'll never get another chance.'

'Do you think we might make some breakthrough that'll save our skins?'

'Dunno about that. But at least we can ask him if he objects to us taking him from the hospital for a bit. If we can get evidence of that, the authorities will be hard-pressed to say we abducted him against his will.'

'Good idea, Ted, in theory. So we haul in the next passing local and get him to witness words coming out of a computer, then send him on his way with a label stuck on his mouth saying, "Do not open except in the event of our arrest"?'

'You can be a sarky bitch sometimes.'

Claire knew Ted did not mean to be hurtful, but the words stung. 'I'm only trying to be realistic. We're in one hell of a mess, and I can't see how we can get out of it.'

'I agree. It's only a matter of time before they identify us, or at least are suspicious enough to come looking here. We made no attempt to disguise ourselves. That was pretty stupid, really.'

'So. The wolves are at the door. Why don't we just let them in and get it over?'

'That's what I'm trying to say. We've got the chance to really *talk* to Paul. No interruptions, no routine to disrupt. We ought to do it *now*, before the boys in blue suss us out.'

'And what do you hope to gain?'

Ted gave her a look of total incomprehension. 'Gain? Christ, Claire! I thought you were a scientist!'

'I am!' She scowled defensively.

'Then where's your curiosity? Don't you want to *know* what's going on in there, in that mind of his?' He laughed coarsely. 'At least it'll give us something to think about while we're doing time.'

Claire rested her elbows on the table and put her head in her hands. She peered at Ted through open fingers. 'My God! A few weeks ago I was day-dreaming of a Nobel Prize. Now I'm thinking of being in gaol.'

'We could always skip the country. You and me. Start a new life together. All that stuff.'

Claire gave him an indulgent smile. 'Don't tempt me. Just 'cos you've got fugitive's blood in your veins already!' Her face became serious. 'Besides, what about Joanne? We couldn't leave her to face the music.'

'No. Course not. But we're wasting time. What about it? Starting right now and having a really long session with Paul? Find out what's going on in there?'

Claire was silent for a long moment. Then she shrugged. 'What have we got to lose?'

'Exactly.' Ted got up from the table and led the way upstairs.

* * *

'How do you know?' Claire spoke into the microphone, astonishment in her voice. She had just told Paul that Lucinda had been found safe. Paul had replied, letter by letter, that he knew.

They patiently went through the alphabet as he spelt out his reply.

'I was listening.'

Ted shook his head in wonderment as the message was completed. 'When Joanne came upstairs. She told us in here!'

'It must be so frustrating for him — and us. If only we could interpret flowing speech —'

'Well, we can't, and we don't know how much time we've got. It's gone six now — so let's get straight to the point.'

'All right, you big bully.'

Ted eased himself to a new position, to help settle the pain in his chest. His breathing was all right, but he had a bit of a cough. He hoped it was nothing important.

Claire positioned herself before the microphone. 'I want to start by asking Paul about that peculiar word, *ALGHRAID*, if it is a word at all. Perhaps it's some initials that stands for something.'

'Well, go ahead. Ask him.'

Progress was laborious. Claire could not guess at what she wanted to know. Yes-No conversation was useless. Every answer from Paul had to be spelled out with their going-through-the-alphabet method. Each word took from one to several minutes to work out.

Although it was a painstaking process, they hardly noticed the passage of time. As it grew dark they put the lights on, but otherwise nothing interrupted their progress. It was only after four hours that they realised the responses from Paul were becoming slower and slower.

Claire looked at her watch. 'Good grief! It's gone ten.'

'Four hours? Paul's obviously struggling.'

Claire addressed the microphone again. 'Paul, are you tired?'

'He says "Yes".'

'Shall we stop for a while?'

'Yes.'

'All right. Good night, then, Paul.' She switched off the microphone, moved to the head of the bed and carefully eased off the headphones.

Despite their tiredness, Claire and Ted were agitated, bright-eyed. 'I just can't believe all this!' Claire pointed to her pages of notes.

'It's fantastic. Let's go through it all, try and make some sense out of it.'

Claire nodded. 'But first, do you think you could check on Maudie and get her something before she goes to bed?'

'Do my best.'

Claire saw him wince as he got up. 'Take it easy. Especially on the stairs.'

'Yes, nurse.'

'I'll do my best for Paul. He's due a tube feed, and the catheter bag needs emptying. You'll have to help me turn him and stretch his limbs, if you can. Joanne said without his ripple bed he might get bed-sores — and he ought to have some physio to stop him getting fixed contractures.'

'Right, matron.' Holding his side, Ted went in search of Joanne's elderly aunt.

CHAPTER 41

Sergeant Clothier never did like the distinctive odour of formaldehyde. It reminded him too much of those rare occasions when he had attended autopsies. Even a whiff of it would turn his stomach. And he didn't want to waste his fried breakfast. He lit one of his infrequent cigarettes. This was a cast-iron excuse — take away the smell. He was desperately trying to stop smoking. His wife, his doctor, his friends who had already given up, all gave him a hard time. All this talk of risk factors, his blood pressure being a bit up, his overweight . . .

The pathologist, tall, gangling, red-haired, came in from the post-mortem room and eyed the cigarette disapprovingly. The policeman stubbed it out. He needed this man's co-operation.

'Dr Hatcher?'

'That's me. You must be Detective Sergeant Clothier.'

'Correct. If you've got a minute —'

'You want to talk about the Sansome woman?'

'It would be helpful.'

'Don't come across one of these very often, I can tell you.' The pathologist sat on the edge of his desk, peeled off his rubber gloves, and dropped them in the waste-bin. 'Take a pew.' He indicated a worn wooden-armed chair. Clothier sat down gratefully. Hatcher looked at his watch, then removed his blood-stained plastic apron and threw it in the corner. 'Eleven o'clock. Might as well have a cuppa. You want one?'

'Thanks.'

The doctor went to the door, shouted at someone for some coffee, and then resumed his perch on the edge of the desk, swinging one wellington-booted foot. 'OK: Cause of death — interesting.'

'The knife wounds?'

'Difficult to be sure. Haven't got any histology yet, of course. It's a toss-up between strangulation and loss of blood.'

'And the little girl —?'

Hatcher looked up sharply, brow creased, then laughed. 'Good God, no! Quite impossible for the kid to have had anything to do with it. Poor little blighter. Bad enough that she saw it.'

'So we don't know who killed her?'

'Oh, yes. I know that all right.'

Clothier nearly stood up, but his legs weren't ready to resume their burden. 'You do?'

'Yes. Obvious. She did.'

'*She* did?'

'Told you it was a funny one. Didn't you know the lady was, to put it mildly, a bit kinky?'

'Well, no. I mean, she was a bit prickly, but I had no idea —'

'Unusual in a woman, this sort of accident.'

'Accident? I thought you said she killed herself?'

The doctor scratched his neck. 'Well, she did, I suppose. But she didn't mean to.'

'Could you — well, could you explain in words of one syllable?'

Hatcher seemed to enjoy keeping Clothier in suspense. 'I'll try. But this is all off the record. Have to put it all in the report, check it over.'

'Yes, I understand that.'

'You noticed her clothing? Or lack of it?'

'Could hardly miss it.'

'That was what killed her.'

'What was?'

'That tight-fitting gold top she was wearing.'

'I — I'm sorry. You've completely lost me again.'

The doctor nodded, smiling. 'All right. From the beginning. You've heard of people strangling themselves by accident, trying to get a sexual thrill?'

Clothier vaguely remembered. 'I — I think so.'

'I'll refresh your memory. Some strange people — usually men, as I've said — get turned on by half-strangling themselves. What they are doing is restricting the amount of oxygen that gets to the brain. Somehow it gives a heightened sense of sexual awareness. They often dress up while they do it. Many a bishop or lord or other such respected gentry has been found dangling in her ladyship's underwear. Usually kept quiet, of course.'

'You mean they deliberately hang themselves — for kicks?'

'Well, they don't *mean* to hang themselves. They set up a hook and a noose, a stool or chair, then just tighten things up enough to turn them on. But it's pretty risky — as you can imagine. Kick over the chair accidentally, the knot slips — and there you are, strung up waiting for the maid to discover you in the morning.'

'It sounds as if they must be mad.'

'Does, doesn't it? Though my shrink friends assure me they're not. Just a form of deviant sexual behaviour, one up from fetishism or masochism.'

'That's *normal*?'

'Well, you or I mightn't do it in Woolworth's on a Saturday morning, but in the psychiatrists' book it's just one end of the spectrum.'

'Is it very common?'

'Difficult to say. It's not something you'd go around talking about at cocktail parties, is it? But deaths are rare. I believe that's because the participants are often intelligent people, and they rig up some sort of safety device. As Mrs Sansome did.'

'You mean she could have prevented her death?'

'Well, she tried. The knife, that was her get-out clause.'

'You mean those wounds –'

'Were self-inflicted. Yes.'

'Jesus! What was she trying to do?'

'Cut herself down, of course. Like I said earlier, it was the fancy gold top that did it. I don't know why they like to dress up, but they do. And this lady, who if not mad was obviously very weird, also wanted the child there to watch. A form of reverse voyeurism, I suppose. And if you recall, just to make sure she had a good time, she was naked from the waist down. That was so she could use the vibrator.'

'Oh.' Clothier's frown cleared momentarily at the recollection. 'The plastic thing on the floor.'

'That's it. Didn't recognise it, eh? I didn't realise you chaps led such sheltered lives.' The doctor grinned.

Clothier began to find his jovial manner irritating. 'I still don't see how the gold top comes into it.'

'Simple. In case anything went wrong, she had a knife in her belt.'

'So she could cut herself down.'

'Correct, my dear Watson. But this fancy top – it was a real tight fit. Restricted the arms and shoulders. It was easy to demonstrate once I had her on the slab. Arms simply wouldn't go up high enough. So she tried to cut through the cord where she *could* reach it – at the side of her neck. She had several goes at it.' He shrugged his shoulders. 'She missed.'

'Jesus Christ.' Clothier felt sick.

Hatcher continued unabated. 'Only just, though. One great gash nearly got through the cord, but severed the internal jugular in the process. That did it. I think the tests won't show asphyxiation. She probably just dangled there, conscious for a bit, and bled to death.' He pursed his lips, nodding his head gently. 'Yes, I think that'll be it.' He turned to Clothier enthusiastically. 'You should see the photographs and the video your people took! There was one hell of a lot of blood on the carpet. And everywhere else.'

Clothier's nervous system gave up the unequal struggle. His eyes rolled up, and he slipped untidily to the floor.

* * *

Once he'd recovered from the nausea and embarrassment, Clothier set off for the hospital to interview Joanne Yeates. He had been told that the child was not to be discharged until the specialist child psychiatrist had assessed her, probably the next day. He knew this was a very tricky situation to handle. God knows what the experience has done to the child's mind, he thought. He remembered the little bundle trembling in his arms, the overwhelming emotion as if it had been one of his own children lost and then found . . .

He presented his warrant card to the ward sister, and was shown to a small waiting-room. After a few minutes Joanne came in, eyes sparkling, face smiling. She extended her hand, and Clothier took it.

'Sergeant Clothier. How can I ever thank you?'

'Thank me?'

'They told me you were the one who found Lucinda. "Used your initiative", I think your senior officer said.'

Clothier grinned. 'I've always wanted to say this.'

Joanne looked puzzled. 'What?'

He put on a North American accent. 'Jest doin' ma duty, ma'am.'

Joanne laughed. They smiled at each other for a long moment, then Joanne sat down.

'Nevertheless, I am so grateful. The last few days have been the worst of my life.'

'It was my pleasure.' Clothier knew it was a trite thing to say, but he meant it. Liberating that child, even in such horrific circumstances, was one of the most rewarding moments of his career. He felt his eyes moisten, and looked away as he sat next to the nurse. 'How is she? Little Lucinda?'

'She looks fine. Not a scratch on her. She seems quite normal, went through the night – with a little sedation. I slept here with her. It's the mental effects of all this they can't assess yet. They think it may take some time before we know.'

'Get the best you can for the little lass, won't you?'

Joanne regarded him carefully. 'You have children of your own?'

'Three. Little tearaways.' His voice was thick. He tried to look jovial, swallowed.

Joanne looked at him, nodded, knew she need say no more on the subject.

'So.' She sat up, spoke briskly. She sounded light-hearted, but deep in her stomach there was a churning feeling, a warning, reminding her of the scene at poor old Aunt Maud's, wondering if they'd been discovered. 'What is the interrogation about today, officer?'

'I'd like to talk to you about Christine Sansome.'

Joanne looked down. 'Yes. Of course.'

'I wanted to know if you could shed any light on why she should choose your little girl as her victim.'

Joanne felt a tightness in her chest. She had been hiding this for so long. She wanted to tell this pleasant, dumpy policeman, get it out of her system. But her loyalty to Paul, as always, stopped her. She wanted to keep silent, forget . . .

'Is it true Mrs Sansome is dead?'

'That is correct, Mrs Yeates.'

'The young officer who brought me here yesterday suggested the circumstances were somewhat — bizarre.'

Clothier nodded his agreement. 'You could say that, yes.' He thought of his recent conversation with the pathologist. 'Very bizarre.' He glanced at her, recognising a look he'd seen before, of someone who was battling with a decision to release knowledge — confess, even. He wanted to take this gently. 'Does that surprise you?'

Joanne looked up sharply, took a deep breath. 'No. No, it doesn't, really.'

'Perhaps you'd like to tell me why.'

'Sergeant, before I say — anything more — will this all have to come out in public?'

'There's bound to be a great deal of media attention.'

Joanne gave a forced smile. 'You're right there. I've practically had to fight off the press and TV. D'you know, one of them tried to sneak in and talk to me in the middle of the night.'

'I can believe it. Haven't any of them waved cheque-books at you yet?'

'So far I haven't given them a chance. I can never understand people who are willing to expose their sadness, or joy, or whatever it is, in public.'

'Neither can I. But don't judge them too harshly. There are a lot of pressures in those circumstances, and often I believe they don't think, just do it because these days it's almost the norm.'

Joanne looked at him. 'You're a very thoughtful man.'

'I try.' He smiled at her. 'But I'm also trying to get your thoughts on Christine Sansome.'

'Sorry. I wasn't being deliberately evasive. But if all this has to come out, be gone over in open court . . .'

'I don't want to be pushy, but you have a duty to reveal any material facts, you know.'

'But what is material? The woman is dead. She can't be prosecuted for anything now. Can she?'

'No. I doubt any court case will follow. But as I said, there *has* to be an inquest. Just how much will have to come out then, I can't say.'

'Oh, dear.' Joanne bit her lip. 'I just don't know what to do.'

'Look. This isn't a threat, it's advice. It's obvious that you know something. And the Court could subpoena you.'

'Force me to attend as a witness, you mean? On oath?'

'That's right.'

She shook her head in distress, knew she was cornered. 'But I promised Paul — ' She stopped abruptly.

'That would be Dr Paul Sansome, would it? Christine Sansome's husband?'

Joanne nodded.

'Present whereabouts unknown?' He posed the question gently.

'Yes. That Dr Sansome.' She dared not look up.

Clothier cleared his throat. 'I think it might help if I told you a little more about what *I* now know about Mrs Sansome. Might make it a bit easier for you, and I think will do no harm, as I'm pretty sure you have some idea of most of it already.'

Joanne eyed him cautiously. He seemed so reasonable, so helpful — or was he just laying a trap for her? But if he *did* know all about Christine, then what was the point of further secrecy? 'Thank you. I'm listening.'

'The search of the Sansome residence was very revealing. For one thing, it would seem Mrs Sansome was an alcoholic.' He watched the nurse nod her agreement. 'We found vodka bottles hidden all over the house. Dozens and dozens of them.'

Joanne murmured so that Clothier had to strain to hear. 'It was always vodka. Paul — Dr Sansome told me. She thought he couldn't smell it on her breath.'

'She also had strange sexual tendencies. A cupboard full of — ah — equipment, clothing, pictures. Including pictures of children.' Clothier could see that Joanne had gone pale, could see that she knew. 'When she — when she died, it was as a result of a sexual game with a rope that went wrong. I expect you guessed that?'

'More or less.' Joanne shook her head, then her face creased in a grimace of anguish. 'Why did the bloody bitch have to make Lucinda watch? Why?' Then she was crying, fighting to stop, sobbing again. Clothier watched sadly, went through the ritual of offering his handkerchief. Joanne took it without comment.

When she was quiet, Clothier spoke again. 'We also found a large quantity of pink notepaper.'

'The witch!' Joanne spat the words. 'The evil witch.'

'Could you be more specific?'

Joanne felt long-suppressed rage build up in her chest. There was no point in holding out now. Soon everyone would know. 'She was the devil incarnate. a nymphomaniac, sexual deviant, a cunning, conniving drunkard. A blackmailer. A bitch.'

'You knew all that — but didn't say anything?'

Joanne could hardly speak. 'No.' It was barely a whisper.

'And you suspected she was blackmailing you, threatening Lucinda?'

She spoke again, barely audible. 'I only had the vaguest notion. But now, after what's happened . . .'

'Then why, for God's sake, didn't you say anything before?'

'I told you. It wasn't much more than an idea. I thought I might just be paranoid about her. But I knew what she was like. Always dramatic, over-playing her part, always the actress, always threatening. But never risking exposure. She needed her public image, the influence and status it gave her. Not to mention the money. I just didn't think she'd actually do it.' She hesitated. 'Besides, I didn't think anyone would believe me, anyway.'

'If you'd told me of your suspicions, I would have believed you. Right from the first attack on your flat, I've known it was a woman.'

Joanne raised her tear-stained face. 'How?'

'From the graffiti on your wall. The hand-writing expert put me on to a psychologist with a special interest in the subject. She was certain it was a woman — though even my own inspector wouldn't listen.'

'I wasn't sure about that attack — surely men did that?'

'Yes, I'm sure they did the damage. She probably paid them. But she was there. I expect watching them smash up your place gave her a kick, too. And she couldn't resist the message.'

Joanne shuddered. 'With the blood of our poor cat.'

'She behaved like that, and you still didn't think she'd really take Lucinda?'

'No, I didn't. Just like I didn't think it was she who cut my leg, or collected the message in the bottle, or —' she trembled again at the memory '— behaved in that disgusting fashion in the car park. I remember recognising a smell, thinking about it afterwards, it was like her perfume. I knew she was depraved, but — those sort of things? I really thought there was someone else involved.'

'I shall want to hear more about all that. But we still haven't touched on the other vital issue: why? Why were you subjected to all this abuse?'

Joanne licked her lips. 'I think there were times when she thought she was invincible, could do anything. I think when that failed, that's what pushed her into taking Lucinda.'

'But *why*, Mrs Yeates? Why did she want to punish you?'

Joanne shifted her position, uneasily.

'Because of Paul. And me. We were — lovers.'

Clothier nodded slowly. 'I see. And she found out?'

'She did, with her usual cunning. Set a trap for us, and we walked right into it.'

'Why didn't Dr Sansome divorce her?'

Joanne breathed in slowly, then out again. Why indeed? she thought. They had gone over this so many times.

Clothier was watching her closely. 'I'm sorry. If this is too distressing for you . . .'

'No, it's all right. Might as well get it over with.' She brushed some hair away from her eyes. 'Obviously, he didn't know what sort of a person she was when he married her. She put up such a good performance to catch him, to get what she was after — the money, the position. And he was completely under her spell. He made every excuse for her, for years. But in the end — some of the things she did, the drinking, the perversions.' Joanne picked at the sleeves of her dress, collecting her thoughts. Clothier waited in silence for her to continue.

'He always thought she must be mentally ill. Always making allowances. I think at first he didn't want to admit to himself that he had made such a horrendous mistake, such an error of judgement. Then he put it all down to something she could not control. He was always trying to get her treatment, but she always refused. Anyway —' Joanne faltered, knew she could not keep the bitterness from her voice ' — anyway, there's no treatment that will change a psychopath. The last thing she wanted was to have anyone try and modify her behaviour. She was addicted to her perversions, just as much as she was to the alcohol. And yet to the world, she presented herself as a model of society. Most of the time.'

'So Dr Sansome thought divorcing someone he regarded as being in some way ill was not the thing to do?'

'Sounds terribly old-fashioned, but yes, it was something like that.'

'And you continued your affair?'

'Yes.'

'You came to some arrangement?'

Joanne flushed. 'Yes. She didn't want a divorce, of course. She would lose her status, be revealed as an alcoholic at the very least, and say goodbye to some of her income and property. Paul didn't want to expose her either, as I've said, and a divorce would not have helped his career. So we had a sort of agreement.'

'But when he went on the skiing holiday, he was with his wife.'

'Yes. I've never really understood that. Why she went with him, why he took her.'

'You don't think it was a reconciliation attempt?'

'I did speak to her on the phone before they left.' She looked embarrassed. 'She was looking for Paul. He was —'

Clothier nodded his understanding.

'She implied she was going to try and make up with Paul. I think she was just trying to hurt me. I know he'd have told me if — if he was going to try.'

'Look, you're doing bloody well. Can I ask you a few more things — if you don't mind?'

Joanne almost smiled. 'There's not much more to tell, but now I've gone this far —' She shrugged.

'How did you and Dr Sansome meet?'

'Oh, at the Neurological Unit. Although he worked out at the Research Institute, he often came onto the Neuro Unit to see patients with particular problems.'

'Did he know Mr Porthenoy?'

'They knew each other, yes, but not that well. They weren't friends. Mr Porthenoy was in Neurosurgery, and Dr Sansome's interests were mainly in the physical line — diseases of the nervous system, like multiple sclerosis, or epilepsy, rather than things that needed surgery, like trauma, or tumours.'

'However did you feel when he came onto your ward to be nursed after the accident?'

Joanne clasped her hands firmly in her lap, then looked Clothier in the eye. 'I wanted it. I asked for him to come on my ward. If anyone was going to be looking after him, I wanted it to be me.'

'That must have been very hard for you.'

'In a way, yes. But it meant I was close to him, could see him. *She* wanted him dead. But I've seen miracles of recovery before from coma. I knew I could keep him alive, and wait and pray for the miracle to happen.'

'Do you think that was why that poor nurse was electrocuted? Was she trying to stop you keeping him alive? Or was that just revenge?'

'That was so awful. I kept wondering if it was meant for me. But it seemed so haphazard. I never touched the special equipment in there.'

'So you think Mr Parkes or Miss Donaldson were the targets.'

'Maybe I'm just trying to kid myself — but yes, I do.'

'Any idea why?'

'None whatsoever.'

'And do you know why she wanted to get copies of the program they were using?'

'No. Perhaps she was hoping to sell it if the technique was a success, something like that.'

Clothier thought a moment. 'Talking of money, did you know she was applying for powers through the Court of Protection for Dr Sansome?'

Joanne frowned. 'No. What's that?'

'It's a way of getting control over someone's estate when they can neither give consent by power of attorney or make any decisions for themselves.'

'Never heard of it.'

'Oh. I just wondered.'

'Why?'

'We found a lot of papers referring to it at the house. A couple of days before you were pushed under the lorry, she'd had a letter from the Master of the Court, telling her she would have to have a character assessment. I don't know if anyone had smelt a rat, or heard a rumour. But the letter said they would have to interview various people — including those who were nursing her husband — and that included you.'

Joanne gaped, open-mouthed. 'And because of that she tried to kill me? My God!'

'That's right. *I* think she hoped to use the computer program to produce evidence that she could use to show her husband was capable of giving her power of attorney.'

'He'd never have agreed, I'm sure.'

'Perhaps she thought she could, well, persuade him?'

'I don't think so.'

Clothier looked sombre. 'Well, anyway, it all went wrong. After the lorry incident had failed as well, my theory is that she flipped completely. Knowing how best to make you suffer, instead of just threats, she took Lucinda. And paid a terrible price.'

'I'm not sorry she's gone. She was evil.'

'How did Dr Sansome take the news?'

'We haven't had the —' Joanne's mouth clamped shut.

Clothier felt a surge of triumph. He smiled gently. 'Haven't had what, Mrs Yeates? The chance to tell him yet?'

Her mind was racing. A trap! Was that all this was about, a long and laborious road to a trap? She tried not to look flustered, but was afraid her face had already given her away.

'I — how could I tell him?'

'Using all that special research equipment that communicates with the deeply comatose. I know all about that. Ted Parkes told me himself.'

'Well, yes, that's *how* we — you'd tell him. But he's missing, isn't he?'

'Yes, indeed he is. I was hoping you might be able to give me some clue as to where he is.'

She shook her head vigorously, in an expression of denial, but also in an attempt to shake off the feeling that her lies were so transparent. She forced herself to meet his eyes. 'I have no idea.'

'Oh.' The sergeant looked genuinely disappointed. 'I was hoping you might. After all, now all this is over, there seems no point in keeping him any more.' He looked up and smiled benignly. 'Is there?'

'I don't see what you're getting at.'

'I've kept asking myself why anyone would want to kidnap a comatose man. There wouldn't seem much point unless you could — well, talk to him in some way? Don't you agree?'

Joanne looked away, shrugged. 'I — I don't know, I —'

'I thought, well, if he knew something about all this, about who might have taken your daughter, for instance, and someone had access to this source of knowledge denied them, well, maybe they would consider abduction of the potential informant an option.' He smiled again.

Joanne wanted to give in, tell him where Paul was, get the whole business finished. Her secret was out, her career finished anyway. But her daughter was alive, in the next room, alive, would need her; they wouldn't send her to prison for her part in the affair, surely she could stay free . . .

She became aware Clothier was waiting for her decision. *Bugger it!* She swore to herself. She just couldn't leave Ted and Claire without a warning. They had to have their chance to get away, if that was what they chose to do. She owed them that.

'I'm sorry. You've been very helpful and sympathetic. But I just can't help you any further.'

She thought he would argue, try and press her, trick her again. But instead he hauled his bulk out of the chair, and extended a hand. 'Mrs Yeates, you're a brave lady. Thank you for all you've told me. You've been a great help.'

Joanne stood up and shook the proffered hand. 'Well, I — I'm glad if I've been of use. I can't thank you enough for what you've done.'

'You take care of that little girl, now. Give her my love.'

'I will. Thanks again.'

Clothier waved a hand dismissively, and left.

Joanne walked quickly back down the corridor to Lucinda's private room. It was nearly lunch-time. Her daughter was watching cartoons on the television.

'Hello, Mummy. Where have you been?'

Joanne forced a smile. 'Talking to that nice policeman, Sergeant Clothier.'

'The fat one?'

'Yes, that's the one.'

'I like him,' she informed her mother matter-of-factly. 'He rescued me from the nasty dead lady.'

Joanne could think of no adequate reply. Her daughter saved her the trouble by changing the subject.

'I'm hungry.'

That she could deal with. 'Lunch'll be here in a minute.' There was the sound of crashes and bangs from the TV set, and Lucinda was soon engrossed once more. Joanne licked her lips, and looked at the telephone on the bedside cabinet. She unclenched her fist, snatched up the receiver, waited.

'Directory enquiries. Which town please?'

Within a minute she had the number of the village store in Kingston Seymour. The woman in the shop was all agog to hear the voice of someone who was so much in the news.

'Ooh! Hello, Mrs Yeates. Oh, we're all so pleased your little girl is all right. We saw it on the telly. Poor little mite, shut up with that dead woman! However's your poor aunt coping, her so frail an' all —?'

Joanne managed to interrupt the flow, and asked if someone would be so kind as to go along to her aunt's house and ask the young lady who was looking after her aunt to call her. Only too glad to help, she was told several times. Clearly, being in the news had its advantages. She made the woman read the number back to her to make sure it was correct, then settled down to wait. She was soon distracted by the arrival of her daughter's lunch, and they chatted happily as the little girl ate her way through her meal.

The tray had just been taken away when the phone rang. It was the hospital switchboard.

'I have an outside call for you.'

There was a click as the connection was made.

'Claire! Is that you?'

'Yes. Hello, Joanne.' She sounded breathless. 'How's Lucinda?'

'Oh, she's fine, just fine.' She glanced across at her daughter, who was once more absorbed in watching television.

'Is everything all right? You sound worried.'

'I am. But not about Lucinda. About you.'

'What's the matter?'

'I've been questioned by Sergeant Clothier. About Christine Sansome's death.'

'Oh, it sounds so *awful*! It's been on the radio.'

'Have you told Paul?'

'That she's dead? No, we didn't know whether we should. But Joanne, you must hear what we've found out! We've been talking to him – all last night, and this morning. It's incredible! You'll never believe —'

'Claire, listen! There's no time!'

'But it's all so fantastic.' Her voice dropped, as she tried to make sure no one overheard her in the shop. 'Did you know Paul had connections with the Ministry of Defence? He's told us all about this man, do you remember how we —?'

'Claire! Please! You must listen!'

'Sorry. No need to shout. But it's so exciting, I —'

'Shut *up* Claire! You're in danger.'

'Danger? What do you mean?'

'I'm trying to tell you, for God's sake! Are you listening?'

'Yes. Sorry. I'm all ears.' She sounded calmer.

'Good. Look, it's probably all my fault, but I think I let slip that I knew where Paul was. Not in so many words, but Clothier, he — he sort of laid a trap for me, about Paul. Anyway, the details don't matter. But I'm sure the police will be checking on the house in Kingston Seymour. You and Ted have to get out.'

'Get out? But we can't just leave. What about Paul? And Maudie?'

'Lucinda seems amazingly well, so I'll come down straight away. I can be there in an hour. You and Ted take everything you can, the data you've collected and the computer, anyway — and get out of there. Now!'

'Joanne, we can't just up and —'

'Claire, please!' She was almost shouting again. Lucinda gave her a puzzled glance, then turned her attention back to the flickering screen.

'But what about you? If the police are coming, they'll find Paul, and you'll be arrested, or something.'

'I don't think so. Not with Lucinda having just been through what she has. They won't keep me from her, I'm sure. Even if they arrest me, I'll be out on bail.'

'But — but we can't just leave you to face the music.'

'I'll be all right. It's all over now, anyway. Christine is dead. She was sending the pink letters, was threatening me, tried to kill me. And now she's dead. We've got to come clean sometime, get Paul back to a proper hospital.'

'Christine! She was behind all that? But from what Paul has told us, we thought —'

'Claire! There's no time! I'll tell you everything later.' She thought quickly, spoke again before Claire could interrupt. 'Ring my sister. Make some arrangement with her about how we can meet or talk.'

'But all this stuff we've got from Paul. We can't just —'

'So take it with you. If you've got to look into it, go somewhere and hide out until you've worked it out. Then get in touch with me.'

There was silence the other end. Joanne could hear the murmur of noise from the shop in the background. 'Claire. Are you still there?'

'Yes. I — I don't know what to say. I feel like a rat, just clearing out. But this information we have, I don't know what we should do with it.'

'Maybe you should just hand it all over to the police. They seem to know pretty well everything.'

'I'll ask Ted. You'll be here in an hour, you say?'

'Yes, easily. I'll catch a train.'

She knew it might take longer, but she wanted them to be gone.

'Why don't we just wait for you to arrive?'

'No! For all I know they're already on their way to you.'

'Christ!' Another silence, shorter this time. 'Look, Joanne, you're a fantastic woman, you know that? We'll do as you say. I'll be in touch.'

'Claire!'

'Yes?'

'Get a local taxi to Yatton, then hire a car. There's a place near the station. The police will know Ted's — is it still in the barn?'

'Yes.'

'Just leave it there. Can I use it when the dust settles?'

'Of course.' Claire started to say goodbye, then stopped. 'Oh, Joanne! Wait a second. There are two things I *must* tell you!'

'Claire —'

'Two minutes. It's important. We asked Paul if he would have consented to us taking him from the hospital so we could communicate with him. He said "yes", twice. Ted recorded the sequence on disk — like he has all the rest. I don't know what a court of law would make of it, but it's something.'

'That's great, Claire. Really great. But hurry — what's the other thing?'

'Ah, yes. Paul gave us a message. For you. Very enigmatic.'

From the tone of her voice Joanne could picture Claire smiling mischievously. She felt an unexpected tingle of anticipation despite her anxiety and desire for haste.

'What was it?'

'Just before we signed off just now. He was tired. We were going to tell him to stop, when he spelled out for us to wait. Then he told us — he said, "Tell Joanne I love her." '

Joanne was speechless, felt weak. The phone nearly dropped from her hand. This time it was Claire who thought she had been cut off.

'Joanne! Can you hear me?'

With an effort Joanne spoke again. 'Yes. Sorry, Claire.'

'What do you think of that, then?'

'I — I think it's — it's very nice.'

'Very nice? You sound all funny. Are you all right?'
'Yes, I'm OK. Now for heaven's sake —'
'All right, all right.'
'Good luck. And *get going*!'
'We will. Thanks, Joanne.'
'Forget it. Now goodbye.' Joanne put the phone down firmly, then went over to the armchair across the room and flopped down. A message from Paul! She could not believe it. She had hoped this system devised by Claire and Ted might enable her to communicate with Paul personally, one day. But to have a message like that! Just when she needed it, to give her strength. More than ever, now, she wanted to get down there, see him, touch him, knowing that even in that shell of a body his mind still thought of her, loved her . . .
She explained to her daughter as best she could that she was going to Great Aunt Maudie's, but she'd be back tonight. Then she popped into the ward office, disregarding the mildly disapproving look the staff nurse gave her as she informed her of her temporary absence, successfully dodged the press outside, and set off for the station.

* * *

Downstairs, in the office that housed the hospital switchboard, the CID man switched off the tape-recorder and grinned at his colleague.
'Bingo! Let's go and get Sergeant Clothier.'

CHAPTER 42

Ted packed all the gear he could into a large hold-all, while Claire summoned a taxi. The computer itself and the terminal just fitted in, with the supplementary 196 Mb hard drive and the two sets of disks wedged between them. They packed them round with some towels as protection from too many bumps.

Claire returned from the phone. 'Ten minutes, they said. How are you doing?'

'OK. It'll be awkward, but as long as I don't drop it . . . You'd better throw a few things in a bag — just the basics, mine and yours.'

'What about money?' she called from the bathroom, throwing toothbrushes, razors, make-up, all in together.

'I've got about sixty quid. Should be enough for now.'

Ted struggled down the stairs with the hold-all. It was awkward rather than heavy, but he was still weak from his recent ordeal, and the rib still hurt like hell when he moved in a certain way. Claire rushed down the stairs with a large shoulder bag, doing up the zip as she came.

'Hope this'll do.' She looked up and saw Ted's drawn, pained expression. 'You're mad. You should have let me bring it downstairs.'

Ted was trying to slow down his breathing. 'Be all right in a minute.'

Claire heard a car draw up. 'Here's the taxi.'

Ted picked up the hold-all and rejected Claire's attempt to take it from him. 'Let's go.'

Claire opened the front door, to see the taxi-driver walking up the path. He took Ted's hold-all, put it in the boot, and helped him into the back of the car.

'Wait a minute,' Claire commanded the driver. She ran back indoors, up to Paul's room. He seemed settled, the drip bottle was full. It should run for at least four hours. He had had a tube feed not an hour before. She went to Maudie's room. She was sitting in an armchair, asleep. She softly closed the door, so did not see Maudie open one eye and smile as she listened to Claire's footsteps descending the stairs.

Outside again, she flicked the lever on the deadlock, pulling the front door shut behind her. When she got back to the waiting taxi, Ted was holding something out to her. 'Keys! To the car. For Joanne.'

Claire snatched them, went back, found the door locked, cursed under her breath, and posted the keys through the letter-box. She jumped in the back of the taxi beside Ted, instructed the driver, and they drove away.

Upstairs, Maudie waited until the noise of the engine faded, then got up from her chair.

* * *

As they approached the garage near the station, where Joanne said they could hire a car, Ted told the driver to pull into the station yard and asked him to wait. He got out, and beckoned Claire to follow.

'What's the matter, Ted?'

'As we turned into the street, I could swear I saw someone in uniform go into the garage.'

'The police?' She glanced round, brow furrowed in concern.

'Looked like it to me.'

'Surely they're not on to us already?'

'Whether they are or not, we can't go in there while they're there.' They spoke quietly, standing with their taxi between themselves and the garage, looking over the roof. Two policemen emerged from the garage; one pointed across the road, then went back inside. The other crossed the road and entered a small newsagent's shop.

'Shit! They're watching the place. I think they *are* on to us!'

'But how?'

'God knows!'

'What shall we do? Catch a train?'

'They might be watching that, too. We can't just hang around in the station – it might be ages before the next train. But they can't have seen us yet.'

'Motorway! It's not far. We'll go to the motorway and hitch. They won't know if we've gone north or south.'

'Sounds as good as anything.'

They got back in the taxi, and headed for the M5.

* * *

The old lady looked down at the sleeping man, a fond smile on her face.

'Don't worry. Auntie Maudie will look after you.' She bent and gently stroked the side of Paul's face with a bony finger. 'But we must get rid of these nasty needles first.'

Her hands moved to Paul's forearm. She had some difficulty getting her fingernails under the tape holding the intravenous cannula in place, but eventually she succeeded.

'There!' she declared in triumph, as she pulled on the thin tubing. It slithered out of the vein and onto the floor, where she left it to drip slowly into a crack between the bare boards. She had already turned her attention elsewhere, ignoring the welling blood trickling down onto the white sheet.

Her eye fixed on Paul's scalp. She shook her head and tutted.

'And as for these. I never did like these.' She went round to the top of the bed, unfastened the steel wire cradle, and began to tug vigorously on the electrodes.

* * *

Joanne sat in the train only a mile outside Yatton station and cursed. This was the third time the train had stopped in the short journey from Bristol. Something about track maintenance. *Why did it have to be today*? She looked at her watch for the tenth time in as many minutes. Nearly two hours! God, I hope he's all right! The train lurched, and then started to roll forward, slowly, not much more than walking pace at first, then gathered speed, slowing again as it pulled in to Yatton station.

No taxis! Why no taxis?

'I can ring for one, miss. But the bus'll be going in half a mo.' The ruddy-faced railway employee pointed to the green and white coach parked nearby.

'Thanks.' She climbed aboard, fretting with every minute's delay. The driver was talking through his window, in animated conversation with another man in a lorry. Eventually he started the engine, but still did not move off. A laugh, a wave of the hand, a crunch of gears, and at long last he pulled away.

Joanne jumped from the bus almost before it had squealed to a halt outside the village shop. Running blindly towards the house, she did not see the men watching, or the cars parked round the corner.

She arrived, panting, sweating. Front door's locked, they've gone! She rummaged in her handbag for the key, rammed it home, turned it, and almost fell inside, not stopping to close it behind her.

'Maudie! It's me. Joanne!'

The house sounded very still and quiet. She dropped her handbag, ran up the stairs. She heard a gurgling sound from Paul's room, rushed to the door, stood there momentarily transfixed.

Maudie looked up at her and beamed. 'I told you I was a good nurse.'

Her aged aunt cradled Paul's head in one arm, and in her other she had a glass of milk. Joanne took in the intravenous drip dangling uselessly, the blood-stained sheet by his arm, his head with its stubby growth of hair, he looked so normal, so much more normal —

'The electrodes! Maudie, what've you done with the electrodes?'

The old lady did not move, but continued to smile with a look of satisfaction at her niece. Joanne rushed round to the end of the bed and stared in horror at the three gaping holes in her lover's skull. She could not move, just stared, kept staring . . .

'I've been very gentle, Joanne. And he seems so thirsty, you know.'

As she spoke she moved the glass to the doctor's lips, and tipped milk into his mouth. Some spilled out, but the rest went to the back of the throat. He had no swallowing or coughing reflexes, there was nothing to stop the white liquid trickling into the main breathing tubes and down into the lungs. The gurgling sound came again as Paul attempted to breathe through the fluid.

The noise seemed to break Joanne's trance-like state. She rushed round the bed, pushed her aunt roughly aside. 'Leave him alone! Get away from him!'

Paul was going a dusky colour, his lips were turning blue. Joanne heard someone screaming, realised it was herself. Her nurse's training struggled to surface. She turned Paul almost onto his front, began to pound his chest with her palm. Bubbly white mucus drooled from his flaccid lips. His colour darkened.

'Oh, God, no! Please, no!'

Then she heard the sirens, the squeal of tyres, many footsteps running up the stairs. She ignored them, kept working, slapping, as the room filled with men, her tears flowing, until a firm but gentle pair of hands gripped her shoulders and pulled her away.

'It's all right, miss, we've got him now.'

She allowed herself to be drawn back from the bed. She stood there, watching through her tears. Fear and hope surfaced in turn as laryngoscopes, endotracheal tubes, suction apparatus and portable oxygen were all put to work.

* * *

'Can I make anyone else some more tea?'

Joanne looked round the room. Heads shook, thanks were murmured, hands held up in polite refusal.

'I don't know how to thank you.' She turned to the uniformed man sitting opposite her at the table.

'We always try our best, miss.' The ambulance man sipped at his mug. 'You should thank the police for making sure there was a fully equipped ambulance in attendance.'

'I didn't know you were trained to intubate.'

'Part of the new training. They do it in the States all the time, the para-medics. We're a bit behind the times here.'

'Well, you certainly saved Dr Sansome's life.'

'Not often we have to suction milk from the trachea.' The man tried to make light of it. 'But I think we were quick enough.'

'You gave him oxygen as well, didn't you?'

'Yes, straight away. His colour returned immediately.'

'So he should be all right?'

He sipped his tea again. 'Difficult to tell, to be honest. Him being, well, comatose already.'

'But he's alive. That's the main thing.'

'Oh, yes, miss. He's alive.'

* * *

Joanne said a silent goodbye to Paul, then stepped down from the ambulance and watched it draw carefully away. As she turned to go back inside, an unmarked police car drew up behind the others down the lane. She recognised Sergeant Clothier immediately. She felt a mixture of emotions: shame, that she had unsuccessfully tried to dupe him, and anger that he had set a trap for her — the policemen who came to the house admitted they had been in waiting before she arrived. She decided she might as well get the encounter over. He was only doing his job, after all.

'Good afternoon, Sergeant.'

'Hello, Mrs Yeates. I'm glad you're still speaking to me.'

'There seems little point in not. We were only doing what we thought was right, but nevertheless from your point of view we were acting unlawfully.'

'I gather from the report I got on the radio that Dr Sansome is going to be all right?'

Joanne went into the house before answering. The policeman followed, and she turned to him.

'In reality, the fact that your men and the ambulance were already waiting probably saved his life.' She went on to tell him about Aunt Maude's well-intentioned but near-fatal attempt at nursing.

'Sounds horrific! Could she have caused more brain damage by removing the electrodes from his skull?'

'I suppose it's possible. But the wires are very thin. I should think the greatest danger is infection through the wounds she left open.'

'Will they be able to replace them?'

'That I don't know.'

'I was thinking it might put an end to attempts to communicate with him again.'

Joanne's eyes moistened at the recollection of her treasured message. 'I hope not. I really do hope not.'

They ended up in the kitchen. Joanne offered the inevitable cup of tea. Clothier thanked her and accepted a biscuit as well.

When he had helped himself to milk and sugar, he sat down at the table. 'What do you propose to do about your aunt?'

'In the long run, I'm not sure. But it's clear she's not safe here alone, and I have to be with Lucinda. In the short term, I suppose she'll have to go into a rest home. There are some nice ones near here. She owns the house, so there'll be enough capital to keep her going for years.'

'What about tonight?'

Joanne looked up at him, a knot of fear in her stomach. 'What are you getting at?' She saw the gravity in his eyes. 'Are you going to arrest me, then?'

He looked slightly uncomfortable. 'I — ah, I have no specific instructions about that as yet.'

'What does it depend on?'

'*Who* does it depend on would be more accurate. I have had no orders from on high. But it might help if you could assist me in locating Miss Donaldson and Mr Parkes.'

Joanne shook her head. 'I can't.'

'Or won't?'

'No, I honestly don't know where they might have gone. You heard what we said when you were listening in.' Clothier avoided her accusing glance. 'Nothing was said about their destination. I'm surprised you didn't pick them at the hire place in Yatton.'

'They never turned up there.'

'Anyway, I can't help you.'

'I also heard that they have some evidence that Dr Sansome was not, in effect, abducted against his will. In that regard it might be in your interest to help us locate them.'

'It might. But I'm not going to make any sort of decision on that now, and I hope you aren't going to try and coerce me.'

'Mrs Yeates, I don't think I am. No one is more relieved than I that you have your daughter back. I shall try to make sure I am not party to you being separated again. Not for now, at least.'

Joanne looked at the dumpy figure sprawled at the table, looked into his eyes, and was certain she saw compassion, sincerity. She felt compelled to touch him, moved and laid a hand on his arm. 'Thank you.'

The sergeant shrugged and looked up at her. There was a long moment of silence, broken by the entry of a young policeman carrying a sheet of paper. He approached Joanne, hesitated when he saw Clothier.

The sergeant nodded. 'Go ahead.'

'I've got that list of rest homes you asked for. Couple of them sound real nice.'

'Thank you.' Joanne took the paper, looked up and smiled at the young man, then across at Clothier. 'I couldn't ring from here, so I asked him to go to the village shop,' she explained. 'They've got a local directory.' She looked down at the list, the constable reading over her shoulder.

'That sounds nice.' He pointed. 'Tradewinds Retirement Home. It's only just the other side of Yatton. My grannie's in one like that. She loves it.'

Joanne stood up and spoke to Clothier. 'Is it all right if I go and see one or two? I'd like to fix something if I can, so I can go back to Lucinda tonight.'

'Of course. I'll run you round myself, if you want.'

'That's very kind. But I think I'd rather go alone. I can use Ted's car.' She went towards the door, and Clothier got up to follow. 'It's all right, I won't try and escape.'

Clothier smiled. 'I know. Just coming to see you off.'

Joanne picked up the keys she had found on the hall floor, and went out to the barn. The police officer helped her open the doors, then after holding the car door for her he waited whilst she got the engine started. It made a lot of smoke, and he quickly went out into the fresh air, down the drive, and then stood across the lane to wave her clear as she backed out. His eye caught something under the car as it rose over the incline from driveway to lane. Loose exhaust. I'll tell her about it when she gets back.

Joanne let the car run to a halt, then engaged first gear. She wound down her window and waved at Clothier. He waved back, called out. 'Take care, now.'

Joanne pulled away carefully, and as she drew level with him, his eye was again drawn to the underside of the vehicle.

Funny, there can't be an exhaust there. Reminds me of something . . . Joanne was past him now, beginning to pick up speed. Something from a recent training film, about looking under cars, suspicious objects . . . The memory focused in his brain, and in an instant he was certain.

'Mrs Yeates! JOANNE!' He started to run after the car. '*JOANNE!*' He screamed her name at the top of his voice, saw the young constable come running out of the house, the brake lights of the car come on, off again.

'Joanne, get out of the car!' He was only 20 feet away now, shouting as he ran. The brake lights came on again as Joanne jammed her foot on the pedal in response to the warning. As she turned to look back at Clothier, the car lurched to a halt, sending a small silver-coloured blob of mercury rushing down a narrow tube suspended beneath her, under the floor. The liquid metal reached the two contacts projecting into the tube, completed the electrical circuit, and sent a current to the detonator.

The massive explosion shattered glass throughout the house, and in the police cars parked nearby, turning one over. The young constable was blown back into the house, the bones in a flailing fore-arm snapping cleanly on the edge of the door frame. Joanne was dismembered instantly by the blast centred directly beneath her. Clothier's eardrums were ruptured by the roar, his eyes blinded by the flash, his hair set alight. He didn't see the section of door-post that drove into his brain, or feel the slice of the shard of steel that virtually decapitated him. He was dead before his disjointed body landed thirty feet away from the scattered remnants of the car and the pieces of flesh that had once been Joanne Yeates.

CHAPTER 43

Claire stood up, paced across the room, turned, flung her arms wide and let them drop to her side again.

'My God, Ted, I just can't believe it!' She walked back again to look over his shoulder at the newspaper he was reading. 'I mean, who would do a thing like that? Why?' She flopped down in the chair opposite and put her face in her hands, unable to stop the tears. 'Poor Joanne. Oh, Ted. She didn't deserve it, after everything she —' She was barely intelligible for a few moments. 'And Lucinda, poor little girl, just when she really needed —'

Ted got up and moved to kneel by Claire's side. He stroked her hair. 'Please, Claire. I — I don't know how to handle this, how to help. Try and calm down a bit.'

Claire turned on him. 'Calm down a bit! Christ, Ted! Don't you *care*?' She looked up into his face, saw the brimming eyes. 'I — I'm sorry!' She leaned on his shoulder, sobbing helplessly. Ted put his arm across her back, waited for her to settle.

'That's better.' He squeezed her upper arm. 'That's more like it.'

Claire pulled away a little. Ted looked at the puffy eyes, the streaming nose. She looked so vulnerable, so like a small child . . .

Claire raised her eyes to meet his, and voiced the thought that they had both kept unspoken. 'The bomb — it was meant — for us, wasn't it?'

Ted looked away. 'It was my car. It must have been me they were after.'

'But why, Ted, why something like this? What have we done?'

Ted was keen to try and analyse the situation, felt more able to cope with that than the emotional consequences of what had occurred.

'The paper says the police don't think it was the IRA.' He went over to his chair and picked up the tabloid, read the details again.

> The car belonged to Mr Edward Parkes (34), an Australian researcher in the new and revolutionary field of computerised neurological communication. He has no known connections with any terrorist organisation.
>
> The dead woman, now identified from dental records as Mrs Joanne Yeates (36), had only just been reunited with her daughter after the Lucinda Yeates kidnapping affair. A police spokesperson said they

would not speculate further until more details were known, but colleagues present at a briefing yesterday afternoon suggested that they were trying to establish a link between the murder of Mrs Yeates and the death of a student nurse at the Bristol Neurological Unit some weeks ago.

There was also speculation that the sexual deviant and child abuser, missing coma doctor's wife Mrs Christine Sansome, who hanged herself in bizarre circumstances two days ago, is also connected to the bombing.

Claire wiped her nose on a tissue. 'Do you think Christine had anything to do with this?'

Ted shook his head slowly. 'It can't have been her. When we heard about her being hanged, when we knew she was dead, I thought somehow Joanne's troubles were over. And ours. I felt certain she was the cause of everything — the threats to Joanne, the attempts to steal the computer data, the attacks on you and me — even though I couldn't explain it all. But now, with what we've just learnt from Paul . . .'

They were both silent, then Claire let out a wail of despair. 'Ted, what are we going to do?'

'I — I'm not sure.' He looked around the simply furnished room. The double bed, two armchairs, a wardrobe. They had arrived here the previous evening after picking up a lift on the slip road of the M5, where the taxi had left them. The lorry driver was going to Cardiff, so they had crossed the Severn Bridge, and from Cardiff had travelled on to Swansea. They were now in Sketty, to the north-west of the city, at the Little Oaks Guest House, a temporary refuge picked at random. 'We need to sort out some sort of plan. I need to think —'

'No! No more plans! Look what a sodding awful mess our plans have got us into already!' She grabbed the newspaper. 'Look! I mean, for Christ's sake!'

Police are looking for Edward Parkes and his associate, Miss Claire Donaldson (28), who it is thought were involved in the disappearance of coma victim Dr Paul Sansome. The senior officer in charge of the investigation has asked anyone seeing them to contact their local station.

She threw the paper down. 'There's even a bloody photograph!'

'So what are you saying?'

'Let's just go to the police and get it over. I can't take any more of this cloak-and-dagger stuff. Joanne's dead, and Paul's probably not far off it if you can believe that.' She waved her hand at the paper. 'I thought we were being so bloody smart!' Her face twisted in a grimace of bitter torment. 'And what have we achieved? Absolutely fuck all!' She collapsed back in the chair.

Ted tried to make light of her outburst. 'Dear me, such language from a lady.'

'Get lost, Ted.'

'Sorry.' He waited a moment. 'Look, I'm just a simple Aussie fella thousands of miles from home. Here I am in the middle of mayhem and murder, and I don't know what to do about it any more than you do.'

'So why don't we just let the authorities take over?'

Ted sighed deeply. 'I guess I'm just shit scared they'll lock us up, and we won't be able to do anything about it.'

'About what?'

'About our own situation, of course. Or about what Paul told us.'

'I knew that was it. You want to go on probing, like some amateur sleuth, to find out what's behind all this.'

'Well you're right about one thing. I sure as hell want to know what's going on. Look at what it's cost us already. Our lives are obviously on the line. And while we're out of sight like this, we're safe. As soon as we show ourselves, the media will have us on every front page, on the box, everywhere. And whoever made a balls-up with the car-bomb will find his task much easier.'

Claire pulled a face. 'Not if we're locked up, they won't.'

'But they'll know where we are. And when we do get out, on bail or whatever, how do we know they won't be waiting round the corner?'

Claire looked up, uncertainly. 'Ted, you're frightening me.'

'I'm only trying to make you see. Giving ourselves up isn't necessarily the best option.'

'Not necessarily? You're considering it, then?'

'I'm not bloody Mephistopheles. I just don't know!'

Claire looked at the floor, head bowed in dejection. 'I don't think we'll last five minutes trying to hide out, anyway.' She got up and walked over to the window, looked down at the busy street outside. 'For all we know the owner is downstairs now, dialling the local police station.'

'That's true enough. We ought to be moving on, trying to hide our tracks.'

'You don't give up, do you?'

Ted got up and joined her at the window. 'Not in my nature.'

'Stubborn bastard.'

'Spoken like an Australian.'

'Perhaps we could go there.'

'Where?'

'Australia, you dope.'

'One day, maybe. I'd like that. But not now. We can't just leave this.'

Claire sighed, turned to Ted and clutched him to her. 'A decision, then.'

'We need to talk to someone we can trust.'

Claire pulled away. 'Who, for Christ's sake? That Sergeant Clothier was the only one I'd have had any confidence in, and he's dead, too!'

'I've been going over what Paul told us. There *was* someone he seemed to trust a lot, and he mentioned him more than once.'

Claire's brow furrowed. 'You mean that Air Force chap — Sir Richard Jacobson?'

'Jacobs. Air Vice Marshal. What do you think?'

'I know Paul used to confide in him a great deal.' She nodded, considering. 'Hmm. It's a thought. But how would we get in touch with him?'

'Shouldn't be too difficult. Phone books, directory enquiries, Ministry of Defence.'

'Oh, come on, Ted. "Excuse me, is that MOD? Put me through to my old chum Sir Richard, will you?" '

'Sarcasm does not become you.'

'And even if your cunning little antipodean brain works out a way to get in touch, what then? Arrange to meet at midnight under Nelson's Column, wearing a red rose in our buttonholes?'

'Look, I'll think of something.' Ted spoke angrily, stung by Claire's derision.

Seeing his tension, she spoke more gently. 'I'm only trying to be practical. Look, let's suppose you fix up a meeting. How do we know he won't have half the RAF standing in the shadows with loaded howitzers?'

'The RAF don't use howitzers.'

'Well, whatever, idiot. You know what I mean.'

'It could be difficult, I admit. But if we choose our meeting point carefully enough . . .' Ted went over to the bed and lay back, hands laced behind his head. Claire left him to his thoughts. She went back to grieving for her friend.

* * *

Air Vice Marshal Sir Richard Jacobs, KBE, QHP, FRCP, RAF, Principal Medical Officer to the Royal Air Force, sat in his office at the Central Medical Establishment in Cleveland Street and peered over his half-moon glasses at the traffic snarled up outside. He was going to be late for the reception at the RAF Club in Piccadilly if he didn't leave soon. His private secretary knocked and came in. Anticipating her business, he turned from the window, saying, 'I know, I know, I'll be late meeting the speaker chappie at the Club.'

'Well, there is that, sir. I've sent for the car. But — there's something else. I've just had this rather curious phone call.'

'Curious? In what way?' He smiled encouragingly at his secretary. He was a handsome man even now, in his mid-fifties, with a full head of silver-grey hair and a smooth, unlined face above a trim body. He was generally liked by his staff for his gentle manner and an unusual degree of consideration for his subordinates. He could see his secretary was worried.

'Someone, a man, says he wants to talk to you, personally. But he wouldn't give his name.'

The PMO waved a hand dismissively. 'Tell the fellow to go away. If he hasn't got the courtesy to identify himself . . .'

'I – I'm sorry, sir.' The woman looked uncomfortable, hesitant. 'He said I was to say to you, remember Paul Sansome.'

Sir Richard frowned, and pushed his fingers through the thick silver hair. 'Really?' He frowned. 'How could I forget poor Paul?' He shook his head in annoyance, spoke briskly. 'Can't stand a mystery. Put the fellow on.'

The secretary left, and a moment later the phone on the Air Vice Marshal's desk buzzed. He took up the receiver.

'Jacobs here.'

'Air Vice Marshal Sir Richard Jacobs?'

'The same. Who is that?' He was sharp, direct.

'I don't think my name will mean much to you. It's Edward Parkes.'

'No, Parkes, can't say it does. State your business, man, I have a function to attend. You mentioned Paul Sansome.'

'Yes. I was doing research with him at the Clifton Neurological Research Institute before his accident. And since then I've been furthering his research and working on a method of computerised electroencephalography. He has been my principal subject.'

The PMO sat upright in his chair. 'Good God! You're the one who –' He cut himself off. 'Where are you?'

'In South Wales. We want to meet you.'

'Impossible.' He paused. 'Who's *we*?'

'Myself and my assistant, Claire Donaldson.'

'You're wanted by the police in connection with Paul Sansome's abduction. I suggest you contact them straight away.'

'He wasn't abducted against his will. We can prove it.'

'How so?'

'We've been communicating with him.'

The Air Vice Marshal considered a moment. 'How do I know you're who you say you are?'

There was a pause. 'Er, well, I suppose I could say you owe me a favour already.'

'Kindly explain.'

'I was at a cocktail party once, at the Research Institute. You were there. I rescued you from the clutches of Paul's wife, Christine.'

Despite himself, Sir Richard let out a chuckle. 'Yes, I do recall something of the sort. Now I can place the significance of your Australian accent.' He leaned forward on his desk. 'And just how successful have you been with your, er, communication, young man?'

'Very successful. Paul mentioned your name.'

'Mentioned my –! But how? I mean –'

'It's too complex to explain over the phone. But we've learnt things, know things, that we need to discuss with someone. In confidence. Paul trusted you. We hope we can.'

There was a long silence, interrupted by bursts of static on the line. 'No.' Sir Richard eventually spoke. 'No, I can't be seen having clandestine meetings with fugitives from the law. It's out of the question.'

He could hear a female voice whispering urgently, 'Tell him. Go on, tell him.'

'There's one thing more, Sir Richard, that I —'

'I've got to go. Turn yourself in to the police.'

'Does the name Al-Ghraid mean anything to you?'

There was another prolonged silence. Sir Richard sighed in resignation. He knew he would have to learn more.

'Where did you hear that name?'

'From Paul. At first we didn't know what it meant, didn't even know it was a person's name. But now we do. Mahmoud Al-Ghraid. He's an Iranian.'

'I — I think perhaps we'd better have a little chat after all.'

There was enthusiasm in Ted's voice. 'Great! The sooner the better.'

'I — we — shall need to be discreet. I should warn you — this is a security matter.' Ted waited. 'Let me see —' Sir Richard opened his desk diary and ran his finger down the page. 'Can you get up to town by tomorrow, that's Thursday, lunchtime?'

'I doubt it. We've got no car, not much money — and we're afraid of Al-Ghraid picking up our trail.'

'Hmm. All right. Let's see. I'm in Guildford tomorrow evening. Perhaps we could meet near there. I shall be driving myself. We could have a talk in the car. Can you suggest a meeting place?'

The Air Marshal could hear a discussion going on at the other end.

'He wants us to choose a place. Somewhere near Guildford.'

The female voice responded. 'I don't know it very well . . . I know! How about the Hog's Back? There's a big sort of lay-by and picnic area on the A31 as you come out of Guildford towards Farnham.'

Ted started to repeat the suggestion to Sir Richard, but the latter interrupted. 'Yes, yes, I heard that.' He considered briefly. 'That'll probably do. Let's say 7.30, shall we? I shall be in a black Jaguar 4.2, registration SRJ 10.'

'Thanks, Sir Richard. You've no idea what a relief it will be to share all this with someone. Paul will be glad it's you.'

'I look forward to our meeting with interest, Mr Parkes. Until tomorrow night, then.'

'See you then, sport.'

Sir Richard replaced the phone, his smile at the familiarity of Ted's farewell slowly fading. His hand remained resting on the receiver until his secretary came to say his car had arrived.

* * *

Ted and Claire felt an overwhelming relief. If they could just get to this meeting, convince Sir Richard of the importance of what they knew . . .

'So how do we get there?' Ted demanded.

'Shouldn't be too difficult. Inter-City coach to Guildford, and I know local buses go along the Hog's Back.'

'He seemed a benign old boy.'

'So you think we can trust him?'

'We haven't much choice. But it won't do any harm to get there good and early and keep a watch out.'

'It's a good venue, Ted. Plenty of people about, but at that time of the evening we should be able to find a quiet enough spot. And he let us choose it.'

'I still think we can't be too careful. We could rig up some disguises as well — glasses, hats, something simple. Our pictures will have been spread around a lot by tomorrow.'

Claire nodded her agreement. 'There's a snack-bar place there. We can get some hot food while we're waiting.'

After dark, Ted went out, being careful to avoid their landlady, and bought fish and chips and some beer. They ate ravenously, and began to feel a little more relaxed, less threatened. Ted's chest injury was much easier, Claire's scars no longer pulled. But the pain of their grief at Joanne's death permeated their thoughts.

CHAPTER 44

Gerard Porthenoy, FRCS, sat at the desk in his study, and slowly put down the newspaper. He had read the same article several times, and his conclusion merely confirmed his initial reaction. There was no way out.

He had experienced a brief period of relief, after his last encounter with the Parkes fellow and Claire Donaldson. He had taken a massive chance, but it had paid off. Once he had faced them out about his homosexuality he had gambled that they would not expose him publicly.

The most senior members of the hospital administration already knew the score, and he was aware of rumours amongst the staff. It was difficult to keep such things quiet in a community as close as a hospital. He could tolerate that, as long as they were just rumours, and knew any 'exposure' to the Hospital Administrator would be old news. He was an excellent surgeon, prestigious for the hospital, had done nothing to break the terms of his contract, and ironically his homosexuality had brought him some powerful and influential friends. He would survive any local attack from Parkes and Donaldson, so long as it did not reach a wider public.

In the event, he had heard nothing more from them. He had not thought them capable of going so far as to remove Paul Sansome from the hospital and had been certain that was Mahmoud at work. After all, he had got the disks for him; now it would be logical for him to have the subject to work on. There had been moments of fury when the corruption of the disks was discovered, but it had been a relatively simple job for a specialist 'disk doctor' to restore the files.

Now he knew why he had had no further approach from Parkes and Donaldson. They had got Paul Sansome, and no doubt they had been too busy extracting data that Porthenoy was certain would implicate him fatally. Now they were on the run, and it looked as if Al-Ghraid and his creatures had tried to get rid of them and failed. So public an attempt at elimination could only mean one thing: Parkes and Donaldson had found out. He, Gerard Porthenoy, would be known not only as a homosexual, but also as a traitor. The media would not fail to pursue such a good story to the bitter end. Every fact would be extracted, every connection made. His ruin was inescapable.

He sighed deeply, and looked about his study; at the richly-bound books behind the glass, the dark gleaming mahogany, the soft leather of the furniture, the hunting scenes in their gilt frames, the cleverly disguised carved panel of his gun cabinet . . .

These few trappings were all he had, now. He had no meaningful relationships since Mahmoud had deceived him, trapped him. He had thought he had formed such a powerful bond with this man, the nearest he had ever felt to a romantic attachment. But it had all been a charade, a clever and cynical performance by a totally unscrupulous manipulator. He knew he would never again be able to trust himself to form any lasting attachment with another human being. His wife, poor woman, was thankfully dead, his son involved in the drug scene and recently tested HIV positive.

His eyes went back to the gun cabinet. Almost subconsciously, he had rehearsed this scenario many times, but not, he was sure, with any serious intent.

Now he wasted no further time debating the matter with himself. He knew, with frightening certainty, that he was going to proceed.

He went to the cabinet, unlocked it. It held two elegant and well-crafted guns. One was a treasured antique side-by-side wildfowling piece by Bonehill, which he used on his annual shooting holiday in Scotland; the other an over-and-under Beretta that he used for shooting clays on a private range. He selected the Bonehill Belmont.

He loaded a single cartridge in the left-hand barrel, and placed the gun carefully on his desk. He then took out his gun-cleaning kit, and assembled the cleaning rod, screwing the two pieces of boxwood together with the ornate brass fittings.

Going to his kitchen, he returned with a short length of string. He tied one end to the left barrel trigger, and the other end tightly to the lambswool plug at one end of the cleaning rod, leaving only an inch or so of string between the two.

He knew the problem with applying shotguns for the purpose he had in mind. The length of the barrel made controlled discharge of the weapon difficult and inaccurate. He wanted no mistakes. He had repaired too many partially damaged skulls and brains following botched suicides to want to join the ranks of those grotesquely maimed and disabled individuals. Nevertheless, he favoured this method: quick, decisive, final. Not for him the slow and occasionally reversible process of overdose, or the inhalation of carbon monoxide.

All was ready. He picked up the gun and the cleaning rod.

The doorbell rang. Porthenoy hesitated. He wanted to finish this, to have no further encounter with other members of the human race.

The bell rang again. If they did not go away, they might hear the shot. He wanted some time, some peace, for his body before it was disturbed. A strange thought, he couldn't explain it. He put down the gun, and went to answer the door.

'Good morning, sir. Registered packet for you.'

Porthenoy looked blankly at the postman for a moment, his eyes going from the proffered book and pen to the postman's face.

'You all right, sir? You look dreadful.'

'What? Oh, ah, just a bit off colour this morning.'

'Could you just sign, then, please?' The book was pushed a little closer. Porthenoy took it, signed where he was shown, and handed it back.

'Thank you, sir.' The postman handed Porthenoy a packet with the familiar blue banding, and turned on his heel. He stopped at the bottom of the steps and looked back at the man still standing there. 'Hope you feel better soon, sir.'

'Yes.' Porthenoy nodded slowly as he spoke. 'Thank you. I'm sure I shall.'

The neurosurgeon closed the door and dropped the packet on the hall table without looking at it. He went straight back to the study, and continued his mission without hesitation. He once again picked up the gun, and placed the barrels carefully in his mouth. He knew the angle was crucial. If it was too vertical, only the non-vital frontal lobes were damaged, invariably leaving the survivor blind; if it was too horizontal the result was total paralysis below the neck but no guarantee of death.

He adjusted the direction of the barrels carefully, holding the gun in his left hand — the blast would go right through the base of the skull and out through the occiput. Thinking only of the clinical details of the task, with his right hand he pushed against the cleaning rod, connected to the trigger.

Nothing happened. He pushed again. Still no report, no — no what? He realised he had no idea what to expect. Would he in fact hear the sound? And surely, he would feel nothing? He removed the gun, hands shaking, feeling faint and nauseated. He sat back in his chair, and laid the gun in front of him. Without looking, he knew what was wrong. The arrival of the postman had interrupted his preparations. He had left the safety on. Even in this moment of Stygian transience he found his lips moving to form a wry smile.

With trembling fingers he slid the catch to the 'off' position. He glanced at his drinks cabinet. A whisky to fortify him, steady him? He had been so close, could he now carry on? He tried to blot out the thoughts. He wanted to do this, wanted to, there was nothing else. He tried to stand, but his legs would not allow it. He pushed himself away from the desk, the stock of the gun resting on the elegant gold-embossed leather of the blotter. He had to proceed, dared not stop again. He adjusted the gun-barrels in his mouth, held the cleaning rod as before, felt the tension on the string tighten. Not quite right! The warning sounded in his mind. He moved the stock and sent a glass and silver ink-stand crashing to the floor. The unexpected noise so close at hand made him flinch — only a little, but there was enough extra pressure on the trigger to release the firing pin. Blood and brain sprayed on the wall behind him, and his body slumped out of the chair and onto the floor.

Porthenoy prided himself on his clinical skill. It was as well that his remaining eye, lying on his left cheek, could not see the result of his careful preparations. The gun had discharged before he was properly balanced, quite exact in his position. The right side of his face had been blown away, part of his forehead with it. The spreading shot had missed the medulla oblongata and other vital areas.

As the effects of the concussive force of the blast wore off, an almost surreal form of consciousness returned to him. There was no real pain, but in the silent darkness in which he found himself there was terrifying mental anguish. He could sense, though not observe, that his worst fears might be fulfilled. He would be paralysed down one side, gruesomely disfigured. Blind. But he would survive.

In a sense, he was lucky. The temporal artery was spiked by an irregular spicule of bone, and was held open. Instead of constricting and stopping the blood loss as his blood pressure fell, his heart continued to force out the crimson fluid. Even so, it took him several hours to die.

CHAPTER 45

Ted and Claire sat on a bench well to one side of the snack bar, nursing their third cups of coffee. They tried to appear relaxed, sitting there in the dark glasses and sun-hats they had bought when the coach stopped at a motorway service area. Already travelling light, they now had only an overnight bag containing bare essentials. The bags containing the computer equipment were in a left luggage locker at Swansea Bus Station. The key was in the hip pocket of Ted's jeans. They had taken the vital data disks with them to Sketty.

So far as they knew, no one had recognised them, although they had spent some anxious moments when a couple in the seat in front had started discussing the case.

For an hour they had been sitting watching the traffic and the trippers from the A31 come and go. The flow was beginning to slacken now. They had seen nothing untoward.

It had been a warm mid-August day, but as the sun dipped below the trees there was a perceptible chill on the gentle breeze. Claire shivered slightly, took off her hat and glasses and put her jumper on over her T-shirt.

'You'd better put them on again.' Ted nodded at the elements of her thin disguise on the seat beside her. She complied.

'It's well after 7.30. Do you think he's going to come?'

Ted shrugged. 'Dunno. We've got to give him some time yet. I'm going to the dunny.'

'Don't be long.' Claire kept checking the cars while Ted was in the lavatory. He had hardly disappeared from sight when her heart turned over as she saw a new black Jaguar glide into the lay-by. It stopped behind another car and she couldn't see the registration plate. Come on, Ted, for Christ's sake. The darkened windows stayed up; she could not see inside clearly.

'Bloody hell!' Claire spoke aloud to herself as she saw the car move out again. She wasn't sure what she should do. Rush out and tell the car to wait? Supposing it was the wrong one? Supposing it was the *right* one and she was taken away in it against her will, with Ted not knowing? She stood up, looked round to the snack-bar for Ted, back to the moving car. It had not returned to the road, but had now pulled into a large parking area to the right-hand side of the buildings. She watched carefully. It was almost too distant to be sure, but she thought the registration was three letters starting with S and followed by the number 10. It must be the one!

'That our man?'

Claire jumped, had not heard Ted approach. 'Yes, I think so. Can you read the plate?'

He squinted. 'That's him all right. Come on.' He set off for the car park, but Claire hung back. 'What's the matter, girl?'

'I'm not sure. How do we know it's not a trap?'

'We don't. But we haven't seen anything funny. And Paul trusted him.'

'He didn't actually say that.'

'He couldn't spell out everything, now could he? Come on, this has got to be our best bet.'

* * *

They sank into the comfortable leather of the seats, Claire in the back and Ted in the front. As soon as they were settled Sir Richard, dressed in dinner jacket and black tie, engaged the automatic gear and the car moved almost silently forward.

'Hey, just a minute —' Ted reached for the door handle.

'Relax. Just adjusting our position.' Sir Richard went down a slope to the edge of the car park farthest from the road, then turned the car round so that they could see the entrance and exit clearly. The engine was turned off.

'That's better. I'm sure I wasn't followed, but we can keep an overall eye out from here. No doubt you have been watching this place carefully?' He raised a bushy white eyebrow at Ted.

'Been checking it out for an hour. Seems all right.'

'Well, now.' He paused a moment, pressed a button to lower his window about an inch, then turned to face them as best he could. 'Perhaps you'd better tell me what this is all about?'

Ted responded by asking a question of his own. 'You knew Paul Sansome well, didn't you?'

'Yes, I did. We met when he took a short service commission in the RAF, after he qualified. I was a wing commander then, a medical consultant. We got on well. Had similar interests.'

'What? In neurological research?'

'Not specifically. But in most things. We've always kept in touch.'

'Did Paul tell you about his breakthrough?'

'I knew something of it, of course. You may recall I helped him with that unfortunate boy Coombes, the coma victim, when he wanted to try and put some of his theories into practice.'

A sudden thought struck Claire. 'I don't want to sound rude — but if you were friends . . .' She felt awkward about the accusation. 'You never came to visit him after his accident.'

Sir Richard raised both eyebrows. 'Oh, but I did, my dear girl.' He gave her one of his benign smiles, to show he took no offence. 'I was one of his very first visitors. Before even his wife, I believe. But I only went the once.' He looked sad. 'Didn't seem much point, frankly, after that.'

'No.' Claire's eyes went down. 'No, I see what you mean.'

At the mention of Christine, Ted took the opportunity to raise another matter. 'Did you know about his wife's — er, strange behaviour?'

'Well, I knew she was always a bit odd. Machiavellian. Tendency to improbity. And insobriety. Not to mention deviation. I recall at one point the intelligence people did a security check, had to have a word with Paul. Let him know they knew, sort of thing, so he wouldn't feel any anxiety if someone outside the Service tried to, shall we say, apply any pressure.'

Claire sat forward. 'Like blackmail, you mean?'

'Well, yes, though I don't think there was any worry about that in Paul's case. That sort of procedure is pretty routine. Then nobody tries to hide anything.'

'He wasn't working for the intelligence services himself, then?' asked Ted.

'Good Lord, no!' Sir Richard looked genuinely amused. 'He was a medical officer, a doctor, pure and simple. Just like me. That's what I was then, am now, except I have to do a deal of administration.' He paused, looked out through the windscreen. 'Mind you, he was a very clever fellow. Very clever indeed.' He looked back at his companions in the car. 'The Service wanted him to stay on, you know. Tried to get me to persuade him.'

'And did you? Try to persuade him, I mean?'

'Yes, as a matter of fact, I did apply a bit of pressure. He was first class. I'd have liked to keep him in. No good, though. He was so full of ideas, raring to go into his research.' He turned his smile on them again. 'Which brings us full circle. What have you learnt from him as a result of his brain-waves, if you'll excuse the *double entendre*?'

Claire leaned forward a little more, resting her arms on the back of Ted's seat. 'We've learnt a great deal. Ted has developed this incredible program that selectively filters out signals from special EEG probes.'

'Yes, I had heard about that.'

'We tried various ways to interpret the responses we were getting, but had to settle for "Yes-No" replies, which meant we could only ask specific questions, or when we got into things we didn't understand we used a technique whereby Paul would indicate letters of the alphabet.'

'Sounds intriguing. Amazing, in fact.' The older man's eyes were alive with interest. 'Tell me more.'

'It was very slow going. It wasn't until we had the chance of many uninterrupted hours with him at Joanne's — Joanne's aunt's house . . .' Claire was still shocked by the death of their nurse friend. She found she could not continue for a moment. Sir Richard leaned over and patted her hand gently.

'Yes, terrible tragedy, terrible.' He glanced at Ted, then back to Claire. 'Take your time, lass, take your time.'

Ted intervened. 'There's one thing we found out some time ago, though.' He was watching Claire anxiously as he spoke. 'Paul told us that his was no accident. Someone tried to do him in.'

The Air Marshal sat up. 'Did they now? And did Paul say who was responsible?'

'Well, we couldn't make head or tail of it at first. He kept mentioning danger, and spelling out these letters that made no sense. It wasn't until three days ago that we found out. He was spelling a name. Al-Ghraid. Mahmoud Al-Ghraid. It's Arabic.'

Sir Richard nodded.

'Paul thought he saw this man in the crowd when he went up in the ski-lift. And then when he took a tumble, someone jumped him. They must have been following, waiting for a chance.'

'To kill him?'

'Or to kidnap him. That's what *I* think. A bungled kidnap attempt.'

'He — Paul — told you all this?'

Claire felt able to continue. 'Not so fluently, not like we are talking now. But he would spell key words, and then we'd flesh them out, and he would respond Yes or No according to whether we'd got it right.'

'All very clever. Very clever indeed.' He put his hand inside his jacket, rubbed ruminatively at his chest. 'And what else did you learn?'

Claire continued. 'That this man Al-Ghraid was an Iranian Air Force officer, who was in England on secondment from the Shah of Iran's forces when he was exiled and Ayatolla Khomeini took over.'

Sir Richard nodded. 'Hmm. Yes. That was in 1979, if I recall?'

'I'm not sure. About then. Al-Ghraid was known as a pro-Shah officer, loyal to his sovereign. He claimed he would be imprisoned and tortured if he returned to Iran under the mullahs. Eventually he was given political asylum. He must have been an outstanding officer, because after extensive vetting he was given a commission in the RAF.'

Ted looked inquiringly at Sir Richard. 'I'm surprised a big cheese like you hasn't heard all this. The RAF's not so big, is it?'

The older man laughed benignly. 'Over eighty thousand men is quite a lot. But you're right, there are not that many officers. In my own branch, of course, I know 'em all, but outside . . . mind you, the business does ring a bell. Tell me more. I'm intrigued.'

'Al-Ghraid left the RAF about two years ago. We think he developed a consultancy, an agency, that sold high-tech equipment to hospitals in this country and Europe.'

'Where did he get the money to get that sort of set-up going?'

Ted shrugged. 'There were some things we couldn't — or didn't —

pursue. But my guess is that he was probably set up with money from the Middle East.'

'I see.' Sir Richard rubbed his chin, shifted his position for comfort. 'When did he come into the picture as far as Paul was concerned?'

'About a year later – about six months before the accident, he approached Paul.'

'Approach? What sort of approach?'

'Somehow Al-Ghraid knew about his research. Paul was obviously shocked at the amount of detail he knew.'

'And what was his angle?'

Ted looked at Claire before speaking. 'Through his agency he offered Paul a job. To go and work in Teheran.'

Sir Richard's shoulders shook gently. 'Shouldn't think that cut much ice with Paul. What incentives were they offering?'

'Half a million dollars.'

The Air Marshal whistled softly. 'That's a lot of money.'

'And also all the Western technology he needed, and as many subjects to experiment on as he wanted.'

'Sounds rather sinister.'

'Doesn't it? Especially as this was a time of no official contact with Iran. There were no diplomatic ties after the Rushdie affair. It was an illegal approach.'

'So presumably Paul reported it to the powers that be?'

Again Ted and Claire exchanged glances. 'No, he didn't.'

Sir Richard's eyebrows shot up. 'Whyever not?'

Claire leaned forward again. 'Look, it's difficult to be sure. Remember our communications were far from full. We got very abbreviated information from Paul that we had to try and expand.'

'You sound as if you are defending him.'

'Maybe I am. But whatever he did, I'm certain it was for the best of reasons.'

Sir Richard smiled. 'I admire loyalty.'

'It's not just that.' Claire felt herself flush, a note of defensive anger crept into her voice. 'We think he was threatened. Probably with exposure of some of Christine's activities. Any hint of connections with illegal deals, or the misapplication of his discoveries, would have risked having his research grant withdrawn, being kicked out of the Clifton Neurological Research Institute just when he was on the point of a major breakthrough. So he just told Al-Ghraid to take a hike, and said nothing.'

'Hmm.' Sir Richard considered. 'I can see that.' He paused. 'What do you suppose the Iranians wanted with this research?'

Ted snorted. 'You're a military man. I'd have thought it was bloody obvious to a clever bastard like you. There surely must be some value in a system that would enable you to extract information from people even after you have rendered them unconscious. Perhaps even only temporarily unconscious.'

'Surely their co-operation is required, whether unconscious or not.'

Ted shook his head. 'I don't think so. A person might be able to stop himself articulating a thought into words, but I don't see how, if a question is asked, he can stop himself thinking of the answer.'

Claire nodded her agreement. 'And a logical extension of what we're doing would be that you could tap into memory circuits in the brain and just draw off the information there, without the need for any form of interrogation.'

Sir Richard absorbed this information and was silent for some time. 'So you are saying that you can envisage a time when, using a more sophisticated form of your equipment, you could kidnap someone, render him unconscious, literally drain off all he knew into a computer, and then restore him to his previous environment.'

Ted's eyes were alight with excitement. 'Too bloody right, mate! And if it was skilfully done, using amnesic drugs that obliterated short-term memory, the subject might not even be aware it had happened!'

Sir Richard was silent again. 'This takes some thinking about. This is a very powerful, very dangerous tool indeed. I think our people should know about it. This is no longer simply an interesting piece of research into the management of coma victims. This is the stuff of national security.'

Ted flopped back in his seat and blew out his cheeks, exhaling the air noisily.

'At last!'

The Air Marshal gave him a curious look. 'I'm sorry?'

'That's what I've been wanting to hear you say. Now perhaps you'll get us some protection, try and get this Al-Ghraid bloke behind bars, or deported or something.'

'Indeed. Yes, indeed.' Sir Richard was still taking in the significance of what he had just learnt.

Ted pressed on. 'I've had this vision of the ultimate power of what we've been doing ever since the Coombes boy.'

Claire looked at him indignantly. 'You never told me!'

Ted gave her a scornful look. 'I'd have thought you'd work it out for yourself.' He turned back to the man beside him. 'I tried to persuade Paul that the Ministry of Defence would be interested, but he always refused. He got very touchy at one point, we had a row over it. I reckon that must have been about the time of Al-Ghraid's second approach. I accepted Paul's explanation that he wanted to remain independent, not just become part of some secret Government department in MOD, where he would lose control over what he did.' Ted shook his head. 'He never said a word to me about the Teheran offer.'

'Second approach?'

'Sorry?'

'You said Al-Ghraid made a second approach to Paul.'

'That's right. Just before he went on his skiing holiday. The approach was made through Christine. Obviously our Iranian friend knew something of Christine's propensities. I should think she was offered money, and the prospect of untold riches to come, if she could persuade her husband to accept the deal. Paul thinks a meeting was set up, in Austria. He remembered being surprised that it was Christine who was keen to go on holiday then. Skiing being such a love of his, I reckon she just conned him into it. I think he was always hoping she would reform, even though . . .' Ted's voice trailed off.

'Even though what, Mr Parkes?'

'Even though he had a mistress. Joanne Yeates, the nurse that was killed. He told us they were lovers. We didn't know before.'

'Well, well. This gets more and more complicated.' He canted his head slightly as he posed the next question. 'Don't you think it's odd he should agree to go on holiday with his wife in these circumstances?'

Claire spoke up. 'Not knowing him, no. He probably felt guilty, anyway. I think he was always prepared to give her a chance.' Her face hardened. 'When in fact the bitch had set a trap.'

'But what would be the point of killing him?' Sir Richard's brow furrowed as he digested this latest information.

'Like I said before, I think the idea was to kidnap him, though God knows how they thought they'd get him to co-operate. Must have been confident in their methods. But they bungled it. And once Paul was in a coma himself, he was no bloody good to anyone, so they dropped the whole thing.' Ted sighed. 'Until we came along, that is, and unlocked his brain.'

'How did Al-Ghraid hear about that?'

Claire's eyes were angry. 'That's what we'd like to know.'

'And now it would seem he wants to kill you. Why?'

Ted wearily wiped a hand across his eyes. 'I must say we've given that a great deal of thought.'

'And your conclusions?'

'Still very indistinct. I can see why Al-Ghraid might want the information even more. Since the Gulf crisis, Iran and Iraq burying the hatchet, you can see how something like this would appeal to jolly old Saddam Hussein and his cronies as well. It's a real bugger's muddle. There have been at least three attempts to get the data from us, and I can't see how they all fit in with Al-Ghraid. And someone tried to kill us off before the bomb — by electrocution. Whether that's a rival faction trying to stop someone else getting the knowledge, or what — I just haven't a clue. It's a complete dog's breakfast.'

Sir Richard showed gentle amusement. 'That's putting it mildly.'

'I can only assume it's because Al-Ghraid is now aware that we have probably extracted enough information to implicate him and his agency, which is presumably a front, and have him exposed, deported, or imprisoned. No us, no testimony. Something like that.'

'Why would he suddenly assume that now?'

Claire explained patiently what had become obvious to herself and Ted. 'Because we kidnapped — well, borrowed, Paul. Why else would we want unrestricted access to our subject? Obviously, because we were in a position to extract everything he knew by using our technique. That would confirm Al-Ghraid's hopes and worst fears — that the system worked, and that we would hear about him and his set-up from Paul.'

'Why a bomb, though? Bit over the top?'

Ted laughed harshly. 'Very funny. Don't know, mate. There are plenty of ways to skin a cat, sure. But that's a typical, final, terrorist weapon. And that, I'm sure, is what our friend Al-Ghraid is: a terrorist, who managed to con HM Government's investigators all those years ago, and whose skill was rewarded with a commission in the RAF.'

Sir Richard breathed deeply, and pinched his nose between thumb and forefinger. 'I must think a minute.'

In the silence, Claire and Ted reached out to each other, and exchanged hopeful smiles. Claire stroked the back of Ted's hand with her thumb. When this nightmare was over, what would happen to them? she wondered. Right now, her tension and anxiety were dominant, but beneath the surface she could feel an almost painful welling of emotion that this man stimulated inside her. She was brought back to reality by a sharp word from the Air Marshal.

'Right.'

Ted stopped scanning the car park entrance, now less clear in the failing light, and let go of Claire's hand. He started to turn towards Sir Richard, but some activity caused his eyes to be drawn back to the entrance. An army truck drove in, travelling fast. It swung round, not twenty feet away, and about a dozen soldiers piled out in camouflage fatigues.

'Jesus Christ!' Ted gripped the door-handle, then relaxed as the men sprinted away, laughing and shouting, towards the snack-bar and toilets.

Sir Richard observed his alarm. 'It's all right. Just some TA's. Probably from Aldershot.'

'Sorry. I'm a bit jumpy.'

'I understand. Look, there are some people I need to talk to. Your priority is to stay out of sight a bit longer.'

'You don't think we should go to the police?'

'Ultimately, yes, you'll have to. But I want to prepare the ground at higher level first. This is top priority stuff, y'know, and if we can get the big boys at MOD on our side, they can handle the police.'

'How long will it take?'

He looked at his watch. 'Can't really see me stirring them up until tomorrow, now. Have you got somewhere to stay tonight?'

Claire looked at Ted. 'Well, there was a place we looked at in — '

'All right, don't need to know. As long as you've got a roof, somewhere inconspicuous.' He paused. 'What about money? Got any left?'

'About £30. I didn't like to go to a cash-point in case it gave away where we were.'

'Quite right. Here.' He rummaged in his inside pocket, came out with a handful of twenty-pound notes. He handed over three of them. 'That'll keep you going.'

Ted did not hesitate to accept the money. 'Thanks a lot.'

'That's very nice of you,' said Claire. 'But how do we get in touch with you tomorrow?'

'Good question. Ring my secretary, Mrs Rafferty, at CME — she'll give you instructions.' He considered briefly. 'Anything else?'

'I don't think so.' Ted held out his hand, and the Air Marshal took it. They shook hands firmly. 'You've no idea how grateful we are. It's been a bloody nightmare.'

Claire leaned forward and kissed the Air Marshal on the cheek before he could take avoiding action. 'Me too. You're a godsend. Thanks for listening.'

Sir Richard's eyes glowed, his face reddened. 'Always glad to help a maiden in distress. Part of an officer's training, don't you know?' He laughed. 'And glad to help our antipodean brethren, too, of course. Though the real person we are all serving here is our sovereign. The country.' He seemed embarrassed by his small display of patriotic zeal. He reached forward and started the car. 'I'll drop you off near the centre of Guildford. Keep your heads down, and your spirits up. OK?'

CHAPTER 46

Ted and Claire walked until they found a street of late-Victorian houses with a profusion of 'Bed and Breakfast' signs. They chose a nondescript-looking guest house in the back streets of Guildford in which to spend the night. The place was scruffy and none too clean, but that disadvantage was outweighed by the fact that the proprietor, an obese and untidy woman who went around with a cigarette hanging from her mouth, barely looked at them, let alone asked their names. All she wanted was the cash, and she was gone, back to her smoke-filled lounge and blaring television.

Claire observed the suspect cleanliness of the sheets and then lay down on the lumpy mattress. Ted climbed in beside her. As he had done before, he traced out the scars on her face and breast with his finger, as if this was his way of reassuring her that the disfigurement was of no consequence. Then he held her, and they rested quietly in each other's arms. She was content to remain there, clinging to him, the only part of her world that remained as a fragile oasis of security. The sound of the television's canned laughter coming from below gradually faded from her awareness, as exhaustion took over.

She could sense Ted breathing deep and slow beside her. Thoughts of their predicament began to return, making her restless. It seemed a long time before she finally drifted off to sleep, and barely moments seemed to have passed before she heard the noise from the door.

She started to sit up, then went rigid as in the half-light from the street lamps outside she saw the handle turn. She wanted to call out to Ted, but couldn't. She was transfixed with fear. The door opened, a hand appeared, then a head. Claire cried out, but it was a feeble sound, choked by the terror that constricted her throat, not enough to wake Ted, still unmoving, lying on his side next to her. The head was covered in black material, only the eyes showing through the mask. The body followed, also in black, and she froze as she saw the gun — a short, stubby affair with a magazine protruding below. She knew it was an automatic weapon, a sophisticated piece of equipment, and as the barrel came up she at last found the strength of will to scream. Ted turned onto his back and began to sit up, but was knocked back as fire spat from the gun and a stream of bullets hit him in the chest. His body jerked as more missiles struck their target, then the weapon moved and gunfire raked across the bed, over Claire and then back to Ted. Incredibly, the bullets passed either side of her, but she ignored the miracle. She flung herself onto the bloodied mess beside her, in a desperate but futile attempt to protect her lover from further harm. Not caring that death would strike her at any moment, she cried out, sobbed, called his name over and over and over . . .

'Claire! Claire! Snap out of it!'

Something, somebody, was shaking her. How had she survived? She did not *want* to survive!

'Leave me alone!' She tried to pull away.

'Claire! It's me, Ted!'

She gasped, disbelieving, moved back, wiped the tears until she could see more clearly. He was there, alive, no jagged holes in his flesh, no blood. Her eyes turned to the closed door, back to the concerned face before her. Then she flung herself on him again, gripped him so tight he complained. She felt the strength of his arms, wept silently as he stroked her hair, stroked away the horror of her nightmare, until she finally entered the sanctuary of dreamless sleep.

★ ★ ★

They rose early, washed in the damp, cramped bathroom, and left before their temporary hostess had risen. Neither fancied any food that might be set before them in this slovenly household, and they breakfasted anonymously in a small corner café a few streets away. They knew it was no use calling Sir Richard's secretary yet. He would not have had time to hold discussions with the 'big boys at MOD' as he had called them, let alone reach any decisions. They decided to wait until lunchtime, and spent the morning wandering round the shops, having coffee, sitting on a bench in Stoke Park, watching and talking in the August sunshine. They did their best to look and feel relaxed, but the spring of inner tension wound tighter with each hour that passed.

They had a snack lunch in a fast food restaurant, then set out for the post office they had noted earlier. The modern phone booths did not look very secure for such an important conversation, but they had little choice. Ted got a handful of change ready, then dialled the number of the Central Medical Establishment.

'AVM Sir Richard Jacob's office.'

'Mrs Rafferty?'

'Speaking.'

'This is Ted Parkes. Sir Richard said to call you.'

The slightly officious tone changed perceptibly. 'Oh, yes, Mr Parkes. I have a message for you.'

Ted gave an OK sign to Claire. 'Great. What does he say?'

'First, if you'll excuse me, Mr Parkes, I am instructed to verify your identity.'

'Oh. How do you do that?' Ted frowned.

'One moment please.' There was a pause and a rustle of paper. 'Here we are.' Another pause. 'It says here that you have to tell me the first name of the coma victim Dr Sansome worked with.'

'Oh, no worries. That was Jason. Jason Coombes.'

'That's correct, Mr Parkes. I'm sorry. I feel a little foolish!' She gave a titter of embarrassment.

'No problem.' He was getting impatient. 'What's the message?'

'He'd like to meet you again. Take you to meet some people.'

'What people?'

'He didn't say. He's been very secretive about all this.'

Ted hesitated. 'Is he there? Can I speak to him?'

'No, I'm sorry. He's down in Whitehall at the moment. I haven't seen him myself today.'

Ted came to a decision. 'All right. Where do we meet, and when?'

'This is all very mysterious, Mr Parkes. He just said, the same time and the same place. Does that make sense to you?'

'Yes, it does. Thanks, Mrs Rafferty. Tell him we'll be there.'

* * *

Ted and Claire had a lot of time to kill. They went to the matinee performance at the cinema and sat through a series of advertisements, cartoons, and a feebly-plotted family comedy, to the accompaniment of much talking, eating and the running around of small children. But they didn't mind. They felt secure in the darkness, and could be inconspicuously close.

When they emerged into the still bright sunlight, Ted bought an evening paper. They walked down to the park again and shared it between them. Ted had the inside pages, and he scanned them for any news relating to themselves. There was nothing. The media soon lost interest, he reflected with relief. Beside him, Claire turned to the inside of the front page and immediately let out an exclamation.

'God! *Look* at this, Ted! It's Porthenoy!'

'What's he done? Got a knighthood or something?'

'Hardly. He's dead. See here.'

> Leading Bristol neurosurgeon, Mr Gerard Porthenoy, was found dead this morning in his house in Clifton. His daily help, who has a key to the premises, found the body in the study. He had suffered gunshot wounds to the head. A police statement said that foul play was not suspected, and no one else was being sought in connection with the incident. There is much speculation locally as to the background to this apparent suicide. There are rumours that Mr Porthenoy was a homosexual, and an unofficial police source said that a registered packet containing photographs was discovered in the house. A police spokesman said that he was unaware of any blackmail allegations concerning the dead surgeon.

So. He topped himself, then.'

'It looks like it.' Claire bit her bottom lip. 'Ted, you don't think . . . ?'

'Think what?' Ted snorted scornfully. 'Think that our little threat to expose him had anything to do with it? No, course not.'

Claire looked miserable. 'I suppose not. But it seems that we *are* under a curse at the moment. People we know dying, being killed. Nurse Marvaine. Christine Sansome. Poor Joanne. That nice detective. And now Mr Porthenoy.'

Ted nodded slowly. 'It's a bit of a facer, that. But I don't think we should lose any sleep over that slimy old bugger.'

'Ted! He may have had his faults, but he was a fine surgeon. Think how many people will never now benefit from his skills.'

'Yeah. I know. I'm not very charitable, am I? Letting me prejudice show, eh?'

Claire gave his arm a squeeze. They sat there in silence for some minutes.

'I feel like a child on a long journey.'

Ted looked puzzled. 'What do you mean?'

'You know, when they want to keep asking how much farther it is. I keep wanting to ask about the time.'

'It's nearly six. We could start to make our way to the Hog's Back, I suppose.'

'Do we need to get there so early this time?'

'I don't really think so. But we might as well wait there as here, and better safe than sorry.'

* * *

This time the black Jaguar arrived right on time. Ted and Claire walked slowly towards it, disconcerted by the darkened glass which prevented them from recognising the occupant. They were right alongside before the window slid down, and Sir Richard's face beamed up at them, this time dressed in a grey lounge suit.

'Well done! Glad you made it.'

'Yeah, no problems. What happens now?'

'Get in, and I'll take you to the meeting.'

Claire climbed in the back, Ted in the front, settling into the fawn-coloured leather seats as they had the evening before. It was cool inside, the air-conditioning blowing softly. Sir Richard accelerated the car out onto the Hog's Back, heading for Farnham.

'Where are we going?'

'It's not far.'

'And who are these people we're meeting?'

'MOD types. Nice enough chaps, even though they're from the cloak and dagger department.'

Claire leaned forward, unable to conceal a feeling of schoolgirl excitement. 'You mean, MI5, intelligence?'

Sir Richard turned his face in her direction, while keeping his eyes on the road. He smiled. 'Not MI5, no. But that's the sort of idea.'

'And this place we're going to,' she asked eagerly, 'is it a — what do you call them in the books? — a safe house?'

Sir Richard chuckled at her enthusiasm. 'In a manner of speaking, yes.'

They turned right just past the Hog's Back Hotel, and Claire thought they must be going to a military establishment in Aldershot. However they turned right again at the bottom of the hill into the village of Tongham, continued through it and out into what was virtually a country lane. After a few hundred yards, the car slowed as a high stone wall dominated the right-hand side of the lane, then Sir Richard braked and pulled in through broken-down iron gates. The narrow, overgrown drive turned a corner, and they found themselves in a small courtyard before a derelict building that looked as if it were once a home of some substance.

Ted felt nervous, but tried to make a joke. 'This isn't *my* idea of a safe house. Looks about to fall down!'

'Don't worry. It isn't all that it seems.' Sir Richard made two very short toots on the horn, then turned to face his companions. 'Someone will be here in a moment.' He looked round, seeming a little nervous himself, then smiled at them reassuringly. It was already warming up with the air-conditioning off, and he took out a handkerchief to mop his brow.

'Ah. Here he comes.'

A man dressed in a suit and wearing dark glasses emerged from behind a crumbling wall, looked round for a moment, then walked briskly over to the car. He got in the back behind Sir Richard. Claire moved over to accommodate him.

'Miss Donaldson, Mr Parkes, I'd like you to meet Mr Marcus Andreas.'

The newcomer took off his dark glasses, revealing an olive skin and dark eyes. He extended his hand to Claire, and shook hers with a little nodded bow of the head.

'It's a pleasure to meet you, Miss Donaldson.'

Claire murmured a response. Mr Andreas turned to Ted, who was studying him closely. The hand which was being extended stopped abruptly as Ted spoke.

'You look familiar, mate. Where have I seen you before?'

'I don't think we have had the pleasure, Mr Parkes.'

'I'm sure it was no bloody pleasure. Where are you from?'

'Why, Greece, of course. From Megara.'

Ted looked at the swarthy skin, the pock-marked jowls, the shadowy eyes below bushy brows. 'Oh, I see.' He relaxed, extended his hand. 'From the north. Near Salonica, isn't it.' He made it a statement, not a question.

Andreas took the hand. 'Precisely.'

Ted snatched his hand away, turned to Sir Richard. 'This man's a fraud. I've spent a lot of time in Greece. Megara's near Athens, in the south.'

'Mr Parkes, I can assure you —'

'And now I remember where I've seen him before.' He looked at Claire. '*This* is Porthenoy's boyfriend!'

Claire stared open-mouthed as the indulgent smiles froze on the faces of Jacobs and Andreas. Ted was speaking again.

'Come on, girl. I think it's time we went.'

He reached for the door handle, but as he did so Sir Richard pressed the catch on his side, and all the doors locked electronically with a soft, uncompromising *clunk*.

'You bastard!' Ted screamed the word, fear and anger mixing to produce an unnaturally shrill sound. He grabbed the Air Vice Marshal by the collar. 'Open the fucking door!'

'Mahmoud! For God's sake —' Sir Richard's skin was white with shock.

'Just let him go, Mr Parkes, if you don't mind.' The accented voice was smooth, icy calm.

Ted tightened his grip. 'You let us out of this —'

Claire cried out involuntarily as the gun barrel was pushed forcibly into her ribs. 'Aah! Ted, please —'

The Australian turned to see the man he was now certain was Al-Ghraid smiling insolently at him. He was holding Claire by the hair with his left hand, and with the right was holding a silenced automatic pistol against her chest.

'I think you had better let Sir Richard go, don't you?'

Slowly Ted relaxed his grip. His anger was replaced by fear, his mouth went dry. Al-Ghraid watched him closely, saw the colour drain from his face.

'That's better.' He nodded at Sir Richard. 'I think we can drive on, now that the formalities are over.'

The Air Marshal started the car, but instead of backing out into the lane as Ted expected, he drove forward, along overgrown tracks at the side of the ruin, and across what appeared to be a disused gravel patio along the back. He stopped the car and flicked the locks undone.

'Now let's get out carefully, shall we?' He spoke smoothly, almost reasonably, but the deadly menace was unmistakable. Ted had no option but to comply. He waited, poised, hoping for some opportunity, as Claire got out. The gun was never more than an inch or so from her body. The three of them stood in a triangle by the front of the car.

'Excellent.' Al-Ghraid smiled, teeth white and gold. 'Sir Richard, would you be so kind?'

The RAF officer moved round the car to an iron-bound door set in a thick, low wall. He produced a large key, and soon had the lock turning. None of it was new, the door in particular looked as if it had not been used for years. In fact it looked from the outside as if it led nowhere, with only a pile of crumbling masonry the other side. But it opened without a sound, and revealed a narrow stairway of stone steps leading down into darkness. Sir Richard stepped forward, flicked a light switch, and then stood aside.

'After you, my dear chap.' He made a formal bow to Ted.

'You treacherous bastard! How could Paul ever have trusted you? You should be —'

Ted's bitter tirade was cut short by another cry of pain from Claire.

Al-Ghraid spoke brusquely. 'Shut up and get down the steps, will you?'

Ted went. The place smelled damp, despite the dry heat outside. Something scuttled away as he reached the bottom. They were in a well-constructed stone-walled room, with rudimentary furniture, a table and two chairs. The cellar was lit by two opaque wall lights that were not very bright. Ted wondered briefly about the power source, concluded they were probably batteries. In one wall were two doors. There was no mistaking their purpose. They were cells.

'Nice little conversion, isn't it?'

Al-Ghraid stood at the bottom of the steps, his own and Claire's silhouettes merging in the daylight from above. Ted looked round more carefully. Everything down here seemed fairly new, the stones well pointed, the timber strong and durable, the fittings modern.

He had no idea what to say or do. He felt weak with the certain thought that they were going to die here, and Claire looked near hysteria. Her eyes were wide, wild, rolling, her chest heaving with over-rapid breathing. Ted was incongruously reminded of a young calf just captured, having its first encounter with man, an image from his farming days as a teenager in his home country.

'Can't you let her sit down?' Ted not only felt Claire was about to faint, but also thought it would get her away from the end of Al-Ghraid's gun, maybe give him a chance to do something. What, he couldn't imagine. His legs felt like jelly.

It didn't work. Al-Ghraid pushed Claire to one of the chairs, and as she fell onto it he transferred the point of his weapon from her chest to her head. She looked at Ted with terrified eyes. He didn't know how to console her.

Sir Richard went past Ted, keeping his distance, and turned near the bottom of the stairs. 'I suppose this is where I should say how sorry I am. But I'm not. I'm afraid my pension and my peerage are just too valuable.'

'Lousy, treacherous bastard!' Ted growled at him.

Sir Richard beamed his benign smile. 'A perfect example of the literary charm and grace of the average antipodean, if I may say so.' As he looked at Ted, his expression changed from gentle amusement to a superior sneer to open contempt. Ted's muscles tensed, his hands shook, his mind went completely out of control. He was overwhelmed by the desire to change that expression, to smash the face that derided him so arrogantly. All thought of Claire and caution gone, he leaped at his tormentor with a bellow of rage. His quarry had no time to turn before Ted was upon him, crashing him to the floor, fist flailing at his face. Claire's scream penetrated his frenzy, slowing his onslaught, but he did not see Al-Ghraid raise his gun, step forward, and calmly shoot him in the back of the left leg.

Ted screamed and rolled over, clutching his knee, aware now only of the agony of torn muscle and tendon, shattered bone.

Al-Ghraid stood over him. 'That is a little lesson for you. The IRA call it knee-capping. A very effective punishment, don't you think?'

Ted could hardly make sense of the words, but did hear Claire's wail, a long-drawn-out cry of his name. She tried to get to him, but Al-Ghraid pushed her roughly back. Sir Richard Jacobs struggled to his feet, wiped his bleeding mouth, tried to straighten his tie, dust off his jacket.

'Man's a maniac. An animal.' He looked down at Ted, his disdain returning with his confidence. He continued to tidy himself as he waited for Ted's writhing and groans to subside. Claire watched, horror etched in her face, tears flowing. Al-Ghraid lounged nonchalantly against the table. Like some grotesque pantomime, the three of them regarded the man on the floor as he moaned, moved, clutched his leg, writhed and moaned again, the movements gradually slowing like a mechanical tableau in which the motor was running down.

Finally Sir Richard decided Ted was likely to be receptive.

'Don't worry, you won't die of that wound. So I advise you to co-operate fully with Mr Andreas.' He laid heavy emphasis on the pseudonym. 'He has far worse in store for you if you don't tell him what he wants to know.'

Ted's head swam with faintness, coherent thought impaired by waves of pain. 'Why?' was all he could manage.

'Why? Ha! I would have thought that was obvious. Killing you seemed the simple option, but that was bungled before. We didn't know then that you'd really plugged in to Paul Sansome's brain. Now we want to know everything you've learnt, as well as how you did it.'

'And then?'

'Then Mahmoud and I shall be a force to be reckoned with in the international intelligence field, and make ourselves very rich indeed. And you and Miss Donaldson will be — how can I put this delicately?' He managed one of his smiles. 'Let's say, together for eternity.'

'Fuck off.'

'Fucking, young man, is one thing *you* will never participate in again.'

Ted's refuelled anger overcame some of his pain, and he tried to rise. Claire went to help him, and this time Al-Ghraid did not intervene. She helped him to a chair, and he slumped forward, gripping the edge of the table. He tried to think of something to say, something to encourage Claire. When he said it, it sounded fatuous.

'The police are looking for us.'

'Indeed they are.' Sir Richard actually chuckled, his earlier humiliation forgotten. 'How fortunate, isn't it? I mean, you are wanted, you and your little concubine here, and hence likely to go to ground.' He smirked. 'Or underground, I should have said.' He savoured his words. 'So if you are never seen again, well, the disappointed constabulary will have no alternative but to conclude that you have outwitted them. A regular pair of second division Lord Lucans.' He laughed aloud this time, the sound echoing briefly. 'No doubt for a while you will be sighted around the globe. But I can assure you, your appearances will be purely imaginary.'

Ted raised his head from the table, hoped the older man could see the hatred burning in his eyes. 'So, if we are to die, there's no point in saying anything, is there?'

Sir Richard nodded his head in an exaggerated expression of concurrence with his own statement. 'Oh, I think you will find that there is. A quick end, perhaps will be your reward. The alternative, well, it hardly bears consideration.' He looked at Claire, and licked his lips. 'Does it, my dear? Hmm?' Claire glared at him, but her eyes betrayed more terror than hate. 'A little rape, eh? A touch of mutilation? Mahmoud – that is, Andreas here, is very good at that sort of thing.'

'Rape?' Ted's attempt at contempt was feeble. 'Neither of you two arse-bandits would know where to start.'

'Despite the veracity of your assessment, young man, I can assure you that anything is possible in the line of duty.'

Ted felt despair overwhelm him. Sir Richard caught the change in his eyes, pressed home his advantage. 'Let's make a start, shall we? Where, for example, is all your equipment? That would be very useful. You must have it hidden somewhere.'

Ted made a desperate attempt at resistance. 'Bollocks.'

'Oh, very original.' He looked across at Al-Ghraid. 'My dear chap. Would you like to open the batting?'

With a confident leer, the Iranian's hand snaked out towards Claire, grasped her by the shirt. She pulled away involuntarily, the material tore, and her left breast with its livid scar was exposed. Al-Ghraid released his grip on the remnant and stared. Claire quickly did her best to cover herself.

'My, my!' Sir Richard spoke first, turning to Ted. 'You're not into sado-masochism yourself, are you?'

Ted felt a fresh surge of rage and hatred, attempted to lunge at the man, but his good leg buckled and he sprawled again across the table. Reacting to the threat, Al-Ghraid turned, saw Ted's grasping hand. He reversed the gun, and brought the butt down hard on the outstretched fingers, smashing them against the wood of the table. Ted moaned, an animal sound, and clutched his injured hand with the other.

Claire shouted, shook her head again and again.

'Stop it! Stop it! Stop it!' She drew a lungful of air. 'The key is in his back pocket, you stupid bastards. You only have to look.' Her sobbing filled the small chamber, as Al-Ghraid moved round the table, keeping the gun trained on Ted as he reached down the back pockets of his jeans. He held the key triumphantly aloft between finger and thumb.

'Well done, my dear.' Sir Richard addressed Claire. 'You're getting the hang of it. Now, where is the container that this key fits?'

Claire almost collapsed into the chair opposite Ted, only the narrow table separating them. Briefly, their eyes met. Ted tried to unclench his teeth enough to speak. 'Don't tell them.'

'Don't be ridiculous, Ted. What's the point?' She struggled to her feet and turned to Sir Richard. 'Left luggage locker. Swansea bus station.'

Ted knew they were near the end. His mind struggled with a kaleidoscope of messages, but one burst through to the fore of his consciousness. He gritted his teeth and looked malevolently at Claire.

'You never could accept it. You always said it was crooked.' He swallowed. 'In my place.'

Claire looked at him, puzzled, made an involuntary step nearer. Ted took his chance. Without hesitation, he released his pulped and broken fingers and reached forward for Claire's arm with his good hand. He pulled her further towards him, raising his chest from the table as he did so. Letting her go again, he swung his open palm as hard as he could at her face. Her head jerked back, and she overbalanced onto the floor, blood pouring from a split in her lip, pain and hurt in her eyes, breast again exposed.

Ted leaned over the table at her. 'You stupid bitch!' Spittle flew in her direction as he raged. 'You've ruined everything!' He sobbed, lowered his head onto the table. He lifted it again, slowly, as their captors looked on, captivated by this unexpected bonus of entertainment.

Ted spoke, more softly this time. 'Everything. Gone.' His head dropped to the table once more, his whole body slumped in the unmistakable posture of defeat.

Sir Richard was greatly amused. 'Poor child. You poor child.' He moved over to Claire as he spoke, the words heavy with sarcasm through his mirth. He reached down to pull her up. Claire once again clutched her torn shirt with one hand to cover herself, but accepted the assistance offered with the other. As she rose to her feet, she clenched her jaw and stepped back. Her foot flew forward as hard as she could drive it into the Air Marshal's crotch, scoring a direct hit on his testicles. He doubled up, expelling air in a rush but then unable to breathe in again. As he sank to the floor Claire dashed past him, going up the stairs two at a time.

From his position at the table, head on one side, Ted saw Claire draw back to aim her blow. As she did so he lunged at Al-Ghraid and grabbed his arm, twisting him round. The table fell over, Ted and Al-Ghraid with it. The Iranian lashed out with the gun, striking Ted on the forearm and loosening his grip, then pulled away, swung his gun arm, and aimed a shot at Claire's fleeing figure, now near the top of the steps. Ted saw her shadow disappear into the sunlight.

Al-Ghraid knew he had to stop the girl at all costs. His other prisoner would not get far. He struggled to his feet, but before he could get clear, Ted, in a last act of defiance, grabbed his ankle. Al-Ghraid tried to pull free, dragging Ted towards the stairs, expecting the grip to be broken. It was like iron. He heard the door of the Jaguar slam, and in one smooth movement turned and shot Ted in the head.

In the car, Claire locked herself in and scrabbled for the keys. She was certain they had been left in the ignition. Her brain was racing, her chest and scalp prickling as if any moment she expected them to be penetrated by bullets. The key turned. For a second she wasn't sure the engine had fired, it was so quiet, but the swing of the rev counter reassured her. Thank God Sir Richard is short, she thought, I can reach the pedals. She engaged reverse, turned the wheel. The lightness of the steering and the power of the engine took her by surprise, and the car spun back almost out of control. She hit something, prayed it would not snag the car, and pushed the lever into drive. As she floored the accelerator she saw Al-Ghraid emerge from the doorway at the top of the steps. Her heart tore at the thought of abandoning Ted. She contemplated trying to run the gunman down, but could see that he would only have to step back into the doorway to evade her easily. She saw him swing up his arms, saw the gunmetal catch the sunlight. The rear wheels were spinning, then they caught, and the car careered and snaked across the gravel. The old chippings undoubtedly saved Claire's life. Al-Ghraid was holding his firearm steady, waiting for a clean shot, when he was showered with dust and stones that stung his face and hands and clouded his vision. He fired blindly into the hailstorm of grit flung up by the wheels, saw the car continue its crazy course and disappear round the side of the house.

Claire did not recognise the reports of the silenced gun above the noise of tyres and engine, but heard the rear window smash. Then she was clear, round the side of the house, moving quickly and just managing the bend in the drive. It was much shorter than she remembered, and when she tried to swing the heavy car to the right into the narrow lane, she was going much too fast. She hit the opposite bank. The engine stalled.

Al-Ghraid was swearing and shouting so loudly for Sir Richard that he nearly missed hearing the engine stop. He realised something was hampering the woman's escape, which at that point he had accepted as inevitable. He sprinted off round the house.

Claire could not restart the car, realised frantically that it was still in drive. She moved the lever into neutral, turned the key. The engine fired immediately. She slammed it in reverse, backed off the bank, engaged drive again. The side window behind her exploded in a shower of glass. She did not turn her head, did not see the Iranian running through the gateway, was unaware he had fired again as she raced away up the lane. Al-Ghraid reached the road, and crouched expertly on one knee. He fired, and Claire saw the windscreen craze, almost obscuring her vision. God! Where's the road! She had gone hardly fifty yards, and there was a T-junction ahead. Anxious not to lose control, unable to see clearly, she slowed the car.

Al-Ghraid seized his last opportunity. He methodically emptied the remainder of the magazine into the back of the car. Claire sensed rather than heard the thump of bullets, felt a tug at her shoulder, but she was past all caution now. She chose left, squealed round the corner, the rear of the car striking the bank as it swung. It won't steer properly! What's the matter? She wrestled with the wheel. She couldn't see that the nearside front and offside rear tyres were flat, but she assumed bullets had caused a puncture. She drove on, the car bumping and slewing as she tried to maintain direction. Half a mile, perhaps more now. Surely she was no longer in range? Could he possibly catch her now?

She passed a sign, announcing 'ASH GREEN'. Smart houses, neat lawns appeared. A truck was coming the other way. She tried to steer to one side, but the nearside wheel caught in a drain and she lost control. The car slewed round, driving a furrow through an immaculate lawn, and came to rest with a jerk against an ornamental tree. She had had no time to put on her safety belt, and the arrest of her progress was enough to throw her forward, striking her head on the fascia of the broken windscreen. She slumped against the wheel, the blaring of the horn announcing her arrival to the whole village.

CHAPTER 47

The nurse leaned over Claire, and looked down at the tear-stained face.

'There's a policeman here to see you, Miss Donaldson. Is that all right?'

Claire turned sleepily from her side onto her back. Her shoulder moved, despite her arm being in a sling, making her wince. The wound wasn't bad, she had been told, but that didn't seem to stop it hurting like hell. She was still nauseated from the anaesthetic required to remove the bullet, but she was hungry for news. She sat up.

'Yes, yes of course.'

The inspector came in, looking tentative. He advanced until he stood by her bed.

'I'm Detective Inspector Howard. CID.'

Claire picked up a tissue with her left hand. 'Yes. I know.' She wiped her eyes, made a token attempt to push her hair into shape. 'You are — were — Sergeant Clothier's boss.'

'Yes.' He cast his eyes downward.

'He was a nice man.'

'Indeed he was. A little unconventional, perhaps, but — as you say, a nice man.'

'Have you seen Ted — Mr Parkes?'

'I've just come from the Intensive Care Unit. But I didn't see him myself.'

Claire hung her head. 'Oh.'

'He's still unconscious. There was no point in —' The inspector stopped, realising his thoughtlessness. 'I believe they propose to transfer him to another neurological unit tomorrow.'

Claire looked up sharply. 'Why?'

'Well, I suppose they think it will be the best place.' The inspector was uncomfortable with the situation. 'I'm sure it's not because of any deterioration.'

'Thank you. For telling me.'

'You are a very brave lady, Miss Donaldson.'

'Bravery had nothing to do with it.' She looked him in the eye, defiantly. 'Frankly, I was scared shitless.'

A twitch of a smile flickered at the corner of his mouth. 'Nevertheless, your actions have led to the uncovering of a serious matter that could have, indeed may already have, affected national security.'

'That makes a change from being on the run because of suspected kidnapping.'

'I think you will find that matter will be sorted out.'

'I suppose I should be grateful. I *am* grateful. But right now, I don't care too much about anything.' She let her head go back against the pillows and closed her eyes.

The inspector was sensitive enough not to need to ask why. He changed tack. 'Sir Richard Jacobs has been apprehended.' This time he did allow himself a smile. 'He was still in great pain. Traumatic orchitis, I think the doctor called it.'

'Good.' Claire opened her eyes and looked up. 'What about the other bastard?'

'No luck, yet, I'm afraid.'

Claire could not hide her alarm. 'Oh, God!'

'It's all right. You are well protected, I can assure you.' He paused. 'And so is Mr Parkes.'

'I suppose you're watching the bus station?'

'I'm afraid Mr Al-Ghraid's network is more extensive than we imagined. We went there as soon as you gave us the information, of course. But he must have telephoned someone. The locker had been broken into very skilfully. It was empty.'

'Oh.'

'You don't seem terribly distressed.'

'Not at the loss of the equipment, no. It can be replaced.'

'So the data programs were not in the same place?'

Claire smiled to herself at Ted's forethought. 'No. Mr Parkes wasn't that daft. We hid them. Under the floor. In one of the places we stayed.'

'In Swansea?'

'Yes.'

'Oh dear.'

'What's that supposed to mean?'

'I'm afraid I may have more bad news for you.'

'Oh, Christ. Now what?'

'A small guest house in Sketty. Last night it was ransacked. The owner was beaten up, and the place was set on fire.'

'Oh, no. Not Little Oaks?'

'Yes.'

Claire closed her eyes again, let her head turn to one side. A single tear spilled over and traced its way down her cheek. Was there nothing left out of all this? All those lives, the pain, the suffering, all for nothing?

Howard shifted awkwardly. 'I'm sorry.'

'How did they know?'

'I was hoping you might be able to answer that.'

She shook her head. 'I can't think . . . It doesn't really matter now, does it?' A thought came to her, nevertheless. 'Ted wrote the address down somewhere. Perhaps he left it in the bag the computer was in.'

'That would have been uncharacteristically careless.'

'It would. But we were under a great deal of stress, to put it mildly.'

'Of course.'

There was an awkward silence, before the inspector spoke again. 'Surely there are other copies. Maybe not so up to date, but . . .'

'Most of the communications with Paul — Dr Sansome — were on those disks.'

'But the basic program — the one that enabled you to communicate? I understood from Sergeant Clothier's records that Mr Parkes stored them safely somewhere, before, er, before Dr Sansome's removal from hospital.'

'He did. In a safe deposit box.'

'Well, perhaps the loss is not so great.'

'Except that I don't know where the key or the box are hidden. He wouldn't tell me. Said it would put me at unnecessary risk.'

'I see.' Howard scratched his neck. 'And Mr Parkes is —'

'Is in no position to tell us where it is. Exactly.' She turned her head away to hide another tear.

There was another silence. Claire tried to turn her thoughts to a less painful subject. 'What will happen to Sir Richard?'

'Difficult to say. Ruined, of course. Gaol. He's being interviewed by the MOD chaps at the moment. Someone in his position, even in the Medical Branch, must represent a considerable security risk.'

'And Al-Ghraid?'

'We're watching all the airports, ports, of course. All the usual things.'

'You don't sound very optimistic.'

'Frankly, I'm not. He has some pretty sophisticated back-up. We've been through the offices of his front organisation. Extensive Middle Eastern connections, evidently.'

Claire suddenly wanted to be left alone. 'Was there anything else, inspector?'

'No, not really. It was mainly the safe deposit box I was interested in. MOD were pressing.'

Claire sat forward, eyes blazing. Howard immediately regretted his candour.

'That's all anybody cares about in this mess, isn't it? What they can bloody well do with Ted's breakthrough! Bugger the medical benefits! To hell with all the deaths, the orphans, the ruined lives! As long as the bloody Government can get their hands on it! No wonder Paul wouldn't have anything to do with the military!'

'I — I'm sorry, really, I —'

'Go away. And don't come back unless you've got some worthwhile news.'

Biting his lower lip, Inspector Howard turned and left.

* * *

Claire slept fitfully for an hour or so after the police officer went, but something kept nagging at her subconscious. Eventually she distilled the thought, and pressed the bell-push. A nurse came almost immediately.

'Who's the consultant in charge of Ted Parkes' case?' Claire wanted to know.

'Mr Rossini is the neurosurgeon.'

'Tell him I'd like to see him.'

The nurse was out of her depth immediately. She went for sister. 'Out of the question,' she was told. Claire was doggedly persistent. The houseman, then the registrar were summoned, Claire all the while getting more angry and upset.

'At least *ask* him if he'll see me, for Christ's sake!' she shouted in frustration. To calm her down as much as anything, they agreed.

Two hours later Mr Rossini came to see her. He was very pleasant, seemed quite young, didn't look remotely Italian, and had an obvious London accent. He came and sat on her bed, and with twinkling eyes and a mock-hollow voice, said 'You rang?'

Claire liked him immediately. 'Yes. Sorry. I made a bit of a fuss.'

He grinned. 'That wasn't quite how sister put it, but never mind. From what I've heard, you deserve a little special attention.'

'Can you talk to me about Ted?' Claire spoke rapidly, desperately. 'I'm not really his next of kin, or anything, but he hasn't got anyone else, not in this country, and not in Australia either as far as I know, and we *are* sort of, well, you could say he's my fiancé, and I only want to know if —'

Rossini held up his hands defensively. 'Whoa, whoa! Steady on!' He smiled at her, put his hands in the pockets of his white coat. 'All right. I'm in the picture. Ethically this sort of situation is always a difficult one — the disclosure of information about a patient to someone else. Your Mr Parkes can't give permission one way or the other, but you obviously have his interests at heart, and I'm sure —' he looked at her pointedly '— will keep any information confidential. So in my judgement I think it reasonable to treat you as I would the next of kin in these circumstances.'

Claire looked grave. 'Thank you.'

'So.' He smiled at her again. 'For what purpose have you summoned me?'

'I just want to know how he is. And where he's going.'

'Ah, so you heard we might move him, did you?'

'Yes.'

'Right. I'll try and put it simply. Let's do the easy bits first. He's got a healing fracture of the ninth rib — previous injury, that, but quite recent. His left hand — several broken bones, won't look very pretty, but he'll get quite good function again. There was also a spiral fracture of the ulna, in the forearm, but that's nothing much. The knee — well, the bullet missed the popliteal artery, but made a mess of the joint.

However, many orthopaedic surgeons in the UK have had a lot of practice at repairing this sort of damage — from the knee-cappings in Northern Ireland — and we've got one of them here. He's made a superb job of reconstructing the joint. Your Ted won't do the hundred yards very fast, and it'll get arthritic in old age, but he'll walk well enough. OK so far?'

Claire looked at him. 'It all sounds fine. But none of that matters if he's got — got —'

'Brain damage? That's what's worrying you, I realise that. That's what all this is about.'

Claire nodded, held her breath.

'Large areas of the brain are pretty redundant, did you know that? Don't appear to have any special function, so we seem to get along without them quite well.'

Claire nodded. 'Yes. Don't forget, experimental neurology is my field.'

'Sorry. Of course it is. I had forgotten.' He moved position, settled again. 'Just try and think of this anatomically, don't visualise it as your man, OK?'

Claire paled. 'I'll try.'

Rossini demonstrated on himself. 'The bullet entered the skull over the frontal area here.' He pointed to a spot on his hair-line, above his right eye. 'It travelled tangentially through the superficial area of the frontal lobes, and came out just anterior to the left temporal artery, here.' He pointed to an area above and to the left of his left eye. 'It was a silenced weapon, and Mr Parkes has a thick skull.' He tried a grin. 'Don't tell him I said that. Anyway, that meant relatively slow speed of bullet, less shock to the rest of the brain, less exit wound damage. It's the high-velocity stuff that really messes things up.' He glanced at Claire, saw her pallor. 'Sorry. I'll try not to be too graphic.'

'No, please. I want to know.'

'It looked quite a mess — no wonder the would-be assassin thought he was dead.' He gave Claire a guarded look before continuing. 'Anyway — we have trauma to part of the frontal lobes, but I don't think that will matter much. The track was clean apart from a few bone spicules that I've removed, and we can repair the skull with grafting later if need be. No metal plates or anything.'

'Will it affect his — his mental capacity?'

'Shouldn't do. Intellectually it shouldn't affect him at all. There just *could* be some personality changes, I suppose. But I think that is very unlikely. No inter-cerebral connections were severed — you know, like they are in those rather empirical lobotomy operations that are rarely performed nowadays.'

'So he could be perfectly normal?'

Rossini grinned. 'As normal as any Australian.'

Claire smiled back, but it quickly faded. 'So why is he still unconscious?'

'That's the sixty-four thousand dollar question. And the answer is — I don't know.'

'How long before you do know?'

'I just can't say. His pupils are reacting. But at the moment there's a fair bit of cerebral oedema, swelling of the brain, if you like, that you get after most injuries such as this. He's got marked papilloedema, swelling of the optic nerves, that we can see at the back of his eyes. It's a good guide to what's going on inside. When that goes down, and we're treating it vigorously, he should show signs of getting lighter, and we can only hope he'll come out of it then.'

Claire digested this information, and Rossini let her think about it for a few moments. 'I hope that helps.'

She gave him a grateful look. 'Yes, it does, really. I can think about something positive now, instead of just letting my imagination run riot.'

'Anything else?' He stood up, took his hands from his pockets.

'Yes. Moving him.'

'Oh, right. I forgot.' He sat down again. 'We've done the emergency stuff here. As soon as he's stable he should go to a proper neuro unit.'

'Where?'

'I was thinking of one of the London hospitals.'

'Oh.'

'Problem?'

'Couldn't he go to Bristol? There's a good neurological unit there.'

'That's where you and Mr Parkes did your research with Paul Sansome, isn't it?'

'Yes.'

Rossini gave her a speculative look, and Claire thought he was going to say something critical about Paul's abduction. Instead he said, 'It's a good place.'

'I know. And it's near where we both live, so I'll be able to visit him. Maybe help him come round if he's still — still . . .'

'Makes sense. I'll see what I can do. Should be in a couple of days, maybe three.'

'Oh. Inspector Howard said it would be tomorrow.'

The doctor looked serious. 'Policemen aren't always right, you know.'

She could tell he was mocking her, and gave him a pale smile. 'I'll remember that. And I'll remember you. I'm sure you've done everything you can for Ted. And you've been very kind to me.' She thought of Porthenoy. 'And you've restored my faith in consultant neurosurgeons.'

He laid a hand on her arm. 'You're a charming and courageous lady. It's been my pleasure.' He went to the door of her room, and put his head round just before he shut it. 'Any time you want to talk — just let me know.'

'Thanks.'

The door closed softly, and Claire was alone with her thoughts. Strangely, the first one she had made her smile. She spoke softly, aloud.

'A thick skull. Just wait till I tell him.'

The smile was only transient, as another thought supplanted the first: *If* I can ever tell him.

CHAPTER 48

Claire recovered quickly. She left hospital after only three more days, and was back in her flat by the time Ted was transferred to the Bristol General Hospital Neurological Unit, six days after his injury. Her police protection was discreet, and she felt increasingly that it was superfluous. Everyone involved seemed to be convinced that Al-Ghraid had left the country.

Going back to the ward that now included Ted as well as Paul Sansome amongst its patients was a difficult experience. A new ward sister was in charge, efficient and kindly enough in her way, but thoughts of Joanne were strongly in Claire's mind. There was fear, too. She had not seen Paul, of course, had not even dared inquire how he was after the ordeal he had suffered as a result of her and Ted's intervention. And she had not yet seen Ted, either.

She braced herself, and made her inquiry about Paul as soon as the formalities of introduction were over. The sister responded with professional detachment.

'Dr Sansome seems quite stable again, now.'

Claire swallowed. 'What was the matter?'

'The traumatic removal of the probes resulted in some infection of the meninges.'

'He got a meningitis?'

'Yes. But it's responded well to antibiotics.'

'Do you know if there was any — any other brain damage?'

'Not that we can tell. He's had a CT scan and EEG which showed no change. I didn't nurse him at all before, you understand, but from what the other nurses say, he seems to be rather deeper. The typical coma sleep-wake cycles are more infrequent, and less prolonged. But even the doctors don't know if that carries a bad prognosis.' The sister sighed, and pulled a face. 'On the other hand, there has been no evidence to suggest he'll ever come out of this.' She looked up at Claire's stricken face. 'I'm sorry. I forgot your personal involvement.'

Claire tried to look composed. 'That's all right.' She forced herself to smile weakly. 'It's Ted Parkes I'm most involved with.'

The nurse had obviously been briefed. 'He's your — your fiancé?'

'Something like that.'

'We'll do the very best we can, you know that.'

'Of course.' She forced the question she was dreading to ask. 'Has he shown any sign of regaining consciousness?'

'Not yet. He coped with the transfer very well. The papilloedema's almost cleared. But he's still unresponsive, I'm afraid.'

'I see.' Claire had to work hard at maintaining her equilibrium. 'Can I see them?'

'Of course. You can come any time you like.'

* * *

She went into Side Room 3 first. She had a powerful feeling of *dêjà vu* that made her feel weak, her scalp prickle. They had put him back in the same room, but the familiarity seemed ominous rather than reassuring. It was so different. There were the naso-gastric tubes, the drip feed, the catheter drainage bag, of course. But no special equipment, no electronic machinery. The room looked bare.

Paul's hair was growing again, and there were no electrodes protruding from his skull, just three patches of scar tissue. Despite the hair regrowth, which removed some of the starkness of profile he had previously shown, Claire thought his face looked thinner, his features more strained, his whole posture, even though he was just lying in bed, less relaxed. She told herself it could only be her imagination, her guilt at the disruption of his care, to which she had been party; but somehow he looked restless, ill at ease — she searched for the most apt adjective, found it: unhappy. You're being ridiculous, she admonished herself. He's deeply unconscious. He can't show his emotions like that. But she had made contact with the inner feelings of this man, knew they existed, however inscrutable the outward mask remained.

She went closer to the bed, and took his hand. Could he still hear? Had he heard that the woman he loved was dead? Did he know about Ted, now lying in the same state only yards away across the corridor? She felt she had to talk to him, say something.

'Hello, Paul.'

Instinctively, she watched his chest, alert for any change in the breathing pattern. She had spoken indistinctly, her voice husky, her mouth dry. She drew breath to speak again, louder, but the door opened and a staff nurse bustled in carrying a kidney dish.

'Oh, sorry. Shall I come back in a minute?'

'No, it's all right.' Somehow the spell was broken. She would not be able to communicate with him now, aware of someone waiting outside, the possibility of interruption hovering in the back of her mind. She squeezed his hand firmly, and left.

She crossed the corridor and stopped outside Ted's room. She had to breathe deeply, summon her strongest resolve, before she pushed open the door.

For a moment she thought she was in the wrong room. She had expected the hand and leg in plaster, the tubes and the drips. But she did not immediately recognise the man who lay with his head supported either side by blocks of foam, with his shaven head, two heavily sutured gashes, uncovered, on the scalp, the bloated face with swelling around and below the eyes, or the distorted eyelids discoloured with shades of blue and yellow. Was this really Ted? She had kept picturing him as a dust-jacket hero, a gallant-looking bandage round the forehead, eyes closed peacefully as if in sleep. But not — not like this.

She stood quite still, just inside the door, waiting for her emotions to settle, waiting for . . . She was ashamed to admit the sensation to herself. Waiting for the nausea to settle, for the bile that had risen to return whence it came.

She approached the bed slowly, and as she got nearer, an almost miraculous change seemed to overcome her perception. She began to recognise features, each one drawn in turn to her attention, as if a zoom lens were homing in to enhance the detail. A mole on an exposed forearm, a blemish on his cheek, an irregularity in his lip, the cleft of his chin. As she approached, the real Edward Parkes seem to crystallise out of this disfigured caricature. Her brain sorted out the aberrations caused by the trauma, sifted them, discarded them, and left her with the image of the man she knew she loved.

She could see then some semblance of the face she had last seen in that poorly lit cellar. She pictured him now, sprawled across the table, their assailants either side and behind him. He was looking down at her as she tried to assimilate the sudden change in his behaviour that had led him to strike her to the ground. She remembered his eyes, flicking sideways from Sir Richard Jacobs to the steps, not realising it was some sort of a message until he managed, despite the pain racking his body, to close one eye in an almost absurd wink; a signal that caused such a surge of adrenaline that she had found the courage and strength to set in motion the means of her escape.

She moved to the bed, leaned over, and gazed fondly at him. Her heart ached to see him like this; she wanted to lift him, hold his head to her breast, caress the misshapen features. She contented herself with bending forward and kissing him so, so gently, full upon the lips.

After another long look, she pulled up a chair, and sat, holding his hand, and talked to him softly until a nurse came in 40 minutes later.

* * *

Claire maintained her vigil for the next three weeks, making a daily pilgrimage to the hospital. Paul seemed to her to be weakening, although she never spent more than a few moments with him. Ted, though gaining strength in body, his wounds healing, his face now almost normal in appearance, showed no signs of regaining consciousness. Claire began to despair. She could see him crossing that undefined border from being a patient whose carers were waiting for a return to consciousness, to one who was accepted as being in a coma.

The very word made her shudder, with the images it conjured up of Jason Coombes and Paul Sansome. She had been fighting the idea for days, but now, as she sat in a train to London for a meeting she had been summoned to attend at the Ministry of Defence, she faced up to the possibility.

Could she, if Ted did not recover, consider trying to communicate with him as they had with Paul?

Once she had allowed the thought to surface, she put her mixed emotions aside and tried to analyse the situation rationally. Was there a neurosurgeon who would be able, or willing, to insert electrodes as Porthenoy had done? Could she find, work with, another programmer for the weeks, months it would take for him or her to learn all Ted's secrets? Was there any possibility of regaining the financial backing of the Clifton Research Institute?

All this was pure conjecture, she knew, unless or until the data disks Ted had hidden away could be found. Searches of the records of the financial institutions he had any dealings with failed to show any deposit box in his name. His flat and all his belongings had been scoured repeatedly, but no key was discovered. Claire could only take some comfort from one piece of information relayed to her from Inspector Howard. A search of the Little Oaks Guest House had revealed the charred remnants of several computer disks. They were beyond any hope of salvation, but they did show that Al-Ghraid's men had burnt the house in frustration, not triumph. They did not possess Ted's secret.

Claire sighed with resignation. Nor, she reflected sadly, did she.

* * *

Group Captain Jonathan Oliver was not looking forward to this particular interview. He had been working in vetting and intelligence for the past three years, and had met all sorts. But to put this girl on the spot when she'd had a good friend killed by a bomb and her man was in a coma in hospital – well, it seemed a bit insensitive. He sighed, and looked out of the window of his office in the MOD building just off Trafalgar Square, to see if he could spot her approaching. Still, the orders came from on high, and he had no choice in the matter. And that damn jumped-up civil servant was going to be there, too. As an observer, they had put it. God! don't they trust me?

He looked at his watch. She was seven minutes late. He decided to go and wait for her downstairs.

Claire entered the building, worrying about the time as much as what was to happen. She had sat in a stationary train on the Underground for nearly 20 minutes, helpless.

As she entered the building and went up to the security guard she looked anxiously at her watch.

'It's all right, there's no panic.'

She looked round and saw a small, broad-shouldered man in RAF uniform approaching, late forties, sandy-coloured hair.

'I'm Group Captain Oliver. Get held up in the traffic?'

'In the Tube. Stuck for ages.'

'Don't worry about it.' He held out his hand. 'Jonathan Oliver.'

Claire shook hands. 'Claire Donaldson.'

He gave her a security badge, spoke briefly with the guard, and escorted her upstairs. He was very considerate.

'Do call me Jonathan,' he said as he led her to a small room furnished only with several armchairs and an occasional table. Already waiting there was a man in civilian clothes, who half-stood as a token of courtesy when she came in.

'I hope you don't mind, but Mr Brailsford would like to be present. As an observer.'

Claire thought it strange that no other comment was made, and only speculated very briefly on what would happen if she said she did mind. She assumed, rightly as it turned out, that he must be some sort of intelligence officer.

The Group Captain used an intercom to organise coffee, and finally they were settled.

'It's very good of you to come all this way.'

'It didn't sound as if I had much choice.' Claire tried to sound light-hearted. 'And a free travel warrant to London as well.'

'Journey OK, was it?'

'Fine, thank you.'

'And how is Mr Parkes?'

'Still unconscious.' Claire forced a smile. 'Group Captain Oliver, can we get to the point?'

'Jonathan, please. Remember?'

Claire merely nodded.

'This is really a sort of de-briefing. Exchange of information. Tying up loose ends.'

'I gathered it would be something like that.'

'There are no doubt things you would like to know, questions you'd like to ask. And we have a few questions for you.'

Claire crossed her legs, straightened her skirt. 'All right.'

'You see, we think it's better to remove any doubts, any speculations, you may have. You've been very co-operative so far in not talking about this to the press, as we requested.' He coughed, obviously a delaying tactic. He seemed to be avoiding looking directly at her. 'We also need to satisfy ourselves that you will agree not to divulge any details — that you are aware of now or may learn this afternoon — at any time in the future.'

'You mean you want me to sign the Official Secrets Act.'

'Something like that.'

Claire considered briefly. She had really been only too grateful to be protected from the attentions of the media by the 'D' notice that was in force until the authorities felt certain Al-Ghraid was no longer a threat. And after that, even when reporting restrictions had been partly lifted, she had been able emphatically to refuse any contact with prying newsmen. She knew she would never want to publicise her experiences. They were too private, too traumatic. And she certainly had an unquestionable desire to know more of the background to the purgatory of the last few weeks.

She made up her mind. 'Where is it?'

'I beg your pardon?'

'The paper you want me to sign. I'll sign it now, if you like.'

Group Captain Oliver looked immensely relieved. 'Oh! Oh, well, yes, of course. If you're sure.' He'd obviously expected a hard battle to get this far. He looked across at the other man. 'Brailsford?'

Brailsford produced a clip-board with papers attached in triplicate, and offered them to Claire with a pen.

She noted that all her personal details had already been filled in. 'Where do I sign?'

'You ought to read it first,' suggested the Group Captain. 'There are certain penalties . . .'

'It's all right. Just show me.'

He pointed, and Claire signed. The clip-board was handed back to Brailsford, who removed the papers, took one, and folded the other copies away. He spoke for the first time.

'This is your copy. I suggest you make yourself aware of your obligations by reading it carefully.'

'Thank you.' Claire took the paper and put it in her handbag. 'Can we start now?'

Oliver glanced at the observer. 'I think perhaps, to save a lot of questions and answers, it will be simpler if I just outline the facts as we now know them. You may ask questions, of course, and there are one or two points we may wish to put to you.'

Claire nodded her understanding, sipped her coffee, and waited for the Group Captain to proceed.

'Everyone thought Sir Richard Jacobs was a fine officer. I never heard anyone speak ill of him. Always so considerate, especially of his junior officers. However —' He paused, as if almost reluctant to continue the indictment. 'However, it seems that he had had an association with Mahmoud Al-Ghraid for many years. He's told us all about it, now.'

He leaned forward, elbows on his knees, and steepled his fingers. 'It all started by accident, as these things often do. Opportunities, that's what these chaps are trained to look out for. Sir Richard met Al-Ghraid on his secondment. He would have denied it to you, of course, but Al-Ghraid was an Admin Officer at an RAF Hospital for a few months. At the time Sir Richard was on the brink of getting Air Commodore, and was moving in influential circles. He wanted to enhance his financial position, thought it would help him get on. He took some bad advice from some of the high-flying friends he was cultivating. It was a disaster. They could afford it, but he couldn't. Looked as if he would be ruined financially. Couldn't keep that quiet, of course. Might have scuppered his chances of Air rank, certainly any further progress. It wasn't just the money, apparently. The deal itself was, er, a bit suspect.' He looked across at Claire. 'More coffee?'

'No, thank you.'

'Where was I? Ah, yes. Al-Ghraid got to hear of it, saw his chance, offered to bail him out. Gave him a story about family wealth back in the Middle East, all very plausible. The way it all worked out was so convenient, I suspect the whole thing may have been a set-up. Anyway, he was a fool, made a grave error of judgement when it came to the choice. Finish his career on a high note, or face the consequences of bankruptcy. He backed the wrong horse. Don't know what sort of a yarn Al-Ghraid spun him about *why* he was helping him out, but the fact that they were both homosexuals, well, bisexuals, actually, was probably not insignificant. Of course, when Al-Ghraid was apparently let out in the cold after the Shah got kicked out, lo and behold, he called in the debt. Sir Richard gave him glowing references, and it was on his recommendation that he got his commission. After that, they did several quiet business deals together, and by the time Al-Ghraid left the service to set up his consultancy, Sir Richard was in a position to put a number of service contracts for medical equipment his way, as well as recommending him to his friends in the other forces.' He sat back, crossed his legs. 'With me so far?'

'Yes. But how does all this tie in with Dr Sansome?'

'Indeed. Well, I think you know he and Sir Richard had kept in touch over the years.'

'We knew that, yes.'

'Obviously when Sir Richard learned something of Sansome's researches, his Iranian friend saw the possibilities at once. Started trying to find out more about it, even made an offer he thought Dr Sansome couldn't refuse.'

'Paul told us. Half a million dollars. He said no.'

'Quite. An honourable chap. Kept it to himself, though.'

'When we told all this to Jacobs —' Claire could no longer bear to grace the Air Marshal with his title '— he acted as though it was all news to him.'

'I'm sure he did. Cool customer.' Group Captain Oliver nodded his head knowingly. 'In the end they got so desperate to recruit Dr Sansome that they set up the Austrian affair. But that all went wrong. When he was in a coma, they backed off, thought it was a cold trail — until you two made it possible to tap Dr Sansome's secrets, proved his ideas could work.'

He took a deep breath. Claire waited.

'At first Al-Ghraid just tried some simple tactics. Thought if one of you met with an accident —'

'Like electrocution?'

'Precisely — then the other would give up. But as your technique improved and the market widened with the ending of the Iran-Iraq war, well, they didn't want to stifle Sansome so much as they wanted the technology. They thought it could be used to extract information about germ warfare, nuclear weapons, you name it.' He paused reflectively. 'They thought it was still a good prospect, especially after Saddam Hussein survived being thrown out of Kuwait in the Gulf War.'

'But how did they know we were getting through to Paul?'

'That's where Gerard Porthenoy comes in. He was known to be a homosexual, too. Apparently Al-Ghraid can be quite a charmer with either sex. It was the old honey-trap routine. Photographs, I think, usual thing. Porthenoy actually dealt with Sir Richard, thought he was doing his country a favour, providing info. and getting copies of the disks — even if your Mr Parkes did corrupt them.'

'So when Ted and I confronted him, he was not really worried about threats from us — it was Al-Ghraid he was really afraid of. That was what drove him to suicide?'

'That would seem to be the case.'

Claire pressed her lips together. 'And I thought it was because of us.'

'I'm sure your influence in that matter was incidental.'

Claire looked across at Jonathan Oliver. 'What about the other attacks on us — when I was cut up?' She absently fingered the livid mark on her cheek as she spoke. Her hand dropped to her scarred bosom as she recalled the horror of the scene in the cellar that had prompted the question. 'I'm pretty sure —' She recalled the look of surprise on Sir Richard's face when he saw her exposed breast after Al-Ghraid had ripped her shirt. 'I'm, pretty sure that wasn't them.'

'This is one of the major areas of difficulty in unravelling all this. There was tremendous confusion about this time, which drove Al-Ghraid and Sir Richard to distraction. There seemed to be someone else in the field, who was apparently terrorising the nursing sister, Yeates, the woman who died in the car bomb —'

Claire wanted to stop his impersonal reference to Joanne. 'She was a wonderful woman. She became a friend.'

'Yes. I beg your pardon. I didn't mean to sound uncaring. But they were thrown into confusion by this intervention, thinking it was a rival. It was, of course, Christine Sansome.' Oliver placed his hands on each arm of the chair. 'It must have been a terrible ordeal for you. Caught in the middle of the activities of a madwoman and a terrorist.'

'It was. And it's not over yet.'

The Group Captain sat up straight. Even Brailsford was moved to react. 'What do you mean?'

Claire looked from one to the other. 'Al-Ghraid is still out there somewhere.'

Oliver spoke soothingly. 'I'm sure you won't be having any more trouble with him,'

'I'm not a child, Jonathan.' She could not keep the trace of derision from the use of his name. 'You don't know where he is any more than I do.'

'We are as sure as we can be that he has left the country.'

'Even if he has — he could still come back.'

'I don't think so.'

Claire nodded, let her breath out slowly. 'You don't *think* so.' There was no reply. Claire spoke again. 'And I am still left with the consequences. My man in a coma. My friend's daughter an orphan. My life's work lost for ever.'

'Yes. I do see all that. And I sympathise.'

Claire had to bite her tongue. She didn't want this man's sympathy. She didn't know what she wanted. She certainly didn't want to stay here. She stood up. 'May I leave now?'

The two men stood also. 'Of course.' He hesitated. 'Just one more thing.'

Claire was moving to the door. She turned to Oliver, raised an eyebrow questioningly.

'The data on Mr Parkes' program. They're still missing?' he asked.

Surely they know that? she thought. They were the ones who went through the flat with a tooth-comb. 'Yes.'

'Should they ever come to light — at any time — you will let us know, won't you?'

Claire felt anger flare in her, unreasonable, uncontrollable. She rounded on them, fists clenched at her sides.

'So that's what this is all about! You use my curiosity to tempt me here, offer an exchange of information. Ha!' She fought back tears of frustration. 'But all you wanted was for me to sign that bloody paper to shut me up, and then make me promise to give you everything Ted's worked for, while he lies there and can't do anything about it!' She tried to force her voice lower. 'Look at the price he's paid! Why should I hand *anything* over? I might as well give you his life.'

'Please Miss Donaldson, calm yourself. We only want to be sure — for the good of the country, of course — that you —'

'God! What do you think I am? You think if I find it, I'll rush out and sell it to the first terrorist organisation that meets my price?'

She couldn't hold back the tears any longer, but she kept her head erect, stared defiantly at the two men.

The Group Captain tried to soothe her. 'Of course not. But just try to remember the importance —'

Claire did not let him finish. 'Get stuffed!'

She marched out of the door, threw her security badge at a bemused doorman, and went back to Bristol.

CHAPTER 49

She woke the next morning with a suddenness that left her heart racing. She had been sweating, and strands of hair were stuck to her face. She sat up, aware of an urge to recall some fragment of the nightmare that had woken her, yet not wanting to revisit the scene again.

She had been in a dark, dank, violent place, a place her subconscious had visited regularly at night: the cellar where Ted had been shot. The action replay began with his striking her, giving her the chance to escape. She hadn't seen the act of his shooting, but her dreams always ended with a vision of Ted's head jerking back as the bullet ploughed into his forehead, blood spraying everywhere, then he was falling, slowly falling, eyes staring sightlessly ahead . . .

But this time — this time it was different. She struggled to remember. It was the beginning of the nightmare sequence that was different. Right at the beginning. She made a mental effort to rewind the tape of her recollection. Right at the start, before he struck her, Ted had said something, something that hadn't made sense until now. What had woken her this time was not Ted's grotesque spasms, but some realisation, some revelation that was important, so very important. Something about being crooked. In his place. *His place!* His flat! Something crooked in his place that she could never accept. It could only be the shelf!

* * *

Claire was due to go to Cheltenham that morning, to see Karen Henstridge, Joanne's sister, and Lucinda. She phoned to say she would be late, then went straight round to Ted's flat.

She had been here only once since his injury, to try and put things back as they were before the place was ransacked. She had not enjoyed the experience, the feeling of emptiness. This time, as she let herself in, her feelings were more those of an uncertain excitement at what she might find. She had an idea already, and she had to make a conscious effort to suppress a sense of mounting anticipation.

She went straight into the lounge, and stood before the shelf holding his record collection. It *was* crooked, one end perceptibly lower than the other. Despite everything, she smiled. She had often teased him about it, his rare effort at home improvement, but he had refused to correct the error.

There must be something very significant about the shelf that he should mention it at such a time of crisis. Something very significant indeed.

She took the records off a few at a time. She had already been through the album sleeves when she had put them back. She knew it was the shelf she had to look at.

It was a simple affair, two slotted metal uprights screwed to the wall, with rigid U-shaped steel brackets that hooked into the slots. The brackets supported a length of veneered chipboard shelving. She removed it, noting wryly that he hadn't even bothered to fix it to the brackets.

She stood back and looked again. Perhaps she had to unscrew the uprights? But first she reached forward, and after a brief struggle, managed to unhook the left-hand bracket. She placed it with the shelving, then turned to the other one. This one came off easily, and as she tilted it something fell out from inside the bracket onto the floor.

She looked down at the piece of card. Picking it up, she saw the key taped to it. On the other side of the card was an address, a 9-digit number, and a name. Even then, Ted's humour had not deserted him. Her lips twitched as she read it.

'Mr. C. Dundee.'

* * *

As she drove up to Cheltenham, Claire was already planning how she could try and get the research project going again. The key would literally unlock the door to all Ted's original programs. She'd get everything ready, then as soon as he recovered . . .

Who was she kidding? Come on girl, be realistic. Recover from having a hole blasted through his head?

But she could not totally reject the possibility. And if the worst came to the worst . . . *Face up to it! Go on!* She allowed the thought to form. If he doesn't regain consciousness, then maybe I could get another computer expert, someone who could make it all work, let me talk to him, just like I talked to Paul. Maybe . . .

* * *

When she finally arrived at Cheltenham, she was delighted with her reception. Lucinda remembered her, was pleased to see her, and didn't even comment on her scar and lopsided face. Karen was equally welcoming, but subdued. Her sister's death had hit her hard.

Joanne's mother was also there, staying with her surviving daughter. Claire sensed a cool response from her, and after a few awkward exchanges, Mrs Bristowe excused herself and left Karen and Claire alone.

They sat on the patio. It was early September now, but the weather was still comfortably warm.

'Lucinda looks settled.' They were watching the child playing happily with a rather tattered teddy bear, giggling as she teased a cat that was trying to sleep in the sun.

'They seem amazingly adaptable at this age. Piers and Steph have been terrific, too. She's really like one of the family already.'

'She'll stay with you now, I suppose?'

'Yes, we'd like that. It'll be best for Lucinda too, I'm sure. We've even talked of adoption. Her father has agreed.'

Claire thought of Joanne's other relative, who would surely be missing her too. 'What about Aunt Maudie? Where is she now?'

Karen smiled. 'She's here, too.'

Claire looked around. 'What? With you?'

'No, no. I mean here in Cheltenham. She's in a rest home, about a mile away. She seems to like it.'

'I'm glad. She was a lovely lady.'

'She still is. In her own little world.' Karen stood up. 'Would you like a cuppa? I usually have one about now.'

'Oh, yes, thanks.'

Claire was left alone, watching the little girl play, knowing another dream had faded. After Joanne had been killed, she had often thought of Lucinda, and in her mind's eye she always pictured the child with herself and Ted, proud adoptive parents, trying to repay their friend by doing all they could for her daughter. Now, it was obvious that this was the right place for Lucinda, and without Ted, the dream was fractured, hollow.

Karen returned with the tea, and Claire had to turn away until the brimming tears had cleared away.

The hours went quickly, and by the time Claire felt she must go, she had decided on a change of plan. Instead of her usual visit to the hospital, she went to the safe deposit box and collected the fruits of Ted's genius.

When she got home, she checked that the disks were uncorrupted, then read through all her own data. She got totally engrossed. At one point she looked up, and was aware for the first time that it was getting dark. She felt suddenly overwhelmed with tiredness. I'll go and see Paul and Ted tomorrow, she told herself, and went straight to bed and a dreamless sleep.

* * *

The security porter at the hospital looked curiously at the olive-skinned man in the white coat and his brow creased in an effort at recognition. It was only just after five in the morning. As the man passed the reception counter, he smiled and lifted up a wire basket containing a selection of different-coloured tubes, swabs, vacutainers, needles. The porter's frown cleared, and he raised a hand in acknowledgement.

'Lucky bastard,' he muttered to himself. He was jealous of the fact that on each occasion the lab technicians were called out at night to do emergency tests, they got overtime payments. It always rankled with him.

* * *

The solitary staff nurse at the nursing station stood up, stretched, and ran her hand over her eyes. She was thirsty again, and went into the ward kitchen to make more tea.

The white-coated figure slipped past the shaft of bright light that emanated from the kitchen and penetrated the gloom of the main ward. A patient moaned softly as he turned noisily in bed, the springs creaking. The figure stopped, frozen for a moment, eyes fixed on the kitchen door. The next sound was of a tap being turned on, a kettle filling. The white coat disappeared into the near-darkness of the corridor, and slipped silently into Side Room 3.

The man looked down at Paul Sansome and smiled. He reached out, stroked the scrawny neck, first with one hand, then with both. Fingers probed gently, until both carotid pulses were located accurately, indicating the site of the main arteries that supplied blood and oxygen to the brain.

Slowly, gently, the fingers increased their pressure. Just enough to stop the flow of life-giving blood, but not enough to bruise the tissues. Death by apparently natural causes would be better, cause less fuss, give him more time. Besides, he was a craftsman, proud of the quality of his work.

He watched as Paul Sansome's breathing became irregular, one rapid intake of breath making a noise like a gentle snore. Sightless eyes roamed, then stilled, staring into infinity. The pressure was maintained for a full three minutes after the breathing ceased, and even when the hands were moved away from Paul's neck, the man watched for further long moments to make absolutely certain life was permanently extinguished, that every betz cell in the brain was dead.

He had been calm, quite calm, but now as he crossed the corridor to enter the room almost opposite, he felt a rage build inside, a fearsome anger directed at the form he now looked at lying helpless in the bed. He wanted to strike out, to smash the sleeping profile, slash the pale skin, literally break the man who had ruined the culmination of 20 years' work.

He turned away, breathed deeply, clenching and unclenching his fists as the desire for violence slowly subsided. Then, when his hands no longer trembled, he turned back to the bed and reached out to locate Ted Parkes' carotid arteries.

* * *

On his way out the porter barely acknowledged him. He was still carrying his stolen wire basket of blood-letting equipment, but he dumped it in the first waste bin he passed that was big enough to hold it. A little further on, he took off his white coat, and stuffed it under a portakabin next to some building works in the grounds of the hospital. From the same place he retrieved his small overnight bag.

Once out of the grounds, he hurried towards an all-night taxi-rank, but then felt compelled to stop under a streetlight and make one final check.

He reached into the inside pocket of his jacket and withdrew an airline ticket. The name matched that on his new passport. He just wanted to be sure of the check-in time, and to savour once more the destination. He nodded, satisfied. By this time tomorrow, he would be back home. He sighed, whispered the word.

'Teheran'.

* * *

Claire moaned in her sleep, a mournful, animal sound of suffering. For the second morning running, she woke abruptly, sweating, trying to overcome a feeling of terror, of some terrible loss. This time there had been no nightmare, so what was it?

She felt for the chain around her neck, to locate the key she had decided to keep as a talisman. It was still there.

She lay back, and tears flowed freely. She could not push away the feeling of desperate emptiness.

She knew, beyond any doubt, that she was completely alone.

CHAPTER 50

Claire sat at her desk in the Neurological Research Institute, unable to concentrate. Even now, four months after the end of the most traumatic period of her life, she was often overcome with memories.

Usually they were triggered by some development in her research, by a trick that Ted had developed in his programming, or perhaps, as now, when another hurdle was overcome by her new colleague and computer expert, Peter Gardiner.

She looked across at him. He was still smiling, a subdued sign of his recent triumph — an important step forward in their bid to create a thesaurus that would enable more straightforward communication with comatose patients. It had proved a major stumbling-block for herself and Ted, but time had been against them. Now, with their new subject, they had time and money. Once the proof of their success had been validated from Ted's computer records, and the Ministry of Defence had given clearance to publish, the technique had become a celebrated success. Claire had been welcomed back into the academic fold with open arms, and money for further research had been made available. She had been repelled at first by this cynical change of heart by her former backers.

She was a pragmatist, however, and also drew comfort from the fact that Ted would approve. 'Take the bastards' money, go on.' She could almost hear him saying it, and had accepted her reinstatement philosophically.

Now she was working hard, successfully, and was getting on well with her new partner. He did not have Ted's rough edges, or his flair, but he was very clever indeed. She knew they would succeed. The keen young consultant neurosurgeon who had been appointed in Porthenoy's place had actually approached them personally to work on a case he thought would be suitable. The electrodes were positioned in the female patient's brain, and their preliminary contacts with the woman's subconscious had been dramatically successful. Claire found it an eerie experience, partly because of the ease with which they had got a response, and also because she felt she was going through it with Ted's ghost looking over her shoulder.

She gazed out of the window, chin cupped in her hands, not really seeing the trees beyond the glass. She sat that way for some time, lost in her thoughts. When she looked back into the room. Peter was working intently at his keyboard, glancing occasionally from his notes to the screen. She leaned back in her chair. At least she could feel a little more relaxed, now. For the first three weeks after Ted's death she had been in a state of constant fear. The autopsies on Paul and Ted had revealed subtle signs of how they had met their deaths, and the evidence of the night security man and the clothing and equipment hidden in the grounds of the hospital had confirmed that these were murders.

After her initial grief and anger, Claire had turned her thoughts to why Al-Ghraid — for she knew it must have been he — should have done this. She was still uncertain. Paul was no threat any more, although his killer might not have known that. Ted could well have recovered. The only motive she could think of was revenge. She had been given police protection, and had hidden herself away, until diplomatic sources reported that Al-Ghraid was back in Teheran. She was still uneasy, but as time went by she worried less about the possibility of being at risk.

She sighed deeply, knew she must stop this retrospection and get on with her work. She glanced at Peter. He was a decent chap, she got on well enough with him. He was her age, and single. But she knew there was nothing there, nothing that matched the interest or excitement she had felt with her coarse but kind Australian. At the moment her energies were absorbed by her work, and by her desire to emulate and improve on Ted's achievements. One day, perhaps, there would be someone else. One day . . .

She returned to her keyboard. Her hands flew over it, touching the keys. She looked at the screen and shivered, felt cold. She couldn't recall typing what she now saw there. Surely it wasn't she who had done that?

It was a familiar enough message. But who had sent it? The cursor winked at her as she stared at the two words. They stated, simply:

'Hello, Claire.'